Also by Thomas Gondo

**An Eighty Percent Solution**

In a world where corporations suborn governments as a part of good business practice and unregistered humans can be killed without penalty, Tony Sammis, a midlevel corporate functionary, finds himself unwittingly a pawn in a guerilla war between a powerful cabal of business leaders and an elusive but deadly underground movement. His final solution to the biological terror unleashed mirrors Tony's own twisted sense of justice.

**Toy Wars**

Flung to a remote world, a semi-sentient group of robotic mining factories arrive with their programming hashed. They can only create animated toys instead of normal mining and fighting machines. One of these factories, pushed to the edge of extinction by the fratricidal conflict, attempts a desperate gamble. Infusing one of its toys with the power of sentience begins the quest of a 2-meter tall, purple teddy bear and his pink, polka-dotted elephant companion. They must cross an alien world to find and enlist the aid of mortal enemies to end the genocide before Toy Wars claims their family—all while asking the immortal question, "Why am I?"

# Demon Holiday

*Bruce H. Graw*

TANSTAAFL PRESS

TANSTAAFL Press
1201 E. Yelm Ave,
Suite 400-199
Yelm, WA 98697

Visit us at www.TANSTAAFLPress.com



Demon Holiday

First printing—TANSTAAFL Press

Front cover art: Tony Foti, www.tonyfotiart.com
Rear cover art: Modified by GNU general public license from
BrooklynBridgeAtNight.jpg by TheGlowingClown
Interior design and layout: Marian Hartsough Associates

Printed in the USA
ISBN 978-1-938124-10-5

# Chapter 1

"How are we doing today, Bob?"

The short, stocky man looked up from his desk and shook his ruddy, almost completely bald head in frustration. "How do you think I am?" he demanded angrily. "You keep me chained here, all the time, and make me work my fingers to the bone—how would you feel?"

"Now, now, Mr. Collins, there's no reason to get upset," Torval replied with a sardonic smile. "That does nothing to foster a productive work environment."

Bob winced visibly at the mocking phrase, which he had used all too often back when he—well, when he still worked for real. Before he came to this awful place. A place he knew the nature of, though he still steadfastly refused to admit it to himself.

"Screw you," he muttered under his breath.

"There is no need to foster an attitude," sniffed Torval, lifting up and inspecting the thick metal links that connected Bob's ankle to the heavy wooden desk. He let them go and they fell to the hard floor with a loud clank, as if to punctuate Torval's words. "At least you are accomplishing something productive, Mr. Collins. These reports do, after all, need to be processed. In triplicate, of course. You are indeed quite well suited for the job."

"No, I'm not," Bob complained, shoving the stack of papers roughly away from him. "I'm a manager, damn you! I'm not some administrative flunky! And this typewriter is a manual one! Are you people still in the fifties around here?"

Torval chuckled reflexively and repeated another of Bob's favorite excuses. "We are upgrading as fast as we can," he said piercingly. "Oh, and here, as soon as you complete those, I have some more forms for you." With that, he dropped a two-foot-high stack of papers in Bob Collins's already overflowing inbox.

The look on the ex-executive's face was one of thunderstruck horror. Torval forced a smile as he turned and tromped off down the hallway. He didn't look back at Bob's tiny office, and didn't need to know that the unfortunate man would begin to feel the pain soon…the terrible, burning sensation in his skin that lessened only with each report he completed satisfactorily and placed in his outbox.

An outbox that would flare immediately, burning the page to ash.

There was a time, not so long ago, when Torval would've appreciated the bitter irony of the punishment being heaped on poor Mr. Collins. Not that the man didn't deserve it, of course. While alive, the career executive had been a cruel taskmaster without the slightest bit of remorse for the misery he caused. And wasn't that what Hell was all about? Making people suffer for their crimes in life?

Of course it was, and Torval, Demon Third Class, Layer Four Hundred Twelve of the Eighth Circle of Hell, had been in the business of punishing sinners for hundreds of years. Or was it thousands? He couldn't be sure anymore. He'd been at it so long, in fact, he couldn't even remember when and how it all started.

Idly, Torval thought back to what he could recall of those earlier times. He remembered something about an argument between the Creator's top servants about what to do with that troublesome new animal they called "Man." Had he actually been there for that, or simply heard about it later? He couldn't recall for sure. The more he thought about it, the more his memories all seemed to blur together. All he knew for certain was the result of that long and bitter fight—humans were allowed to make their own destinies, and those that chose poorly wound up in Hell, where demons like Torval oversaw their punishment.

For as long as Torval could remember, he'd been a Punisher. That's all he ever wanted to do, all the way back through all those endless blurry centuries. His job defined his existence—it was his purpose, his reason for being. Something seemed different now, though. Something didn't feel quite right. What it might be, he didn't know, so he tried to put it out of his mind as best he could. The uncomfortable feeling remained, though, nagging at the edges of his consciousness, distracting him ever so slightly as he went about his daily business.

It'll go away eventually, Torval told himself as he strode alone down the long, twisting hall. He turned a corner and stepped into sunlight. No distinct gateway or door separated Bob Collins's environment from the next, and the demon felt no change upon moving into the cell. He also didn't feel any heat from the swollen orange sun hanging high in the sky above, for it was but an illusion. Nothing in this place was truly real, except in the minds of its occupants. Torval could see and experience everything the victims did, of course, in order to move through the zone without disrupting the effect, but he sensed nothing he didn't choose to feel.

This particular cell's occupant was one Michael Rubin, a victim of that deadly sin known as "greed." In life, the wealthy businessman had surrounded himself with expensive things and coveted possessions above all else, even the love of his wife and family. For his punishment, he now occupied a tiny desert island with only the barest minimum of water and food, and no hope of rescue. Sometimes tantalizing visions of ships would appear on the horizon, but Michael long ago gave up chasing those mirages. Nowadays, he simply sat motionless on his narrow strip of beach, staring into the distance and brooding.

Torval approached him from behind, stepping up onto the low dunes from the surface of the water, leaving no footprints in the sand. While in Bob Collins's cell, he had appeared clad in a trim business suit, with a neatly cropped head of black hair and the look of an executive. Now, transitioned into the island illusion, the demon appeared as a surfer bum, with bleached blond hair, richly bronzed skin, and a thin, wiry frame.

He forced another smile as he stepped up next to Michael. "And how was the sunrise today?" Torval asked automatically, his voice assuming a degrading tone without any thought on his part.

Michael Rubin didn't respond for a long while. Normally, Torval would prod the poor man at his feet, either verbally or physically, with automatic taunts drawn from the sinner's memories and life experiences. Today, though, the demon held back and waited. He had no idea why, but he seemed to sense something was different now. Something…

Something significant.

Gradually, with deliberate slowness, Michael stood and turned to face Torval. The unfortunate man looked impossibly thin and emaciated, almost literally a walking skeleton, but he always retained enough strength to get around in his prison of the mind. His skin was scorched and burned red from the terrible sun that never set, but only circled and climbed across the sky in an endless meandering oval.

"You know," said Michael after a protracted pause, "for the longest time I thought you were just a hallucination."

"No," replied Torval, still a little bit baffled by the unmistakable, yet equally indefinable, change in the prisoner. "I am as real as you are."

"Yeah," the scrawny man replied with a sigh. "I know. That's what finally made me understand."

The demon cocked his head and gave Michael a sideways look. The cell illusion hadn't provided him with the usual taunting reply. Torval found himself treading on uncharted ground, with no idea what to say.

"Understand what?" he asked, clearly at a loss.

"Who you are, and who I am," said the tortured soul. "And why I'm here. You know," he said with an air of unseemly confidence, "for a long time, I just couldn't figure it out. What did I do to deserve this? Why were you making me suffer? And then you came in yesterday. Or was it a month ago? I can't really tell. Anyway, you said something that made it all clear."

"And what was that?" wondered Torval, trying to figure out where this conversation could possibly be going.

"You said I was in a prison of my own making," Michael told him.

"I said that?"

"Yes. Don't you remember?"

"No, I do not." Of course, with so many souls to visit, how could Torval remember everything he said? He might've, once...but now, it all seemed like a blur. Always a blur.

"Well," Michael went on, taking a few steps and slowly circling around the surfer-demon before him, "that's what got me thinking. Not about how this was a prison, though. Or even that it was of my own making. I think I knew that all along. I just—I just never accepted it before, you know? I never really, truly understood."

Torval just stared at him for a long moment. "Understood what?" he asked at last, in an uncomfortably low voice.

"That I deserve this!" said Michael resignedly. "All of this! I really do, don't I? I'm in Hell, and this is my penance for a wasted, selfish life! And you know what? There's nothing I can ever do to make up for it, to repay those I hurt, or pay back those I stole from or ruined to earn this fate for myself. I just wish there was something I could do."

His head hung low, and his eyes glistened in the bright sunlight.

Torval realized those eyes were actually rimmed with tears, and not from suffering or pain this time. These were different. They were tears of genuine regret.

"I wish there was some way I could just say I'm sorry," Michael concluded miserably.

This would've been a wonderful opportunity to rub it in, as the cell's programming usually insisted, but Torval could only stand there, a befuddled expression on his face, as he found he had no words to say. And then a strange thing happened, something he'd never witnessed in all his centuries of service in the Lower Realm. Something he didn't even know was possible.

Before the surprised demon's eyes, Michael Rubin began to disappear. He became transparent, and as he did, the edges of his sunburned flesh began to glow brightly. After a moment, all that remained was a shining white silhouette, and then this congealed into a single star-like shimmer that winked out as if it had never been.

Torval blinked. Around him, the beach environment gradually faded into a blank nothingness, leaving him standing within a featureless white cube. His illusory surfer attire melted away, leaving him naked and unadorned with anything save his natural, scaly, humanoid form. His snakelike tail twitched with uncertainty, and stubby, slate-gray horns glistened weakly in the pale, ambient light.

He stood there for a long while, trying to understand what just happened. He could think of only one explanation at first—Michael somehow found a way to escape. Yet that simply wasn't possible. The damned couldn't escape a place like Hell! This is where the souls of the wicked belonged—where they'd been consigned upon their death ever since the passing of the very first deserving sinner—what was his name? Oh, yes. Cain. That's what the legends said, anyway. Didn't he even now languish in the original cell on Level One of the First Circle? If he couldn't find a way out, how could someone like Michael Rubin do it?

Torval shook his head and tried to put that out of his mind. *It doesn't really matter,* he told himself. He still had his rounds to make, after all. He'd just have to notify Landri that this cell was now unoccupied. Surely the foreman would know what to do about that, or if he didn't, he'd contact the baron and let him know.

*Perhaps this sort of thing happens from time to time,* Torval mused, *and I just haven't encountered it before. Yes, that must be it,* he convinced himself. *My superiors will know how to proceed from here.*

With that in mind he turned and strode in the direction of the next cell, trying to forget the strange disappearance of Michael Rubin. And, for a while, he did.

But only for a while.

* * *

"Come in and have a seat, would you?"

The bloated form of Foreman Landri scarcely moved from within the depths of his colossal, overstuffed chair. Whether or not he even had the ability to stand was a mystery. "Well, come on, I don't have all day," he insisted brusquely.

Torval half walked, half crept into the spacious office, sinuous tail firmly planted between his legs. He could only think of one reason anyone of his rank would be called into the foreman's office—punishment for some transgression. The phenomenon of reward for good work was completely unknown to either demon.

The trip to the small chair in front of the massive ebony desk seemed to take forever. Upon reaching his destination, Torval kneeled quickly, not waiting to be told again to be seated. The chair bent forward at an unnatural angle, for he couldn't sit properly thanks to his tail, and had to struggle to balance himself.

"Yes, Foreman Landri?" he asked weakly, wondering just what form his discipline would take this time. After all, in a place like Hell, the possibilities were endless.

"Torval," pronounced the immense figure seated before him. Fat seemed to roll around on his body in little waves. Landri's voice, deep with authority, came from within a rippled mountain of brick-red flesh. "How long has it been since I've had to speak to you? At least a decade, I think."

"I do not know, sir," Torval muttered. "About my performance lately, sir . . . I know I have been slow making my rounds. It's just that—"

"Yes?" asked Landri curiously. "Go on. Don't let me stop you."

"Well, you see, I—well, it's hard to explain, sir. I just do not feel quite right somehow."

The corpulent mass in front of Torval made a motion that looked very much like a nod. The scarlet ribbons of blubber encircling his neck jiggled about repeatedly.

"Might this have anything to do with that prisoner's disappearance the other day?"

"No!" Torval blurted, but immediately regretted his hasty response. Shifting uncomfortably in the hard metal chair, he spoke again before the foreman could put in another word. "What I mean to say, sir, is that I felt like this before he—before he vanished. I've been trying to figure out the reason, but I cannot."

"And you've never had these feelings before?" wondered Landri aloud.

"I might have," sighed Torval. "In fact, I am certain I have, but they always go away. Just... just not this time."

"Because of Michael Rubin." The massive tower of fat shifted and jiggled on its throne. "It happens, Torval. It's called 'transcendence.' Did you really think these souls are stuck here permanently, for all eternity? That Hell is the only destination they'll ever know?"

"I, uh, well, I never thought about it much," answered Torval weakly, not meeting his superior's gaze.

"Of course you didn't. That's not your job, is it? You're a Third-Class demon because you're not supposed to think. That's what the foremen and managers are for. Don't forget that!"

"I—I will not, sir. I meant no disrespect." Torval hung his head, fearing the punishment he knew would soon come. Perhaps it would be best, he thought, if I just shut up now and don't try to explain any more. Anything I say will only make things worse.

"All right," said Landri after a moment, his voice taking on a lecturing tone. "Let me explain something for you, just on the off chance it might help you with your little problem. Punishment is of no use unless it teaches something. Surely even you can understand that! Haven't I punished you before? And don't you learn something from it?"

"Y-yes, sir," mumbled Torval, his voice barely audible.

"Good." The foreman continued as if giving instruction to a schoolchild. "For souls, you see, it's not just about lessons, it's about preparation. Hell isn't a final destination, Torval, it's just another path in the journey they all take. Where they go from here, I don't really know, nor do I care. It's not important to me, or to you either, only that sooner or later, they all go. It might take them hundreds or even thousands of years—but that's what eternity's for, right?"

"Y-yes, sir," uttered Toval weakly.

Landri acted as though he didn't hear those words at all, but continued his lecture unabated. "Presumably, Heaven—if it truly exists—has its own method of preparation for a different kind of person," he explained. His vast bulk shuffled slightly, as if he might be uncomfortable with this particular subject. "Anyway, I always thought the place would be incredibly boring, if the stories I hear are accurate, but that might well be an obstacle in its own right. Are you getting all this?"

Torval nodded and tried not to look directly into those sunken black eyes. He said nothing, but absorbed every word. The foreman's statements only led to more questions, but he didn't have the courage to ask them.

"Good, I see that you are." Landri coughed. "Do you understand now, Torval? Does comprehending why you do your job help you in any way at all?"

"I—I do not know, sir," Torval heard himself saying. The questions in his head were just too strong to ignore, and some of them clawed their way out despite his attempt to hold them inside. "But why, sir? Why do we torture those people? Why put them through such misery? Surely there must be a better way!"

Silence reigned for a long moment, until Landri shifted in his huge chair once again. For an instant Torval thought the massive demon might pull himself forth, presumably to crush him under that colossal bulk, but instead Landri merely clasped his beefy hands together under his multitude of chins.

"Very well," he seemed to sigh, "I can see there's only one solution to this problem, if you are to be salvaged. I've seen this before, you know. After decades of the same old thing, year in and year out, you're bound to get a little stir crazy. It happens from time to time, and it's nothing I can't deal with. After all, I'm the foreman here for a reason! I'll just need to shuffle the work schedules a bit, but it can be done."

This left Torval a bit befuddled. What was his boss talking about now? "I—I am sorry, sir, but I do not understand," he heard himself mutter.

"Of course you don't!" barked Landri gruffly. "How could you? Let me explain it to you, then. You see, you've forgotten what kind of people these humans are. Or maybe you just never knew in the first place. Either way, I can't just tell you. You have to see them in action for yourself. That's why I'm authorizing some time off for you."

"Some... time off?" Torval stared at the foreman in disbelief.

"That's right." Landri chuckled, and his massive form quivered as if from an earthquake. "That's right, Torval. You're going on vacation!"

# Chapter 2

Torval paced back and forth in his rest-cube, whip-like tail twitching and snapping behind him. His meal sat on its tray half-eaten, the remaining white worms wriggling about in a desperate, vain attempt to escape the high ridge surrounding the plate. He paid them not the slightest heed as he worried and fretted in silence.

A vacation! It was unheard of. In all his time here he'd never heard of anyone getting any kind of time off. From what Foreman Landri said, though, it had to happen occasionally. Perhaps no one ever bothered to mention it before—it wasn't as if Torval had friends, after all. When he spoke to other demons of his class, it was only to discuss his current assignment, or to give advice if a transferee or visitor from another Layer asked for it. Carrying on small talk didn't appeal to him at all, and in fact, he found it quite uncomfortable.

What really bothered him was the destination. Landri didn't give a lot of details, but Torval knew full well where this holiday would take place—Earth, the proving ground for souls! How could Torval accomplish anything in the Middle Realm? What would he do? And why, in the name of Lucifer himself, was he going there in the first place?

Well, the answer to that is obvious, Torval thought irately, his tail smacking the wall as he turned quickly on his heels. He was going because the foreman told him to, plain and simple. If Landri thought one of his workers needed to go on vacation—well, who was Torval to argue? He might not like the idea, but then, it wasn't his job to make that decision. If nothing else, he knew his own place in the hierarchy.

If he could deal with that, where's the problem? Torval couldn't understand why he should be so agitated. In fact, he couldn't recall a time when he ever felt this way. He wouldn't really be in any danger on Earth, after all. He didn't have a soul, so he didn't have to worry about dying and winding up being punished for eternity—well, okay, not eternity, he knew now, but for an awfully long time! Until he transcended, whatever in Heaven that meant. So why all this nervousness?

All of a sudden it came to him, and he almost banged his bony head against the wall in frustration. He was going somewhere new, someplace different...someplace mortal. Put simply, he'd be leaving his comfortable, familiar home and entering a strange, alien world. Oh, he'd transferred around between Layers occasionally, perhaps once or twice each decade, at the whims of his superiors, but nothing more. In fact, in another hundred years or so, assuming all his transfers got approved, he'd be eligible to visit the deeper Layers, where the torments became more elaborate.

Actually, that's about as far ahead as Torval ever thought about his own future. Working as a tormentor in Hell wasn't just a career to him, but a definition of his life. He had no aims of ever achieving a promotion, or permanently transferring to a more presitigious Circle. Some of his fellows occasionally talked about such things, and he overheard their conversations, but he had no such aspirations. Why should he? He was comfortable enough making his rounds and torturing sinners. He was good at it, and he liked it. Or so he kept insisting to himself, anyway.

So why must he be so wary of going to Earth? Did the trip represent some kind of threat to his way of life? Was he afraid that humans might show him he'd been doing things all wrong? He shook his head violently as he rejected that thought. He couldn't possibly be afraid.

Demons didn't feel fear... did they?

The entry-wall of his cube dissolved away, interrupting his brooding. A demon with pitch-black skin stood waiting, clawed hands clenched together expectantly in front of him. Sharp white teeth stood out in relief against the dark shadow that formed his face. "Demon Third Class Torval, I presume?" he asked in a voice that hissed like steam from the Fire Pits.

"I am he," Torval replied, doing his best to keep his shoulders from slumping in resignation.

"Good, good. I thought I'd never find you. This is the fourth cube I've tried. They really pack you in down here, don't they?"

Torval shrugged. "It is comfortable enough," he replied in as even a voice as he could muster. The ebony-skinned demon before him seemed awfully cheerful, and considering what awaited Torval, he found that attitude quite irritating.

"Well, be that as it may, I am called Geezon. I am a Transitioner... are you familiar with the posting?"

Torval suppressed a sigh. He had no interest whatsoever in carrying on a conversation with this demon—he only wanted to get on with it and get this ridiculous holiday over with! Still, Geezon was his superior—a Second-Class demon, by the way he carried himself. He might not be in Torval's chain of command, but his words carried a tone of measured authority. Best to humor him, Torval thought.

"No, I am not," he answered blithely. "I am not given many opportunities to leave my assigned area."

"Oh, of course, how silly of me. Well, you see, I'm in the department that handles arriving souls. We see to it they receive a suitable space on the proper Circle. We don't have anything to do with their actual punishment, though, mind you. That's what the Judgment Center's for, after all."

Torval just nodded resignedly. He really had no idea what the black demon was talking about, and didn't much care. He had no reason to expect he'd ever interact with that department, and while he had a vague inkling that something like it existed, it didn't matter to him one whit.

"Anyway," Geezon went on amiably, paying no attention to the way Torval shuffled his feet in obvious impatience, "normally all I do is sort out new arrivals, but I also happen to be the only one on duty right now who can do a reverse transference. When your manager contacted me, I hopped the next inter-Circle transport, and here I am. I hope you haven't been waiting too long."

"No, that is quite all right," said Torval with a sigh. "It is just strange to sit in my cube and not walk my route. It feels . . . well, wrong somehow."

"Yes, I can imagine," Geezon told him in a tone that suggested he really couldn't relate at all. "Well, don't worry, your vacation doesn't actually start until the reversal, so my keeping you waiting hasn't affected your time allotment. Come along, Torval. You have quite a journey ahead of you."

With that, the midnight-black demon turned and strode off along the passageway, his lean legs propelling him ahead with surprising speed. Torval hurried to keep up, and dropped into step behind his guide, taking up a half-jog to stay on pace. As he followed, he was glad of two things. First, he was happy to be underway at last, for the sooner he got this torturous vacation over with, the better.

He was also very, very glad that Geezon finally decided to shut up.

* * *

Torval stared at the black section of wall dubiously. He could see nothing there, just an inky shadow with no surface texture whatsoever. The black circle comprised a portal, he knew without asking. He could feel the shadowy vortex tugging ever so slightly at him even now, as Geezon manipulated the energy flow nearby. The entrance would accept Torval only after being attuned to his particular essence, or so his guide explained. Otherwise, crossing that barrier would lead only to Oblivion.

Geezon was silent now, arms and tail moving swiftly about as he communicated wordlessly with the yawning black portal. Torval sighed, glad for the break. As he discovered during the interminably long journey to the First Circle—the only part of Hell that actually bordered the Middle World—Geezon remained quiet only while actually doing something. When he walked (at an annoyingly quick pace, as if on a tight schedule), the much taller demon never spoke and in fact didn't even seem to hear Torval when he asked to slow down. The instant Geezon reached the transport, though, he began to blather incessantly. Torval eventually resorted to ignoring him, concentrating primarily on not showing his discomfort during the ride.

The steamship was something relatively new, actually. Developed sometime in the last few centuries, it was one of a number of things in Hell that took inspiration from humanity. Demons were notoriously poor thinkers, with little in the way of imagination, but once they got an idea, they ran with it. The transport replaced the slow, pole-driven ferryboats that once crossed the wide expanses of water bordering the zones, and Torval was glad for that. Some of those seas, like the Styx or Lethe, were dangerous. He had no interest in accidentally touching those foul liquids and forgetting who he was.

Torval tried not to cringe when he saw the transport for the first time.

The thing resembled a fallen building partially immersed in the bubbling waters, its wide, flat deck bordered by walls on all sides. In the center, a pair of grimy silver cylinders jutted up, belching white smoke as if one of the Pits itself resided underneath. Upon boarding the strange vessel, Torval found the wooden floor vibrated and shook under his bare feet, even before the journey began. Once they got underway, the shaking became more pronounced, and something in the interior emitted a loud whine that grated endlessly on his ears. Torval spent most of the trip grinding his teeth in discomfort and trying to avoid the company of the insufferably chatty Geezon.

There was little to do aboard the steamship, though, and nothing to see outside except the mists that bordered the Circles. In some way Torval didn't understand, the transport could reach the shore of any other Circle simply by sailing in a particular pattern. Geezon tried to explain it to him, but he barely paid attention. Something about traversing overlapping sub-dimensions, whatever the Heaven that meant.

In any event, after what seemed like a century, the transport docked and Torval finally exited the obnoxious craft. His ears were still ringing when, after a walk as brisk as it was long, Geezon arrived at the entrance to the Transition Center. The cavern looked much like any of the other winding passageways that lined Hell's innards, but there was a difference this time—the entrance was guarded.

Torval had never seen a warder before. They were huge, towering over him by at least twice his height. The two creatures, scowling down doubtfully as he approached, were golden-skinned, with plates of bony armor covering their bodies. Long, wickedly curved horns adorned their scaly heads. Torval had little doubt the monstrosities could use those sharp, powerful-looking weapons in battle just as well as the immense, barbed swords they held in their meaty hands.

The swords came up as Geezon approached, but the black demon waved a hand and muttered something quietly. The guards retreated, though their eyes never left the pair as they ventured past. Torval heard a growling then, and in the darkness behind each guard he saw a shaggy black shape larger than himself. Six pairs of red eyes stared out at him from those shadowy corners, and he knew the glowing orbs belonged to cerberi, the dreaded hounds of Hell. Torval shuddered and hurried along, sticking close to Geezon's heels.

In due course the travelers arrived at the black portal. "This is the way to the Middle Realm," said the dark demon. "Stand before it, and do not move until I tell you. Is that understood?"

"Yes, sir," Torval replied, and with that Geezon started making some strange motions with his hands. He kept this up for quite a while, until Torval began to feel the pull of the black opening. After a while this tugging became more and more difficult to resist, but because he'd been ordered to stand fast, Torval simply shifted his weight to compensate. So conditioned was he to obey a superior's orders, the thought of doing otherwise never crossed his mind.

Eventually, Geezon stopped his weird antics and seemed to relax. "Finally!" he said in relief. "I hate doing that! Do you realize how much effort it takes to open up all those locks and set up the return path?"

"No, sir," said Torval with a sigh. Another long-winded explanation was on the way, he could tell already.

"Well, how could you?" Geezon laughed for a moment. "This is the first time you've even gone on holiday. I keep forgetting that. Most demons of your rank have taken a couple of vacations by now, you know. Why haven't you?"

"I never needed one, I suppose," replied Torval. "I was not even aware that such a thing was possible, until my foreman told me."

"Well, you Third-Class types don't get nearly enough time off, I say. If it were up to me, I'd make sure you all knew a lot more about how this place operates. Landri told me this happened because you witnessed your first transcendence. Is that right?"

Torval shuffled his feet, finding it difficult to stay in place with that portal pulling at him, but he managed to persevere. "I guess that is the word for it," he muttered.

"Well, I'm sure the foreman explained it all to you. I just want you to understand something, Torval. You did nothing wrong. In fact, it speaks volumes that you haven't seen a transcendence yet, after all these centuries of service. You must be pretty good at tormenting if you can keep all those souls from thinking about anything else but their pain. They do get used to it after a while, you know.

"Anyway, let me explain a bit more, if I may. Souls can move on to the next phase of existence at any time, but not until they've been properly prepared. Earth provides their trials, and Hell their punishment for failure. Heaven, I'm told, is its own reward, but I wouldn't know. No demon has ever seen the place, so we don't even know if it's really there, or just a story the religions tell the humans in order to cover up the truth. After all, no human is without sin, so theoretically they should all end up here, in one Layer or another."

"But, sir," said Torval in the brief silence that followed that cryptic statement, "if I am not being disciplined, then why am I here? What purpose does it serve to send me to Earth?"

Geezon laughed again, making a noise rather like a buzz-saw tearing into a piece of wood against the grain. "Now, now, it wouldn't do to tell you everything." He chuckled. "You'll be debriefed when you come back, and we'll explain then. Just keep your eyes open and pay attention to what goes on around you."

"I still do not understand," whined Torval. "What am I supposed to do? Who gives me orders while I'm there?"

"Nothing, and no one," Geezon answered patiently. "You don't have to do anything specific, Torval, and no one is going to tell you what to do. That's why it's a vacation, you see? The humans have a saying for this sort of thing—'getting away from it all.' I know that doesn't make much sense, but then, very little about Man makes sense. You'll see what I mean when you get to Earth."

"But, sir, if I have no task—" Torval began, but was cut off by a swift gesture from his dark-skinned superior.

"You have no tasks to perform, and that's the point!" explained Geezon rapidly. "Listen, I know you're confused right now, but take my word for it, this is exactly what you need. The humans have something we demons don't really enjoy. It's called free will. Do you know what that is?"

"Not exactly," admitted Torval freely. "Should I?"

"It means they're free to make their own choices. They can do whatever they want, for good or ill. That means they have to suffer the consequences when they choose poorly, of course, although you won't have to worry about that. I do recommend you try to make the right decisions while you're on Earth, though, because it'll make things easier on you for the duration of your stay, but it's up to you. Experiencing free will is what your vacation is all about, after all, and it's all you need to know if you want to truly understand humanity.

"Now, let me tell you a few more things and then you can go. You'll be in the Middle Realm for two weeks, as the humans measure time. After that, the portal will reappear for you. Make sure you enter it—I don't want to have to send in a team to hunt you down."

"Do not worry about that," Torval insisted quickly. "I'll be looking forward to getting back! I do not even wish to go at all. Are you sure I have to do this?"

"Sorry, you have to go, by order of Foreman Landri. I'm not in your chain of command, so I can't overrule him." Geezon shrugged away the idea without further comment, although he would've been within his rights to log the complaint and report it. "Anyway, another detail you need to keep in mind—you're going to take over the body of a human when you get there—someone who just recently died, and who has few or no mortal connections to confuse things. Since you've never been in a real human body before, you'll likely find this strange at first. Just remember, the flesh is mortal, and the world is real—you can't just ignore external stimuli like you can in the cells. If you get injured, it'll hurt, and if you die, you'll just wind up back here and I'll have to send you out into another body. You can't get out of your vacation that easily, I'm afraid."

Torval didn't say anything, but inwardly, he was frowning. So much for that potential loophole, he thought sadly.

"In any case," Geezon continued, "you'll have a limited access to your body's memories and reflexes, but only enough to get by. Those memories will fade rapidly, but you'll still retain the basic knowledge of how to use your mortal form—how to eat, sleep, excrete, things like that. And don't worry about our breaking any rules here. The Compact permits this sort of thing, but you don't get to go around mucking up the natural order with stuff a supposedly dead man knows, got that? I expect you to avoid attempting to find out your 'true' identity—just head off somewhere and don't get involved with your host body's former life, all right?"

"Yes, sir," said Torval. He still didn't quite understand what he was supposed to do on Earth, but he really didn't want to ask any more questions, thereby inviting another rambling diatribe from Geezon. He'd already grown quite uncomfortable, leaning backward like this, and by now he just wanted to jump into the portal and get the whole holiday business over with as quickly as possible.

"Okay, we're almost done," the black demon went on. "Just one other thing to mention. We do have agents out there, you know, doing their best to spread as much evil and temptation as they can. If you run into someone who isn't really human, you'll see his true form when you physically touch each other. If that happens, you're expected to keep his true identity to yourself and don't ask questions. Just tell him you're on holiday and move along. I don't want to have to discipline you for interfering with an operation in progress. Is that clear?"

"Yes, sir!" Torval snapped off the answer quickly, the response all but automatic. "Is there anything else, sir?"

Geezon rubbed his chin with a couple of long, slender fingers. "No, I don't think so," he said after a moment. "That about covers it. I'll see you back here in a couple of weeks for your debriefing. Unless, of course, you have any further questions?"

"No, sir, I do not."

"Then go," said Geezon with a smile. He made another waving motion with his hands, and suddenly the pull from the portal became inexorable. Torval didn't resist this time, as per his orders, and instead eagerly fell forward into the inky blackness.

As the Third-Class demon's form vanished from sight, Geezon's grin widened, his pointed teeth gleaming in the cave's bright light. "Transitioners," he muttered, shaking his head slowly. "They never know what they're in for, do they? Well, he'll find out soon enough."

After a few final adjustments, Geezon turned on his charcoal-black heels and left the chamber, still chuckling softly to himself.

# *Chapter 3*

Torval remembered a sensation of falling, and a strange numbing sensation all over his body. Then, with a violent twitching, he awoke.

The first thing he realized was that he felt cold—blessedly cold! His breath formed into a white cloud upon exiting his mouth, and he shivered involuntarily. Pale flakes of frosty snow swept all around, driven by a bitter wind that cut him almost to the bone.

So this is what it's like, he thought at once, realizing he couldn't simply deactivate or dismiss the terrible, biting cold that assaulted him from every direction. This is what humans have to put up with, every single day! Sensations they can't ignore with a thought, even when they're in misery.

Looking down, Torval found himself clad in several layers of ragged, filthy clothing. His hands wore mismatched gloves with holes in the fingertips. The shoes upon his feet were but shredded clumps of leather, the soles worn so thin they offered almost no protection from the numbing frost. His head and shoulders were wrapped in a wretched windbreaker hood that only served to form a surface for the snow to collect upon.

Involuntarily, he clutched himself with his arms, shaking and trying to keep warm. Well, he thought sourly, there's no mistaking how the previous occupant of this body died. He surely froze to death.

Torval slowly struggled to his feet, and suddenly found himself wracked with a paroxysm of coughs and gasps for breath. Thick globs of some gelatinous substance came up from his throat, and he spat them out disgustedly. I'm sick, he realized—another sensation he would gladly do without. He'd seen such things in some of the cells—men who visited pain upon others in life were often punished by various plagues and other ailments. Torval, however, had never experienced such a thing for himself, and he didn't like it at all. His head hurt terribly, and he couldn't seem to stop shaking.

So, he thought disgustedly, this is my punishment! Instead of disciplining me back in Hell, Landri decided to do it here, on Earth! Two weeks of this, Torval grumbled to himself. I have to suffer for two weeks as a mortal!

There was little he could do, however, except endure this trial and learn whatever lesson his foreman saw fit to teach him. After all, the only way off the Earth was death, and Geezon already warned him that doing so would just get him stuck in another body. What if that one was worse? Although, at this moment, Torval found himself hard-pressed to imagine something less appealing than being deathly ill, and freezing cold to boot.

He couldn't do much about being sick, he realized, but perhaps he could find shelter somewhere and get out of the weather. He looked around at his surroundings, noticing them for the first time, and realized suddenly that this time what he saw was real. This was no illusion, like the cells of the damned he visited every day on the job. The gray brick walls that rose around him now were no creation of thought, but physical reality. He couldn't simply walk through them or ignore their existence any more than he could shut out the uncomfortable feeling of coldness that penetrated his skin.

Bless it all! Did Geezon and Landri really send him here on purpose?

Still somewhat woozy, Torval stared up and around at the snow-flecked walls on either side of his quivering body. To his left, a barrier of metal chain links rose over his head, blocking access to a series of doors that lined another bleak gray wall. In the other direction, the alley opened up onto a street black with slush. Even as he watched, a vehicle of some sort shot past, a yellow blur he barely recognized as what the humans called a "car." Melted snow splashed up as the construct of metal and glass rolled by, the rumble of its engine fading into the distance.

Torval watched the vehicle pass in amazement. He knew what cars were, of course. He'd seen visions of such things in cell illusions, and thanks to the memories of his host body, he felt no fear of them. Yet, even so, he still found himself enthralled. Here was something no demon could possibly build or understand—a technological creation sprung entirely from the mind of Man.

Every now and then, a human idea found its way into Hell, resulting in new innovations like the Circle transports, but those were few and far between. How could men, with lifespans measured in decades, produce such fantastic creations? Why was it so easy for them, when the entire assembled host of demonkind couldn't fathom such things if they tried? Torval had no idea. In fact, the very question was so vast in scope, so completely unanswerable, that he dropped it from his mind almost automatically.

Instead, Torval shifted his mind back toward the goal of finding some sort of shelter, someplace warm and comfortable. He took a couple of wobbly steps and nearly tripped over a shape that blocked the alley, something covered with scraps of newspaper, wrinkled cardboard, and a light dusting of newly fallen snow. To Torval's surprise, the lump shifted and let forth a grunt of surprise.

"Wha—?" came a man's raspy voice. "Lemme 'lone. I'm sleepin' here."

"Sorry," muttered Torval automatically. "I did not know anyone was under there."

The cardboard shifted away and an old man's face peered out, a look of wonder in his bloodshot eyes. Long, ragged gray hair surrounded a mass of wrinkly, battered skin and a nose so red it might be sunburned.

"Izzat you, Joe?" he said in amazement. "I thought you was dead! Ya stopped breathin' an hour ago!"

Torval coughed a couple of times. Remembering what Geezon told him about keeping his true nature to himself, he replied, "I was merely sleeping."

"Ya sure coulda fooled me!" said the old man with a chuckle. "I thought I'd lost another one! Well, good ta have ya back, and I'm sorry I took yer box, but I thought ya wouldn't be needin' it."

Torval shrugged. The flimsy-looking cardboard didn't look to be all that useful for warmth, anyway. "You can keep it, Marty." Now that's odd, he thought suddenly. Where'd I hear that name? Oh, yeah, right, it must be my host body's old memories creeping in. Good, that'll make blending in with these people easier.

"Where ya goin'?" Marty asked after a moment, reaching for a brown paper bag near his side. Yawning, he sat up and put the sack to his lips, and Torval realized then that the crinkled wrapping concealed a bottle. There's a word for a person like this, he thought, trying to remember one of the punishments he'd seen inflicted a long time ago. Oh yes, that's right. Wino. Alcohol was one of those things a tortured soul loved to blame his problems on, but that excuse never worked. Not taking responsibility for his own actions was one of the surest ways a man could guarantee a one-way trip to Hell.

"I do not know," Torval answered after another bout of coughing. "Someplace warm. Do you have any suggestions?"

"Damn, yer talkin' funny," said Marty, taking another swig out of his bottle. "Well, whatever ya want, I guess. Y'can go try the shelter 'gain, if ya like, but they'll jus' throw ya out like last time. Anyway, while yer out, pick me up s'more slosh, 'kay? I'm almost dry here."

Shelter? Slosh? What was the old man talking about? Torval started to ask for clarification when Marty took another drink from the bottle that still lay hidden within its crumpled paper sack. A strange feeling swept over Torval and he licked his lips unconsciously, remembering the taste of liquor through the memories of his host body. All at once he wanted to wrest that bottle away from Marty and suck down as much of the burning liquid as he could. The alcohol would warm him, no doubt, and make him forget. Forget everything. All the guilt and pain, all those things he did wrong in his life...

No! Not my life! Torval shook his head and pushed those memories away. That was Joe's life, not his. Joe was on his way to the afterlife now—to his reward, or quite possibly his punishment. Only his shell remained, a shell now occupied by a demon who felt lost and alone and very, very cold.

Suddenly Torval took another look at the clothes he wore, and then back at the clear spot on the ground where he awoke just a few minutes ago. Already a coating of white snow collected there, in amidst the gray newspapers and onto the bag that lay there on its side. A brown paper sack he knew contained an empty bottle.

So that's it, he thought. They sent me to Earth, to take human form, and turned me into a bum. A drunk, sick, and freezing homeless person with nothing to look forward to except two weeks of shivering in some frosty alleyway, alongside an old man who can barely speak coherently.

Maybe I should just kill myself, Torval's meandering mind suggested. Surely another life somewhere else couldn't possibly be worse than this!

* * *

After what seemed like an excruciatingly long walk, Torval stepped through the shelter door and sighed with relief as the gloriously warm air washed over him. He thought he'd never felt something so wonderful in all his existence, though of course that was an exaggeration.

Or perhaps not. He couldn't be sure. His job rarely drew any emotions from him anymore. Had he ever felt anything quite as intense as the relief he felt now, as he finally came in from the cold? After so many years of mindlessly walking his route, he just couldn't remember.

The shelter was small and crowded with humans, virtually all of them dressed in rags like his own. All wore pitiful, broken expressions of hopelessness. Very few spoke. Mostly they just lolled about in chairs, sipping slowly on a liquid that occupied a bowl in front of them. A few lounged up against the wall or in the corners, sleeping, or trying very hard to do so.

Torval only barely remembered the interminable walk through two disgustingly dirty alleys filled with trash, debris, and drifting snow. Left to his own devices, he would've had no clue where to go to find the place, but the memories in his human brain knew the way. He simply let his body shuffle along, and his weary feet brought him to the rickety building of their own accord.

What he did recall of the trip was a sense of amazement at the city that surrounded him. Before today, all he knew of human places were the illusions that appeared in the Layer cells. To actually see one for real took his breath away. The streets were endless, stretching into the distance as far as he could see, all filled with cars, trucks, and other strange vehicles of all shapes and sizes. Above him, immense buildings of steel and glass stretched toward the sky, vanishing into the gray clouds and swirling white snow.

As his frail human body stumbled its way along, all Torval could think was how fantastic this place was. The humans built this with their own hands! They had nothing to help them but their own brains and muscles, and look at what they had created! How many centuries must it have taken? Any one of the dozens of buildings he walked past was more awesome than the greatest accomplishment of demonkind throughout all their thousands of years of ruling Hell.

He shook those thoughts away as his body finally stopped shuffling in front of a rickety-looking table. A large pot sat on a tablecloth, manned by an overweight black woman who stared at him with disdain. He hardly noticed her irritated gaze, though. His attention became fixed on that steaming silver pot, for his nose detected the most amazing aroma rising forth from within. He felt his stomach rumble in anticipation, and his mouth filled with saliva of its own accord. By the Pits, he was hungry! He hadn't realized that until just this moment, but his desire to eat some of that soup nearly overwhelmed him.

"Lemme guess," complained the dark-skinned woman behind the table. "You want some more, don't you?"

"Yes," Torval answered without looking up, completely fixated on the steaming soup before him. "Yes, I would like some very much."

She put her hands on her hips and scowled in his direction. "Goddammit, Joe, I told you earlier today, you only get one free meal at a time! Now go away and don't come back until tomorrow. If you want more to eat, you oughta spend some of those coins you scavenge on food instead of booze!"

"Please," he replied desperately, having no idea what she was talking about. Joe might've been here earlier, but Torval wasn't, and only vaguely recalled meeting this woman before. "I'm so hungry." He began to cough, loosening up more of that strange sticky goo from deep in his throat. "I have to eat," he went on pathetically, wishing he could just turn off these terrible feelings like he could back home.

"Oh, for the love of Christ, cover your mouth!" the woman all but shrieked at him. "You wanna ruin it for everybody?"

"Come on, Lakisha, have a heart," said a woman's voice from close by. "Can't you see he's sick? Go on, Mr. Sampson, have a seat. I'll see if we can spare anything for you."

Torval turned to see who spoke, for her voice sounded much younger and less antagonistic. When he saw her, his eyes widened. The woman was lovely, with dark brown hair pulled back behind her head, the russet color in sharp contrast to her wide, almond-shaped, sky-blue eyes. Meeting his gaze, she smiled at him, and Torval suddenly felt quite a bit warmer than before.

He heard his body say, "Thank you, Christine," but he hadn't spoken those words consciously. He was too surprised by her simple beauty, and the kind way she overruled the unpleasant black woman in order to help him.

"You're welcome," Christine replied, still smiling pleasantly. "Now go on, Joe, have a seat. Don't make me drag you over there!"

"Sure," Torval answered dully, shuffling away in the direction she indicated. His body once again took over, automatically sitting down on the nearest bench. Using a high-backed piece of furniture like this would've been difficult in his natural form. His thick, sinuous tail would've gotten in the way without some sort of hole or gap to slip through. As a human, though, the motion felt perfectly natural. He pushed his back right up against the bracing, something he'd never done back home, and yet he never even noticed the difference.

While he waited, Torval craned his neck to watch the pretty young woman draw a ladle full of soup and pour it into a bowl. She continued arguing with Lakisha, but never once did Christine seem upset or angered by the other's attitude and the affable smile never left her face.

After a moment Christine came over with the bowl and set it down in front of Torval, along with a spoon and a thin white napkin. "Here you go," she told him comfortingly. "You don't pay any attention to her, now. You're still sick, and some more hot soup'll do you good."

"I hope so," answered Torval, drinking down a spoonful of the thick, warm broth. Back home, he would've preferred something alive and squirming, but now, trapped in this pathetic body, this would have to do. Besides, the soup tasted wonderful. He coughed again, several times, but not so much of the chunky mucous made its way up this time. Perhaps he was already getting better. Since entering the warm shelter, he could already sense the difference. He could almost feel himself growing stronger with each spoonful of soup he downed.

"Well," said Christine after a moment, "you know I'm not going to let you get away with this for free, don't you?"

Torval looked up at her curiously. "What do you mean?" he asked. "I have nothing with which to pay."

She laughed. "Oh, Joe, you know I'd never ask you for money! I'm going to make you listen to another lecture."

"Oh, I see," he replied between spoonfuls of soup. Now that he'd warmed up, and the initial excitement of just getting something to eat wore off, he found himself really enjoying the broth's odd, tangy flavor.

Certainly it was like nothing he'd ever experienced before. After all, he always ate the exact same kind of worms every day in Hell. The concept of variety meant nothing to him.

Christine put her hands on the table. "All right, I guess you aren't going to argue with me today, huh? Your little reverse psychology trick won't work, though, 'cause I'm giving you the speech anyhow."

"All right, go ahead," said Torval, having no idea what she was talking about. He actually didn't mind hearing her voice, for he found it quite soothing, and she was pleasant to look at, too. He'd seen beautiful women before, of course, for they were quite common in Hell, but that's while they were being punished for their sins. To see such a lovely young creature in the midst of life, still in control of her own destiny, was somehow much more intriguing.

Christine rolled her eyes. "Come on, Joe," she said sternly. "You've heard me ask this a hundred times. Why don't you stop drinking, get cleaned up, and find a job? You and I both know you can do it if you want. It breaks my heart to see a man like you throwing your life away!"

Torval just stared at her, even pausing in his efforts to shovel the excellent-tasting soup into his mouth. He had no idea what to say to that. How could he find a job, anyway? He only knew how to do one thing, and somehow, he doubted there were too many opportunities for a Torturer here on Earth.

After a moment of awkward silence, Christine finally gave up and slapped her palms on the table. "Ohh! You're just impossible!" she hissed at him in frustration. "Go on, then! Go back out there and beg for nickels, and waste them on hooch if you want! I just hope someday you realize what you're doing to yourself and turn it around, or you'll find yourself dead in an alley somewhere!"

Torval almost responded this time, because she hit pretty close to home with that comment, but he was too busy swallowing another helping of soup. By the time he licked his lips and started to reply, she'd already stormed off toward the back of the shelter. He watched her go, her hips swinging hypnotically back and forth in her long gray skirt, clearly frustrated at her failure. Torval sighed and shook his head sadly. What would she say if she knew the man she thought of as Joe had died, his body now inhabited by a demon from the pits of Hell? She probably wouldn't be all that amused, he thought idly.

"Feisty, ain't she?" a voice rasped next to him.

Torval glanced over to see a middle-aged man dressed in a heavy parka staring at him. Not a single strand of hair adorned his shiny head, and his craggy face bore a beaming smile.

"What?" mumbled Torval, annoyed at being distracted from the pleasant view of Christine's departing figure.

"You know what I mean," came the reply. "I see you lookin' at her, Joe. You know you wants her."

"Huh?" Torval's eyes narrowed, and for some reason the man's words irritated him. Joe's memories, however, immediately confirmed that statement. When he was alive, Joe frequently stared with longing at the lovely Christine, and in fact, she was one of the reasons he lingered in this section of town, without moving along like so many other transients.

Torval pushed those memories away and concentrated instead on the man speaking to him now. He knew this person: Drew Phillips, a fellow street bum.

"Yeah, so do I," Drew went on with a wistful sigh. "She really makes this place worth visitin', don't she? Like any of us gots a chance!"

"I don't understand," said Torval, his spoon now scraping the bottom of his bowl. He coughed a couple more times, the sound much clearer now, as if his lungs had finally freed themselves of the junk collected there. "Why is she here? Surely someone like her can find someplace better than this to live her life."

Drew cackled a couple of times. "I think we've all wondered that, my boy," he replied. "She's just a bleedin' heart, that's all I know. And I'm glad for it. Sometimes I get so lonely, and just seein' her brightens up my spirits, y'know?"

Torval tried to understand, and once again his host body's memories kicked in and translated for him. "You mean she just does this on her own?" he asked, surprised. "She receives no reward for it?"

"Nah," said Drew. "Them's all volunteers, all of 'em, even that bitchy Lakisha. I guess they think they can earn bonus karma points by workin' here on their off time. Christine, though, she's here a lot more than the others. If she didn't have a job, I think she'd live in this place. Whatever. I don't know or care, I'm just glad she comes."

Torval nodded in agreement, pushing the empty bowl away from him and leaning back in his seat. His stomach felt warm and satisfied now, and even the ache in his temple seemed to have faded. As he relaxed, his eyes sought out the svelte form of Christine again, just visible in the distant kitchen, preparing another batch of soup, a happy smile brightening her face.

Perhaps, thought Torval, being trapped on Earth won't be so bad after all.

# Chapter 4

After a few more minutes of idle conversation, Drew got up and took his leave. Just the right time, too, Torval thought, because he'd started to get bored with the older man's banter. The way he just carried on about the cold and snow, and how much money he made begging on the street, reminded Torval of the equally talkative Geezon. Perhaps that's where the dark-skinned demon got the idea to speak all the time—from watching humans too closely.

The bald-headed man's departure also meant Torval could watch in silence as Christine worked. She went about preparing another pot of hot soup without any further complaints, emitting a strange high-pitched noise by pursing her lips. Joe's memories informed Torval that this was called "whistling," an act normally performed by someone happy and content. Torval didn't understand, though. Everything he knew of humanity suggested that to them, labor represented hated drudgery that brought out the worst in people. Why would anyone enjoy it?

That's not all, Torval realized as he observed Christine's actions with curiosity. From what Drew said, she was a volunteer. Torval only vaguely understood that concept, for the act of volunteering is all but unknown in Hell. Torval had never done, or even contemplated doing, such a thing. After all, Third-Class demons didn't have initiative, nor did they seek out work. They did what they were told, nothing more and nothing less. None would ever think of volunteering for anything. Christine, by contrast, was here on her own initiative, expecting nothing in return—not even the currency that humans seemed to find so important. Wasn't the purpose of work to earn money in order to buy food and shelter for oneself? Why do it, if there was no reward?

Then again, why did humans do anything? Torval leaned back in his seat, eyes following Christine's movements as she set up a fresh batch of soup and began serving it to a waiting line of homeless people. He remembered something that had happened a long time ago, so long he couldn't recall exactly when.

He was doing his rounds and noticed that one prisoner—Gregor Pyrzeschi or something like that—kept trying to escape. Gregor's cell provided an environment much like a real prison, with barred walls, cruel guards, and meager rations at best. No matter how many times Torval told Gregor the place was escape-proof, or how severe the pain and torture was each time he failed to break out, the pitiful wretch kept right on trying. He even continued using the same methods that bore no fruit, steadfastly refusing to give up.

Torval remembered that particular prisoner well because that was one of the few times he actually went to his foreman to ask what to do. Torval's job was to torment sinners, but Gregor kept torturing himself on his own, leaving the demon wondering how to respond. Of course, Landri just said to carry on and watch the fun—a predictable answer, naturally, but he also added something else, too. He said something like this: "These humans, they do whatever they want, no matter how stupid it seems. That's one thing I've learned about them. They're unpredictable like that. Even if you hold their salvation right in front of them, they'll as likely refuse to take it as not. I gave up trying to understand them centuries ago."

That turned out to be one of the longest conversations Torval ever shared with Landri. In fact, shortly thereafter the pudgy demon figuratively booted his subordinate from his office. After that, Torval just didn't bother trying to figure out what humans were all about. He had no reason to, really. He wasn't involved in determining their punishment. All he had to do was administer it. Inevitably they complained, pleaded, cried, and did a thousand other things to try to earn his mercy, but Torval never wavered. They could've chosen to avoid this fate, but they failed, he always reminded himself. He didn't know, or even comprehend, the foreign emotion of pity.

Well, everything seemed different now. Studying the lovely Christine as she handed out food to the needy, he wished he'd taken the time to try to understand human motivations. To a demon like himself, who lived in a cause-and-effect universe, the thought that someone would do something without good reason left him totally baffled.

He watched her for some time, trying to understand. Perhaps, he thought after a while, the problem is I don't have the proper frame of reference. After all, he'd never seen live people before, only dead souls being punished. These humans, he reminded himself, didn't know anything about that. In fact, they had no knowledge of what lay beyond the veil. Sure, virtually every religion taught about Heaven and Hell, or some reasonably similar concept, but living souls couldn't really know for sure what the afterlife was like. In fact, some were so convinced that only Oblivion lay beyond that they lived a life of hedonism, and then were shocked to discover the truth when they arrived in Hell and began a pseudo-eternity of torture.

So, he thought analytically, if a human happened to believe in the afterlife, or at least that they'd receive some kind of punishment for a life lived poorly, why would they sin? Because the flesh is weak, as he'd heard more than one soul argue. A person might want to live a good life, but they made mistakes, or fell victim to their own passions. If they didn't resolve those problems during life, then they wound up in Hell.

Things seemed clearer now, and in fact, Torval sat up in his chair as the obvious answer finally occurred to him. Christine volunteered here to help her soul go to Heaven! Yes, that explained it—the only answer that made any sense, really. She probably figured if she did enough good deeds, they'd cancel out whatever sins she may have committed earlier on in life—or might commit later.

Torval raised his eyebrows as he thought of something else. If he'd worked this out correctly, then that meant Christine was performing a good deed right now! He'd never experienced such a thing in all his lonely years of existence. The phenomenon of good was unknown in Hell, where the various demons simply went about their business without any concern for their fellows. Some, in fact, openly schemed and plotted to move up in the hierarchy, building immense power bases and trying to take over their own personal Layer. Failure meant a return to the Pits, to begin again as a lowly Fourth Class—or, if they annoyed someone really powerful, the final, true death of Oblivion. Needless to say, Torval had no interest in such games, and until recently was perfectly content to walk his rounds each day without any higher aspirations.

He continued to observe the smiling Christine as she ladled soup into the bowls of each and every bum who stepped up to her table. So... this is "good," he thought. She is a good person!

So "goodness" was defined by working for nothing, and helping others with a smile on one's face. That didn't seem so hard.

Still, if she did such things just to ensure she got into Heaven, was that really goodness, or simply selfishness of another sort? He could recall several religious zealots being tortured, all of whom insisted they were in Hell by mistake. Surely, they complained, someone as righteous as they couldn't possibly deserve to spend eternity in torment! Was that the fate that awaited Christine? He had no way to tell, at least without being able to discern her true motives.

Well, I have two weeks to figure out what those are, he thought to himself. Two weeks to find out more about Christine, and learn what it really meant to be "good." After all, that's what he was here for, right? To understand humans as best he could, so he could go back to his job with the right attitude. Perhaps if he knew what human souls could've done in life to avoid their fates, he could use that knowledge to torment them further. Yes, that was perfect! That's the lesson he could show Landri he learned, to prove he'd been paying attention during his little vacation.

Besides, he thought as he let his eyes linger on Christine's beautiful blue eyes, I certainly wouldn't mind having someone like her for a teacher...

For an instant, his body's memories ran away with him. He remembered better times, and the feel of a woman's body against his own. What would it be like to take Christine in his arms and press his lips to hers? He could almost picture it in his mind... the silky-smooth texture of her skin, the warmth of her body heat, the flowery aroma of her perfume, the touch of her tongue to his...

He jerked his head away and blinked rapidly. That wasn't Christine, he told himself. That's someone Joe knew long ago, in another life no longer of any consequence. And he didn't really desire Christine, either. How could he, a demon, want anything to do with a human, no matter how attractive she might be? After all, he'd seen more than his share of female flesh in torment over the centuries, and never felt the slightest hint of interest. No, this was just another weakness of the miserable body he wore.

Putting the lovely Christine out of his mind, he looked around the crowded shelter and frowned. The place became more and more packed with bodies as the sun began to set outside. Soon, he'd be kicked out to face the cold and snow once again. What should he do then?

He searched his body's memories, but found little of use. His best bet would be to find a barrel-fire and try to stay warm that way. That's why he slept during the daytime, of course, because he stayed up all night to avoid freezing to death. Too bad that didn't work once Joe got sick, Torval thought. In the end, the combination proved to be the end of him.

Joe's life, it seemed, consisted of an endless series of begging for coins, getting drunk, and sleeping in an alley underneath whatever scraps of cardboard he could find. Truly pathetic, Torval considered. This is the man they dropped me into! Was Joe's soul in Hell now, reaping a just reward for a wasted life? Or was this miserable experience here, on the city streets, the only punishment he really needed?

Well, Torval mused, I'll probably never know. None of that matters, anyway. This body is mine now, and Joe is gone. In fact, perhaps it's for the best that he'd been such a worthless, unnoticeable person in life. That means I can blend in here without any real trouble.

Yet none of this answered the real question: What do I do now?

One thing he did know was he didn't want to spend the next two weeks begging, drinking, and sleeping in the cold. There must be something else he could do to ensure he got through this with a minimum of pain and suffering. But what?

Again, he searched his body's memories for some clue. Joe had once been something called a "truck driver," whatever that meant. Trucks were one of those amazing vehicles, he discovered as he rummaged through the catacombs of Joe's mind. Really big vehicles, in fact. Images of driving along a highway came to Torval, causing him to shudder and shove those thoughts away. By the very Gates of Hell, how could anything move so fast? All those cars and trucks, all screaming along down the road together! How did they avoid colliding?

Actually, they didn't, Torval realized suddenly. A stab of guilt tore through him as a darker part of Joe's life surfaced. His truck, jackknifing, crushing two cars... the dead woman and her baby... the terrible, soul-wrenching funeral... Joe's life was never the same after that. He lost first his job and then his wife, turning to alcohol to drown his sorrows. All this because of a single mistake. His fault... it was all his fault! If only he hadn't tried to stay on the road just one more hour! If only he'd pulled over for a nap when he felt the warning signs of exhaustion! But he hadn't—and two innocent people paid the price.

No, not two people. Three. The third just took longer.

Again, Torval shook his head to recover his senses. I am not Joe

Sampson! he shouted inwardly. Joe is gone! He made a mistake and destroyed himself because of it. I'm not that man! I'm Torval, a demon from Hell, and I'm on vacation, for Lucifer's sake! Now I just have to decide what to do next.

I will not be like Joe, he told himself. I'm not going to just let myself waste away.

Well, of course he could, but when Landri saw how little his subordinate learned of humanity, the punishment would be severe. Torval knew instinctively he couldn't just lie around uselessly. But what can I accomplish? Joe's only skill was something I don't want to do, and he's been a bum for so many years I probably can't recover those reflexes anyway. Still, I have to try something... but what?

Sitting there, thinking about it, Torval remembered something he heard Christine say earlier. She suggested he clean himself up and get a job. Great, just great! That's all well and good, but how can I possibly do that? If getting a job is so easy, why are all these homeless people here? Wouldn't they all prefer to be somewhere else, other than this place? Surely they don't all have stories as pathetic as Joe's!

As he pondered, the large woman named Lakisha sauntered over, a scowl painted on her dark-skinned face. "What the hell do you think you're doing?" she said angrily, and for an instant she reminded him of his corpulent boss back in the Underworld. "Can't you see you're taking up a seat? You already had your soup, now get out!"

"Yes, ma'am!" Torval replied automatically, snapping to his feet so quickly that his vision swam from dizziness. Old habits die hard, apparently.

"Ma'am, is it now?" Lakisha laughed. "This ain't the army, son! Just put your bowl where it belongs and go! Come back tomorrow if you want, but leave the rest for the other hungry folks!"

"All right, I will go," said Torval, starting to move toward the exit. Without thinking about it, he picked up the empty soup bowl and set it in the stack near the sink.

Suddenly, he turned back to Lakisha. "Wait," he said somewhat nervously, "I want to ask you something. How can I go about finding a job?"

For a moment, she just stared at him as if he'd gone crazy. Then, without warning, she burst out laughing. "A job?" she snickered, as if he'd just said the most ludicrous thing she ever heard. "You? Oh, wait just a second, let me get a tape recorder!"

"Why?" he asked curiously, having absolutely no idea what that was. "Will such a thing help me become employed?"

Lakisha was by now laughing so hard that Christine took notice, walking over to see what was going on. "Whatever is so funny?" she asked curiously.

"Oh, wait till you hear this!" Lakisha guffawed. "Joe says he wants to get a job! Ain't that the most hilarious thing you ever heard?"

Christine chuckled weakly and turned to Torval. "Is that true?" she asked. "Are you serious, or is this some kind of joke?"

"No, I am quite serious," replied the demon. "I want to—well, I do not want to have to go out in the cold again. I need to have a job so I can get a place to live. Is that not how things work?"

"Well, yes, of course," said Christine, a curious expression on her face. "I just never thought I'd hear you ask, Joe. You've always been so adamant about not going back. Didn't you say this was how you wanted to be? What you deserved?"

She had her hands on her hips now, and Torval wasn't sure just what she meant by that. Vaguely, Joe's recollections reminded him that he did, in fact, say that to Christine. He never told her the reason, though, despite her seemingly endless attempts to pry that information out of him. Perhaps that's what she's trying to do now, Torval thought. Best to get her off that line of questioning.

"Maybe so," he replied, "but I died—well, I mean, I thought I was going to die, and that made me reconsider. I do not want to be cold and hungry any more."

Lakisha continued to laugh. "Oh, listen to him now! A changed man, just like that! Don't listen, Chris—this is some kind of game!"

"Is that right, Joe?" She was studying him carefully now. "Are you just fooling around? You've been acting funny all day—your voice seems wrong, and you don't hunch over like usual."

"I told you," he replied, "I am trying to change my ways. I do not want to live like this any more. Please help me."

Lakisha just kept on laughing. "Yeah, go on, help him," she said derisively. "Don't buy it, girl. Seriously!"

Christine rolled her eyes. "Just go back to the line, Kisha," she scolded. "I'll take care of this."

The black woman moved away, still shaking her head and snickering. As soon as she moved out of earshot, Christine said, "Are you serious, Joe? No, really, don't play with me now. Do you really mean that?"

"Yes," Torval told her. "How can I make you understand? I want to be warm and comfortable, not cold and sick. Tell me what I have to do."

Christine looked at him doubtfully. "Well, I don't know," she replied with a shrug. "I don't have any jobs to give you. I'm just a social worker, not the employment bureau. But, if you want, I'll stop by and see if they have any postings. What are you looking to do? What can you do?"

"I do not know," replied Torval. "I do not care what it is. I would do anything you want."

"Sheesh, you're desperate now, aren't you?" Christine smiled. "Well, if this is a joke and you make me waste my time tomorrow, I'm going to stop sticking up for you in front of Lakisha, understand?"

"I assure you, this is no joke," Torval said with a hint of frustration. Why was this so difficult for her to believe? Didn't she always beg Joe to change his ways and find a job? Now, he was doing it, and all she could do was doubt him.

"Wait—why tomorrow?" he asked suddenly. "Can you not help me find a job right now?"

"It's almost dark, silly," Christine replied with a laugh. "No one's interviewing this late in the day! Lucky for you, I've got nothing going on at the office tomorrow morning. Be here at eight, and we'll see what might fit you. We're going to have to do something about those clothes, and that scraggly beard of yours. And for the love of God, don't show up here drunk! If you do, I'll throw you out and never speak to you again!"

"I will not drink," he promised. "But what do I do now? I do not want to go back out there!"

"Well, you have to," she told him. "We can't put you up here, you know. You can always check one of the other shelters, if you can find one that'll take you. If not, just build yourself a fire like always and make sure you're here in the morning. Oh, I do hope you're serious, Joe! I just knew you could pull yourself together if you really wanted to. Now look, I have to go get some more soup ready, okay? See you tomorrow!"

Just like that, she was gone, leaving Torval standing there alone. He glanced over at the door again, watching the snow follow the newest homeless arrival inside, and shuddered at the thought of returning to that frozen wasteland of a city. Yet what choice did he have? At least tomorrow promised to be a better day.

Pulling his tattered coat around him, he left the shelter without glancing back.

# Chapter 5

"Damn, you're lookin' better, Joe," mumbled a heavily bearded, dark-skinned man dressed in ragged jeans and a heavy jacket stained almost black with grime. "Hard t'believe you were almost dead yes'day."

Torval shivered slightly as he huddled next to the rusted barrel and the soothing warm flames that flickered within. His memories informed him that the black man addressing him was named Carl, but Joe's brain revealed nothing more. Accessing those buried thoughts seemed harder now, so unless he really concentrated, Torval could only remember the most basic things about himself, his surroundings, and his acquaintances. He felt certain he should know more about Carl, but whatever tidbits remained in his human mind were elusive and quickly forgotten.

"Yes, I do feel much better," Torval said listlessly. He enjoyed the warmth emanating from the barrel, but didn't like the idea of having to carry on an inane, pointless conversation in order to enjoy it. All he really wanted was to be left alone.

"'Tis good, 'tis good," went on Carl, nodding and rubbing his hands together in front of the orange flames. "We already lost Harry t'this damned blizzard, and I don't think Hal's gonna last much longer."

Torval shivered again. The heat from the barrel-fire stood out in amazingly sharp contrast to the biting wind coming down the alleyway. Several other barrels lined the snow-covered street, creating the appearance of a snake-like string of flickering lights winding their way through the darkness. Absently, the demon turned to the side, rotating his body so every part of him could enjoy the heat, but with each pivot the bitter wind cut through his meager clothing, lashing at his skin. He found himself longing for the shelter, where the warmth wasn't quite as localized.

"Somethin' wrong, Joe?" asked Carl, making Torval wish the man would take the hint and quit talking. "Oh, I get it, yer worried 'bout Hal, aincha? Yeah, we all is, an' that's the truth. I gotta tell ya, I don't think he's gonna make it. If ya wanna say anythin' to 'im, he's down thataway."

Carl pointed a gaunt, rag-covered arm toward the end of the alley, where a trio of barrels stood guard over a cluster of pitiful-looking homeless people. Although the multiple fires promised greater warmth, Torval preferred to be as alone as possible. The fewer people he had to interact with, the better.

Still, he thought, Carl isn't showing any sign of shutting up, so being around others couldn't be any worse. Besides, if what the black man said was accurate, Hal might actually be nearing the end of his life. Torval hadn't ever actually witnessed a soul ending its mortal travels and transitioning to its next destination. That might well be something worth observing. Humans only died once, so this might be the only chance he had during his vacation to see the phenomenon.

"All right, I should speak to him," Torval agreed, moving away in haste, reluctantly leaving the warm barrel behind. The chill felt even worse as he left the fire's soothing aura, and he tried to hurry as much as possible. The snow, built up in foot-deep drifts, crunched loudly under his feet.

Although he only had to walk a dozen yards through the dark alleyway, the trip seemed to take an eternity. Once again the cold assailed Torval from every direction, reminding him how precarious his situation was. All around him rose the immense spires of concrete and glass that made up the vast city he had yet to actually identify. Torval found it quite ironic that, despite the fact that perfectly comfortable dwellings surrounded him, his presence within those structures would be most unwelcome.

Before coming to this alley, he actually had tried to make his way inside one of the impossibly tall spires. A uniformed man, armed with a short stick and bulging muscles, met him at the door. Torval found himself reminded, for a brief instant, of the massive gold-skinned demons guarding the Transition Center. The human guard wasn't twice his size or backed up by deadly cerberi, but might as well have been.

Torval knew without even thinking about it that the bulky security man could crush his fragile, illness-weakened frame with little effort.

After that failure, Joe's memories pointed out that a bum wasn't welcome in any building, except those set up specifically to deal with street people. An ordinary human kept himself clean, dressed in well-kept clothing, and took care of his own personal hygiene. Those who didn't follow these rules were, quite simply, outcasts.

This attitude reminded Torval of a Fourth-Class demon after its initial spawning in the Deep Pits. Once formed, such a creature experienced a period of mindlessness, where it roamed about in the lower caverns, completely driven by its own limited wants and needs. In such a state, it wasn't welcome anywhere else in Hell, and was shunned by all, even the lowest Third-Class demon. Only after decades of wandering would a mindless Fourth-Class drone develop any thoughts beyond its most basic drives. Eventually, when one began to show true curiosity, a recruiter would bring the creature into service for the lowest menial labor. Fourth-Class demons were little more than slaves, which was all they deserved to be, until such time as they advanced themselves to the next level of existence—a process that could take hundreds of years, if it happened at all.

Torval didn't even remember his own time as a Fourth Class demon. He'd been a Third Class so long, he couldn't even recall if he started existence by clawing his way out of some pool of slime, or was simply part of the initial crop of demons planted by the Creator. Not that it mattered much to him, anyway. That was centuries ago, and he had no intention of ever going through such a trial again. This sojourn on Earth, however, felt very much like he imagined life was like for a Fourth Class—treated with no respect, without even a place to call home, and forced to prove himself worthy before he could even get a job.

Of course, a Fourth-Class drone had no idea that anything better awaited it. Torval knew otherwise, and so did these other bums and castoffs in the frosty alleyway. They, like Joe, seemed to prefer this existence over any alternative, and Torval simply couldn't understand. Why would anyone choose to live like this?

Joe, at least, had something of an explanation. The ex-truck driver once made a huge mistake, all those many years ago, and fled his old career for this pathetic existence. Because of his guilt, he punished himself by becoming a burnt-out wino. Why would he torture himself during life, though? That was what Hell was for! Oh, that's right, Torval reminded himself—humans didn't know for certain that an afterlife awaits them. So, not sure that he would be punished in Hell, Joe Sampson created his own version of it right here on Earth.

Torval nodded slightly to himself as he made his way through the last snowdrift. Maybe that's why all these people are here—self-induced torture. He found himself wondering, even as he stepped up gratefully to the nearest warm barrel, if upon their death these bums would be granted any compensation upon their sentencing in Hell.

"Hey, Joe," said a hooded man close by as Torval rubbed his hands quickly together near the flames. "'Nother cold night, eh?"

Torval nodded absently. He knew Jake, he reflected, upon glancing briefly at the old man's hollow eyes. The face, with its scattering of wrinkles, possessed a thick growth of graying beard and mustache, flaked with bits of snow despite the protective hood. Jake was something of a leader among the homeless community, having been here for years. No one really knew anything about him, which was just the way he seemed to like it. While other bums had little trouble relating their sad stories to anyone who would listen, Jake never spoke a word about his own background. In that, he had something in common with Joe, Torval reflected.

"Oh, 'ey, Joe," said a withered woman clad in what looked like several layers of heavy coats. She, too, was old, with claw-like fingers and a hooked nose that looked as though it had been broken several times. Ethel was her name, and she used a different method of speech than the others, although Torval didn't know what that meant, exactly. In Hell, each demon sounded pretty much like any other, and there were no languages or accents to cause confusion. Here in the Middle World, the spoken word worked differently—it had to do with something in the Compact called Babble or Babel or something like that, but Torval couldn't remember the details.

"Come t'see 'al, 'ave ya?" Ethel went on in that strange, curious burr of hers. "We're tryin' to keep 'im warm, 'ere in the middle, but 'e's pretty weak."

With his fingers and arms warmer now, Torval stepped around the rusty cylinder and looked down at Hal. The middle-aged man lay amidst a pool of melted snow, covered in moth-eaten blankets and soggy cardboard scraps. His face was drawn and pale, and his breath came in ragged gasps. Thin, half-gloved hands clutched weakly at his chest, shaking noticeably in the cold.

Immediately, Torval felt a twinge of sadness flow from what remained of Joe's mind. Hal was a friend—a good friend, Torval realized in confusion. The concept of friendship shook him momentarily. In all his life, the demon never felt such a thing. He simply didn't associate with others all that much, certainly not enough to have a "friend," or even really understand the concept. Now, though, looking down at the sick man at his feet, Torval felt a distressing wave of distinctly unpleasant anxiety.

Reflexively, he sorted through Joe's memories as best he could. The recollections were much more difficult to reach than they were upon his arrival—Joe's personality seemed to be slipping away, out of Torval's reach. Even so, the demon quickly realized that Hal was someone of value. Someone he knew for—how long? He couldn't remember, but as he thought back to Joe's worthless, wandering existence, the face of Hal Sommersby was usually there, somewhere in the background.

Yes, Torval recalled slowly, Hal befriended him shortly after his arrival on the streets. They "hung out" together, if Torval understood that particular euphemism correctly. Not all the time, but more frequently than anyone else Joe knew. When Joe got sick several days ago, Hal brought him some booze to "warm him up," but after Hal started to show symptoms, he wandered off to try to beg for medicine. That's the last time Joe remembered seeing him.

"Hey, Hal," Torval heard himself saying, after trying unsuccessfully to draw forth any further images from his host body's brain. "You all right?"

The sick man coughed twice, a rasping, throaty sound that sounded vaguely familiar. Torval recognized the noise as one that came from his own chest shortly after his arrival here. So... he and Hal had the same illness, probably picked up from the same location while they meandered around the streets together. That's how diseases work, Torval knew. They spread from one human to another, through the air or by physical contact. That's what made them one of Lucifer's most insidious creations. Torval had no idea how plagues transmitted themselves, exactly, only that they existed as a means to spread chaos and fear, and enough death to make humans desperate and weak without killing them all—which, of course, exceeded the scope of the Compact. If Armageddon came, it would be at a time of the Creator's choosing, not any of his subjects.

"Joe," gasped Hal weakly. "I'm g-glad you're h-here. I'm g-gettin' through this, b-buddy. I'll be okay t-tomorrow, just like you."

Torval nodded, but inside he wasn't so sure. The disease had, after all, killed Joe in the end. "Just stay still," he said, rattling off the first thing that came to mind. "You need to rest."

Ethel leaned over slightly. "What 'e really needs," she intoned almost accusingly, "is a warm bed, but th' bloomin' shelters won't take 'im. No sickies, they say. Some kinda bug goin' round, and they don't want 'im infectin' the whole bloody city."

"I'll be fine," wheezed Hal. "Just keep me warm. And I'm hungry. So hungry . . ."

"'e needs some-a that soup," Ethel stated. "That's the best thin' for 'im roit now. It'll warm 'im up inside."

"That is true, the soup was very good," agreed Torval, fondly remembering the way the thick broth tasted on his tongue. Taste—there's another thing he just wasn't used to. For his demon form, taste existed only to tell him when his crushed grubs were ready to be swallowed. He didn't normally derive pleasure from that particular sense. For mortals, taste served a valuable purpose—picking out which foods are good to eat and which are bad. As a demon, Torval always ate the same thing. With no variety, he had no reason to ever consider taste as anything other than vestigial.

"Blimey, you're daft," muttered Ethel after a few seconds of silence passed, punctuated only by a couple of coughs from Hal. "Do I need t'spell it out fer ya, you bloomin' idiot? If you don't want yer friend t'croak, go fetch 'im some-a that soup!"

Torval stood up straight, automatically responding to Ethel's orders, completely by reflex. For hundreds of years, he'd taken commands without hesitating or questioning them, and that ingrained impulse proved difficult to ignore. He opened his mouth to say the automatic "Yes, sir!" that hung on his lips, but suddenly stopped. For the first time in his existence, Torval had the opportunity to refuse a direct order.

Ethel wasn't his boss, or in his chain of command—nor was she a Second-Class demon, or anything remotely similar. Torval had no reason to accept her orders, but her stern voice threw him off. Where he came from, only those with authority gave orders—others would never consider doing so. That wasn't the only reason Torval paused, though. He was a mortal now, on Earth, and as Geezon told him, no one gave him orders here. He could do whatever he wanted.

One thing he definitely didn't want to do was trudge off into the cold, windswept night just to fetch some warm soup for a sick human. Hal might've meant something to Joe, but, as Torval had to keep reminding himself, he wasn't Joe! He had no reason to help the friend of a man now dead and on his way to his final sentencing.

Torval turned to Ethel, opening his mouth to refuse her command, and suddenly halted. The look on her face was one of—what? Expectation? Did she expect him to help Hal automatically, because they were friends? No, that wasn't entirely it. She expected him to help because it was the right thing to do. The good thing to do.

*Good.* There's that concept again. Torval knew about evil well enough, for that's what brought souls into his care back home. Good, though, still eluded him.

Torval knew how it all was supposed to work, of course. Good people were rewarded in Heaven, while the evil languished in Hell. Since no one reached Hell as a reward for good deeds, Torval had no understanding of exactly what it meant to be "good." Is that what Ethel wanted from him now? For him to undertake an action simply because it would help Hal, at no benefit to Torval himself? Is that what it meant to be good—to perform a selfless act? To help Hal for no reason other than that he needed help?

Torval considered that for a fleeting moment. Helping Hal would, on the surface, do nothing to serve his own interests. Yet, as far as Joe was concerned, Hal was his friend. If Joe helped his companion now, he could expect similar aid in the future. So, did that mean people did good deeds in expectation of reciprocation later on?

He'd seen one other person doing something good today, Torval remembered—Christine, the lovely social worker back in the shelter. Maybe, if he asked her why she volunteered at the facility, she'd give him further insight into the phenomenon of "good." He couldn't just jump out and ask, of course, without revealing he was more than he appeared, but perhaps if he phrased the questions properly, he might learn something more.

Besides, he certainly wouldn't mind another opportunity to interact with Christine. Even putting Joe's lascivious memories out of his mind, something about her still intrigued him. She just genuinely enjoyed helping people, and stood up for him in front of that other, much more unpleasant woman. Christine was just—nice. Yes, that's the word. Nice.

Torval never met anyone "nice" before.

"All right," he said after a brief moment. "Stay here, Hal. I will try to get some soup for you."

* * *

With a grunt of final effort, Torval forced his weary legs up and over the last snowdrift and exited the alley. Ahead of him, the black street loomed, half filled with idling cars waiting at a light. The molten snow glinted under the pale streetlamps, which lit up the city like miniature suns. Vehicle engines rumbled as they idled impatiently, and several cabs moved by in the opposite direction, splashing oil-slicked, salty water onto the curb. Passing pedestrians avoided the brackish liquid, muttering under their breaths and clutching their heavy coats around their bodies to protect them from the bitter cold.

Torval stopped momentarily, just taking in the scene. There was so much here he just didn't understand. Joe's fading memories told him everything looked perfectly ordinary and normal, but Torval's demonic mind saw things differently.

For example, how did those tall metal poles produce such bright, steady lights from their tips? Apparently Man long ago mastered some sort of semi-magical force called electricity, or so Joe's vocabulary suggested. The streetlamps weren't the only source of light, either—it was everywhere, coming out of seemingly everything. Some of the windows on the buildings high above, for example. Signs advertising various products and services. The front and back corners of cars and trucks idling on the road. Even some of the people walking by carried personal light sources in their hands.

The colors, too, were amazing. Reds, yellows, greens, and more glowed all about him. A car's rear had red lights, compared to white and yellow on the front. A flashing amber light from a bumper signaled a pending turn. Hanging above the street, a series of red, yellow, and green lights told the cars and trucks when they could move. Most spectacularly of all, a huge sign hanging on a building some distance away seemed to glow with an unearthly blue aura, spelling out the name of some business or other entirely in gigantic letters.

The phenomenon of artificial light was but one of the mysteries Torval couldn't quite grasp. The cars themselves were another amazing human creation. How did they move? Where did they come from? Who figured out how to make them? Torval wasn't naïve enough to believe this was really some sort of magic. Perhaps in Hell, where illusion was the way of things, a magical self-propelled vehicle might be believable, but not here. In the mortal realm, things operated by specific natural laws. Magic didn't really exist, despite how often Lucifer's agents tried to convince people that it did.

Torval remembered quite a few inmates who insisted they were witches or warlocks who must be the victim of some sort of failed magical spell. The punishments for such charlatans were usually quite elaborate. For putting their belief in a nonexistent force, and seeking to control others through these "dark" powers, they were often tortured by giving others power over them. One prisoner, in fact, found herself trapped in the form of a mouse, transformed thus because of the way she tried to dominate others with the aid of nonexistent sorcery.

Equally amusing were the hard-core scientists, who refused to believe in anything other than the universe's rules. They denied the very existence of a Creator or an afterlife, simply because they refused to believe in anything they couldn't see or measure. More than a few such humans now sat idly in empty cells, with nothing to study or observe—nothing to do but think, for all eternity. Or until they transcended, of course, Torval added automatically.

So, he thought, without magic, cars could only function if Man himself harnessed the natural laws of the universe. How did humans do it? Where did they find the time? Living less than a century, always at odds with each other, not knowing why they were here? Baffling, totally baffling…!

The mysteries just went on and on. Even the simple things were beyond Torval's understanding. Clothing, for example. He knew about metal and stone, but what created the strange garments people wore? And the shiny packages the women carried over their shoulders, in all those odd shapes and sizes—what were they made of? Or the metallic frames worn over the eyes of the occasional human passing by? He knew the names of these things—purses and glasses, respectively—but had no idea how they came to be.

These things weren't new to him, of course. He remembered all of them, in various forms and shapes, from illusions back in Hell. Yet until now he'd never stopped to contemplate their existence or purpose. He'd always just assumed they were merely props used to torture inmates, like the rickety old typewriter in Bob's cell. Not so, he realized now—they were part of the Middle Realm, a world Torval simply couldn't relate to or comprehend. Even something as simple as why the snow formed huge immobile piles everywhere, yet melted instantly upon hitting the street, eluded him completely.

The demon shook his frost-coated head and shivered as another gust of wind swept down between the buildings, knifing through his tattered garments. Without wasting any more time, he hurried down the avenue, avoiding the passersby who alternately ignored him, turned their gaze away, or scowled at his ragged figure. Even at the corner, where he waited for those amazing and incomprehensible traffic lights to turn and let him cross, the other pedestrians shied away from him as much as possible.

Finally, after far too long in the bitter wind, Torval made it to the alley where the soup kitchen waited. He shuffled up to the door, glad to be back here once again, only to find the portal securely locked.

He fought with the doorknob for a moment, thinking it might be stuck, only to pause as he saw the hours posted clearly on the door. The place closed at 10 p.m., the sign said. Torval knew, thanks to Joe's ingrained memories, how to express time in human terms, but he had no way to actually tell what hour it was. Late, he was sure—several hours had passed since he left the shelter before, and that was close to sunset. How late was he? Maybe someone was still inside. Maybe Christine was still there, cleaning up the place, he thought hopefully.

Torval banged on the door several times, and called out as well, but no one came. After a few minutes, he gave up and turned away. How was he supposed to get soup now? And without Christine there to talk to, should he even bother? No, of course not. All he wanted to do now was get warm at another barrel-fire. Lucifer willing, after this long night was over, he'd have a job and a place to live, and he wouldn't have to endure this miserable cold any more.

He started back toward the alley, but as he did, he began to think about what he was going to tell the other bums. What would they say when he came back empty-handed? Well, it doesn't matter, he told himself, wondering why he felt a sense of nagging discomfort in his belly. They'd just have to understand that the kitchen was closed.

Torval let his mind drift as he made his way back to the street. He pictured himself pushing his way through the snow back to the trio of fires, where he would look down at his coughing friend Hal and tell him the bad news. He could almost hear Ethel lambasting him for giving up so easily, and could virtually see the disappointed look on Jake's wrinkled, bearded face. Worse still, he could see Hal's gaunt eyes staring up at him, pleading for food.

In his mind's eye, Torval saw himself turn his back on Hal. Then, with a choking gasp, his friend and companion shuddered and died.

Torval came to a halt and steadied himself against a nearby wall. The feeling that washed over him caught him totally by surprise. He felt remorse—the same thing that pierced Joe's heart whenever those memories of the truck crash came flooding back. Torval tried to push those thoughts away, but couldn't. He didn't want to see Hal die, especially if he had the means to prevent it. He didn't want to feel that same pain felt by Joe when he stood alone at that terrible funeral, watching the coffins lowered into the ground, unable to face the families of those he'd wronged...

Bless it all! Torval shook his head and swore to himself. I don't want these stupid feelings! I'm a demon, for Lucifer's sake! I've got no connection to this world, or to these people. I shouldn't feel any sort of responsibility for any of them, certainly not if it causes me any discomfort at all. Yet, thanks to Joe's memories, he had no choice. He knew if he didn't help Hal, and the man died tonight, he'd feel that same annoying, soul-gouging, Satan-blessed remorse in his chest for the rest of his time here on Earth.

Still swearing, Torval started along the street again, hands automatically reaching into his well-worn pockets to check for change. He found a dime and several pennies—not enough to buy anything at all, he knew, assuming he could find an open establishment at this hour. That meant he only had one alternative open to him, distasteful as it was.

He stopped at the corner where he had crossed the street earlier and looked around. A coffee shop on the other side appeared closed, judging from the lack of interior lighting. No other stores appeared capable of serving food. He searched Joe's memories, but as a street bum, the man didn't go in such places, so he didn't take much notice of them during his wanderings. There were many restaurants and diners in the area, but their exact location eluded Torval.

The light turned red before he could cross, so the demon stood there, waiting. As he did, a man approached, dressed in a heavy trench coat and studying a sheaf of grayish paper. He didn't see Torval immediately and stopped close by, only to glance up and back away suddenly. As they made eye contact, the demon decided to take the plunge. "Excuse me, sir," he said as amiably as possible, "can you tell me where—"

"Get a job!" barked the man quickly, turning his back and stepping further away.

"No, you do not understand," Torval went on. "I need to find a place to get some food for my sick friend."

"Stop bothering me or I'll call the cops," came the angry reply. The man looked back over his shoulder warily, as if afraid Torval would accost him at any second. The pedestrian's face twisted into an expression of utter disgust and contempt, and then he hurried off into the darkness.

Torval sighed. Joe's memories seemed full of similar failures. Only one person in dozens ever succumbed to his pathetic attempts to scam enough money to buy another bottle of booze. He just had to keep trying, even if all he wanted now was information. Persistence usually paid off, although it could take a while.

He stood at that corner for quite some time before a passing woman finally stopped to listen. "Please," he implored her, rubbing his icy hands together, "my friend is sick and needs some soup. Can you tell me where I might find a place to get some this late at night?"

The old woman, bundled up in a long brown coat, leather gloves, and earmuffs, leaned close to hear him. "That's all you want?" she asked curiously, looking surprised. "You aren't going to bug me for money?"

"No," Torval admitted truthfully. "I just want to find a place where I might find food for my friend. I tried to go to the soup kitchen, but it was closed."

She nodded. "Who did you say was sick?"

"My friend Hal," said Torval honestly. "He is too weak to move, so I left him between the fire-barrels to stay warm."

"That poor dear," said the woman, still studying Torval curiously. "You don't sound like any street person I've ever met. You're too—what's the word I'm looking for? Innocent—yeah, that's it exactly."

"Innocent?" Torval raised an eyebrow. Well, perhaps that's a good way to put it. He certainly was new to this world, although this old lady surely couldn't know that. "I'm new here," he confided after a moment's reflection. "Tomorrow, I'll get a new job, so I can get a place to stay. I do not like the cold, and I definitely do not want to get sick again."

She nodded. "Okay, you've convinced me," she told him. "You're either the worst beggar in the history of this city, or you're one of the best. I don't know which, but I'm in a good mood, so I'll take door number two. Anyway, there's an open diner two blocks that way." She pointed a hand in one direction, and then reached into her purse. After a moment of rummaging, she withdrew two green sheets of paper Torval immediately recognized as money. "When you get there, buy your friend a nice meal, okay?"

"I shall do so," said Torval, taking the two one-dollar bills and stuffing them in his pocket. He then realized he should respond appropriately, using a strange human custom—but he couldn't quite remember it. "I am not sure what else to say," he added with uncertainty.

"Don't worry about it," she replied with a shrug. "Someone did me a favor yesterday, and what goes around, comes around. Now, good luck with your job tomorrow. Just remember, practice random acts of kindness, okay? I hope your friend feels better!"

The light turned green as she finished speaking, so the old lady crossed quickly while she had the chance. She almost seemed uncomfortable in her haste to depart. Torval watched her go, idly running his chilly fingers over the bills in his pocket. He didn't even ask her for that money—she just gave it to him for no reason! Why? Why did she do that?

By far, money brought the most sinners to Hell. Humans just seemed to go crazy for the stuff. They worked all their lives to earn it, then either hoarded their gains until death, or spent what they had too frivolously. Sometimes they stole even more, or cheated other people out of what they'd legitimately earned. Once, when Torval noticed that ten of the souls in a row on his route were all being punished for money-related crimes, Foreman Landri said, "You know, Satan didn't invent money, but I hear he really, really wishes he could take the credit for it."

Indeed, thought Torval. Money would've been the greatest invention of evil in all of history, but if Landri spoke the truth, Man created it for himself! So why would this old woman simply hand him two dollars for no reason at all? Was it, as she said, a "random act of kindness"? Or was this just an attempt to earn points toward a lesser sentence in Hell when she finally passed beyond the veil?

Torval shook his head. He still didn't know enough about goodness to know for sure, but he certainly appreciated the woman's gift. The green pieces of paper seemed warm in his pocket, although of course that was just his imagination. He felt seized by the impulse to do something nice for the old lady in return, but by now he'd missed his chance.

She was gone, already out of sight around the next snow-blanketed corner. Even if he could find her again, what could he possibly do?

Besides, he thought, as the wind buffeted him again, I'm too cold to worry about it now. Maybe the money will be enough to purchase two bowls of soup, so I can warm up again before returning to Hal. Yes, that's perfect, he thought eagerly. He very much wanted to taste soup once more. Just the memory of that savory broth coating his tongue was enough to make him wish he never had to chew on another food-grub again.

Without another thought, he turned and hurried down the street in the direction the old woman indicated. Maybe the diner will be warm, he thought hopefully. Maybe I can stay there long enough for the numbness to fade from my fingers and toes, too.

# Chapter 6

THE SIGN ABOVE THE FRONT DOOR read "Diner Forty-Niner." Torval took no notice of the rhyming name, hurrying inside with thoughts squarely focused on the warm air emanating from within.

Small round tables surrounded by empty barstool-style chairs took up most of the restaurant's tiny interior. As Torval stepped inside, a jingling bell sounded above his head, taking him by surprise. He stood paralyzed for a moment, wondering if he might've triggered some kind of alarm, when a youthful, bearded man dressed in a collared beige shirt and matching slacks stepped into view from behind the counter. A cheerfully colored yellow tag on his lapel identified him as Alan Ferrell, the store manager.

Alan held a moist rag in one hand and a pail in the other, obviously intent on cleaning something, but he set his implements down the moment he saw his would-be customer. "We don't give handouts here," he grumbled in a somewhat strained voice, frowning at the sight of a ragged street bum in his doorway.

"I do not want a handout," explained Torval, taking out the green strips of paper the humans valued so greatly. "I have money. I wish to make a purchase."

"Oh," replied the manager, relaxing noticeably but still casting a wary look in his customer's direction. "Well, I don't sell alcohol here, either. Unless you want some coffee or food, you're out of luck."

"Food is what I need," said Torval. "Specifically, some soup, if you have it. My friend is sick."

"Really?" Alan appeared surprised. "You just want soup? That's it? Okay, well, I suppose I can do that. A lot of people want hot soup this time of year. I've got chicken noodle, bean, and vegetable, take your pick."

Torval searched Joe's fleeting memories. Which type did he sample at the soup kitchen? He really liked that kind, but didn't know if any of the types just named were the same variety. "The same as the shelter serves," he answered, unable to come up with anything better to say.

"Oh, I wouldn't know what they've got in that place," the man said distastefully, stepping close enough to his guest to identify the bills in Torval's hand, but going no further than he had to. "How much you got there? Two bucks? Tell you what, I'll give you a take-out bowl of each, okay? I've had it warming on the burner all night, but I've got more than enough to last till midnight, when those damn health bureau watchdogs make me trash it."

Torval had no idea what a health bureau watchdog was, but the man's offer sounded reasonable. If he understood correctly, he'd now exchange these two one-dollar bills for three bowls of soup. So... that's how money worked! How very simple and convenient.

"Yes, that will be adequate," the demon replied carefully, hoping he had the gist of things down properly.

"All right, hang on a sec while I get your stuff," said the proprietor, heading back behind the counter and through a swinging door. His young face appeared momentarily in the round window atop the portal, as if still suspicious of his visitor, but vanished a moment later.

Torval looked around. As the only patron in the diner, no one else could see him as he studied the place. The tables nearby looked clean, but the surface of the counter just ahead still harbored a few stains and crumbs scattered here and there. A rectangular container with white papers sticking out topped each of the dozen or so round tabletops. Studying the tables more closely, Torval also observed two smaller cylindrical objects, one marked "S" and the other "P." The significance of these eluded him completely.

The demon shook himself, causing the residual flakes of snow and drops of water to break free of his rags and join the growing pool of moisture at his feet. He found the warmth in this room most welcome, and particularly appreciated the lack of any significant wind. Already he felt much better about undertaking his soup-fetching journey. The barrel-fires, while hotter close up, didn't warm all sides of him like the diner's air did. Although, he realized after a moment, there did seem to be more heat coming from one direction. A very light breeze washed over him from a metallic grating along the right-hand wall.

Immediately, Torval moved toward the metal panel, finding the air coming out of the tunnel wonderfully hot. Where was it coming from? He stared into the blackness through the grate, but saw nothing. The warmth on his face felt soothing, though, and he shivered again at the comfort it provided.

This is what I want, Torval told himself. A room of my own inside a comfortable building, where I can huddle up next to a warm vent like this and not have to worry about the elements. That, and plenty of food and drink to keep this body going until my two weeks of torture are up.

Food and shelter, he thought idly. Those are the basic needs of humanity, are they not? Many of his charges back in Hell constantly reminded him of that, especially when consistently denied one or the other. Michael Rubin, in particular, often complained that he needed shelter from the unending sun.

Surely food and shelter shouldn't be that difficult to secure, Torval considered as he warmed his body in front of the heating grate. The basic necessities seemed easy enough to acquire—simply find a trade or skill with which to earn money, and exchange that for food, as he just did a few moments ago. That didn't seem so hard. A race of people who could construct such immense buildings couldn't have that much trouble affording a place to live, could they?

"Enjoying the heat?" asked a voice behind him. Torval turned to regard the proprietor, who held a bulging white bag in his right hand. "Yeah, I don't blame you. It's damn cold out there tonight."

"Yes, it is," replied Torval, raising an eyebrow at the man's use of the word "damn" again. That's the second time he'd heard that epithet spoken by this particular individual, and others he'd met earlier in the day seemed to use it with abandon. Humans, apparently, were familiar enough with the concept of damnation to include it in their everyday vocabulary. "I wonder if I might stay for a few more minutes," the demon asked hopefully.

"That's fine. You're a paying customer," answered Alan, reaching out his open hand. "I need those two bucks first, though."

"Yes, of course." Torval handed over the green bills and took the food. How elegant and simple, he thought. Now the man would take the cash and use it to buy something he wants at a later time. The ordered simplicity of money appealed to Torval's regimented demonic lifestyle. How could such a straightforward concept cause so many problems? He wanted to know, but didn't know how to ask without revealing his true nature. Not yet, anyway.

"May I sit down here?" he asked after a moment. "I would like to consume some of the soup myself, before I proceed further."

"Damn, you're the strangest-talking homeless guy I've ever met," said the man, again invoking that word, as though doing so wasn't in the least bit unusual. "Sure, go ahead. You should save the chicken soup for your buddy, though. That's the best for a sick person, or so they say."

Torval sat down on one of the bar stools and opened up the bag. He found three round containers inside, each with a lid on top. Two plastic spoons sat on top, along with a couple of napkins. All three soup bowls appeared identical. "Which one contains the chicken?" he asked.

"Oh, sorry, I don't remember," answered the proprietor. "You'll have to look yourself. I think I put the bean soup in first, so it should be on the bottom."

Torval selected the first Styrofoam bowl and lifted the lid, revealing a layer of creamy white broth dotted here and there with chunks of pale-colored plant roots. A rich, spicy aroma entered his nostrils, and he felt his mouth watering immediately.

"Oh, you found the veggie soup," said the owner. "Not as many vegetables as I would've liked. It's mostly potatoes tonight. Anyway, give it a try. I hope it doesn't have too much salt."

Torval pulled out one of the spoons and removed the useless clear wrapper. This implement reminded him of the metal one he used back at the shelter, only lighter and flimsier. He had no idea what strange substance it might be made of, but at the moment that didn't matter. He cared only about sampling the pasty white liquid inside the bowl. The aroma rising up from within caused his stomach to rumble with anticipation.

He dipped the plastic spoon into the thick soup, drew forth a sample heaping with chunky potatoes, plus a few flecks of orange that Joe's memories told him were called "carrots." Torval put the whole spoonful into his mouth without comment. The hot food tasted nothing like the shelter's broth, but he found it just as satisfying. Torval swallowed and quickly scooped out another helping, chewing the vegetables only briefly before repeating the process. With each bite, his stomach craved another all the more.

"I guess it's all right, I see," said the man with a smile. "You act like you haven't eaten in days!"

"It is very good," mumbled Torval between swallows, amazed at both the similarities and differences between this food and what he ate earlier in the day. Both were merely soup—mostly liquid, made from heated water and other products—but with wonderfully stimulating flavors. The vegetable soup's variety intrigued him, though. The white broth had its own appeal, but each of the bits inside added different tastes and textures that worked together to produce something greater than they would alone.

*So this is what it's like to taste different things simultaneously,* Torval thought in appreciation. Already, of all his experiences on Earth so far, taste was definitely his favorite.

"Well, don't choke yourself," the store manager added with a chuckle, walking back to his counter and picking up his rag once more. He proceeded to clean the countertop surface meticulously, wiping away the crumbs and spills left behind by earlier patrons. The room fell into silence, save for the humming of the wall heater and Torval's hasty slurping.

After a few minutes, the demon finished his meal and set down the spoon. A little bit of soup remained inside the cup, so he scraped it out with his fingers, determined to enjoy every last drop of the thick white stuff. As he did, the proprietor shook his head, but allowed a knowing smile to briefly cross his face.

Finally, Torval pushed the empty container aside. Two soup bowls still awaited him inside the bag, but he decided not to touch them for now. He no longer felt hungry at all. When he reached Hal, perhaps he'd eat one of the other helpings—the one that wasn't chicken soup. What was it again? Oh, yes. Bean soup, whatever that was.

Reluctantly, he stood and regarded the door. Through the glass front, he could see snowflakes blowing past in the harsh wind. He didn't want to go back out there.

"You gonna be all right?" the diner's owner called out.

"I think so," Torval replied. "It is so very comfortable in here. I wish I could stay longer. However, my friend is hungry, so I must go."

Alan nodded in understanding. "Anything else I can help you with?"

"No." Torval started toward the door, but paused. He could almost see the coldness emanating from the pale street outside. As much as he didn't like the idea, if he could strike up a conversation with this human, he could buy some more time in the warm and comfortable room. He turned back to regard Alan, who looked at him expectantly. "Actually, there is one thing," Torval explained. "It regards money."

"Money?" The man took a step backward, and his hand disappeared underneath the counter. Torval had the distinct impression he was gripping something tightly, just out of sight.

"Yes, I do not fully understand how it works," said the demon, figuring he might as well ask for more information on the subject. What harm would it be if this one human being thought him aberrant, anyway?

"You don't know how money works? What country are you from, anyway?" The proprietor seemed very worried now, and his hands remained hidden, clutching something out of view.

"I understand how to buy things," Torval went on, paying little attention to the veiled threat before him. He had no idea what Alan was doing, but even had he known about the shotgun there, he would've had no fear. After all, dying meant little to a demon trapped in human guise. "That part is easy," he went on curiously. "What I do not know is where money comes from."

"Oh," replied his host, appearing to relax ever so slightly. "The government prints it up. You should visit the Treasury Department in DC if you want to find out more."

Torval had no idea what any of that meant. "Treasury Department" and "dee-cee" were meaningless terms to him, and Joe's fading memories provided no answer this time. Although he found himself curious about those odd phrases, he pressed on instead with his original line of questioning. "So you are saying the government simply creates it at will and gives it to people?"

"Well, not exactly. It goes to banks, and places like that, so if people want their money, they can get it whenever they need to."

Torval stared at Alan and searched his host body's memories, which now seemed only able to provide data on the most basic concepts. Banks... they were places where people stored money for safekeeping, he realized. Yes, that made sense. He could recall several inmates of Hell being punished for robbing such places. Still, that didn't answer the most basic question of all. "If the government, as you say, can print what they need, where do they get it from?"

The man looked up at the ceiling for a moment. His tense expression seemed to quickly evolve into thoughtfulness. "You know, I really have no idea," he answered after a moment. "I seem to remember it's supposed to have some sort of basis in gold. Like, money represents gold somehow. I must admit, I don't understand it completely. Anyway, I figure there's only as much money as there is gold."

"Gold," Torval repeated. Just what he needed, another complication thrown into the mix! Like money, gold was another one of those valuable things that men stole and killed for with wild abandon. In the ancient depths of Hell, there were more souls imprisoned for gold-related crimes than virtually anything else. Newer inmates rarely sought that metal any more, just money. But if humans based their money on gold, then they were one and the same, were they not?

"Yeah, all that glitters," the proprietor went on with a quick shrug. "It's been a long time since I took high school economics, but I remember now. Money is like a promise of gold, or something like that. Theoretically, you can exchange dollars for gold any time you want, but nobody ever does. Money's so much easier to deal with. Hell, nowadays you don't even need cash. Most people have credit or debit cards, and one of these days there won't even be cash at all. Everything you buy will be done with some kind of electronic transfer via the Internet."

Once again, Torval had no idea what the man was talking about. Electronic transfers? Internet? Credit and debit cards? What were those? Joe had no experience with such things, at least not in the memories Torval could still find, which became harder and harder to access with every passing minute.

Before he could inquire further, the man gave a loud sigh. "Well, this has been an interesting conversation," he admitted, "and you've given me something to ponder for the rest of the night, but I can tell a stalling tactic when I hear one. You should go, my friend, and before your soup gets too cold."

"Very well," agreed Torval. "I have many more questions about the subject of money. You mentioned something called 'high school economics.' How can I learn more of this?"

"Try the library," was the response. "Now go on, go! I've got to start cleaning the floors, and I can't do that with you adding more melting snow into the mix. Come back next time you need to buy some soup, and maybe we'll talk more. You'll find me here most nights—the name's Alan, like it says on my tag."

"I am T—I mean, Joe Sampson. Goodbye, Alan Ferrell."

"Have a good evening," said Alan, turning away and retreating further into the diner. The phrase he used seemed odd, but the meaning was plain—Torval was dismissed.

The demon stood there for a moment longer, gathering his strength. The infusion of more soup into his stomach seemed to boost his spirits. He also knew more about how money worked—surely that would be useful information when Landri debriefed him upon his return. The more he found out about such things, the better off he would be. In fact, he now knew there was a place called a "library" that could provide even more data. Perhaps after he secured his job, and a warm place to live, he would locate and visit this mysterious institution.

Steeling himself against the cold, he pushed his way out the door into the snow, clutching his bag as tightly as he could.

* * *

The aging, poncho-enshrouded bum named Jake looked surprised as Torval shambled up to the trio of fire-barrels. He pointed at the sack in the demon's snow-coated hand. "Whatcha got there, Joe? Take-out?"

Nearby, Ethel snickered. "Toldya 'e wouldn't let 'im down. Joe 'n' 'al, they stick together. Guess the kitch'n was closed f' the noit, eh, Joey?"

"Yes, it was closed," said Torval, opening up the bag and withdrawing one of the containers. "I told people on the street about Hal, and a woman gave me money. I purchased the soup from Alan Ferrell."

"'oo?" asked Ethel, eyeing Torval curiously.

"Doesn't matter," insisted Jake before the demon could reply. "You got it, and that's what counts. You're a good man, Joe. I wish I had a friend like you."

"Really? I am good?" Torval looked at the old man with a surprised expression. "That is all it takes to be good? To perform a service such as this?"

"I guess so," replied Jake, staring at the demon through narrowed eyes. "You're actin' real funny tonight, Joe. Are you all right?"

"Yes, just cold," Torval replied, stepping close to the nearby fire. As he did so, Ethel snatched the soup container from his hand and opened it up. Another astounding odor emanated forth, making Torval's mouth water once again. He looked longingly at the cup the woman now held, noting how this particular batch of soup appeared more watery, with some kind of long, white ribbons of food scattered amidst chunks of grayish meat. Chicken soup, he knew at once, reaching for it automatically.

"Now, now," she cautioned with a wave of her hand, "this 'ere's for 'al, see? You 'ad your chance to eat some. Now stay still while Nurse Ethel takes care of 'er charge."

Torval nodded and watched as the bag lady began to spoon-feed the reclining form on the cold ground. The demon shrugged and set down his sack, along with the other container of soup still tucked away inside.

"Th-thanks, buddy," Hal managed between a few rheumy coughs. "I owe you. I owe you big."

The demon just nodded. He'd just done a good thing, or so Jake insisted. So bringing food to a sick friend was a good act! How interesting! Torval did indeed feel better for doing so. Or at least Joe did, despite the fact that the dead man's personality had nearly faded from Torval's mind. Was it only Joe who felt this way, or was there something more? He didn't know.

"Are you all right, Joe?" asked Jake curiously, still studying him with a curious eye. "There's somethin' different about you. I don't know what it is, but I'll figure it out."

"I was sick," suggested Torval, "but I am quite better now. Perhaps you remember me in my weakened state, and now that I am healthy, I look better."

"That's not it," Joe replied, now appearing openly suspicious. "Your speech . . . you never talked like that before. You always slurred, even when you weren't drunk. It reminds me of—oh, shit!"

"What? What is it?" To his surprise, Torval saw fear in the old man's face. Jake began to glance hastily from side to side, as though afraid of something only he could see. He looked ready to bolt, although he had nowhere to go at the end of the dark, snow-filled alleyway.

"You!" Jake replied accusingly, wagging a finger in Torval's face. "I know what you are! Stay away from me! I'm not going back! You can't make me! I made the choice of my own free will! I followed all the rules!"

"Wot's the problem, Jake?" asked Ethel, still spooning servings of chicken broth between Hal's quivering lips. "It's just Joey-boy, same as always. You're spookin' 'al now! Settle down!"

Jake continued to back away, up against the frosty bricks that lined the rear end of the alley, acting like a cornered animal. "N-nothin', Ethel," he stammered. "You just keep on feedin' Hal. I need to go. Just keep him away from me!"

Torval stared at Jake in confusion. "I do not know what you are talking about," he explained. "I assure you, you have nothing to fear from me."

"Y-you're not here to take me back?" asked Jake worriedly. Most of the other street people in the alley watched his antics with concerned expressions, while some backed noticeably away. "You aren't part of a hunt team?" Jake went on, relaxing ever so slightly.

"I do not know what that means," said Torval truthfully. "There is nothing special about me."

"Oh, really?" demanded Jake. "Very well, if that's true, come over here right now and shake my hand."

"What?"

"Shake my hand. I won't know if you're really my friend until you give me a really good handshake."

Torval shrugged. The request seemed innocent enough. Handshakes were normal behavior for humans, after all. Taking a few steps away from the comfortable barrel, he crunched through the snow to Jake's side and extended his hand. The old man reached out and took it in a firm, solid grip.

And *changed*.

Suddenly, Jake no longer looked like a withered old man wearing a ragged, heavy overcoat and snow-encrusted hood. Instead, the figure standing there shifted, becoming a gaunt, bony creature with a thick, ropy torso and no discernable neck. A spade-like, angular face stared unblinkingly back at Torval through eyes of purest black. The sharp chin beneath those bulbous eyes ended in a pointed tip, atop which protruded a round mouth lined with needle-like teeth. A pair of foot-long, folded ears twitched nervously in the dim firelight.

*A demon!* Jake was another demon!

But—but why? How? Even as he realized what he was seeing, Torval remembered Geezon's explanation that other demons might be found scattered about on Earth. Physical contact would reveal their true form, as it had just now. Yet, these other demons were supposed to be involved in plots to spread evil and temptation. Taking the body of a street bum, living apart from society, made no sense at all.

Jake released Torval's hand almost instantly, jerking it back as if burned on contact. "I knew it!" he half-shouted, now once again appearing totally human. He seemed on the verge of panic. "Your voice! That's how I spoke when I first got here! I'm not going back! You can't take me!"

"I do not want you," said Torval honestly. "I do not know who you fear so greatly, but I assure you, I am here for my own reasons. I am on vacation."

"You're—you're on—?" Jake hesitated, staring at Torval with a goggle-eyed expression. Almost immediately he relaxed, deflating noticeably and taking a deep breath. "Vacation, you say? Yeah, they let you Hell-bound types have time off every now and then, don't they? I remember hearing about that a few times. Oh, wow, what a relief!"

The old man put his hand over his heart and began to hyperventilate. As he did, he noticed the small crowd forming around him. "Don't worry, everybody!" he called out. "It's nothing! I'm all right now. Go back to the fires!"

The other homeless people nodded and grunted in his direction before turning away. A few lingered, but Jake shooed them off with a wave of his hand. Torval watched them go, surprised they weren't a bit more taken aback by what they'd just seen. "I do not understand," he said as soon as the others were out of earshot. "I was led to believe they are not aware of the existence of demons. If they just saw our true forms, why are they not afraid, or at least upset?"

"What? Oh, they didn't see us," explained Jake. "You and I, we saw our own forms in our minds, but the others just saw two men shaking hands. That's how the Compact set it up, remember? We can't journey to Earth in our natural shapes. To come here, we have to take human form. Even the Creator Himself followed that rule when he paid this place a visit two thousand years ago."

"He did?" Torval raised an eyebrow. "Really? The Creator Himself took a mortal shell?"

"Yes," insisted the demon known as Jake. "Or at least that's what they say. Didn't they give you some kind of orientation before they sent you here? You shouldn't act so innocent and curious—it's gonna give you away."

"I do wish they'd told me more, it is true," agreed Torval. "Who are you, anyway? Why are you here, in that particular body?"

Jake sighed. "I shouldn't tell you," he replied. "You're only Third Class, though, so you're conditioned to obey, aren't you? When you go back, you're going to blab all about me. That means I'm going to have to move again, and I really like it here. Wait! I know—I'll give you an order. Yeah, that should work. You recognized my form, right? I am—well, I was—a Second-Class Tempter. That means I'm your superior!"

"That is so," Torval answered. "However, my Transitioner told me that I need not follow orders during my vacation. In fact, he told me that if I encountered another demon, I was to pass him by. I suppose I should leave you to your business." He turned to go, not relishing the idea of trudging through the snow once again, but intent on following his instructions to the letter.

"No, no, don't do that!" said Jake quickly. "It's been a long time since I've been able to talk honestly with anybody! I couldn't tell most—er, any of these humans who I really was, you see. They wouldn't believe me, and if they did, I'd be in real trouble."

"You want me to stay?" asked Torval. "But I was given orders—"

"Screw that!" Jake insisted. "Your orders don't mean jack shit here—you just said so yourself! But they will mean something when you get back. So here's what I'll do. I'm ordering you not to tell anyone back home about me. Those orders hold no sway now—but when you die, or your vacation ends, they'll be solid. You won't be able to talk about me to anybody. Got that?"

"Yes," Torval agreed. It seemed like a decent enough solution, as far as such things went. Although, of course, if his superiors asked him sufficient questions, their presence in his chain of command would override Jake's orders. Torval saw no reason to point that out now, though, so he proceeded along his previous line of questioning. "You still have not told me who you are, or why you are here."

"All right, my name is Prelz," replied the demon in Jake's body. "Like I said, I was a Tempter. I was here on Earth doing my job, which of course is to try to convince mortals to sin. I was pretty good at it, too. I worked at the post office, deliberately damaging and mishandling the mail."

Torval cocked his head, for he didn't know exactly what a post office was, but Prelz completely misread the expression. "Don't look at me like that!" he argued defensively. "You'd be amazed how much a shredded piece of mail can tick somebody off! Besides, the Compact is a lot more specific these days. Time was when we could offer 'deals with the Devil' in exchange for souls. Not anymore. Now we have to be a lot more subtle."

"So if you were so good at temptation," asked Torval curiously, "why are you not still doing it now?"

"You would ask that," sighed Prelz, slumping his shoulders. "Look, I'll tell you, but it's freezing over here. Can we go to one of the barrels?"

"Please," agreed Torval eagerly.

The two demons shuffled out of the snow bank to the nearest fire. Two other street people were there, warming their hands and bodies. "Get lost," Jake ordered, changing his voice subtly so that he sounded once again like an aged street person. "Joe and I here have somethin' private to discuss."

"Okay, whatever," muttered one, and the pair backed away, moving over to the next barrel, where Ethel continued feeding the ailing Hal.

"Anyway," Prelz went on after his hands warmed up, "I got sick of it. I kept wondering why I bothered. Men don't need us to convince them to do evil. They're plenty good at it on their own! Of course, I took the job hoping to get promoted, but after a few hundred years of bouncin' from body to body, I could tell that wasn't going to happen. I was weary, Joe. Say, what's your real name, anyway?"

"Torval, of Layer Four Hun—"

"Save it," interrupted Prelz with a wave of his hand. "I don't give a crap what layer you're from! Anyway, don't you ever stop to wonder why you do what you do, Torval? You're what, a Torturer, by the look of you? Yeah, that's right, I could tell by the horns and tail. That's how humans think of demons, you know. If they saw your true form—which they can't, at least most of them anyway—they'd know what you were immediately. It's in their psyche somehow."

"Yes, I am a Torturer," Torval admitted, "and, since you asked, yes, I have occasionally wondered why I do what I do. The reason I am here is because my supervisor recently noticed a decrease in my performance."

"Ah, so he thought a trip to Earth would fix you, huh? Not a bad idea. He dropped you into a bum, too. Slick. Your boss sounds like he's got real baron potential."

"I do not know," said Torval. "Perhaps he does. It is of little importance to me."

"Yeah, well, for me there weren't any holidays," Prelz went on. "I just got sick of it, Torval. I started looking for a way out. And you know what? I found it."

"A way out of what?"

"A way out of work, idiot!" Jake snapped. "A way to get out of an eternity of abusing and harassing these people. They don't deserve it. Haven't you ever thought about that? Why these souls exist? Why the Creator put them here? Why He makes them suffer here, on Earth, and then again, in Hell? What purpose does it serve?"

Torval shrugged. "My foreman said it is to teach them something," he answered. "What that is, even Landri did not know."

"Yeah, well, I couldn't figure it out, either," muttered Prelz. "I tried. I read, and studied, and asked. I even went to churches to try and experience religion, but I got no answers. I've debated philosophy with priests and rabbis, for God's sake, and gotten nowhere. Nobody knows, I tell ya! I wonder if even Lucifer himself truly understands."

"Perhaps he does," suggested Torval insightfully, "and that is why he rebelled against the Creator."

"Yeah, that could be it," Prelz agreed thoughtfully, "but who knows? He never told any of the rest of us, and since I'm never gonna get promoted, I'll never get to ask him. So anyway, after a while I started thinkin' about getting out, and I found out how to do it. I renounced being a demon, and accepted mortality."

Torval was momentarily stunned. "You did what?"

"You heard me!" insisted the grinning Prelz. "I gave it up. It's an option, when you're in human form. You can relinquish demonhood and accept the shell as your new self. Oh, you still look like a demon to other demons, as you just found out, but that's about it. You're mortal for all other purposes."

"But you have no soul. When you perish, you face Oblivion!"

"Ha!" Prelz chuckled at that. "Think, my Third-Class friend. Humans have souls. You're in a human body. Ergo, you have a soul."

"But I'm not a—"

Prelz interrupted him with another quick wave. "Look, we can argue this all night, but trust me on this. You've got to have a soul to take human form. Those are the rules. If you didn't have a soul, you couldn't be here now."

Torval stared at him uncomprehendingly. A soul? How could I have a soul? That makes no sense. Demons don't have souls. That's the way things are. As a demon, he was essentially immortal, unless sent to Oblivion, which destroyed him utterly.

Didn't it . . . ?

"Anyway," Prelz went on, paying no attention to the befuddled look on Torval's face, "whatever you want to call it, soul or life-force or whatever, the thing that makes you *you* is in that body. Because it's a human body, you can choose to accept humanity, and your life-force takes the form of a normal soul. That's what I did, and it's the best decision I ever made."

"But why?" Torval asked, still reeling somewhat from this new revelation. He would never even contemplate such a thing. Being human was, overall, the worst experience in his entire existence. "I do not understand," he went on, trying to wrap his mind around the thought of being this way forever. "Why would you do that?"

"Freedom," came the immediate answer. "That, and lots of other little things you can't understand until you've experienced them. Mortality's not to be taken lightly, I'll tell you, and I had to start taking a lot better care of myself after that. My boss, though, wasn't too keen on my idea of freedom. When I didn't report in, he sent hunt teams after me."

"So that's why you thought I was a Hunter," noted Torval, putting aside the distasteful thought of being permanently mortal. "You thought I tracked you down."

"Yes, but I can tell that's not the case, or you would've transitioned me right back to Hell already. If they did that, before I died naturally, I'd revert to demonhood in the process. You know what they'd do then? Torture, no doubt, and then either Oblivion, or the Deep Pits."

"But will they not get you eventually? When you perish here, will you not return to Hell, and be captured?"

"No, no, you don't get it," Prelz explained, gesticulating wildly as if to punctuate his words. "I'm mortal now! If I die here, my soul goes to its final reward, just like any human's would. At Judgment, it won't matter that I used to be a demon—they only care about what I've done as a human. Anyway, I've tried to live as good a life as I can, while staying under the radar of the Hunters. I'm not a drunk, and I don't steal or beg any more than I have to. If I got noticed or reported, a hunt team would snap me right up. Why else do you think I'd stay a bum like this? Hopefully, when I finally go, I'll be taken to Heaven, and from there, find out what this whole existence thing is all about."

"But if you do not go to Heaven, assuming it exists at all," protested Torval, "you could wind up in the layer cells. Humans are said to be sinners by nature, so what if Heaven is not real? My foreman seems to believe it is just a wild story the religions tell humans here to keep them in line."

"Yes, don't think that hasn't crossed my mind," Prelz remarked with a roll of his eyes. "I think I could endure it, though. After so many years here in these alleys, I think I could take any torture they can dish out. In any case, when I die naturally, I'll go through to the afterlife as a human soul, not a demon shape. After that, there's nothing they can do to me that they couldn't do to a human, and at least I won't face Oblivion. Besides, I know it's possible to transcend out of Hell. I'll figure out how, eventually, and move along to the next stage, whatever that might be."

"Something else I do not understand," said Torval. "If death releases you, why not simply kill yourself? You would avoid the Hunters that way, and proceed more quickly toward your goal."

"Because, dolt, suicide is a mortal sin!" barked Jake. "I don't want to wind up in Hell if I can avoid it! Besides, how many other demons have a chance to visit Heaven?"

"I suppose I could kill you," suggested Torval after a moment's consideration. "That would release you from this mortal shell, would it not?"

"Sure, sure, but you'll just get in trouble here on Earth," replied Prelz with a shrug. He coughed a couple of times, as if delaying the conversation long enough to gather his thoughts. "Maybe when you're about to finish your holiday, you can do it. I can't ask you to, though. That's the same thing as suicide." He was silent for a moment, thinking, and finally nodded in agreement with his own statement. "Yeah, in fact, you'd better not. I'm still not sure I'm sufficiently good to wind up in the right place."

"Very well, then. I will not kill you."

"Thanks, you're a pal." Jake slapped him on the shoulder, briefly touching his neck, so that he flickered momentarily into demon-form before reverting to human. "Say, that reminds me. If you're in Joe's body, that means he must be dead. Shit! That's too bad! I really liked him. How long have you been in there?"

"Since earlier today," Torval answered. "I am not sure of the time, but the sun set soon thereafter. I awoke in an alley. Since then, my illness faded quickly. I visited the soup kitchen, and then made my way here."

"Decent start," said Prelz with a nod. "You've got the good deed thing going on, too, don't you? I saw you go get the soup for Hal. Or was that just your former body helping out a friend?"

"Yes," said Torval. "Well—yes, and no. I felt some impulse to aid him, but it was not just Joe. Getting food for him seemed right somehow, and when I returned here, there was an odd sensation in my chest that I have never felt before."

"You were pleased with yourself," Jake explained. "That's one of the great things about being mortal—you can feel happiness! I'm not surprised you never felt it before, back in Hell. It's not a very happy place." The demon chuckled to himself, as though he'd made a personal joke. "Anyway, when you're human, you've got access to a lot more emotions than we demons do. That's one reason I wanted to be a Tempter—field work has its rewards. Anyway, what else do you like about mortality so far?"

"Taste," answered Torval immediately. "The flavors of soup I tried are—I cannot describe them. I have no words for such things."

"Yeah, you can't describe senses. They don't lend well to spoken language. I know what you mean, though. Soup is just the tip of the iceberg. You should try some of the other things humans can cook up. If you're going to have a real vacation, Torval, you can't spend it in these alleys! You need to get out into the city!"

"I know. I have already spoken with someone about that. Tomorrow, I am going to try to get a job. I do not wish to stay in the cold any longer than I must. And, as you say, I must try to taste more things. The sensations foods bring are most pleasurable."

"Good for you," said Prelz. "You're taking advantage of your holiday already. I'd come with you and help out, but if I tried to do something like that, the Hunters might find me. Tell you what, though. I'll answer what questions I can, if you don't mind listening to me babble on all night."

"No, I would not mind," replied Torval, and in fact, he found it surprising that he wouldn't. Normally, he hated interacting and speaking with others. This was different, though. Prelz possessed vital information about being mortal and interacting with humans. With Joe's memories fading, Prelz might be the only source of such knowledge for the foreseeable future.

"Well, then," said the temptation demon, "go ahead. Ask me whatever you want, and I'll tell you what I know."

"Very well," said Torval, his voice filled with anticipation. "First of all, on the subject of money . . ."

# Chapter 7

Prelz proved to be quite the expert on money. After all, he'd been a Tempter for a long time, and what he called the "almighty dollar" provided a powerful influence on people. Men didn't call money "the root of all evil" for nothing, it seemed.

Unfortunately, Prelz didn't seem to understand that Torval had no concept of monetary issues. The higher-ranking demon didn't slow down to make sure his "student" kept up, and every time Torval asked a question, it just made the Tempter more and more irritated. Eventually, his audience of one simply quieted down and tried to follow as best he could... which wasn't very well at all.

Somewhere around the sixth or seventh long-winded anecdote about a man who wanted to get more money for some obscure reason, Torval began to notice a strange feeling coming over himself. His eyelids became steadily heavier, and his mouth kept opening involuntarily to let out long, weary breaths. Joe's mind told him this "yawning" was totally normal, but it seemed very odd. During each yawn, Torval's eyes involuntarily squinted, so much so that tiny drops of water came squeezing out the corners. Furthermore, the more this happened, the more his eyes stung and his head drooped.

After a while his body also became heavier, as though gravity somehow increased beneath him. To reduce the load on his already tired feet, he sat down on the ground next to the fire-barrel. Prelz did the same, crossing his legs in a position Michael Rubin and many other inmates used when contemplating something. The temptation demon had no interest in thinking, though. Instead, he seemed caught up in a long-awaited opportunity to talk openly, from one demon to another. Prelz didn't even seem to notice Torval's progressive drowsiness, or perhaps he simply didn't care.

While Prelz droned on about the "stock market"—something that totally confused and baffled Torval—the vacationing demon noticed a wet slab of cardboard nearby. Without even thinking about it, he pulled the makeshift mat over and unfolded it over the pool of melted snow next to the barrel. For some reason the spongy, corrugated material looked comfortable, so he gradually stretched out along its length, pulling his hands inside his coat to keep his fingers warm. The last thing he remembered of that night, besides Prelz trying to explain the phenomenon of "insider trading," whatever that might be, was that the snow had finally stopped falling.

* * *

Something tickled his face. Torval blinked and opened his eyes to find a gray, furry, bedraggled-looking creature blocking his vision. With a start, he sat up quickly. Startled, the scrawny alley cat scampered away, disappearing into the collection of garbage cans that lined the farther wall.

Nothing to fear, Torval told himself. It's just a cat—a friendly one the bums of this alley refer to as Felix, for some unknown reason. Why he should know the creature's name, or its harmless nature, was the sort of detail that no longer seemed important. He just accepted that he knew, and moved on.

Torval yawned again, an act that still seemed strange to him. The sun shone brightly in the morning sky, and his eyes took a moment to adjust. The barrel-fire no longer burned, and he felt cold, but not as much as he would've expected after having slept all night on the street. The snow, strewn about in windblown piles, seemed to be melting off, for rivulets of water lined the asphalt, draining away into regularly placed sewer grates.

Torval stood up, and his body automatically stretched and twisted a few times of its own volition. So, he thought, that's what it felt like to sleep! As a demon, he had no reason to do so. Instead, during his rest-cycle, he usually sat idly in his tiny chamber, letting his mind go comfortably blank.

That, as he'd already learned, was something a human simply couldn't do. While he slept, time seemed to pass almost instantly—and yet, paradoxically, he could still recall other things that happened in the interim. He remembered awakening a few times, briefly, as he turned over and shifted to avoid uncomfortable positions. Unusually loud vehicles passing, or sirens nearby, also jolted him back to consciousness a few times.

Those weren't the disturbing memories, though. Torval remembered seeing strange things, and visiting places he knew nothing about. Disjointed visions, scraps of meaningless conversation, instantaneous changes of scenery . . . his mind kept trying to tell him a story, making things up as it went along. Curiously, though, he didn't remember any of the details now. In fact, as the seconds ticked by, Torval lost track of those last indistinct memories, leaving him with a vague recollection that he'd seen and experienced something—but with no idea what that something was.

The whole incident left him somewhat rattled. He didn't know if these mental wanderings were a natural phenomenon, or if something might be wrong with him. Perhaps he didn't quite transfer correctly into Joe's body, and the shell was still dying. Or, more likely, more of Joe's thoughts fled from his mind while he slept, and he caught the last vestiges of them as they departed.

Joe's thoughts . . . Torval reached for them, but they were gone. He could no longer access any details of Joe's life. He remembered a few important things he'd brought to the surface the previous day—such as the man's full name, and the accident he had while driving a truck—but nothing more. Perhaps they faded completely during the sleep-cycle. Yes, that must be it. Joe Sampson finally passed on, and only Torval remained.

That will be for the best, he decided after a moment. The less he knew about his host body's former life, the better.

The demon looked around. Several other bums lay curled up on their own makeshift beds, or underneath piles of snow-slicked cardboard. He didn't see Ethel, Hal, or Jake, or anyone else he recognized from the day before. Where could they have gone? Perhaps to the shelter, he thought, to acquire another meal.

The shelter! Torval jerked to attention instantly. I'm supposed to be there at eight o'clock this morning! What time is it now . . . ? He had no idea, and no way to tell. There were no timepieces available to check the hour.

Quickly, he started moving down the alleyway, worrying and wondering if he was late. If so, what would Christine say? He almost cringed at the thought of how disappointed she would be. She'd seemed so pleased the day before that Torval wanted to get a job.

Strange that I should think of that first, Torval thought. The important thing, he reminded himself, isn't what the human female thinks about me, but rather my ability to find employment and a place to live. He knew that's what he should be concentrating on—getting work, so he didn't have to spend the rest of his vacation sleeping in alleys. Whether or not it made Christine happy made no difference.

When he reached the street, he found Prelz standing by the sidewalk, holding a paper cup in his right hand. A veritable river of humans flowed by in each direction, almost obscuring the view of the road beyond. The temptation demon didn't seem to notice Torval's approach, instead concentrating on shaking his cup and looking as weak and pathetic as possible.

Torval stopped, curious to observe this strange behavior. As he watched, the form of Jake repeatedly shook the container in his hand, producing a rattling sound. After a few moments of this, one of the passing pedestrians dropped a coin into the cup. "Bless you," offered Jake, a strange thing for a demon to say.

Eventually, Prelz glanced over his shoulder and saw Torval standing there. "Mornin', Joe," he muttered feebly, as if still somewhat groggy from the long, cold night. He looked a bit pale and seemed to be wobbling from side to side, although this might've been part of an act to garner sympathy from the passersby.

"Lookin' to get some change?"

"No, I am not," said Torval. "I only wish to know what time it is. I must be at the shelter at eight o'clock."

"What, you got an appointment?" Prelz scoffed, steadying himself by leaning against a nearby railing.

"Actually, yes. As I thought I explained earlier, I am attempting to find a job and get a warm place to live for the remainder of my vacation."

"Oh, good for you," replied Prelz, letting out a couple of short coughs. "I wish I could do that, but I gotta stay invisible to you-know-who. Anyway, don't worry about it. You've still got half an hour. See?" He pointed across the street at a large clock hanging on a wall sign.

Torval automatically read off the time of "7:10" without worrying about how he understood the clock, in much the same way as he didn't bother wondering how he could speak and understand the language of this city.

"Good," he replied, relieved that he wasn't late after all. "I wish to eat more soup before my meeting, and to prepare myself further." With one hand, he indicated a spot on his lower abdomen. "There is a pressure here, and I sense it must be relieved. Where can this be done?"

Prelz laughed. "This must be your first time takin' a piss, huh? It's not like how we demons do it back home, is it? Don't worry, you'll get used to it after a while. Just go back in the alley there, pull your pants down, and let go. Try to do it so's nobody can see you, understand? And you don't want any of it on you, though. At least, as much as you can avoid it."

"Very well," replied Torval, heading back the way he came. There was something vaguely unsettling about pulling off his pants in the open, but he didn't know why. He came from a place where the only clothes worn were those of illusion, or for specific purposes. He shouldn't mind taking off his ragged garments, but he did nonetheless.

Glancing from side to side nervously, to make sure he was alone, he relieved himself as Prelz instructed. Once again he found himself amazed at the strangeness of his human body's sensations. As the pressure from within lessened, he felt oddly satisfied. The smell wafting up from the yellow pool forming in the snow by his feet had a curious kind of sharp sweetness that reminded him of other, less intense odors from the alley the night before. Those, too, were urine, he realized now, but the splatters at his feet were his, recognizable as such by their distinctive scent.

Though recognizable, the odor still repelled him. The sharp, unpleasant smell acted as a warning, in direct contrast to the enticing aroma of soup or other food. That a sense could provoke such different responses seemed like second nature, yet Torval found it interesting nonetheless.

In fact, thinking about this further, some of the events of the previous day made more sense. Now he understood why no one wanted him inside any of their buildings, and people on the street shied away and avoided him whenever he approached. He smelled bad! So did all the bums, of course—one reason why they were so universally detested.

Well, Torval thought, if all this is true, and I really do stink as much as these others, I cannot find a job like this! I will need to cleanse myself first. But how?

"You look worried," commented Prelz as his fellow demon stepped once again out of the alley. The Tempter chuckled softly at Torval's concerned expression. "What's the matter, did you pee all over yourself?"

"No," replied Torval, feeling a brief hint of irritation for some reason. "I am concerned about my appearance and odor. If I am to try to find a job, I need to look and smell like a normal human."

"Yeah, I know what you mean," Prelz replied, turning up his nose in an exaggerated fashion. "I haven't had a bath in years, either. You'll probably clog up the drains if you take a shower. Not that it's your fault, of course. That's the body you got dropped into, that's all."

"Be that as it may," went on Torval, "what can I do about it? I sense that I must wash myself, but I do not know how or where to do so."

"There's no easy way," Prelz replied. "Unless you want to go for a swim in Central Park, you're going to have to sneak into a gym or something—but even then, I don't know where you'll find fresh clothes. Where are you interviewing, anyway?"

"I am sorry, I do not know what you mean. Interviewing?"

"Yeah, where's your job interview? You know, the place you're going to try to get work."

"Oh, I see. I am going to the soup kitchen."

Prelz looked confused. "What, someone's meeting you there? Or is that where you're working?"

"I am meeting someone there who is taking me to find a job," answered Torval, not mentioning Christine for reasons he didn't fully understand. Did he think Prelz wouldn't believe him, or was there some other compelling reason not to mention her name? He didn't know for sure, but he left her out of the conversation anyway.

"Oh, gotcha. Okay, then, maybe they'll take you to get a shower someplace. I sure hope so, unless they want you looking like that for some reason. What kind of job is it?"

"I do not know," said Torval with a shrug. "I suppose I will find out when I get there. Is there anything else I should know?"

"Well, probably," Prelz answered with a shrug, glancing down in his cup after another pedestrian dropped a quarter inside. "After last night, though, I don't know if I should bother."

"What does that mean?"

"You weren't exactly listening," the temptation demon answered, in a tone that suggested annoyance. "I was right in the middle of a really juicy corruption story and you started snoring! You fell asleep while I was talking to you. That's very rude, Torval. Very rude."

"I am sorry," said Torval honestly, immediately chagrined about having shown disrespect to a superior. "I did not mean to. This body I wear betrayed me."

Prelz laughed derisively. "Ha! Don't give me that! You weren't listening even before that. I could tell." He sighed, turned back to the crowd, and made a sort of moan while deliberately shivering. None of the pedestrians seemed to notice.

"Oh, well, I suppose I shouldn't blame you," Prelz went on after a moment. "You Third-Class types just aren't made to absorb knowledge and wisdom."

Torval bristled at the insult and started to bark off an angry reply, but controlled himself just as quickly. Prelz was right, of course. As a Third-Class demon, Torval excelled at repetitive tasks and applying punishment, but not at absorbing information or solving problems. Back home, being told this simple fact wouldn't bother him, but here, on the frosty street corner, he found himself quite irritated.

"Don't get mad, you know it's true," Prelz continued, raising an eyebrow curiously, as if at some unvoiced realization. "What you're feeling right now is anger, Torval. It's natural, but don't give in to it. That's one of the things we Tempters love to use on people. If you really want a job today, don't let yourself be insulted by anything anybody says about you."

"Very well," Torval answered, taking a deep breath and trying to relax. His chest felt unusually constricted, but this faded quickly. These strong emotions he'd observed since his arrival here—guilt at the thought of Hal dying, gratification after giving the man food, and now anger at being slighted—would take some getting used to!

Prelz paused a moment as he dumped out his collection of coins and counted them. "Good, that's enough for a cup of coffee and a bagel for breakfast," he remarked, pocketing the change and handing the cup to Torval. "I never really feel good in the morning till I've had something to eat. You should probably get some money, too. Go on—we'll grab a bite before your big appointment."

"Why?" asked Torval. "I am going to the shelter in any case. Can I not simply have soup again? I really like soup."

"Yeah, well, you can't eat the same thing all the time," the Tempter explained. "You need solid food, too. Sheesh, I'm going to have to teach you everything, aren't I?"

"Only what I need to know," Torval answered. "I do apologize for last night, but I am not used to conversation, and you continued to add more and more details—I was quickly overwhelmed."

"Yeah, you're probably right," Prelz agreed reluctantly. "You just don't know what it's like for me—I can't talk to anybody about any of those stories I was telling you. It's like the floodgates opened and I just dumped it all over you, all at once. Anyway, if I start to do that again, just smack me upside the head or something."

"If you insist, that is what I shall do," replied Torval, taking the former demon's words literally. "In the meantime, I suppose I should get some money, as you say. How is this accomplished?"

"Just put the cup out there and wave it around," Prelz replied. "Try to look as hungry as possible."

Torval did his best to comply, but the vast majority of the passersby avoided him. One man dropped in a coin, but only a single penny. "Rattle it around," suggested Jake, showing no surprise or disgust at the meager offering. "Don't look at anyone, though. They hate that. Stare at the ground as much as you can, but keep watching the cup. Sometimes people knock it out of your hand for fun, or just snatch it from you."

"Why?" Torval asked. "Surely they are not as desperate as us. They cannot need the coins more than we do."

"Because, like I said, humans don't need demons to tempt them," came the reply with a sincerity borne from experience. "They've got enough evil in them already."

Torval nodded. If good and evil were constantly in conflict, as he understood was the case, this made sense. Good humans would try to help him by giving a coin or two, while others would evilly strike at him or steal what few possessions he had. This, of course, assumed he really understood what "good" was, which he didn't. Perhaps this was the time to find out what that word really meant.

Before he could ask, though, a man in a long winter coat reached out and dropped a handful of change into his cup. "Damn—I mean, bless you," Torval said quickly, but the pedestrian was already gone into the crowd. Whether he heard the demon's mistaken comment went unknown.

"Watch your phrases," Prelz warned. "Humans say 'damn' as an expression of surprise, or as a violent insult, and 'bless' as a thank-you. That's the opposite of how we think of them, and it does take some getting used to."

"I noticed," Torval agreed, examining the contents of his cup carefully. "It appears that I have over two dollars here. Is that enough for a—what did you call it?"

"A bagel," replied Prelz, rolling his eyes. "Yes, that's enough. You lucky bastard—it took me twenty minutes to get that much! He must've just wanted to empty his pockets or something. Come on, let's go. I guess you don't want any booze, huh?"

"No," Torval replied, but as soon as he heard that word, his body gave an internal shudder. "How strange," he added, shaking his head. "I do not want any liquor, but this body does. I find myself wishing I had some even now."

"You've been drinking for a long time," explained Prelz as he walked across the street toward the coffee shop Torval had noticed the night before. "Your body's used to it, and wants it—badly. Whatever you do, don't drink any more alcohol! Not even a sip. It's very addictive stuff."

"Yes, I have seen many souls imprisoned because of alcohol," agreed Torval, "but I did not know how much a human body could crave it. If it is so addictive, is it truly evil to become dependent upon such a substance? Why would the Creator make such a thing available, and then permit those who fell under its influence to be punished so harshly?"

"Who knows?" asked Prelz rhetorically. "That's just the sort of thing I kept asking myself when I was a Tempter, though. You might as well just ask why good and evil exist."

They entered the small coffee shop and moved to a table set off to one side, apart from the others. There was a familiarity about this place, as if he'd been here before, but Torval didn't remember any more details about it. He sat down automatically, just reveling in the feeling of warmth inside the enclosed building. Not as much as the night before, though, when the wind outside made the air even colder. Today the air was still, the snow had stopped, and the temperature outdoors seemed noticeably higher.

"Well," Torval said once he settled into the hard wooden chair, "I must admit I do not fully understand 'good.'"

"Of course you don't," replied Prelz haughtily. "You're a Third Class, so nobody ever explained it to you. You don't know what evil is, either, do you? Not really, anyway."

"Well, I do punish souls for evil deeds," Torval reminded him.

"Oh, really? That makes you an expert, I suppose? All right, go ahead, define it for me. Define 'evil' using human words."

"Very well. Evil is..." Torval halted, his weathered brow furrowing in thought. As he considered how to answer, he ran his gradually warming fingers through his scraggly, itchy beard. Suddenly he realized he didn't exactly know how to answer the question. He knew that evil people were consigned to Hell, and that they were punished in ways befitting their crimes. He also knew what those crimes were. But as to why they were crimes—well, he couldn't answer that.

"See what I mean?" Prelz chuckled. "What they did is evil because you were told that, but you have no frame of reference to connect it to. No social upbringing that teaches it to you."

"True," replied Torval, at once embarrassed by his own lack of understanding in what, to him, should've been a fundamental tenet of his very job. He simply never had a reason to know more, though. In Hell, Evaluators determined who got punished and Judges pronounced sentence, or so he'd been told—he'd never met such demons, though he knew they existed, somewhere in the deeper caverns. Torval wasn't qualified to perform such duties, and never had any need to really know or care why they did things the way they did. Punishment was his job, and that's all he'd ever focused on for his entire existence.

Until now.

"There's a legend among these people, you know," Prelz went on, automatically launching into another story to illustrate his point. "According to this tale, back when the Creator placed Man on the Earth, the first humans didn't have the knowledge of what was good or evil. This is before He decided to give them souls, I guess. Anyway, there's supposedly a tree that had this knowledge, but Man was forbidden to eat its fruit and learn the secret. A serpent—Lucifer, at least in some versions of this story—tempted the first woman into trying it, and she gave it to the man, and suddenly they knew they were naked, and a bunch of other things too. Anyway, that's what got things started the way they are. The Creator could've taken that knowledge away, or struck Adam and Eve down where they stood, but He didn't, apparently content to let the universe run its course once it started on its path."

The demon paused, as if considering what to say next. Torval nodded and listened carefully, much more interested in this one than any of the anecdotes he'd heard the night before. "Anyway," Prelz continued after a moment, "there's a lot of variations on the story, and of course we all know that Lucifer disagreed with Gabriel on what to do with Man once he started to spread across the world, but any tale that survived this long has to have some roots in truth. I don't know how true it is, but the basic point stands: Man knows in his soul what is good and what is evil. You and I, as demons, don't. We have to figure it out for ourselves. The only way you're going to do that is to watch humans in action."

While Prelz explained all that with his usual wordiness, a waitress approached and placed a glass of water on the table next to each of the two demons. She didn't seem upset by the presence of two filthy, smelly bums in the building, which surprised Torval. She looked young and reasonably attractive, but appeared somewhat sleepy. Her nametag identified her as Kimberly, and she wore a tight pair of blue jeans and a simple T-shirt, plus an apron with prominent front pockets. Her brown hair was bound up behind her head in a kind of lumpy-looking bun, with a few lazy strands of hair spilling out in several directions—whether intentionally or an accident of styling, Torval didn't know.

As soon as Prelz paused in his storytelling, she broke into the conversation smoothly. "The usual for you today, Jake?"

"Yeah," he answered with a nod. "I brought my friend Joe with me, too. He'll have the same."

"All right, coming right up," Kimberly agreed with a pleasant smile.

As the waitress turned and departed, Torval asked, "Why is it we are welcome here, but nowhere else in the city?"

"Oh, I've helped them out a few times," Prelz replied. "I know a lot of people in town, y'know. They move this table over here for me in the morning. Kimmie's a nice girl, too, and easy on the eyes, if you know what I mean."

Torval didn't, although as the young lady walked away, his gaze automatically traveled down to her wide hips and swaying rear end. Something about that particular part of her anatomy drew his attention, but he didn't know what it was. The curve of this human woman's backside definitely intrigued him in some unnerving way, and made him think immediately of Christine.

Quickly, Torval pushed that thought away and returned to the previous issue. "I still do not understand how it is I am to learn about good or evil," he complained. "How can I tell which is which by watching human actions? Will I be told the answer during my debriefing?"

"Well, if you had no experience at all, you'd be screwed," Prelz said, "but fortunately, you've had centuries of torturing to back you up. It should be easy for you to figure it out. You know what the penalties for sinning are, right? And why people got sent to your layer? Sure you do. So, here's the thing. When you see a human do something, ask yourself, 'What sort of penalty would that be worth in Hell if they died right now?' If you can determine a suitable punishment, then it was evil. However, if you can't, it was at worst neutral, or possibly even good."

Torval nodded in understanding. "So, as you say, if someone had stolen my cup of coins," he suggested, "his punishment in Hell might be to sit hungry while scraps of food were taken from him."

"Exactly!" agreed Prelz. He suddenly became very thoughtful again, and then regarded his lower-ranking companion in a different light. "You should be a Sentencer, Torval. I'm sure that's what one of them would've thought of for someone like that."

"A Sentencer?" Torval shook his head. "I am only Third Level, sir. I am not fit for higher duty."

"You say that now, but think about it. How long have you been a Punisher? A century or two? A millennium, possibly? Longer, I'll bet. You told me you were on vacation now because you started wondering why you do your job. That means you're evolving, Torval. You're getting close to a promotion, and your boss knows it, so he sent you here for field experience. When you go back, you'll be evaluated to see if you're ready for advancement."

Torval just stared at Prelz doubtfully, unable to think of what to say in response. As he did, the pretty young waitress returned, placing a plate in front of each demon. The trays contained a donut-shaped grayish object, covered with some sort of pasty white substance. Prelz immediately picked up his cream-cheese-covered bagel and began gnawing on it while Kimberly concluded her trip by depositing two cups of steaming coffee on the table. Without another word, she turned and departed, followed by two pairs of eyes unabashedly watching her curvy derriere sashay into the distance.

Torval didn't care about Kimmie's behind, and didn't know why he watched her go—just another automatic action beyond his control, like when his mouth watered at the smell of soup. And at the coffee on the table before him, he noticed suddenly. Cautiously he sipped at the hot liquid, licking his lips in appreciation as its bitter, yet pleasurable warmth flowed into him.

The two demons enjoyed a moment of silence while Prelz devoured his breakfast and Torval sucked down the tasty coffee. The Tempter's earlier words confounded him. How could he, Torval, be close to advancement? He didn't want to move up to Second Class! He liked being a Torturer, and that's all he ever wanted to do. If he advanced, they'd make him do something else. He'd become a Supervisor, like Landri, or a Transitioner like Geezon. Or possibly a Tempter, or, as Prelz suggested, a Sentencer. A Second-Class demon couldn't remain in Punishment, unless he wanted to supervise other Punishers.

Still . . . perhaps Prelz's theory would explain Torval's recent problems on the job. Becoming Second Class involved more than just an increase in rank. A demon could potentially exist forever in a static state, but most eventually evolved into higher forms—the upper classes. This "advancement" resembled a kind of rapid evolution. Upon confirmation of a promotion, the demon's body underwent a physical change, shifting him into a shape best suited for his new role in the hierarchy. Theoretically, Torval had no choice but to transform into the state he needed to be in to perform his duties, but years or decades might pass before that happened. Furthermore, the exact selection could be modified by actions and training prior to the actual event. As he understood the process, his superiors would run him through various tests and trials designed to usher in his new form, and upon the conclusion of his metamorphosis, he'd officially become a Second-Class demon.

Torval picked up the bagel and nibbled on it as he mulled all this over in his mind. He found the thick bread somewhat rubbery and hard to chew, but it had a satisfying taste enhanced all the more by the white substance spread atop the surface. Without thinking about it, Torval found himself wolfing down the bagel quickly, chasing down each chunk with more of the amazingly delicious coffee.

So, he thought, there's more to this vacation than I was led to believe! Landri didn't send him here on a whim, or to give him some lame "time off." This was a test to see if Torval might be ready to advance! Presumably, what he did and learned here would come out in the debriefing, and they would use that to test him without his knowledge. If this proved to be a false alarm, Torval could go back to his duties without ever knowing he was being investigated. On the other hand, if he was about to advance…

No, Torval thought. I'm not going to worry about that! I don't want to advance, and I have to go through this hoping it's not what this is really all about! I'll just put those thoughts out of my mind. Yes, I'll just forget entirely about that unpleasant prospect.

If only it could be that easy…

# Chapter 8

After Torval devoured his meal—a "breakfast," or so it was called—the pleasantly attractive Kimberly dropped off a slip of paper and bade both bums farewell.

Torval stood up to leave, but Prelz stopped him. "Not so fast, my friend. We have to pay the bill."

Torval nodded in recognition. "Oh, yes, I forgot. The money we begged for earlier. We use it now to purchase our food." He reached into his grit-filled pockets and withdrew the change, automatically counting out enough to match the tab. "These coins," he said as he set them down on the table, pointing at specific ones with an outstretched finger. "These are called quarters, and these are dimes, and these nickels. I somehow know the denominations—"

"Yeah, the body you got provides you with all that helpful stuff. Convenient, isn't it? If you couldn't recognize money, you wouldn't get very far on Earth, y'know."

"Yes, but why do they have these names and values? Why is a nickel five cents, and a dime ten? The dime is smaller and thinner—should it not be worth less? And yesterday, I had pieces of green paper that were called 'dollars.' These are flimsy and could be easily torn or damaged, yet one of them is worth four quarters. Why—"

"Enough!" Prelz interrupted, putting his hand on Torval's shoulder. Were it not for the Tempter's ragged overcoat, his demon form would've become readily apparent. "Look, my friend, I have no idea. These are things humans make, remember? They're the ones who came up with the details. Although, of course, you have good questions . . . hmm . . .

you know, if a demon really did come up with this stuff, I wouldn't be surprised. Not that it matters. Anyway, leave a tip and let's go, or you'll be late."

"A tip?" Torval's eyebrows went up, and he looked at Prelz uncertainly.

"Yeah, you know, a—oh, right, you don't know, do you? I'll bet that poor sap whose body you're wearing didn't leave a tip in years. Anyway, you give tips to people who serve you. Sort of like a reward for good service. If you think Kimmie did a good job bringing you your food, give her a reward. About fifteen percent of the tab should do it, but I usually round up to the nearest convenient coin value."

"How can I tell if she gave me good service? I have not been given service by anyone else." Suddenly Torval realized that wasn't true—the people at the soup kitchen, and the man last night at the diner. Should he have left a tip then? No, he told himself, shaking his head sharply. The first time, the soup was free, so fifteen percent of zero would still be zero. The second time, he wasn't served at a table, but given his food in a sack. Alan Ferrell wasn't waiting tables like Kimmie, so he wasn't entitled to a tip.

Prelz shrugged, answering Torval's original question. "Then just give her the standard amount. Coffee and a bagel is a buck sixty, so I usually just make it an even two bucks. That's why I said we needed that much, remember?"

"Yes, I see," replied Toval, dropping the rest of his coins on the table. The amount actually added up to two dollars and ten cents, but the last dime didn't seem all that important, so he left it with the others.

"Now come on, let's get you to the kitchen. You've got a job interview to look forward to."

Torval nodded and moved toward the exit, passing through the door and out into the sunlight. The melting snow transformed the streets into slushy rivers, and the sky above was a brilliant blue, flecked with clouds. He stared at the tranquil colors for a moment, amazed at how absolutely peaceful the sky seemed. Although he'd seen plenty of cell illusions that mimicked the sky, the real thing seemed somehow different. There was something else, something…what? He struggled to find the word, but couldn't, and then Prelz said it for him.

"Beautiful, isn't it?"

Torval turned to look at the older man. "Yes, I suppose that was my impression. I was trying to think of how to explain it, even to myself."

"Yeah, you don't see a lot of beauty in Hell, do you? It's not a pretty place. Just another reason I wanted to stay here. If you think the sky looks good now, you should try going out of the city for a while. Or better yet, up on one of the observation platforms. Yeah, we'll do that later." He started to chuckle. "I can't wait to see the look on your face! Now come on, move it, or we'll be late!"

Torval agreed and started walking, letting his body's reflexes guide him toward the soup kitchen. Seemingly instinctively, he knew the way, just as he knew the names of the streets in the area, as well as the best places to find shelter, and the spots that were best for begging at certain times of the day.

"So what are you thinking?" asked Prelz as they shuffled along. He already looked better, his color having returned, and he no longer walked unsteadily. The breakfast worked as expected, it seemed. "Are you excited? About finding work, I mean."

"It is strange," replied Torval. "I have toiled my whole life, such as it has been. Now, I am without work, and it feels... different."

"So that's why you're getting a job? So you won't be bored?"

"No, not exactly. I just do not want to be out on the street, in the cold, being miserable for my entire vacation."

"Ah, I see. Makes sense. I'd do that if I could be sure I'd be safe from the Hunters."

Torval turned toward him as they stopped to wait for a light to change. "How long has it been, Prelz? How long have you been on the run?"

"What?" The older man shrugged. "Oh, I don't know. Ten, twelve years, maybe. What difference does it make? Hunters don't care about time, and they won't just give up, you know. They've got me on their list. They won't rest until they find me, or it's clear I'm dead and my soul has passed on, beyond their reach."

"And this is worth it? Living like this, in this cold and wet, just to avoid becoming a demon again?"

Prelz nodded vigorously. "Yes. Hell yes! I'm never going back there, Torval. Never. I'll face Oblivion first."

"They must know that," Torval continued, crossing the street along with a crowd of other pedestrians, all of whom took great care to keep as far away from the two malodorous bums as possible. "Why do they not just let you go? Will not another simply rise from the Pits to take your place?"

"I don't know. Who does? Supposedly there are just enough demons in Hell to run the place and no more than that, and Lucifer knows enough of us have been consigned to the Great Blackness to remake our population three times over. I think it's the principle of the thing. You just can't escape Hell."

"But it can be done," put in Torval. "I have seen it happen myself."

"You have?" Prelz looked confused for a moment, before realizing what his companion was saying. "Oh, right, a transcendence. Yeah, you mentioned something about that."

"Yes, one of the prisoners in my patrol area simply . . . disappeared. I think I understand why, now. That event is what precipitated my downturn in work performance, and resulted in me being sent here."

"Figures. You went for what, hundreds of years without seeing a transcendence, didn't you? I can imagine why it would be a shock. When I started coming to Earth, and realized how different things were than I really thought, the same thing happened to me. Watching people do good and evil on their own... that's what made me realize they didn't need us to tempt them. Ah, but I'm boring you, I can tell. Why do you keep looking around like that?"

"I wish to know what time it is," Torval replied worriedly. "To see if I am late."

"Oh, that?" Prelz lifted up his arm and pulled back the arm of his ragged coat. He wore a watch—a silver one, with an expensive-looking fancy wristband. "It's ten till. You've got plenty of time."

The glimmering device on the old man's arm looked strangely out of place. "Where did you get that?" Torval inquired.

"What, the watch? Oh, yeah, I found it. No, really! Don't worry about it. After you start collecting a paycheck, you can buy one for yourself."

Torval nodded. "That is another thing I find strange," he said, still staring at the shiny watch. "Some of my prisoners, back in Hell, are being punished for wasting time, or for paying too much attention to it. That always seemed unusual to me, but it was not for me to judge. Yet now, I have an . . . appointment, I suppose it is called. I must be somewhere, by a specific time. I find myself... what? I cannot find words for all these strange new emotions I am feeling."

"Concerned?" offered Prelz. "Frightened? Anxious, maybe?"

"Anxious. Yes, that is the word, if I understand the meaning correctly. Anxious."

"Another reason I like being a bum, my boy," said Prelz with a grin.

"No deadlines or schedules. If you want to work, you'd better get used to racing the clock. Now, look, there's the shelter. You go on in—I'm full, y'know, and they only let us in there once a day, so I'll come back later and catch up with you. Say, at six o'clock. Sound good?"

"Yes," Torval agreed. "Perhaps by then I will be, as these humans say, gainfully employed."

* * *

The soup kitchen was, as usual, extremely warm and inviting. The huge crowds of decrepit bums that had swarmed about the place the day before were gone, leaving the tables mostly empty. Apparently few homeless people bothered with breakfast. Or, more likely, they were all out on the streets begging money from people heading to work.

Glancing around, Torval didn't see either the caustic Lakisha or the attractive Christine, leaving him both pleased and dismayed at the same time. He wanted very much to see Christine again, but not with the annoying dark-skinned woman there to insult and deride him at every turn. He hoped she only volunteered later in the day. The only workers here now were an old woman wiping down tables and an elderly man mopping the floor in the far corner. They seemed familiar, so he knew Joe had encountered them before, but their names escaped him.

Torval felt himself getting anxious again. Unless Prelz had deliberately misled him, he was on time. Early, in fact. Wasn't that important?

More disconcerting feelings followed. Torval's chest began to tighten, and he felt the urge to pace about. His heart raced so fast he could hear a thumping in his ears. He had a strange compulsion to scream, but fought it down. Anxiety was an emotion he did *not* care for!

Fortunately, Christine came to his rescue, stepping out from the back room. Her head faced another direction, so she didn't see him right away. "Make sure you order some more potatoes," she called out to someone outside of Torval's view.

Upon hearing her voice, Torval immediately let out a long, relieved breath, and his muscles relaxed of their own accord. She's here! In the scant minute that he'd paced the floors, a dozen scenarios flew through his head. She didn't believe him and wasn't coming . . . he was late and blew his chance . . . something happened to her on the way to the shelter . . . but with her welcome appearance, all those unpleasant possibilities faded away, just like that.

"Joe!" she called out, interrupting his protracted sigh of relief.

"You're here early! I was just getting the morning stew started. Say, do you want some? I won't count it as your meal for the day, no matter what Lakisha says."

"No, I had a—" He tried to remember the name. "Bagel, yes, that's what it was. And coffee. Very hot. It is hard to believe something so bitter could be so satisfying."

Christine gave a melodious chuckle. "Haven't you had coffee before, Joe? It's a strange thing for a homeless person to drink, but I figured somewhere in your life you must've tried it."

Torval studied her for a moment, which was very easy to do. In fact, he realized, he'd been staring openly at her since she arrived. Christine wore a gray overcoat that hung halfway open, revealing a navy blue blouse and skirt that made her look curiously businesslike. Black calf-high boots, still glistening with moisture from outside, concealed most of her legs. A thin gold chain dangled from her slender neck. The shape of her face was very pleasing, as well, but it wasn't just her appearance that intrigued him. He liked the way she just seemed interested. She actually wanted to help him, out of simple kindness.

She also, he now recognized, kept trying to pry into his previous life. She did that once before, after he first arrived, but the Joe persona immediately resisted. Torval knew he should do the same, mostly because he no longer remembered Joe's life, but also because he didn't actually have a past she would want to hear about.

"No, I have not," he answered with a shrug, still staring at her. Her bright blue eyes seemed to sparkle, even in the gloomy interior of the soup kitchen, with a piercing effect that all but hypnotized him. Absently, he managed to add, "I mean, I may have, but I do not remember."

"Well, how is it that you happened to drink coffee today?" Christine inquired pleasantly, moving over to one of the tables to pick up a few scattered pieces of old, donated silverware. "Did you need a caffeine boost for your job interview?"

"A what?" Torval had no idea what she was talking about. Caffeine? What is that? Yet he realized quickly that Christine expected him to know, so he hastily added, "Oh, that. No, no, nothing of the sort. A friend of mine showed me a place to eat breakfast."

"A friend? Who?"

"His name is Pr—I mean, Jake. I told him last night of my decision to get a job and this was his way, I think, of celebrating."

"Oh, yes, I know Jake. That was very nice of him, I must say. The begging must've gone well for you this morning. I'll be so glad when you don't have to do that anymore, Joe! Watching you waste your life has been very painful for me, you know."

"Why?" Torval asked sincerely.

"Excuse me?"

"I said, why? I mean... why do you care so much?"

Christine turned to face him, looking ready to give him a stern rebuke, but then stopped. "You're serious, aren't you? You aren't just pulling my chain. You really want to know."

"Yes. Yes, I do."

Christine narrowed those piercing blue eyes of hers so that now they seemed to bore directly into his skull. "Joe, I think maybe you really have turned over a new leaf. There's something very different about you. You're standing up straighter, and talking without your usual slurring—and you're sober, and want a job! Whatever could've changed you so quickly?"

Torval shrugged, feeling very uncomfortable under her gaze. He began to stammer, which was very strange to him. In demon form, he only stuttered in the presence of a superior. "I—well, I was sick, you know, and came very close to death. When I woke up, I realized just how miserable I was, and decided to do something about it. Is that so hard to believe?"

"No, I guess it isn't," said Christine. "I believe in miracles, Joe. I think God may have spared you for a reason. He sent you a message. A warning. That was your wake-up call from the Almighty."

Torval nodded in agreement. Of course, it was no such thing, but he didn't mind if she thought otherwise.

How interesting, though, that she should choose to believe the Creator had a hand in Joe's redemption. That wasn't a tactic Torval would've considered at all. He knew God existed, of course, unlike these humans, who had to take it on faith. Yet, Torval also knew that once God set the universe on its course, He retreated from it entirely. His angels and demons had their part in the way things worked, just as the beasts and plants and men had their places, but God never intervened directly.

At least, that's what he'd always been told...

Humans, Torval also knew, worshiped a wide variety of gods, from Buddha and Allah to Jehovah, God of the Israelites, and any number of similar variations. Every single one of those religions was in its own way right, and yet wrong at the same time. A great many of the souls in Torval's layer were there for religious reasons, but none of them seemed to realize that no one way to worship took precedence over any other.

Christine is probably talking about one of the Christian religions, Torval thought. Christians usually spoke of "God" without giving Him another name.

"Yes, it might have been God," the demon said after a brief pause the social worker must've thought indicated private introspection. "All I know is that I made a decision, and now I must follow through with it. You did not answer my earlier question, though."

"What question?" asked Christine, now turning away again, looking a little uncomfortable under his gaze.

"Why do you care about me?" Torval inquired curiously. "Why do you care about any of us? You are here every day, and you speak to us, but I do not understand why."

Christine had her back to him now. "I can't explain," she said quietly, almost too softly to hear. "Look, I just believe in people, you know? I have faith in humanity, and to see you suffering so just tears me apart. Can we just leave it at that?"

Torval started to press for more information, but realized that she'd basically just asked him to end the conversation. "Very well. I am sorry if I have offended you, Christine."

"Not at all." She turned to look at him once again. "I'd love to tell you more, Joe, but I really can't, so please don't ask. Anyway, we're wasting time here. I've set up an interview for you at eleven, but first we have to get you cleaned up. That means a haircut and shave, because we're definitely not going to the employment office with your beard like it is. But first, we have to do the most important thing of all."

Torval nodded, for he'd already identified the problem and knew it had to be dealt with one way or another. "I need to be washed, don't I?"

"Yes, very much. Now come on, let's get you to a shower!"

# Chapter 9

Christine led Torval out of the soup kitchen, turning right and heading along the cracked and broken sidewalk. Runoff from melting snow transformed the ground into a slippery mess of shattered ice and accumulated slush. Torval acutely felt the holes in his shoes as he walked, for with each puddle his feet became wetter and colder. To his left, Christine's tall leather boots splashed heedlessly through the water, and the demon could only wish he had footwear as practical as hers.

"Don't you want to know where we're going, Joe?" asked Christine from beside him. She smiled in that decidedly unsettling way of hers, and he deliberately avoided looking at her because of it.

"Not really," the demon answered. "I had not really thought about it. I have no idea of the process we are about to undertake, so I will follow your lead."

"Yeah, I guess you've been out of the job scene for a while, haven't you?" she inquired amiably, managing to avoid sounding condescending. Not that Torval would notice such a thing, of course.

He sidestepped one of the larger puddles and tried not to fidget. This sort of small talk always made him uncomfortable back in Hell. Christine's enticing presence produced an equally disquieting effect, thus doubling his nervousness. "Yes, it has been a long time," Torval muttered weakly, not sure of what else to say.

Christine let out an audible sigh, still looking at him in that disconcerting way. "Look, Joe, I know something hurt you, a long time ago. I don't care about that. If you wanted to talk about it, you would've told me already. I just need you to understand that when we go to the unemployment office today, they're going to ask questions about your past. Your social security number, for example. Is that all right? Are you going to want to give that out?"

Once again, Torval found himself not comprehending her words. This "social security number," whatever it might be, sounded like a detail left over from Joe's life, which he could no longer access. He couldn't just ask, either, so he went with the only response he could think of on the spur of the moment. "I—I just don't remember," he told her, unwittingly covering up his lie with a believable stammer of uncertainty.

Christine nodded. "Okay, I understand, Joe. Maybe you really don't remember. Maybe you don't want to be found. I won't press you any further. When you get to the unemployment office, they're going to give you a form. Just fill it out as best you can. Leave the social security space blank. I'll just tell my friend you don't remember it, okay?"

"Sure," Torval agreed readily. The conversation stalled as they came to a corner and turned right. Once again he beheld a seemingly endless vehicle-clogged street, bordered by sidewalks covered in melting snow. Towering buildings of steel and concrete rose into the clear blue sky all around him, and Torval struggled to contain his awe. Joe, pathetic as he was, should act like a native of this place.

For a minute or so, as he shuffled along dodging puddles as best he could, Torval found himself enveloped by the sounds of the city. Honks and engine noises echoed all about, threatening to overwhelm him. Although he couldn't make out any specific words, the chattering of pedestrians and passersby seemed like a baleful cacophony to one so used to quiet surroundings. He found himself wanting to restart the conversation, if only to distract from all the other noises. Besides, for some reason he sensed she expected more, as though he'd forgotten something important and she wanted to give him the chance to remember.

After a moment's thought, Torval recalled that humans usually expressed gratitude for favors. Hal Sommersby, for example, said something specific upon receiving his soup. Furthermore, while begging that morning, Prelz uttered a distinctly un-demonic phrase. How did it go again? Ah, yes.

"Bless you for helping me, Christine," he said with some uncertainty.

She raised an eyebrow, but still smiled. "No problem, Joe. I just wish you'd come to me a lot sooner. Here, up these stairs. This is my apartment."

They climbed a set of crumbling concrete steps, arriving at a heavily barred door with a large, conspicuous lock. Christine used a key and ushered Torval inside. He expected to see the interior of a home of some sort, like many he remembered from cell illusions, but instead found himself in a hallway, with numbered doors on the walls. Christine led him onward to another stairwell, and they headed upward.

The steps were dirty, the walls encrusted with peeling paint and crumbling plaster. Torval barely noticed this, however, because he could barely breathe. The higher he climbed, the heavier his legs felt, and the more his chest burned. Finally, gasping, he reached the end of the line, the third level, where he sank to his knees and hyperventilated in desperation.

Christine waited patiently. "Sorry, Joe, I forgot you've been sick. I should've let you rest on the second floor."

Torval tried to reply, but couldn't. His breath still came in ragged gasps. After about a minute, he finally managed to recover. "I… apologize," he wheezed. "I am… weaker than I thought."

"Hmm, well, no construction jobs for you," Christine remarked with a chuckle, moving to a door close by and unlocking it with another key. "Here, this is my place. Welcome to my humble abode, such as it is."

Torval nodded. Still holding one hand over his chest, he shuffled inside. A soft white rug covered most of the floor, so Christine removed her boots, setting them aside to keep from soiling the carpet. Observing this, Torval felt he understood the custom and reached to take off his own shoes. All at once he realized he didn't know how.

"That's okay, Joe, just go on back to the bathroom," Christine told him. "Don't worry about leaving tracks. This carpet needs a good shampooing anyway."

"Very well," he agreed, not quite understanding what she meant in any case. Looking up, he saw that she was pointing.

"Straight that way," she told him. "First door on the left. You do remember how to take a shower, don't you?"

The smile returned to her face, and Torval felt a tightness around his mouth as his muscles pulled his lips to the sides. "Uh, yes, I think so," he stammered quickly, trying to keep his mind off what was going on below his nose.

"Why, Joe! Was that a smile?" Christine looked awestruck. "That's the first time I think I've ever seen you do that!"

Is that what it was? Torval massaged his lips with his hand. "I'm sorry," he mumbled. "I did not mean to offend—"

"No, no, it's fine! You can smile if you want to, Joe. It's all right. I didn't mean to embarrass you. Go on, get a shower so we can go get your haircut. Go on. Go!"

She waved her hands out in a shooing motion, so Torval didn't argue. He made his way down the hall, past a variety of common types of furniture. Christine didn't decorate much, but the place seemed positively opulent compared to his featureless domicile back home. Torval knew what most of the objects were for—couches to relax on, a television set to view human entertainment broadcasts, lamps to provide light at nighttime, and so on. Such things existed in plenty of prison cells, so he knew their purpose. To Torval they were always nothing more than props, but to Christine, they defined her living space. They were a part of her life.

One day I will have such things, the demon thought to himself. I will sit on a couch and watch television, in a warm apartment such as this. That's what I want. That's all I want, until this terrible holiday is over and I can go back where I belong.

He found the room Christine indicated and stepped inside. The small, cramped bathroom featured a narrow sink, small toilet, and just enough room for a tub with a built-in shower. Numerous small items, such as towels and toothbrushes, occupied ordinary places about the little chamber. However, the first thing that drew Torval's attention was the mirror—or rather, the reflection within it.

He stood, staring at the image looking back at him. This is my human guise, he realized immediately. He was tall, about six feet, and so thin as to be almost emaciated. The clothes he wore were worn and ragged from years of abuse, barely covering weathered, scarred skin spattered with dirt and grime. A scraggly black beard peppered with gray obscured his harried face, framed by long, unkempt hair of a similar color. Brown and empty orbs of russet stared vacantly out amidst crinkled skin aged well beyond its years.

So this is Joe Sampson, Torval thought. This is the homeless bum whose shell I now wear. A pathetic specimen of humanity, indeed.

Without another word, he turned away from the image in the mirror, disgusted by what he saw. To think that he had to spend more than a day in such a form! Not for much longer, though. Soon, he would no longer appear quite as foul—but first, all that dirt had to go.

The shower came next. Torval glanced inside the tub, a white porcelain oval with a drain at the far end. Another human creation, he thought. He'd seen such things at work in cell illusions. Turning the knobs made water spray forth from the nozzle above his head. First, though, he had to remove his clothes.

The overcoat came first. Underneath, he wore a sweater crusted with the remains of sweat and grime from dozens of nights on the street. As the ragged garment peeled away, he heard the sleeve tear with a ripping sound. He didn't care. He just wanted it off.

Below the sweater, he wore a shredded mat of cloth that might once have been a T-shirt. As he removed the rags, they fell into pieces, leaving sections stuck to his filthy, gaunt flesh. He peeled the remainder of the shirt away, exposing his chest and arms to the air for the first time in what might well have been years. The skin underneath was pale and sickly-looking, even wrinkled in some places. He remembered seeing a number of his prisoners in a similar state, but never imagined he would look down upon such flesh as though it were his own.

Next came his pants, but first he had to figure out the shoes. The laces, tied into permanent knots instead of removable loops, were soaking wet. Tugging on them in confusion, he made no progress. In the end, he simply kicked the shoes off by the heels. Underneath he found soggy socks made of a gray woolen cloth. Perhaps they were once white—he had no way to be sure. His pale and wrinkled feet sported thick, broken calluses marring the surface in every conceivable location. The middle toe on his right foot had no nail at all, while the big toe on the other side was nothing but a gnarled mass of flesh, obviously the result of some long-ago injury.

Standing back up, Torval undid the piece of worn rope that served as a belt and let his pants fall to the ground. These looked like the newest items of the lot, but even they suffered from numerous holes and worn spots. Beneath those, he wore some strands of elastic and cloth, the remnants of a pair of underwear. He'd encountered these before, earlier that morning, when he emptied his bladder in the alley. The jockey shorts were almost nonexistent, serving only to keep his genitals from rubbing together uncomfortably. The elastic waistband, nearly worn through in several places, slipped off his hips easily.

Now totally nude, he considered the shower. He knew he had to turn a dial to make the water issue forth, but when he tried, nothing happened. Another spigot protruded below, made to fill the tub, and Torval tried the lever on top, but that didn't do anything, either.

Flummoxed, he continued staring in confusion at what should've been simple controls until Christine called out behind him. "Are you okay in there, Joe?" her melodious voice asked. "Do you need any—oh!"

Torval turned around. Christine stood there, shielding her eyes and looking away, clearly embarrassed. "What is it?" he asked, almost panicked by her fearful reaction. "Have I frightened you?"

"No! You should close the door!" she insisted. Keeping her back to him, she reached inside and yanked the door shut. "Sorry, Joe, I just didn't expect to see you—well, you know. Naked."

Oh, yes. Nudity. Torval realized he'd forgotten all about that. Humans weren't supposed to see each other unclothed—that's one of the things about the Tree of Knowledge legend that Prelz had described earlier. After Man ate the forbidden fruit, he realized nudity was wrong. "I am sorry to have offended you again, Christine," he said quickly, with a depth of feeling that surprised even him.

"No, no, it's my fault, I shouldn't have just looked in like that." Christine seemed to recover herself, at least as far as Torval could tell from her voice. "Look, I just realized, if you haven't had a shower in a long time, you might not know how mine works. See the big dial? You pull it toward you. Lift up on the lever to make the shower come on. Then hot is left, and cold is right. Okay?"

"Yes," Torval replied. "You were correct, Christine. I was indeed trying to understand that just now."

"All right, good luck. I'm going to make a couple of phone calls. When you come out, use the towel on the wall outside the shower."

"Very well."

He heard Christine's footsteps retreating and turned back to the shower. The controls, he found, worked exactly as she explained. Within moments he had the water streaming out of the spout above, and turning the dial to the left did indeed make it warm up.

When he found the right temperature, Torval stepped inside. His skin suddenly felt alive with tingling, as though thousands of tiny pins jabbed at him simultaneously. He found himself shuddering, but not from cold. The warmth of the water, and the steam beginning to rise about him, felt truly invigorating. All at once, Torval felt better than he had at any other moment since his arrival on Earth. In fact, he couldn't remember ever feeling anything remotely as pleasant as this in all his long centuries of existence.

For a few minutes he just stood there, gazing down at the sight of water streaked with years of grime streaming its way toward the drain. For the first time, Torval thought he understood why Prelz would want to remain in human guise. If he could feel like this, even for a brief time... it just might be worth it.

The feeling couldn't last, Torval knew, and it didn't. After a few minutes, the tingling seemed to numb his skin, and the invigorating massage faded away. Now, he understood, was the time to get down to business. He had to wash himself.

Fortunately, he knew how this should be done. One of his prisoners, a woman named Caitlin Spears, had spent her life obsessed with cleanliness. For her punishment, she lived in filth and mire, emerging only to wash herself for brief periods before becoming dirty again. The bar of soap she used was shot through with jagged stones and laced with salt, so the very act of cleansing left her skin lined with painful, agonizing cuts. As far as punishments go, that's one of the more inventive ones, Torval thought appreciatively. To change such a pleasant experience into something so awful...she must've been a miserable example of humanity in life to deserve such a fate.

The soap on Earth wouldn't be an instrument of torture, fortunately. Torval lifted up the gold-colored bar and started to rub it over himself. Sure enough, he felt no pain at all. In fact, he quickly found his skin coated in a white, bubbling froth that, once washed away, left him clean and slick. Gradually, the water running off his body grew less and less black with dirt, until it cleared completely.

Now on to the hair, thought Torval. Back in her cell, Caitlin used a shampoo made of acid that burned her scalp and left it covered with itchy scabs. The kind in Christine's shower, by contrast, had a pleasant, sweet scent and formed into more of the cleansing white suds. Torval rubbed the sticky goop into his hair and beard, occasionally opening an eye wide enough to check the color of the water by his feet. After a while it cleared up again, signaling the end of the cleansing ritual.

How strange, he considered as he turned the shower off, to think of Caitlin Spears at this moment. In life she was a lovely woman, much like Christine, although back in Hell he hadn't really noticed. Yet Caitlin's self-absorbed vanity drove her to her fate, which she completely deserved, didn't she? Of course she did. Torval would've been hard pressed to come up with a more fitting torture for someone like that . . . although perhaps surrounding her with mirrors, so she could always see how grimy and disgusting she was, might've improved things a bit.

Stepping out of the shower, Torval took the towel from the wall and started drying himself off. The remnants of water rolling off his newly cleaned body collected in a puddle around his dirty, ragged clothes. Suddenly he found himself repulsed by his earlier attire. He didn't want to put those things on again. Once clean, he no longer desired to be anywhere near anything dirty, just as Caitlin Spears must've felt in her cell—but for her, she had no choice. Now, seeing things from that point of view, Torval understood far better the depths of her torture.

What of Caitlin now? Did she still find herself trapped in the mire of her cell, becoming dirtier and grimier, unwilling to use the hated soap and shampoo? Or did she stand once more under the water—either ice cold or scalding hot, but nothing in between—dreading the application of the only instruments she had to wash away the muck? Or had she finally transcended out of Hell at last?

Transcendence. Torval realized now just how little he truly understood the concept. Michael Rubin broke free from his cell by coming to some kind of revelation. He found the way out. Did that mean all cells had a key, like the one Christine used to enter her apartment building? Was that the reason Hell existed—so a soul could find that key? If so, what was Caitlin's key? To linger in the dirt without accepting the soap? Or to shower without it? Was it that simple, or did it take something else? Some greater understanding he had yet to fathom?

Torval couldn't grasp the concept any further. His thoughts seemed to freeze up for a moment, and he completely forgot his surroundings. Suddenly, he saw Christine in his mind, entering the hog wallow that served as Caitlin's cell. In his mind's eye, Christine dressed Caitlin's sores and wiped away her tears—helping her, in other words. Comforting her.

Torval frowned and shook the vision away. Actually helping someone in that way was preposterous! Hell permitted no aid or succor of any kind. No demon had ever considered such a thing. There wasn't room in Hell for acts of kindness. Of... of goodness.

Goodness! There it was again. The foreign concept once more intruded upon his thoughts, intriguing him with its alienness. Here on Earth, he had to remind himself, good was common, perhaps even in the ascendancy. If not, would Man be able to build a civilization? A city like this one? Surely not!

Come to think of it, how had Man built this city? Not to mention all of his other wonders. Torval couldn't imagine where they found the time to do so. They lived for only a hundred years, if that long. All the demons in Hell, since the beginning of time itself, hadn't come up with a single useful innovation. Every item of technology they possessed had been stolen from ideas brought there by Man.

So how did the humans accomplish so much in their short lifetimes? There had to be some way to find out the answer to that question. He couldn't just ask Christine, of course. Perhaps Prelz would know.

"Joe?" Christine's voice called out. "Are you done in there?"

"Yes," he answered immediately. He had, in fact, been standing idly in the bathroom for over a minute now, since he finished drying himself. Unwilling to put on those disgusting, shredded clothes, he was at a loss.

"Good. Look, I hope you don't mind, but I picked up some things for you to wear. It's not much and I wasn't sure of your size, but they should fit well enough. I'm leaving them outside your door here. Just leave your other things on the floor and I'll get them later. I'll head into the kitchen so you can come out, all right?"

"Yes," he agreed at once. Aware now that she didn't want to see him naked, he waited until her footsteps receded into the distance. Only then did he open the door. On the carpet outside, carefully placed to one side of his still-moist footprints, he found a pair of pants, a shirt, undergarments, and even a pair of shoes. All of them looked new.

And she was just giving them to him!

Humans didn't just give things away, did they? Well, perhaps a little soup now and then, but nothing material. He vaguely remembered something about this, something buried deep in his human brain. He searched his memory, trying to remember. A human concept—something that would never happen in Hell. After a moment he had it. The clothes were a gift!

Torval felt mesmerized. In all his hundreds of years of existence, he'd never received a gift. No demon gave anything, or did anything, unless ordered to do so or to cover a debt. Torval did his job because that was his purpose, and obeyed orders because to do otherwise invited punishment. Why would Christine just give him clothing for no reason? Did she have an ulterior motive that would become clear in time? Or was this just another selfless act, like the old woman who loaned him the money to help Hal?

Still somewhat perplexed, Torval picked up the clothes and pulled them on, starting with the underwear and T-shirt. The pants seemed long, so he pulled them up as high as he could. After some fiddling, he figured out how to use the belt. After that, he put on the wool turtleneck sweater, suddenly feeling warm and cozy, almost to the point of being uncomfortable. Lastly, he donned the black socks and shoes, finding to his satisfaction that the latter didn't use those confusing laces. Instead, they used strips of some kind of furry material that peeled loose with a tug and ripping sound, and then fastened down automatically when pressed upon. Another amazing human invention, Torval realized, accepting it at face value and moving on.

He stood. The shoes felt tight, but still far better than the shredded lumps back on the bathroom floor. He took a few steps, and then, unsure of himself, went back to the mirror again. Although his hair and beard remained scraggly, his clothes made him look and feel much better about his appearance.

In fact, as he stood there, he felt that tugging on his lips again. As he watched, the corners of his lips turned up in a smile. Ah, so that's what this looks like, he thought. The expression came automatically, almost beyond his control. By smiling, he denoted satisfaction or pleasure, something rarely seen in Hell, except over someone else's suffering. In his true demon form, Torval had no way to smile, for his bony face lacked the proper structure. His illusionary form could do so in the cells, of course, but he couldn't feel or experience that directly.

The curious movement of facial muscles intrigued him. He experimented for a few moments, deliberately exaggerating the grin. As he did, his teeth showed, momentarily startling him with their appearance. The ones he could see were yellow and dirty, as if they too needed washing. *Should I use soap on them?* Torval shook his head, automatically realizing that wasn't an option. *No, definitely not. There's something else for this, a device called a toothbrush. In fact, there's one right here, next to the sink. Should I use it . . . ?*

In another of his cells, Torval used to visit a dentist who, in life, regularly bilked his customers out of thousands of dollars for unnecessary procedures. As punishment, he was forced to brush his teeth constantly. Failure to do so caused his teeth to rot away, and as near as Torval could tell, the poor man suffered pain that bordered on the exquisite. Furthermore, the toothpaste itself consisted of a disgusting blend of insect parts and castor oil, which, as the unfortunate dentist frequently reminded him, was truly horrific.

Thinking back on this, Torval knew what it was to brush his teeth. The only question was whether he should try. Christine brought him here to cleanse his body and his hair, but not his mouth. When he called out to inquire, though, she didn't answer, meaning she'd moved too far away to hear. Surely she'd want him fully cleaned, wouldn't she? So of course she wouldn't mind, he concluded at length.

Torval picked up the brush, spread some paste on it, and started rubbing the bristles about in his mouth. Once he was sure he'd covered every tooth as best he could, he spit out the frothy, mint-flavored water and looked into the mirror once again. The teeth remained yellowish, but most of the grit was gone.

Now he noticed something else, looking inside his mouth. Some of his teeth showed the glint of metal. *Ah, yes, dentists again,* Torval thought. They filled holes in teeth with some kind of metal substance. More than a few cell punishments involved dentistry, after all. Very few tortures in Hell were as painful as a whining drill piercing a rotten tooth. Torval found it ironic that humans had designed one of the best instruments of pain available to demonkind.

As he washed out his mouth with some water, Torval heard Christine's voice again, coming from elsewhere in the apartment. "Joe? Are you done? We should get moving, or you'll be late."

"Yes, I am finished," he replied, stepping out of the bathroom and moving toward her. She stood there, smiling as he approached. At once he felt uncomfortable again, glancing away reflexively. "I apologize for the delay. I was brushing my teeth."

"Oh, great idea!" Christine agreed. "Good thinking, Joe. And I must say, you look fantastic! Well, those pants need some tailoring, and I'm sorry about the shoes—I didn't know your size, so I had to get Velcro ones. They'll fit a wider range of people, you see."

"I understand," said Torval, although that was only barely true. "Thank you, Christine. I appreciate the clothing very much." At that, he found himself even more uncomfortable. The idea of accepting a gift felt somehow unpleasant. Back home, at a minimum such a thing would leave him in the other's debt. "When I have earned enough money, I shall pay you for them," he added hastily.

"No, no, that's all right. This is the least I can do, Joe. Seeing you off the streets is reward enough for me."

"Very well," said Torval. Her statement automatically released him from any future service, but he still felt bad about it. He found himself thinking back to the old woman who handed him the money the previous night. What was it she said? Oh, yes, someone did her a favor the day before, and so, he should pass it on. A random act of kindness, she said.

So here was another random act of kindness, this time perpetrated by Christine. Both ladies had done him favors, asking nothing in return. That meant, using the old woman's logic, that he should now perform two corresponding randomly kind acts. Perhaps that was the nature of goodness—to ask for no reward, knowing that someone else would eventually pay you back.

Yes, that made sense! Torval understood things clearly now. Goodness involved the passing on of a positive act, and receiving one later as reward, even if not from the same individual. Furthermore, Torval found himself in arrears. He owed the humans two acts of kindness. If he didn't provide them, would he upset the balance somehow? He didn't know for sure.

Now all he had to do was figure out exactly what qualified as a good act, and how to judge if something he did counted as an appropriate exchange. The old woman's gift seemed easy enough to manage—all he had to do was give a similar amount of money to someone needy. Christine's was more difficult to quantify. How much were all these clothes worth, anyway?

"Well," said Christine, walking around Torval with one eyebrow raised, "you do look a lot better, but this needs work. Your sweater, for example, is a bit askew. Here."

She reached up and tugged on the collar, pulling it sideways. The sensation of her slender fingers, so near to caressing his face, left Torval paralyzed. A scent washed over him—sweet, like the shampoo, only more intense. He felt something very much like the imagined taste of alcohol that still lurked in a distant corner of his human brain.

Now Torval understood why he felt so uncomfortable around her. Like the booze that still called to his weak human flesh, Christine's presence was intoxicating.

Torval stepped away, eyes wide with horror. Fortunately, Christine had moved behind him, and didn't see his reaction. Inwardly, he cursed himself. Bless this human body! It is drawn to her, just as it was that first day! Joe wanted Christine—desired her, in a carnal sense—and that desire still haunted Torval, much to his chagrin.

I must resist, the demon told himself. She is only a mortal, and I am a demon! I am not a man. Not . . . a . . . man . . . !

"Something wrong, Joe?" asked Christine, one gracefully curved eyebrow raised curiously.

"No, no, I am fine," stammered Torval. "It is just that—I—I mean, it has been so long. Since I have—you know. Been . . . clean."

"I can imagine. You actually smell all right, for a change. You could use a manicure, too, but that's just not going to happen. Let's just concentrate on doing what we can for now. Come on. There's a barber shop down the street."

Cheerfully, she led him out of the apartment, almost bouncing in her steps as she moved along. For some reason, helping him in this manner made her happy. Torval shook his head and followed her, unable to fully comprehend what would make her feel that way.

*I will never understand good*, he thought as he made his way down the steps and out onto the cold, soggy street.

# Chapter 10

The barbershop was nothing like Torval expected.

One of his cells back home contained a man named Larry Vanderwahl. Mr. Vanderwahl had murdered someone—Torval never knew or cared who it was—by slitting his throat with a razor while he sat in Larry's barber chair. Torval couldn't recall the reason for the killing, but it hardly mattered. One of the surest ways to get to Hell was to commit murder.

In any event, Larry now spent his personal eternity cutting endless heads of hair in a replica of his shop. His scissors were dull, the customers constantly fidgeted and complained, and their inane conversations endlessly repeated themselves over and over again. Worst of all, for every inevitable mistake the unfortunate barber made, his customers sliced a chunk of flesh from his body in exchange. The wounds healed quickly, of course, but left the poor man in constant pain.

Torval didn't care about Larry's agony, of course, but he could still picture the barber shop—a country store with a large glass window, two chairs, and a few seats scattered about. Outside, Larry could always see children at play, friends having fun, and beautiful, sunny weather he could never experience for himself. After all, he was chained to his barber's chair, and the windows were unbreakable.

The barbershop Torval found himself in now looked nothing like Larry's place. Six chairs, most of which were occupied, extended in a line along the far wall. Behind each of the oversized chairs sat a messy desk covered with barber's tools. Above these hung a wall-length, streak-covered mirror. Larry's shop, despite the constant work that faced the tortured victim, produced a distinct feeling of small-town charm. This colorless place had an assembly-line air about it, lacking even a place to sit while waiting one's turn.

A single barber chair sat open. "Go on up, Joe," Christine said from behind Torval. "I made an appointment so there'd be no waiting."

Joe took two steps forward, and the barber blocked his path with an outstretched hand. The heavyset black man turned to Christine. "You've gotta be kiddin' me, Chris," he said with a scowl. "This is the one you made the appointment for? Look at that beard! I'm not doin' it. No way, no how."

"Oh, come on, Ross, surely this isn't the worst you've ever seen. Besides, you'll be doing me a huge favor. Please? Pretty please?"

"Nope, you can't sweet-talk me this time, honey. No chance." Ross crossed his arms, set his jaw, and looked adamant.

To Torval's right, Christine smiled brightly. "You know there's a big tip in it for you, Ross. Now cut the damn hair!"

The big man shook his head and threw up his hands. "Oh, all right, since you put it that way! You know I can't stand to see a pretty lady get mad. Come on, you. Sit down here in Uncle Ross's chair, and I'll make you look like a real man again!"

Torval sat. Ross wrapped a paper cowl about his customer's neck and then flung a white sheet over Torval's chest. From the events in Larry's shop, the demon knew this would catch his falling hair. Then the black barber began to cut. And cut. And cut. Pretty soon Torval's lap held nothing but a mass of salt-and-pepper trimmings.

After several minutes of this, during which Christine watched with obvious amusement, Ross sprayed some mist on Torval's hair and started combing. Now things got painful. What was left of the bum's hair remained matted and tangled from years of absent hygiene. Each time the comb moved, it made a sharp yank on Torval's scalp, causing the demon to wince. Ignoring the frequent grunts of pain, Ross kept spraying and combing, occasionally trimming away what he couldn't deal with, until finally he seemed satisfied. Then he cut some more, evening out the areas around the parts he'd been forced to trim.

After that, Ross brought out a razor and cleaned up the edges. While he did so, Torval noticed that Christine was smiling again, looking at him. She seemed very pleased, but not with herself this time. Torval didn't know what could possibly be so fascinating, but once more he found himself becoming uncomfortable under her piercing blue-eyed gaze.

Now Ross got to work on Torval's beard. Once again, those deft scissors snipped away what took Joe Sampson years to accumulate. The cutting seemed to go on for quite a while, until finally Ross brought out another electric device and trimmed away the remainder. Finally, he lathered Torval's face and cleaned up the rest with a long-handled straight razor. As he did, Torval found himself reminded of Larry Vanderwahl again. This, supposedly, was the implement Larry used to kill another human being and land himself in Hell.

Of course, if Ross did the same thing now, spilling Joe's blood all over the floor, Torval would simply wind up back in the transition gateway. Yesterday, when he first arrived on Earth, he might not have minded that so much. Now, though, he felt like he'd made progress here. He already felt better about being a human, and with Christine's help, he'd surely find a job and get a place to live.

If only she weren't so appealing to this human body, he thought. Joe wanted her still, even now. The way she smiled at him seemed to increase the effect. He had to find some way to control these impulses!

Finally, Ross finished his work. "Well, boy, you ready to see what you really look like under all that fur?" he asked with a hearty laugh.

"I suppose so," Torval replied, not really meaning it. What difference could it possibly make?

Ross turned the chair to face the mirror. Torval now saw Joe's face bereft of hair. The skin there seemed surprisingly youthful, though still marred by weather-inflicted wrinkles and several small scars. The chin looked lighter-colored than the rest of the face, probably because the beard had blocked the sun. This made him look like he'd put on a tan-colored mask.

Ross did an excellent job trimming the bum's hair to a short, fashionable style. The beard's absence made Torval's face seem chilly, even in the warm barbershop. As he ran his hands over his strangely smooth chin, Christine stepped up beside him, staring at the reflection in the mirror. "Wow," she said in appreciation. "You're not as old as I thought you were, Joe. You can't be more than what, forty?"

"I do not know for sure," the demon replied truthfully.

"You've forgotten your age?" asked the barber, shaking his head. "Man, I sure as hell wish I could. I'm sixty goin' on ninety, or it sure feels like, anyway."

"Oh, don't worry, Ross, you're still awfully spry," Christine chided jovially. "Besides, you know you're only as old as you feel."

"Yeah, well, I'm feelin' older every day. I can't imagine throwin' it all away, though. 'Specially not if I looked like this guy."

"What do you mean?" Torval inquired.

"You kiddin' me, boy? Look at you! If you weren't a bum, you'd have chicks hangin' all over you. Know what I mean, Chris?"

She slapped at his shoulder, reddening slightly. "Stop it, Ross! You're embarrassing me. Now, are you finished? What's the tab, anyway?"

"I should charge you twice as much for this, y'know," said the big man, still chuckling over the way he got Christine's face to darken just a bit. He removed the sheet and the neck guard, taking out one of the electric razors to make a few final runs down Torval's neck. The demon felt a sudden chill, and little bumps appeared all over his flesh. He stared at them absently, wondering why he'd feel cold in this comfortably warm place, as Ross continued talking. "Tell you what, just for you I'll only charge twenty bucks for the package deal."

"Thanks, Ross, you're a pal," agreed Christine readily, taking out her purse. Torval only just now noticed that she'd been carrying the small, black accoutrement. She must've had it on her opposite side while she walked, tucked under her arm. Reaching inside the purse, she withdrew a twenty-dollar bill and handed it over, followed quickly by a five. "This is for putting up with me," she added with another of her sweet, entrancing smiles.

"Thank you, my dear," Ross replied with a slight bow. "I give you a hard time, y'know, but you can bring in customers anytime. Next time you've got one with five years' growth, let me know first, okay? See, my ten o'clock's already here waitin'."

Christine glanced back and saw a man in a crisp black business suit by the front door. "Sorry about that," she replied. "Is it really ten already? Come on, Joe, we've got to get moving. We're already running behind. Thanks, Ross, I'll talk to you later, okay?"

"You have fun now, y'hear?" the barber called out as they both hurried out of the shop.

* * *

To Torval's surprise, they didn't immediately start walking again, toward some as yet unknown destination. Instead, Christine moved a few steps out into the street and put up her hand, waving it in the general direction of the approaching vehicles.

Torval watched her curiously, afraid to inquire for fear of revealing his ignorance in some well-known human custom. Instead, he occupied himself thinking about the expenditure of cash a few moments before. As he sat there in the chair, massaging his naked face and looking at his neatly trimmed hair in the mirror, Christine had spent twenty-five dollars on his behalf.

Judging by how much it cost to buy food on two previous occasions, Torval imagined she just spent the equivalent of ten meals. Why was she doing this? Why help him so much, when she knew he could do nothing in exchange? If his earlier theory about passing along random acts of kindness proved correct, was she simply making up for similar acts sent her way, or did she intend to get ahead? Or was his theory flawed in some way, and she had some other motivation in mind?

The lack of answers was positively maddening!

Of course, if Torval's original theory held up, he now owed yet another favor to someone—an act of kindness in the amount of twenty-five dollars. He might be able to beg for that much money, as he had at breakfast this morning, but that would take some time. Perhaps when he had a job, the pay would be sufficient to buy his food, pay his lodging, and pass along Christine's latest act of kindness. Or perhaps repay her directly.

Yes, that will work, Torval thought. I'll pay her back the money she spent today. That would be a simple matter to arrange, and then he wouldn't have to worry about whether he properly followed the rules of goodness. Of course, he still had to reconcile the encounter with the old woman the night before, but then, that was just another form of begging, now that he thought about it. Torval begged that morning and received coins from several individuals. Were those also good acts as well, deserving of a like act of kindness in return? How far would this eventually go? Could he even keep track of them all?

As he mulled that over, Christine's semi-frantic waving finally had the desired effect. A yellow car pulled over to the curb, and without hesitation Christine opened up the back door and climbed inside. "Come on, Joe, get in!" she urged.

Torval balked. He'd seen some of these human vehicles in action in cell illusions. Usually the prisoners in question were there because they had raced cars in life, often illegally, leading to the deaths of innocents. One man in particular, David Griswold, had to relive his wife's unfortunate demise as he wrecked his car over and over. No matter how hard he tried, he couldn't keep the vehicle from crashing.

The memory of that tangled wreck seemed fixed in Torval's mind. Of course, he didn't mind death, but he didn't want to spend the rest of his time on Earth injured and in great pain, either.

"Come on, Joe!" Christine insisted. "What are you waiting for?"

He took a hesitant step toward the cab, and stopped again. These vehicles are safe, he told himself. Even as he looked, he could see dozens of them driving past in both directions on the street. Only the ones driven recklessly were dangerous. So why couldn't he enter? Was it because they were so strange to him? Yes, that must be it.

While he hesitated, Christine suddenly emerged from the cab. "Joe?" she asked worriedly. "Is something wrong? Oh, no, I didn't realize—this has to do with your past, doesn't it?"

Ah, yes, Torval thought. Joe's truck accident. Perhaps that explained his revulsion. He could no longer feel Joe's thoughts and memories, but considering the body's attraction to Christine, some echoes of the bum still lingered. Well, thought the demon, I can't seem to figure out how to deal with the Christine issue, but I can at least squelch this inane fear of motor vehicles.

"No," said Torval. "It is nothing. I just have not been in a car for so long. Come, let us depart."

Christine nodded and climbed back in the cab. Torval entered after her, sitting down on the torn seat. For a moment nothing happened, and then he remembered the door. Reaching out, he grasped the handle and pulled. As soon as the door closed, the vehicle started forward.

"Where to, lady?" asked the cabbie. Torval looked into the front seat, where a small, greasy-looking man sat amidst a pile of discarded food wrappers. Some sort of machine, on which numbers glowed, occupied the dashboard nearby. As Torval watched, the red digits changed, increasing noticeably. All at once he realized that these numbers corresponded to an amount of money. That explained why the vehicle drove where Christine wanted it to go. Just another use for money, it seemed. With enough cash, people could go where they wanted without walking.

And, he thought morosely, this is yet another purchase Christine is making on my behalf. More funds I will owe her in the future.

"The employment bureau on Forty-Fifth," she told the driver. "You know where that is?"

"Yeah, yeah," replied the dour man. He seemed rather annoyed at the destination for some reason. "Just a few blocks. Won't take long."

Christine nodded and sat back, turning her gaze once again to Torval. The demon tried to ignore her stares and looked out the window. As the cab drove, it gathered speed, so that the buildings and people outside seemed to fly by. Other cars followed along, matching speeds with the cab or even passing it. A great many of them were also yellow, with little signs on their roofs advertising their availability for hire.

Again Torval felt concerned by the speed of his vehicle and the proximity of the others. How did they avoid hitting each other, or his own car? There seemed to be no rhyme or reason to the way they traveled down the street, accelerating and decelerating, turning and dodging other vehicles and people.

The initial fear and anxiety about the car ride faded only through diligent concentration on Torval's part. As soon as he realized that the other vehicles weren't going to slam into his without warning, he started to grow more comfortable. There must be some unspoken rule that governed their travels—a rule he didn't understand, but one that definitely existed. Otherwise they'd be bouncing off each other with wild abandon.

After about a minute, he let out a breath and relaxed. He felt better now. Just like that, he'd obviously conquered Joe's lingering fear of cars. Easily, too. Would putting off Christine be so simple? Perhaps controlling these unfamiliar emotions could be accomplished with the mind alone.

"Joe, are you all right?" she asked, interrupting his thoughts. "You're very quiet. What are you thinking about?"

He glanced over at her. She was smiling again. Did she ever stop doing that? "Nothing," he answered. "Just noticing how fast everything is passing by."

"My, it has been a while since you've been in a car, hasn't it?" Christine asked. "How long were you out on the streets, Joe? Was it five years like Ross said? Or have you been out there even longer?"

"I do not remember," he replied. That excuse hadn't let him down yet, so he went with it once again. This time, though, Christine didn't let the issue drop.

"Sure you do. I can tell. You know exactly how long you've been out of society, Joe. A lot of homeless people lose track and become hopeless, but not you. I could always tell that somewhere inside there was a man who wanted to escape that life."

"That certainly seems to be the case," Torval agreed.

"I'm so happy you've turned over a new leaf," Christine went on, "but you know you have to face your old self before you can really move on. Come on, Joe, open up a little. Tell me what happened to you. I think you really want to tell me."

Torval sighed. He could remember the part about the truck accident, but he couldn't speak about that experience. He was, after all, given strict orders not to involve himself in his body's old life. If he started spilling details, he'd be violating that edict. He couldn't simply ignore the command—obeying it was his only option.

Before he could think of a response, Christine shook her head and gave up. "Okay, I can see you're still not ready. That's all right, Joe. Just remember, if you ever do need to talk, I'll always be here for you."

Torval decided this would be a good time to show gratitude again. He had done it wrong earlier, though. Some of the exchanges he'd seen in Ross's barbershop showed him the proper procedure. This time he tried expressing himself a different way. "Thank you, Christine," he said as honestly as he could.

She smiled at once, thereby telling Torval he'd delivered the message adequately. "You're welcome."

At that, she fell silent. The cab drove on, the only noise that of the car's engine and occasional crackles from the driver's two-way radio. Once again, Torval found himself thinking about Joe. The poor bum wasted at least five years when Christine was right there, willing to help him out at a moment's notice. All he ever had to do was ask. Yet he wouldn't, for whatever reason. Did he now reside in Hell, as penance for his stubbornness? Perhaps so. If so, what might his punishment be? Did he remain a bum on some frozen, windswept street? Would he even be able to tell the difference between this vast city and his illusory prison cell?

It all seemed so senseless, and yet, Torval didn't really know Joe at all. He hadn't lived the man's life. How could he judge him by the slight facts he knew? Upon his arrival in Hell, Joe Sampson's soul would be evaluated based on his entire life, not simply his last few years. Perhaps he wasn't in Hell at all. He might be in the other, supposedly better place.

A strange feeling stirred in Torval's stomach. The sensation began when he started thinking of Joe's wasted existence. Another human emotion, he realized, but which one? He didn't feel that tightness in his chest brought on by anxiety, and his mouth didn't want to curl into a smile as it did when he felt satisfied or happy. So what was going on now? He looked down at his stomach and gave it a few experimental prods, but nothing changed.

Christine, of course, picked up on this right away. "What's the matter now, Joe? You look uncomfortable. Nervous?"

"No, I do not think so," Torval answered. If he understood the term properly, nervousness was just another kind of anxiety, and he'd already ruled out that emotion.

"Well, what were you thinking of just then?" asked Christine curiously.

Torval sighed. For a few brief moments, he'd actually managed to avoid more annoying small talk. Still, this wasn't nearly as bad as Geezon's chattering or Prelz prattling on about one of his temptation experiences. Christine had a way of communicating that strangely made him want to answer. "I was thinking of J—of myself. Of how much has been wasted. As I considered that, I felt something in my stomach. Painful, almost, but not quite."

"Did it feel hollow, like you were empty down here?" she asked, putting her hand on his belly. The movement came swiftly, before he could protest. Even through the new sweater, the pressure of her fingers caused his flesh to tingle. More of Joe's accursed attraction to her, Torval thought, fighting the urge to react. Fortunately, the desire to grasp her hand and hold it tightly was neatly cancelled out by his need to back away from her at high speed—just as well, considering he'd already pushed himself all the way back into his corner of the cab.

After a moment, Torval realized she awaited his reply. "Uh, yes, I believe that is a fair assessment," he stammered.

"You feel guilty," she pronounced, giving him a surprising slap on the stomach before withdrawing her hand. "Don't worry, Joe, there's nothing to feel guilty about. What's important is you're leaving that all behind you now."

Guilty? Torval rubbed his smooth chin, which still felt unusually cold, unlike the rest of him. He looked away from Christine and started to think about her words. He didn't understand guilt very well. Prisoners always claimed they felt guilty about the things they did in life, but such complaints never helped their situation. Guilt was something one felt about oneself, not about others. So how could he feel guilty about something Joe did?

Not guilt, he realized then. Pity. He felt pity for Joe Sampson. He almost wished he could bring Joe's soul back to his body, to show him what he could've done if only he cared to try.

What a strange emotion, pity. What purpose did it serve? Torval had seen thousands of prisoners, each suffering for uncounted years in their private hells. What if he, as a demon, felt pity for them? What if all demons could feel this strange, agonizing emptiness in their guts? Why, they would be unable to perform their duties! Keeping order in Hell would be all but impossible.

No, Torval was glad he didn't have to feel pity as a demon. Now if he could just make it go away, he'd be much better off. So far, the best way he'd found to change his emotional state was to think about something else. So, with that in mind, he turned his attention once again to the vast, sprawling city out the window.

The cab came to a stop behind several other similar vehicles. Although the natural sun shined overhead, and most of the city's artificial illumination had faded, one set of lights remained active nearby, currently displaying a glowing red circle. Beneath that, the words "Don't Walk" glowed in crimson. Apparently ignoring the warning, numerous pedestrians rushed across the intersection, drawing irate honks from motorists trying to turn down the street.

After a moment, the red light turned green and the virtually meaningless ban against walking lifted. Now the cab started moving again. Torval cocked his head sideways, not quite understanding the procedure. The "Walk" sign clearly referred to the pedestrians on the sidewalks, as he knew from his own experiences the last day and a half, but except for a few people, it held no power. However, the vehicles obeyed the glowing commands, at least at first. Yet at the next street, the "Don't Walk" command flashed brightly, obviously to attract one's attention, and the cab blithely ignored this and continued on.

Somehow, he knew, all of these things regulated the traffic, preventing cars from striking each other. He couldn't fathom the means, though. Clearly he had a lot more to learn about human policies and procedures. If only he could ask Christine . . . but then he would show too much naïveté. He filed the query away for later, when he saw Prelz again. Even if Torval had to endure more of the ex-demon's long-winded tales, at least he would provide a small amount of useful information.

Torval looked out the window once more, watching the people and buildings pass by. For a few moments, he found himself mesmerized by the seemingly endless stream of humans and their creations. After a couple of blocks, he turned his head both directions and realized that the rows of high-rises and skyscrapers continued on seemingly forever. Just how big was this city?

When he first arrived on Earth, Torval found himself awed by the sheer size of the buildings around him, but he assumed there were only a few. Now he knew they just went on and on. He couldn't imagine the effort needed just to construct one skyscraper, let alone hundreds of them in such close quarters. How did the humans do it?

Another question for Prelz, he reminded himself.

The cab suddenly swerved to the right, causing Torval to jump in surprise. Before he could say anything, the vehicle pulled up to a curb and slammed to a halt. "Here we are, lady," said the driver. "That'll be three eighty-five."

Christine got out of the car, took out her purse, and handed a five-dollar bill to the man. That is the cost of another favor, Torval thought, mentally adding to the steadily growing tally in his head. Then he tried to open the door, and realized he didn't know how. Christine did so easily, but he didn't see how she pulled it off.

*Yes, I still have a lot of things to learn about human procedures,* Torval thought as he slid across the back seat, following Christine around the back of the cab toward the sidewalk.

# Chapter 11

Dozens of people packed the inside of the employment bureau. Most sat in one of the half-dozen rows of chairs in front of a long counter, behind which stood several bored-looking clerks. A few customers chatted in low voices, but most remained silent, reading or busying themselves with some electronic device to pass the time. In one corner, a numbered strip of paper protruded from a desktop-mounted wheel. Each waiting customer held one of these strips of paper, which explained the lack of lines or queues.

Torval knew the "take a number" scheme well. One of his prisoners, a man named Karl Gruber, was in life a bureaucrat who worked in a tax office. There, he did everything by the book, never bending a rule or showing any sympathy for anyone. As his punishment, he forever struggled to push meaningless documents through an endless series of equally meaningless offices. Each time he moved to the next step in the process, he had to take a number and wait. Inevitably, he found himself in the wrong line, or unable to speak to the right person, and then he had to start all over.

Watching some of the people waiting here, Torval thought he understood what Karl had to endure. According to the sign, the number "24" was currently being served (although he saw no evidence of this), but the tag sticking out of the number wheel read "73." Since only four attendants were on duty, Torval expected the wait would take hours.

Not for him, though. Upon his arrival, Christine informed him that they had an appointment, and to stay where he was. Torval agreed and waited patiently in the crowded room, exactly as instructed. Meanwhile, Christine disappeared through a door marked "Employees Only." After five minutes, Torval felt the first stirrings of boredom.

Despite the sheer number of people in the waiting room, the place remained mostly quiet. Torval glanced around, studying the individuals in the seats, as well as the few standing in back. Most were shabbily dressed, but none looked like bums. Men comprised the vast majority of waiting patrons, but only a few were clean-cut. Some wore hats, and one black man had a curious kind of woolen skullcap wrapped over his bald pate. A Hispanic woman standing close by featured skin peppered with a striking variety of tattoos.

As Torval studied the markings curiously, she turned toward him, crossing her arms in obvious dismay. "You gotta problem, asswipe?" she hissed, surprising Torval with her bitterness.

"No, I do not think so," Torval answered, glancing down at his new clothes to make sure nothing had slipped out of place.

"Whaddaya starin' at, then?" she snapped back.

Torval shrugged and answered honestly. "The markings on your arms and neck. They are quite intricate."

"You dissin' my tatts, man?" the woman growled.

Torval had no clue what she meant by that. Had she lapsed into another tongue? In Hell, he always understood what any prisoner said, because language was moot. Here on Earth, things worked differently, thanks to that whole inexplicable Babel business.

"I am sorry, but I do not understand," the demon tried to explain. "I was just admir—"

"Well, knock it off!" she barked. Some of the other people in the room glanced curiously in her direction. "They're not for dickweeds like you to stare at, okay?"

"I apologize again," responded Torval, trying to calm her down. "I was not aware that appreciating the art on your skin was wrong. I will stop." He turned his eyes away.

"Wait a minute. You tellin' me you was really diggin' my art?"

"Yes. I have seen many tattoos. In H—I mean, where I come from, they are quite prevalent." In fact, sometimes such art directly involved a prisoner's punishment, but Torval didn't mention that. One tortured soul, flesh covered by tattoos in life, was forced to suffer through endless additions of new ones on one part of his body while they were forcibly removed somewhere else. Torval always imagined the peeling, burning, and boiling must be quite painful, and now that he'd experienced human form, he could understand why. The very thought of such torture made his skin crawl.

The woman relaxed and leaned back against the wall. "Okay, you can look if ya want. No touchin', though. You look all right, but ya never know 'round this place."

Torval took a step closer and studied her left shoulder, the part of her body closest to him. The woman tensed up, but didn't try to move away. She wore a flimsy powder-blue blouse held up by thin spaghetti straps, probably the better to show off her tattoos. She also revealed a considerable amount of cleavage, and despite the fact that Torval truly wanted to study the image on her skin, his human eyes kept drifting downward of their own accord.

*Self-control*, he told himself, clenching his fists together and forcing his eyes back to her neck, where a spectacular eagle dove in midflight, beak open and wings spread wide. The feathers even had ribbing marked in exquisitely fine lines. *Whoever drew this must be quite skilled*, he thought appreciatively.

Even as he followed the eagle's talons downward, the woman turned her head and gave a brief snort. "Like what ya see?" she inquired haughtily.

Torval's head snapped back upright. "Yes, it is very . . . impressive," he said truthfully.

She smiled suggestively at him. "Damn straight it is. I'll bet ya wanna piece, don't ya?"

"A piece? What do you mean?"

"I saw where yer eyes was goin', mister. Ya can't fool me." She shifted and crossed her arms, and Torval realized she'd been studying him. Although she looked somewhat haggard, with dark circles under her eyes and the hint of age in fine wrinkles just beginning to form, her face had a certain beauty to it. He found himself appreciating the way her long, straight black hair left just a few locks dangling strategically about her eyebrows.

In the back of his mind, Torval knew his weak human shell was attracted to this woman. She had the sort of attributes that made her appealing to his male form—full lips, ample breasts, a narrow waist, and wide hips. The skintight blue jeans and flimsy blouse did little to hide these attributes. She would indeed be a good bearer of children, Torval thought, but of course that wasn't what his body cared about at that moment.

He could feel the male reaction beginning. Startled by the strange pressure and uncomfortable feeling, he stepped back. "I apologize once more," he protested. "I did not—"

"Oh, don't worry 'bout it, man. You're cool. You ain't so bad lookin' yerself. Kinda prettied up for this kinda place, though. What's yer name, anyways?"

"Joe," said Torval. "Joe Sampson."

She extended her hand. "Pleased ta meetcha and all that crap. Name's Shelly Mendez."

Torval returned her gesture, discovering in the process that she had a very firm grip. She wasn't a demon, either. The last time Torval shook hands with somebody, he discovered Prelz's presence. Shelly, it seemed, was merely human.

"It is good to meet you as well," Torval replied, releasing her hand. "I have not met many people since coming here."

"Yeah, nobody talks much 'round this place," Shelly agreed. "We're all, like, rivals, y'know? Fightin' for the same jobs. How 'bout you? What you lookin for? And if ya say waitin' tables I'm gonna kick yer ass."

"If by that you mean what sort of employment I am seeking, I do not care. I will take anything."

"Oh, desperate, eh? Didn't see that comin'. You look awful fresh for a down-and-outer. Smell good, too." She moved closer to him, and Torval felt his skin prickling. "Yeah, real good," she confirmed with an appreciative nod, obviously detecting the fresh scent of his recently cleansed skin and hair.

"I suppose desperate is an accurate representation of my situation," Torval agreed, still struggling internally with his body's reaction to her nearness. Shelly also smelled good, which he couldn't help but notice. The spicy, tantalizing odor didn't remind him of food, but made him hungry anyway—a totally different kind of hunger.

Shelly clapped him on the shoulder. "Ha! I love the way ya talk, Joe!" she said with a chuckle. "You gots a real v'cab'lary in that head-a-yours.

Ya sure you ain't a reporter or sump'in, slummin' down here with us lowlifes?"

"I assure you, I speak truthfully," said the demon. "I am—or was, until today—what you would call a homeless person."

She laughed again. "You? A bum? Lookin' like that? Whadya do, win the lottery or sump'in?"

"No, nothing like that. I just decided it was time to get a job."

"Oh really? Just like that? Yer gonna come walzin' in here and get one, eh? Ha! Better get in line, man! All these people here, and hundreds more, and me too. Heh heh. Good 'tentions don't cut it in this town, y'know."

"It is not easy?" Torval didn't like what he was hearing. He expected to come here today and get employment at once! "How long will it take to become employed?"

"I dunno," Shelly answered with a shrug, "but I've been comin' here on 'n' off for weeks. Somma these peeps, they been here for a lot longer, or so's they tell me."

"This cannot be!" the demon complained. "I cannot wait that long! I must be employed immediately. I need money so that I can purchase a place to live!"

"Oh, yeah, good luck on that too," she replied doubtfully. "You ain't gonna get paid for least a week, y'know. Nobody in this town's gonna give ya a place without a down payment."

Torval scowled. That wasn't what he wanted at all! "This is not fair," he complained. "I do not want to spend another night on the street."

"Well, life ain't fair," said Shelly. "Ya oughta know that, if ya really was out there."

He sensed her disbelief and tried to shore it up with an embellished version of what his life had been like over the last day or so. "I was," he insisted. "I nearly died. I was sick, and when I awoke, I knew that I was finished in that place."

Shelly nodded. "Yeah, it was kinda like that with my ex. I just sorta woke up one day and said, 'That's it, I'm done with this bum.' Sorry, man, no 'fense intended, y'know? Anyway, he was screwin' every girl in sight anyway. So I started screwin' other men, ha ha! That showed 'im! We was done after that, y'know. Y'shoulda seen that fight we had! It was awesome! Ah, well, good riddance to 'im. I'll screw whoever I want now, an' he can't stop me." She halted her tirade for a moment, studying Torval again. "How 'bout you, man? You look hot, and I love that way of talkin' ya got. Smart guys with big words always turn me on. Ya wanna blow this place and go get nasty?"

This time, Torval felt fairly certain he understood her strange speech. If so, she just clearly had offered him sex. Torval's body certainly wanted it, but he knew he couldn't leave. "Not at this time," he replied, with a noticeable air of disappointment in his voice. He didn't put that emotion in consciously, but there it was anyway. "I really must attempt to find employment."

"Oh, yeah, right," said Shelly, looking crestfallen. "Shit, now yer makin' me even hotter! Smart guys with 'sponsability! My hero, and all that crapola! Maybe later, huh?"

"Perhaps so," agreed Torval, and he meant it. An opportunity to study human mating practices simply couldn't be passed up, after all. "I would like that very much, Shelly."

"Heh. You don't know how right you are, man." She threw back her shoulders and shook herself, causing her considerable bosom to bounce about suggestively. "I ain't failed ta satisfy a man yet, even skinny rails like you. Hey, how long ya been on the street, anyway? You ain't all shrivelly, are ya?"

For a moment he didn't understand, but then he saw her eyes meandering downward until she focused squarely on his crotch. Judging by the sensations presently coming from down there, he knew the answer to her question. "I am not, I assure you."

"Good! I'd hate ta think I'd be wastin' my time. So how long, man? How long you been out there?"

"On the street?" Torval thought back to what he recalled of Joe's past. "Years," he admitted. "I cannot remember the exact number."

"Oh, years, eh? You gotten any in all that time? Prob'ly not, huh? Oh, yeah, this is gonna be fun! Here, lemme write down my addy. Yeah, it's a crappy shithole, what with the divorce 'n' all, just till I get on my feet, y'know? Don't worry, though. I gots the place all to myself. Nobody ta cramp my style."

She jotted down some information on a piece of paper and handed it to Torval. He studied the address for a moment and then pushed the slip into his pocket. "Thank you, Shelly. I will certainly seek you out."

"One thing I don't get," she went on. "If you was really a bum 'n' all, how'd ya wind up lookin' like that? All prettied up and such, with them duds you got? Ya didn't beg for that kinda cash, I know. Whatdya do, roll somebody?"

Torval tried to picture himself pushing somebody along on the ground, and found the idea ridiculous. More slang, he determined. "No, I was aided by a—a friend," he replied, not sure if Christine could really be referred to by that term. She was indeed friendly, but the emotional attachment he felt to Hal suggested that a true friendship developed over more than just a single day of interaction.

"Oh really? A friend, eh? What'd he do, spot ya the cash? Trusting, ain't he?"

"Not a he, a she," corrected Torval. "Her name is Christine, and she works at the soup kitchen where I eat."

"Oh, a bleedin' heart! I get it! What a sap!" Shelly started laughing. "Ya really put one over on her, didn't ya? Well, don't think yer gonna get anythin' like that on me, man! I'm smarter than that! I don't want no 'lationship, and I ain't givin' you nothin' but one great night-o-lovin'!"

"I do not want a . . . 'lationship," explained Torval. "And I am not, as you say, putting one over on Christine. I am serious about wishing to be employed."

"Hey, now, don't get yer panties all in a bunch! I don't give a shit 'bout yer bleedin' heart friend. Do what ya want! Oh, hey, don't look now, I think ya got a fan."

"What?"

She was pointing. "Look behind ya."

Torval turned, and Christine stood there, eyes narrowed as she watched the tail end of the preceding exchange. "Sorry, I don't mean to interrupt," she said, for once not smiling. "Joe, the friend I was talking about is ready to meet you, so if you'll come along . . ."

Shelly grinned. "Lemme guess, you're Christine, eh?"

"Yes," replied Torval, suddenly feeling very uneasy. "I am sorry, Shelly, but as I explained, I must attempt to find employment."

"Yeah, right, whatever. Good luck, man, and don't forget, yer gonna need it. Catch ya later!" She gave a little wave.

"Goodbye," Torval replied, turning to follow Christine. Before disappearing through the door supposedly intended for employees only, he took a glance back over his shoulder. Shelly stood there, watching him and grinning. As he lost sight of her, she waved again.

Without thinking about it, Torval automatically returned the gesture.

* * *

"Who was that, Joe?" Christine asked as soon as they were by themselves. She actually stopped in the hallway, making Torval come up short, surprised at her sudden halt.

"Her name is Shelly Mendez," Torval answered honestly. "She, like me, is unemployed. We were talking about our predicament." Abruptly Torval realized he'd actually been making small talk—exactly the sort of thing he always hated to do. Yet, with Shelly, as with Christine, he didn't really mind all that much. How strange! Was it the fact that both were women who interested him, or simply that they were humans? Perhaps other demons simply bored him, and humans didn't.

"Yeah, well, I can tell what she was thinking," said Christine warily. "You do realize she's a prostitute, right?"

Torval just stared at her. Former harlots were quite common in Hell. How could he not recognize one by sight? Or was Christine simply guessing? "I do not think so," he countered. "As I understand it, to be a prostitute one must offer sex for money. Shelly offered sex, as you surmised, but did not ask for any payment."

Christine's eyes went wide. "She propositioned you? Just like that? I was only gone five minutes, Joe. Doesn't that strike you as unusual?"

"She explained that her former husband left her recently, and—" Torval began.

"I don't care what she told you, Joe," Christine went on, interrupting him sharply. She looked quite agitated, which seemed rather uncharacteristic for her. "I've seen her type, you know. Didn't you see how she was dressed? She was looking for a mark, and that's you. Let me guess, she gave you her number, right?"

"She did give me an address, that is true," Torval admitted.

Christine nodded vigorously, as if this proved her case. "See, she wants you to come over. She may even give you a freebie once or twice. Then, when your guard's down, she'll empty your wallet and kick you out."

"If that is so," said Torval, "why would she seek one such as I? I told her I was a homeless person, and had no job. How could she expect me to have money?"

"I don't know. Maybe she didn't believe you. Maybe she just thought you looked like an easy mark, with new clothes and all. You do look much better than the others in that waiting room, you know."

"She said the same thing, actually," Torval pointed out.

"Yeah, I'm sure she did. Well, look, Joe, I'm not saying for sure that's what she was up to. Maybe she's on the level. You really should look out for yourself, though. You should concentrate on getting a job and not getting distracted by some tattooed hussy."

"Very well, that is what I will do," Torval agreed, although his mind kept going back to Shelly's proposal. He and his human body both wanted to experience the mating ritual she suggested. Besides, if Shelly's plot was really nothing more than to string him along until he became wealthy, she would be disappointed. Torval only had thirteen days left on this mortal sphere.

"Good," Christine replied, and her smile returned. "Now come on, there's a clerk here I need you to meet. His name's Simon Spencer, and he's done favors for me in the past. I already explained your situation, and I think he's amenable. Here, through this door."

She indicated a windowed door upon which hung a large tag marked "Employment Evaluation." Several empty chairs lined the walls nearby. Through the glass, Torval could see a tiny office containing a desk, several file cabinets, and a single chair, with little room for any other furniture. A narrow-faced man dressed in a tweed outfit sat behind a computer, staring at the screen through bespectacled eyes. After a moment, he looked up and motioned for Torval to enter.

The demon did so and immediately felt comfortable. The little room reminded him of certain cramped cells back home, mostly occupied by small-minded people who spent their lives focusing on work to the exclusion of all else.

"Hello," said Simon Spencer, standing up and extending a hand. "Welcome to the employment bureau, Mr.—Sampson, is that it?"

Torval shook the hand, relieved to see Simon didn't turn out to be another demon in human form. Having found Prelz already, Torval would be perfectly happy not meeting another demon at all during the rest of his vacation, if he could possibly avoid it. "Yes, my name is Joe Sampson. I require employment."

"Yes, yes, don't we all," said Simon with no hint of amusement in his voice. "Can I ask you what your job skills are?"

"Job skills?" Torval turned his head as he thought about that. Joe Sampson had been a—what? Truck driver, yes, that was it. Torval, on the other hand, knew nothing about driving a truck. From what he recalled of Joe's memories, the task seemed quite unpleasant. "I am not sure," he answered. "I have not... I mean, it has been a long time."

Simon sat back down with a disappointed sigh. "Yes, I suppose so. Let me try this another way. What can you do, Mr. Sampson? Think back to any jobs you've done in the past. What can you do that someone might wish to pay you to do today?"

"I do not know," replied Torval. Perhaps trying to use Joe's past experiences wouldn't work here, so he tried another tack. "In my previous lif—I mean, once before, I was a . . . guard. Yes, that is the proper term."

"Guard?" asked Simon. "What did you guard?"

"Prisoners," answered Torval, which of course was correct, as far as that went. "I was responsible for making daily rounds, administering punishment, and so forth."

"Hmm. Well, I don't have any openings for prison guards, but a career in security could lead somewhere. Nothing like that today, of course. I was thinking about something a little less flashy. Can you wash dishes? Sweep floors? Clean toilets? Anything like that?"

Torval thought about that for a moment. While he'd never actually performed such menial tasks, there being no reason to do so in Hell, he certainly knew plenty of souls forced to undertake such labor as punishment. That made him at the very least familiar with the jobs in question. "Yes, I believe I could," he answered.

"You don't sound enthusiastic," said Simon. "Well, of course you wouldn't be. Are you serious about this, Mr. Sampson? Do you really want a job, or is this just an excuse of some kind?"

"I do desire employment," replied Torval, catching the urgency in the question at hand. "I am tired of sleeping on the street. I want to have a place to sleep, and can only have one if I can earn money for rent. That is my purpose in coming here."

"Yes, well, you certainly speak well. You're obviously better educated than most of the lowlifes that come through here. No offense intended." He glanced away, as if momentarily embarrassed by his own words. "Anyway, here, fill out this form in the hall outside while I talk to Christine for a moment. If you don't know the answer to any of the questions, just leave them blank. When you're done, knock on the door."

"Very well," replied Torval, taking the clipboard and pen. He turned to leave and saw Christine standing there. As she moved to get out of his way, he realized she'd overheard the entire conversation. That meant she must've caught the part about being a prison guard. Had Joe ever told her he drove a truck? If so, he may well have blown his cover.

She didn't seem suspicious, though. Instead, she stepped into the room without comment as the door shut behind her, leaving Torval alone in the hallway.

Shrugging, he sat down in the nearest chair and looked at the form. The first line was easy—it asked for his name. "Joe Sampson," Torval wrote. Unfortunately, most of the items on the rest of the page meant nothing to him. Address? Phone? Previous employment? He left all of those things blank. He did notice the line for "Social Security Number," as Christine warned earlier, but he left that space empty as well. In fact, by the time he'd finished reading the page, the only thing besides his name that had any writing at all was gender, which he dutifully entered as "Male."

As he sat there, trying to decide if he should write anything in the space marked "Personal References," Torval realized he could hear Christine's voice through the door. The conversation within seemed quite animated. Without even thinking about it, he started listening in.

"Look, Chris, I appreciate what you're trying to do," Mr. Spencer told her forcefully. "You know if it was up to me I'd give a job to everybody in that room out there, but there just aren't—"

"Come on, Simon, this is important," she interrupted. "Joe's been on the streets for years. He's finally willing to come in from the cold—you can't turn him back out there now!"

Simon sighed, loudly enough that Joe's ears could hear the noise all the way out in the hall. "Chris, do you know how many times in the last year I've knuckled under to your charms and given a job to some hopeless bum?"

"No, I haven't been keeping track," she replied casually, waving a hand next to her face, as if shooing away a bothersome insect.

"Well, I have. Ten, or eleven if you count Mr. Sampson out there. And do you know what all of them have done so far? Yes, that's right, they stay on the job long enough to get one paycheck, if they're lucky, and they go out and blow it all on booze. Then they never show up again, and I look like a complete idiot."

"I'm sorry, Simon," Christine replied. "This one's different. Joe's really changed. If you could've seen him yesterday, and again today—and he's sober—"

"Save it," interrupted Simon. "You said that about all the others, too. Why should I believe this one?"

Christine hesitated, and Torval worriedly could feel his opportunity for employment fading fast. He stood and knocked on the door, waiting patiently until Christine opened it.

"Here, Mr. Spencer, I have filled out the form as you requested," he explained, holding out the clipboard. "I am sorry I do not have more information."

Simon took one look at the mostly empty page and shook his head. "See what I mean, Chris? No social, no phone, no address, no history . . . nothing. How am I supposed to give anyone a job with no background information? Besides, he doesn't really care. Not really."

"I assure you, I do wish to have a job," offered Torval. "As I said before, I want to get off the street, so I can sleep somewhere comfortable, instead of in the cold."

"Like I said, he—" began Simon, but then he stopped, putting his fingers on his chin and rubbing it in obvious curiosity. "Wait a minute, Mr. Sampson, you're saying you don't care about getting paid? You just want a place to stay?"

"Yes," Joe replied. "That is what I want most of all."

"See?" Christine interjected proudly. "I told you, Simon. He doesn't want to get drunk again, do you, Joe?"

"Believe me, that is farthest from my mind," Torval answered honestly. His body said otherwise, but he felt confident he could keep such impulses under control.

Simon nodded. "Well, then, if that's the case, I may have something you could try. Could be right up your alley, too, with your security background. You know the Roxton Auto Parts warehouse down about five blocks from here?"

"No," stated Torval truthfully.

"I do," Christine replied. "We drove right past that street on the way here. Why do you ask, Simon?"

"Well," he went on, "they need a night janitor, but it doesn't pay much, and the catch is, they want whoever it is to live on the premises. There's a room downstairs—Mr. Roxton called it a 'flop,' if you can believe that. The old guy's still living in the Twenties, it seems like sometimes."

Torval started to agree at once, but Christine interrupted him. "Okay, what's the catch?" she demanded.

"Well, first off, it's for no pay—just a place to stay and some meals provided," said Simon, "although if you're a good worker, you can earn bonuses, or so Mr. Roxton tells me. Also, since they've been ripped off by the last four people working the job, you have to agree to be locked up in the basement all night. No going in or out. The shift runs from eight P.M. to six A.M. weekdays, and since you can't leave, you can understand why I'd understand if you don't—"

"I will take it," Torval interjected eagerly. "Please. That is exactly what I want. Food, a place to stay, and a way to earn money besides. That is perfect."

"Oh, come on, Simon, surely you have something better than this!" Christine argued. "You know as well as I do that's a terrible job!"

"Yes, I do," he agreed. "I haven't been able to give it away. Joe here seems to like it, though, and there's no way he'll be able to sneak booze into that place. Roxton is fanatical about security these days. You sure you want it, Mr. Sampson?"

"Yes. Definitely. What must I do now?"

"Just head over there," said Simon with a smile, looking relieved that he'd found some measure of success. "You can probably walk if you want. That'll give me time to call Mr. Roxton and let him know he's got a suc—er, a potential employee. Heh heh." He chuckled to himself for a moment, while Christine flashed him a scowl. "Sorry, Chris, you know I hardly ever get to laugh around this depressing place."

"Joe," she responded, turning away from the bureaucrat and his computer, "are you sure about this? I mean, as jobs go, this is literally scraping the bottom of the barrel."

"All I want is a place to sleep," Torval repeated. "Shelly said that getting an apartment takes a down payment of some sort. Is that not so?"

"Yes, it's true," said Christine with a sigh. "If you can find a place at all around this town. I have to admit, this does get you off the street, if that's what you really want. You should keep your eyes open for something better, though."

"Yes, I shall," said Torval eagerly. "Now, let us go. I am anxious to get started!"

# Chapter 12

Mr. Lincoln Roxton turned out to be an old man—a very old man, in fact. His leathery skin clung to his bones in age-speckled wrinkles, and his head, craggy as the moon's face, showed only a few tufts of spiky gray hairs. Yet despite his obviously advanced years, Mr. Roxton stood up straight and grinned at Torval with a gleam in his eye as he shook hands with the vacationing demon.

"So, you're my new night janitor!" said Lincoln as he shook vigorously. The touch of his hand proved beyond a doubt that the man was completely human. "Found another one to try it, did they? Well, I hope you're up for a challenge, my friend. I'm going to put you to work!"

"Good," said Torval plainly, withdrawing his hand and flexing his fingers. Although he had no way to judge, he felt certain Mr. Roxton was well past his prime, yet he possessed a surprisingly firm grip. "I need work. I need a place to live for the next—" He paused and glanced over at Christine, who watched the exchange with a judgmental eye. "For the foreseeable future," he added hastily.

"Well, good for you, my boy. Glad to see somebody still has a work ethic out there. Nobody these days is willing to work for just some food and a place to live. Why are you so interested?"

"Because it is cold," said Torval, succinctly explaining the situation in a few quick words.

Lincoln massaged his wrinkly chin and smiled. "Yes, it is at that, isn't it? And you have nowhere else to go?"

At that, Christine broke in. "I guess Simon didn't explain on the phone," she responded. "Mr. Sampson here has been homeless for some time. As you can see by his appearance, he's trying to turn his life around."

"Even better, even better," said Lincoln, his grin widening. "Well, come in, then, and I'll show you around the place."

The old man walked with an easy grace, belying his many years. The warehouse was just that—a huge open building, lined with pallet racks and containers of all shapes and sizes. All of them seemed to contain automotive parts of one type or another, from small cogs all the way up to axles, wheels, and even frames. Several other employees, dressed in light blue collared shirts with sewn-on nametags, scuttled about on various errands, most around the loading dock about a dozen yards away. Mr. Roxton led the trio toward that area first, describing some of the containers as he went. Since Torval had no idea what a carburetor was or what one could use a constant velocity joint for, most of that information went by the wayside.

Finally they reached the dock, where another man approached. He was tall, with black hair, sweat-coated skin and bulging muscles. "Hey, boss," he said jovially. "What's up?"

"Pete, I want to introduce you to Joe Sampson," Lincoln said, sweeping his hand to indicate Torval. "He's taking on the night janitor job, starting tonight. Joe, this is Pete Roxton, my grandson. He pretty much runs the place, except when I'm here interfering."

"Ain't that the truth!" Pete laughed. "Anyway, nice to meet you. Sorry, I'd shake your hand, but I'm pretty dirty. Lots of orders going out." He turned to Christine, studying her with undisguised interest. "And who's this? You getting a new secretary, Grandpa? If so, great choice!"

"Oh, yes, you'd like that, wouldn't you?" said Lincoln with a chuckle. "No, no, this is Christine Anderson." At that, Torval suddenly realized that this was the first time he'd actually heard her last name. For some reason that seemed significant, but he didn't know why. Meanwhile, the elderly Mr. Roxton continued on. "She's the social worker who's helping Mr. Sampson here get back on his feet."

"Oh, that's great!" Pete went on. "My grandmother was a social worker, you know. That's how she and Gramps met."

"Really?" asked Christine, glancing over at the old man. "When was that?"

"After the war. You know, the Big One. Ahh, you young people don't know what I mean when I say that! How quickly they forget. I'm talking about World War II, of course. I didn't have a job when I came back, and she helped me find one. We—"

"Now, now, c'mon, seriously, you'd go on all day if nobody stopped you," interjected Pete quickly. "You can bore 'em with stories later. I'm sure you want to show them the rest of the building, and besides, I've got to get these shipments on the truck."

"Yes, yes." Lincoln nodded. "Yep, that's why I've got my grandson here managing the place. He keeps things moving. Just so you know, Pete, he's starting at eight tonight, so be here to show him the job, all right?"

"Sure thing, Gramps. See ya!"

He gave a quick wave and flashed a grin at Christine, which she returned. Torval suddenly felt a distinct stirring in his chest, and his mouth tightened into a frown. All at once he no longer liked Pete Roxton very much. Why not? He seemed nice enough, and looked like a good, hard worker. Why would a simple exchange of smiles with Christine alter that perception?

He thought about it for a moment, as Lincoln led them about the warehouse, and very quickly figured it out—he actually felt jealous! In the male form he inhabited, he had an attraction to Christine, and that made Pete a rival for her potential affections!

Well, best to squelch that feeling right now, Torval told himself. He really didn't care what Christine thought or did, anyway. Or at least he shouldn't. After a short while, though, he realized the feeling would be harder to get rid of than simply willing it away. Whenever he thought of Pete now, he found himself envying the man's superior physique. Given a choice, he felt certain Christine would prefer a strong, capable male over someone as weak and frail as himself.

Again, he shrugged that off. Let her take up with him if she wanted, he told himself. What does it matter?

Unfortunately, it did seem to matter, no matter how much he didn't want it to.

* * *

By the time Mr. Roxton finished showing off the entire warehouse, Torval felt overwhelmed. The sheer quantity and complexity of vehicle pieces, parts and components left the demon baffled. Their purpose eluded Torval entirely, but Lincoln Roxton seemed immensely proud of each and every overstuffed shelf, halting on numerous occasions to run a hand across some dusty object that meant nothing whatsoever to his new employee. The stories that accompanied these pauses were equally mind-numbing.

Through it all, Torval forced himself to remember that Mr. Roxton was now his boss. He served the same purpose as Foreman Landri back in Hell—he gave the orders, and his underling followed them. If Lincoln felt the need to describe these automotive parts and their history to his subordinate, then by Lucifer, Torval was going to listen, even if he didn't understand why.

Back home, he never really had to understand the reason for anything he did. That was part of what made his job bearable. He had only to follow the same procedure here on Earth, and all would be well.

So why did he find it so difficult? As his new employer droned on and on about the advantages of stainless steel engine parts and the wide variety of radiator hoses available for trucks, Torval tried very hard to focus on this issue. Was it his weak human body, or had he already started questioning his motivation before even coming to this alien place? The lines were already beginning to blur.

"Anyways," Mr. Roxton concluded at last, reaching the back end of the warehouse, "I'm probably boring you to death, aren't I? Let me take you downstairs and show you your flop. I don't suppose you have a lot of things to move in, now do you? Hmm?"

Torval shook his head. "No, sir, I do not." He glanced down at his brand-new clothes, which until now he'd almost forgotten about. They were certainly comfortable, if nothing else. "What you see is all that I possess."

Lincoln nodded. "Figures. Ah, well, you look a lot better than the last few who've come through here. Follow me."

Drawing a key ring from his pocket, the old man popped open a heavy lock and opened a metal-bound door that looked out of place on the scarred and pitted back wall. A single weak light bulb, dangling on a long wire, illuminated the compartment beyond. A dark staircase receded into the ground, and Mr. Roxton advanced downward at a quick pace, heedless to the creaking and popping of the ancient steps. Torval followed at what he hoped was a safe distance.

A dank and poorly lit basement greeted him below. Once a single open chamber, the area was now divided by crude wooden walls into a series of storage cubicles. One compartment held row after row of file cabinets, while others were stacked to the top with boxes containing small automotive parts. Another cubicle, off to the side, partially concealed a softly thrumming heater the size of a large refrigerator. Lincoln bypassed all these, heading for the back, where a crude masonry wall blocked access to the rest of the basement.

There were two doors attached to this wall. One, solidly closed and barred, bore a sign with the warning "KEEP OUT" in large red letters. The other stood wide open. The space beyond opened into a communal bathroom, with a pair of toilets, a single urinal, a curtained off shower area, and a wide sink. The faucet dripped steadily, making a kind of plinking noise audible even over the heater's constant hum. The room reeked of urine and other bodily waste.

Mr. Roxton held out a hand. "This is your first assignment," he said with a wide, toothless grin. "Get it clean, then you can get some sleep. I assume you've done janitorial work before?"

"No," admitted Torval at once. "However, I have supervised many who have." This much was true—there were plenty of souls being tortured in Hell in just this sort of way.

"Were they good at it?"

"Yes." Torval nodded, remembering some of what those unfortunates had to go through. "I would say they are experts."

"Good, good." Lincoln nodded. "I'm not gonna lie to you—this isn't gonna be easy. I expect you to make a good effort. Me and my boys are no good at cleaning up after ourselves, I'm afraid. Never have been, never will be. No shame in admitting it."

"No, sir." Torval already found himself slipping back into his familiar subservient role. There was something very comforting about that. For perhaps the first time since coming to Earth, he didn't feel all that out of place.

"Anyways," went on Lincoln, "once you've put in the ol' college try, you can come back here. Follow me."

He took a few steps to the right and pointed into one of the last cubicles in the semi-finished basement. Unlike the others, which contained either machinery or neatly stacked supplies, this seemed filled with trash. Several open boxes lay scattered about amidst crumpled food wrappers. To one side, a square garbage can, studded with dents and rust spots, overflowed with refuse. A cheap hammock made of nylon netting lay stretched across the open space, attached from one corner to the opposite side by bungee cords.

"Here you go," said Mr. Roxton. "Home sweet home. The last occupant wasn't terribly nice to the place, I'm afraid. Feel free to straighten it up if you like. The hammock should be comfy, and it's quite warm down here, close to the heater and all."

Torval reached out a hand and tested the improvised bed, causing it to swing back and forth in the still air. He'd never seen such a thing before, but then, it could hardly be less comfortable than a soggy piece of cardboard on half-frozen asphalt.

After a moment he realized his employer was waiting for him to say something. "This will do," he mumbled, unsure of himself. Then he remembered that odd phrase that seemed to mean something to these people. "Thank you," he added hastily.

Lincoln's bushy white eyebrows went up. "Really? You aren't going to bitch about it?"

"No, sir," Torval replied. "You promised me a warm place to sleep in exchange for work. I am out of the cold, as we agreed. You have fulfilled your side of the bargain."

"That I have, my boy. That I have." Mr. Roxton nodded appreciatively. "I think you're going to work out just fine here, Joe. Now, a couple of other things I should mention before I cut you loose till later. First off, like the job description said, you'll be locked in here for the night. No coming and going, and no friends over when you're on shift. Got that?"

"Yes, sir." The response was all but automatic.

"The deal also involved food," went on Lincoln. "We'll start you off with a box dinner when you get here tonight, and depending on how well you did cleaning up, you'll get breakfast in the morning. Other than that, if you want anything to eat or drink, you better bring your own. No booze, though! There's a fridge over in that corner, but it's empty, so unless you like drinking tap water, you better bring some of the bottled stuff."

"Very well," agreed Torval.

"I expect you to stay out of the other junk you see down here," went on Lincoln steadily. "You have no reason to get into these boxes, or mess with the heater. You can clean up if you want—I'll make you do it eventually as part of your job, but for today just focus on the bathroom. Oh, and one other thing—this door here." He slapped his hand on the "Keep Out" sign. "It's barred for a reason. Don't go in. Ever. Got that?"

"Yes, sir."

"Good." Mr. Roxton checked his wristwatch in a quick motion. "All right, then, it's almost noon. The late shift will be leaving at eight o'clock tonight. Be here before that so Pete can lock you in. If you're late, he'll probably take your box dinner home and eat it himself, so consider that your motivation to be on time. Got it?"

"I will not be late, I assure you," said Torval, a bit of disappointment creeping into his voice. He'd hoped to be allowed to stay here all day, in the pleasing warmth. Now he would have to wander the windswept streets for many more hours. At least the cold isn't nearly as bitter with the sun out, he consoled himself.

"Excellent. Now out with you—I've got things to do 'round this place. Go on, go! And be back by eight!"

His demonic employee obeyed immediately, hustling to the stairs and climbing them without delay. Mr. Roxton was indeed the earthly version of Foreman Landri now, at least as far as Torval's automatic reflexes were concerned.

The demon scurried out of the warehouse, heading back toward the entrance he'd first come through. The workers he passed didn't give him a second glance as he emerged into the surprisingly warm sunlight. Torval stopped at the doorway, glancing about, wondering where Christine had gone.

"What's up?" asked a voice from nearby. Pete Roxton stood there, pausing in his efforts to load large boxes onto a truck. "Everything OK?"

Torval's voice betrayed his distress. "I am looking for Christine," he complained. "I thought she would be here."

"Oh, right, she left," explained Pete with a shrug. "Sorry, man, she said she had to get to work. You took too long, I guess. Sorry 'bout that. I shoulda warned you, Grandpa's pretty proud of this place, so he tends to talk your ear off. I swear he loves every nut and bolt in sight. 'Course, he did build it all up from nuttin', y'know."

Torval nodded and sucked in a deep breath. That feeling of tightness in his chest returned without warning. Anxiety, again. Why should he feel that way? Because Christine left without a word to him?

He closed his eyes and struggled to control his emotions. How could humans stand them, anyway? I'm not human, he insisted to himself. There's no reason to let myself be controlled by this body's feelings.

The uncomfortable sensation in his chest subsided. Vaguely, he became aware that Pete hadn't stopped speaking.

"... seen peeps like you 'round before, y'know," the muscular man continued, voice punctuated by occasional grunts as he hefted another heavy box into place on the short-bed truck. "Gramps has been tryin' to fill that job for ages. He's got a soft spot for bums, 'cause he knows what it's like to be down on his luck, like you."

Torval didn't respond, but continued to stare out into the noisy, vehicle-choked streets. He knew he had to go back out there, and find some way to occupy his time. Gaining a job didn't solve all of his problems, apparently.

"So anyways, I seen her here before, with some wino she's tryin' to clean up, but never had a chance to talk to her," Pete rambled on. "Such a cutie, that one. I feel sorry for her, I really do. I think she really cares, y'know? I hope you don't disappoint her, like the others."

Torval glanced back over his shoulder. "I assure you," he said truthfully, "I have no intention of that."

"Good," replied Pete, smiling good-naturedly even as his words were laced with threat. "See to it you don't."

* * *

Torval shuffled along, avoiding the puddles that persisted here and there on the broken sidewalks. He knew, from the brief instructions provided by Pete Roxton as he departed the warehouse, that the soup kitchen he frequented lay somewhere in this general direction. All he had to do was walk nine blocks, whatever that meant.

The world wasn't nearly as cold as he remembered. The jacket Christine so kindly provided kept the occasional blast of arctic wind at bay. The lack of snow allowed him to stay dry, and the sun, now high overhead, provided a small measure of warmth.

As he walked, Torval let his eyes wander about. The people, who seemed endless in number, ignored him completely, apparently intent on their own lives. Some talked amongst themselves as they walked, but no one so much as waved in his direction. The previous day, when

Joe Sampson looked and smelled like a bum, he seemed universally reviled, but now he'd been accepted as one of the masses.

He plodded on, following the crowd. So many people! Torval had never had to deal with so many at once. At streetlights, he felt them all about him, though nobody ever actually physically contacted his person. When he walked, he had to avoid stepping on the feet in front of him and occasionally dodge a pedestrian coming in the other direction. He had no idea so many humans could be together in one place like this.

He remembered a sinner in Hell whose punishment was to watch as dozens of people ate the food that should've been his. Another, a woman, relived an embarrassing school dance called the "prom" over and over. In still another, a man waited endlessly at an airport, unable to board his plane due to overcrowding. In each of these cases, there were numerous illusory humans about, but they were just figments and easily ignored. Torval couldn't dismiss the herds of people all around him now. He could only endure their presence, and try to control the breathing that seemed increasingly difficult with each step.

In due course, he found respite on the side of a parking lot, where the few open spaces adjoined a low fence. He stepped out of the flow of human traffic and stood there, panting.

The city was endless. He knew that now. The high walls that surrounded him went on and on forever. There must be tens of thousands of people living in this place. He tried to wrap his mind around the enormity of it, and failed miserably.

At least he understood the term "block" now. Each time he came to one of the red, yellow, and green lights that signaled a safe time to cross, that marked the end of a block and the beginning of the next. Signs also identified the streets, helpfully counting the distance traveled, which explained why Pete said to go to Forty-Ninth Street. According to the last placard passed, Torval had reached Forty-Third Street, and the numbers kept climbing. At least he knew he was on the right path.

As his normal breathing resumed, he glanced back at the last block. The sign clearly read "43rd St." Something about that tickled Torval's memory. Why should that number be important?

Shaking his head, he started to put it out of his mind, but something stopped him. He'd seen that number written somewhere—on a piece of paper, in fact.

Fumbling through his pockets, he found a folded note written by a woman's hand. Ah, yes, the tattooed female he'd met in the employment offices, he recalled immediately. Her name, "Shelly Mendez," written in a lazy scrawl, preceded her now recognizable address. Underneath that, the final words: "Come see me sometime, sexy!"

So, Shelly lived here, on this very road! She seemed quite willing to demonstrate the human mating ritual back when they first met. Perhaps she'll be just as accommodating now, thought Torval, already contemplating what the experience might be like.

Vaguely, he recalled the short-lived images from Joe's mind when he first saw Christine. Memories of physical encounters that brought flashes of emotions: anxiety, excitement, frustration, stimulation, rapture . . . the last one ever so brief, yet the most desirable of all. Still, those recollections seemed foreign to Torval now—fleeting and nebulous, like the dream he experienced while sleeping in the alley his first night in human guise. Something he couldn't quite grasp, yet wanted very much.

He frowned. Why should the possibility of having sexual relations be of such interest to him? He was a demon—as he constantly had to remind himself—not a person! His fragile human form wanted the experience, not Torval himself.

Still, why had he come to the Middle World at all? To understand what it was to be human, presumably. At least, that's what he guessed, from the nature of his vacation. He knew humans needed to procreate, a distinct difference from demonkind, who spawned naturally from oozing pits deep within Hell. For a human to reproduce, a man and a woman had to copulate. This much Torval knew, along with the fact that children were later born of such a joining, but the rest of it remained a mystery.

Back in Hell he'd seen numerous prisoners punished for sex-related crimes. From the kind of tortures they had to endure, he felt reasonably sure he understood what the act of sex supposedly involved. At least, without the punishment part. Yet the fact that people were incarcerated for having sex bothered Torval. There was a right way and a wrong way to go about it, clearly, and he simply didn't know the rules.

Furthermore, Christine had warned him about Shelly. That worried Torval most of all. Christine said Shelly was a prostitute, and would attempt to trick him so she could steal his money. A fool's errand, obviously, as Torval had none to steal. So in the end he had little to concern himself with, didn't he?

Still he hesitated, however. Christine's warning kept replaying in his mind. She wanted to help him, as she had since the demon first walked into the soup kitchen. She hadn't stopped trying to help him, either by giving him food, or money, or clothes, or a job, or...

Why? Why would she help him? Torval struggled to understand. Why would one person help another? There was no reward to be had, other than the vague promise of possible good fortune in the afterlife. Christine spent her hard-earned money buying Joe Sampson clean clothing, a shave and haircut, a taxi ride, and expected nothing back.

She was good. That's all there was to it. Torval didn't know why, but the very prospect of good fascinated him. Christine, too, fascinated him in a way he couldn't comprehend.

She was pleasing to the eye, yes, but there was much more to it than that. The way she spoke to him, never condescending, truly desiring to help get a hopeless bum back on his feet—those were the things that intrigued Torval the most.

What would it be like, then, to copulate with Christine? The thought sprang unbidden to his mind, and he caught himself flushing momentarily with embarrassment. Why should he have such thoughts? His frail body again, obviously. And yet, why not? Torval knew enough to understand that sex was something intimate shared between two humans, and from Shelly's enthusiasm, the female clearly enjoyed the process. Perhaps sex would be a proper way to repay Christine for her earlier aid.

Still, he didn't know enough about human mating to truly understand the procedure. Christine seemed dismayed to hear how quickly Shelly propositioned him earlier. The ritual must involve more than just a simple question, at least most of the time. Furthermore, although Torval had witnessed an illusory facsimile intercourse, at least in a limited fashion, he hadn't actually experienced it himself.

Well, the demon decided at last, perhaps there's something I can do about that. With newfound determination, he set off to locate Shelly Mendez.

# Chapter 13

Somewhat anxiously, Torval waited at the door, shuffling and twitching with a nervousness he felt but didn't quite understand. Had he not spoken casually with Shelly just a short time ago? Their conversation had been perfectly forthright. She had made him an offer, and he'd come here to accept it. So why should he be concerned?

Torval understood the need for mating, of course. Bringing new children into the world allowed the human species to continue to exist. Yet, unlike animals, which had simple mating rituals that rarely changed between individuals, humans chose to cloak the act of copulation in a complex web of social and physical interaction.

That, Torval guessed, explained his nervousness. He'd be expected to understand how the whole process worked, seeing as how he'd clearly been a part of such things before, and yet, being a demon, he had little in the way of actual experience. There were plenty of sex-related criminals undergoing punishment in Hell—in fact, the number was second only to monetary offenses—but that didn't exactly explain how sex actually took place. Thinking back on some of the punishments he remembered, Torval couldn't actually recall any of them that actually involved the direct act of intercourse.

Still, Shelly seemed eager enough. Perhaps she'd explain it to him if he asked. She recognized right away, during their earlier encounter, that he probably hadn't experienced copulation for some time. Yes, that's the answer, thought Torval. I'll simply explain that I am out of practice, and she'll tell me what to do.

After knocking again, and waiting a few more moments, he finally heard footsteps approaching behind the door.

A woman's voice, immediately recognizable, called out through the thin wood frame. "Yeah, what izzit?" Shelly demanded. "Go 'way, I'm tryin' to get a nap in here. Whatever yer sellin', I ain't buyin'!"

Torval hesitated for a moment, trying to figure out what to say. Finally he simply announced himself. "It is I, Joe Sampson," he called out. "We spoke at the employment office."

"Employment office!" She suddenly sounded very excited. "One sec, lemme unlock this thing!"

After a few moments of fumbling around with the chain, she managed to get the door open. She still wore the same low-cut blouse and blue jeans, but was barefoot this time. While hurriedly trying to puff up her black hair around her shapely art-covered shoulders, she stepped into the doorway and looked at him with an expectant expression. "Yeah, whatcha got?" she demanded eagerly. "Someone finally find a job for me?"

"I do not have a job as such," Torval replied, holding out the handwritten note she'd provided him a couple hours before. "I am here to respond to your earlier offer."

"What's that?" She looked at the folded paper in confusion, and then her eyes brightened as she remembered. "Oh! It's you! The dude who liked my tatts! Sorry, man, didn't rec'nize ya!" A knowing grin began to spread across her pleasantly attractive face, making her look quite comely. "Ya had me all 'cited there, thinkin' I had a job or sumpin', but you'll do nicely! Guess ya need some lovin', eh? Well don't just stand there, get yer tight li'l ass in here!"

She all but dragged him through the door, yanking his arm hard until Torval stumbled across the threshold. With a quick snap of her other wrist, Shelly caused the door to bang shut, then continued the motion to seize the back of his neck. Before Torval knew what was going on, she'd locked her lips on his, fiercely sucking and probing with her tongue, all the while holding their faces firmly together with a tight, clawlike grip.

Torval's first impulse was to jerk himself away from this sudden, unexpected physical contact, but he forced himself not to move. The rational side of him explained, in that brief moment of extended time, that he needed this very thing—for Shelly to take the lead, and show him what to do. Besides, the human part of him put in, there was something quite pleasurable about it, despite the unfamiliar feeling of fluids exchanging inside someone else's mouth.

In fact, he reminded himself, perhaps he should reciprocate. Not really sure if he was doing the right thing, he pulled her body close, echoing her tight grip as best he could. Meanwhile, he explored with his tongue, tasting the warm saltiness of her saliva, twisting and parrying wildly, as if engaged in some kind of complex dance.

In due course she pulled her face away from his, grinning and licking her lips with a wet smacking sound. In a deep, sultry voice, she rumbled, "Man, yer a feisty one! Lotsa guys don't like that shit, but not you! I bet yer gonna love what I got fer ya next. Let's stop wastin' time and get down ta business!"

She pulled him further into the building, down a dark hall to a poorly lit back room. Torval didn't bother to glance around at the rest of the cramped little apartment, at the unwashed clothes scattered all about, or the dishes piled up on the sink in the kitchen. He didn't care about the grime or even the rank smell pervading the unkempt place. He kept his attention entirely focused on the beautiful tattooed woman in front of him, who even as she tugged him along, quickly stripped off her clothing.

Like her arms and shoulders, the rest of Shelly Mendez was covered in intricate art, all the way from head to toe and everything in between. Torval stared appreciatively at the way it all wrapped and flowed about her, following her graceful curves, using the natural parts of her body like shaped canvas. Her ribs were the wings of birds, her navel a jewel set within an enormous ring. One breast seemed held by a ghostly hand; the other trapped within a spider's web. The rest of her flesh, just as beautifully decorated, was nothing short of overwhelming.

"Like whatcha see?" asked Shelly in that disconcertingly low, throaty voice as she removed the last of her underwear. She glanced down at the crease forming rapidly in his trousers, and grinned. "Yeah, I can see ya do."

Torval felt strangely hot, and thought perhaps it best to remove some of his own sweltering clothing. The jacket and sweater were first to join a pile near his feet. Shelly helped with the belt, which was fine with him because he couldn't quite seem to recall how the buckle worked. For some reason Torval's normally acute ability to think rationally no longer functioned properly.

He was, of course, by now fully erect, so getting out of his own undergarments proved challenging, but Shelly didn't seem to mind. As her slim hands helped with the process, she remarked, "My, yer salutin' pretty good for such a skinny guy! Just goes ta show ya, can't judge a book by a cover, don't it? Now here, put on yer raincoat, then we can get to bangin'."

So saying, she presented him with a flimsy-looking white ring with some sort of springy material in the middle. With his mind clouded by the sight and smell of her, Torval looked at the condom dumbly. She grinned, obviously pleased with the effect she was having on him. "Here, lemme do it, since yer all dazzled by the sighta me an' all."

She slipped the prophylactic over him, a not altogether unpleasant experience, and then stepped over to the bed. Holding up her index finger, she waggled it in his direction. "Now come on, Joey baby," she intoned huskily, "time to show me whatcha got!"

This was what Torval dreaded, for he didn't exactly know what he should to do next. Shelly, meanwhile, leaned back on the bed, stretched out, and spread her legs invitingly, so he stepped forward with a boldness he didn't really feel, determined to see this through. With a clumsy motion he climbed onto the bed, planted his knees carefully near hers, and leaned forward, hesitating.

"'Nuff foreplay!" gasped Shelly between desperate breaths. "Take me now, 'fore I essplode!"

Reaching up, she seized his shoulders and drew his face to hers, again kissing and sucking on him with wild abandon. Surprised by this, Torval lurched forward, and her hands, sweeping swiftly down below his waist, helped him find his target. Suddenly he was inside her, and she began to thrust and bounce upon the bed, all the while gasping and biting at him with something akin to desperation.

At that point the last remnants of coherent thought left him. His body, it seemed, knew what to do from that point on, so he allowed it to do so, drifting aimlessly into a sea of pain and pleasure. His muscles, unaccustomed to this sort of treatment, quickly began to cramp and tighten, but the feel of her flesh on his, and the building sensation of impending ecstasy, kept him locked in place. He became, for all intents and purposes, a slave to his human body. He couldn't have controlled it if he tried.

For how long this encounter lasted, Torval didn't really know. He lost all track of time. The heat of her skin, the screeching of rusty bedsprings, and the mutual gasps and moans echoing through the room were just a few of the things he perceived, noticing them as if detached from reality. Finally, after a momentary eternity, he experienced an instant of absolute bliss, and then he collapsed onto her heaving form, coughing and wheezing desperately for breath.

He became vaguely aware of Shelly disentangling herself from his wasted shell and slinking swiftly away, but he didn't care. For perhaps thirty seconds he wondered if he would die. Every piece of his frail body (save one) screamed in protest at what he, and she, had just put it through. That single happy part congratulated him on a job well done.

So that was sex! Torval snapped back to reality then, shaking his head and wiping away the perspiration from his face with a bed sheet. So much effort and trouble for just a few seconds of ecstasy! And yet that's exactly what drove so many sinners into semi-eternal torture in Hell. An endless nightmare of punishment hardly seemed a fair tradeoff for a few moments of hard-earned pleasure.

Even as he thought that, however, he found himself wishing to try again. He was inexperienced, and she obviously desperate; perhaps there was more to it, some way to make it last longer or be more enjoyable. Maybe he didn't do it correctly. Surely if he'd failed, Shelly would tell him, so that he could perform better next time.

He sat up, looking around for her, but she'd disappeared from sight. After a moment he heard the sound of water running in the nearby bathroom. She emerged a moment later, wearing only an oversized shirt, one arm resting lazily on the doorframe. What he could see of her body glistened with sweat, and she took a few heavy, satisfied breaths. "Not bad," she told him with a seductive smile. "Not bad 'tall, for a man so outta practice. I can tell you was gettin' tired, so I let ya off the hook this time."

Torval sat up wearily. His gasps continued, and he felt quite dizzy, so he knew better than to stand. "I apologize if I did not live up to your expectations," he told her honestly, gradually getting control over his breathing. "It has been, as you surmised, some time since my last copulation."

"Yer last what?" She waved a hand at him as she walked across the room, stopping when she got to the pile of clothes they'd both left near the entrance. "Joe, ya gotta stop usin' them big words on me. I don't know what yer sayin' half the time! Just say you ain't done it for years and that's good enough, y'know? You get some more practice and you'll be makin' me scream fer twice as long next time. I won't ask if I was good 'nuff fer ya, though, cuz I know I was better." She punctuated that comment with a short laugh, even as she started to pick through the clothing on the floor.

"I have no frame of reference with which to compare you," admitted Torval, "but I have no complaints. I do wonder, however, what the purpose of this garment is." He unrolled the condom, now filled with a sticky substance not at all like the urine he'd expelled from the same orifice that morning. From what he knew of mating, this gooey material must function in some way in the conception of a child. "I would think you would not wish to impede the progress of this liquid."

Shelly chuckled, momentarily pausing her exploration of his clothes, then continued to search around. "Ha, that's a good'n, like I'd really wanna spawn some rugrat from some one-night, or rather one-day, stand! 'Sides, who knows how many diseases ya got? Better t'be safe than sorry, I always say. Just throw that thing in the trash, and dontcha dare spill it on my sheets!"

Torval nodded and stood carefully, wobbling on trembling knees, and made his way to the bathroom, where Shelly had been a few moments before. After doing as she instructed, he wiped his face with a handy rag and looked at himself in the mirror. His white skin had turned a flushed shade of red from the exertion, and now that his blood wasn't pumping as fast, he felt a sudden chill that made him shiver. Nonetheless, there was an unsettling feeling of satisfaction, as if from a great accomplishment, but that sensation came not from within, but from a place below his waist.

He glanced again down at the trash can, where the messy remnants of his tryst glistened in the pale bathroom lighting. Shelly hadn't been interested in the procreation side of intercourse at all, had she? She'd only wanted the experience, not the result. Now Torval began to understand why people wound up in Hell because of sex. This wasn't what copulation was all about, at least not at its fundamental core. What he and Shelly just did could've been considered a sin, depending on whom you asked. They were having sex purely for the fun of it.

Yet, what was so wrong with that? If it was so pleasurable, and in such an intimate way, why should it be a sin? Especially if, as had just been demonstrated, it could be performed without any risk of unhealthy or undesirable consequences? In fact, if with practice it became even more enjoyable, why didn't humans perform this ritual whenever they could? Torval could tell already, from the fading sensations below his belt, that he would have to wait a while before trying again, and presumably Shelly would as well—but why not go again as soon as the waiting period ended?

Again, he had more questions than he had answers. Perhaps Prelz would be able to help him once more. With a sigh, Torval mentally added another stack of queries to his ever-growing list of things to present to the more experienced demon.

Feeling another shiver, Torval decided to retrieve his clothing, so he stepped out of the bathroom, only to find Shelly there, holding his pants and scowling. "What the hell's the matter witcha, anyways?" she demanded, throwing the garment at him angrily. "Hidin' yer wallet! Whatsa matta, dontcha trust me?"

"My wallet?" inquired Torval, somewhat surprised by the sudden and complete change in her demeanor. "What wallet?"

"Don't what wallet me!" she hissed, kicking at the rest of his clothes. As Torval gathered them up and started getting dressed, she crossed her arms and frowned. "Ya know well and good ya hid it 'fore ya came here! Damn ya anyways!"

"I do not understand," replied Torval, glad to be clothed once more, for the room was really quite chilly. "I do not own a wallet, but even if I did, why would it be of any importance?"

"Cause a girl's gotta eat, ya idiot!" she shouted. "God, yer the densest hunka rock I ever met! Ya see, I give ya some love, and ya give me some cash, got it? I thought we had an understandin'! An' then ya show up with nothin'!"

She began to pace back and forth, cursing, while Torval finished dressing. "I am sorry, Shelly," he said honestly, "but I do not recall any discussion of payment."

"It shoulda been obvious!" she complained, and now she didn't look angry any more, but on the verge of tears. "Dammit! I got no food left and there ain't no jobs! I was hopin' ta get some quick cash, that's all I needed, and ya got nothin'! Now I gotta hit the streets again! See, that's what I get for not checkin' first, but I thought—ah, forget it!"

Torval remained silent for a bit, watching the tears forming in her eyes, and felt a sudden and unfamiliar pang of remorse. Still, he told himself, he hadn't done anything wrong. No contract had ever been expressed or implied by anything he said to Shelly before their brief tryst, that much he knew. Yet Christine did warn him that Shelly might be a prostitute, so the fact that she expected money shouldn't come as any sort of surprise. In fact, now that he could think clearly again, he realized she'd been going through his pockets without his consent. If he did own a wallet, she could've lifted whatever cash he had on hand and taken it for her own—and that's obviously exactly what she'd intended to do.

So why did he feel sad for her? He looked around at the cracked plaster and worn furniture that surrounded him, noticing for the first time how pitiful this dwelling was. Yet this was her home, and she had to pay for its upkeep. If she had no job, she might go homeless, as Joe himself had done, as well as all those other transients back at the shelter. Shelly, apparently, would do whatever it took—even sell her body—to keep that from happening.

He thought about what Prelz had told him: If something warranted a punishment in Hell, it was probably evil. So how would he punish Shelly, if he had to judge her? She acted out of desperation, trying to avoid the fate of so many other homeless people in the city. Was there no other way to escape the way of the prostitute, or the thief? Did she take the easy way out? Or was this, itself, her only alternative? Would that warrant punishment, even if it was a sin?

Torval found himself glad he wasn't an Evaluator. He would hate to have to be the one to determine good or evil in this case.

He felt like he should help Shelly, despite what she'd done in the past, and tried to do to him just now. Yes, that's what he should do, if he wanted to be "good"—he should perform a selfless act, without expecting anything in return. This would be the perfect opportunity to start working on some of the debts he owed to others. But what could he do? He had no money, and as far as he could tell, that was the only thing that had any meaning to her at this moment.

"Shelly," Torval finally said, "I am truly sorry for your situation, but I cannot help you at this time. I will, however, attempt to do so in the future, as soon as I have the opportunity."

"Oh ya will, will ya?" she hissed, suddenly becoming angry once again. "Oh, great, just what I need, more goddamn empty promises! Well, thanks fer nothin'! Just go! Get the hell out and don't come back! You ain't gettin' no more freebies outta me! Go on! OUT!"

She all but shoved him through the apartment, and he didn't try to resist. Even as he shuffled across the floor, trying to avoid tripping over furniture and trash on his way to the exit, he tried to think of something to say, but no words came.

Finally Torval found himself pushed all the way outside, into the cool afternoon air, as the door slammed loudly behind him. Shelly's final words echoed in his ears: "And one more thing! You suck in bed! The worst I ever had! Total shit, you hear me? Total shit!"

He could only stand there helplessly, listening to the distant sobbing just barely audible through the thin wood, until the unpleasant sound finally faded away.

# Chapter 14

AS HE RESUMED HIS JOURNEY BACK to the shelter, where he hoped to find Prelz and unload a veritable shopping list of questions on the hapless ex-demon, Torval experienced a strange mixture of feelings. Obviously Shelly became distraught there at the last, but her words haunted him nonetheless. Of course he had little experience with the intercourse ritual, but was he truly as horrible as she insisted? He supposed so, and for some reason that shamed him. He felt the painful sting of failure, and although no authority figures were present to punish him, he nonetheless felt disappointed with himself.

In addition to that, he also felt the strange hollow emotion called pity. Pity for Shelly Mendez, and the life she had to lead. Whether she'd wind up in Hell for her actions wasn't for him to say, since he knew only this small fraction of her life. In the end, though, her choices brought her here, one way or another, so she'd surely be held responsible for them, as it should be. Yet, still, the pity remained, a strange emptiness in the depths of his stomach that simply didn't belong.

His body hadn't quite recovered from his recent, unusual exertions, but walking through the noisy streets of New York seemed to help work out the kinks in his muscles. The flow of people around him swelled with the arrival of the lunch hour, and on more than one occasion the crowds all but swept him along of their own accord. The crush of humanity at least brought his mind off the troubling experience with Shelly and kept him focused on the present.

A couple of blocks from his goal, he managed to slip into an alcove between two storefronts, where he stood for a moment, catching his breath. The cold that overwhelmed him on his first day on Earth no longer bothered him, judging by the way he perspired under his sweater and jacket, so he loosened the front buttons to let in some air. Far from feeling unpleasant, the soft breeze seemed quite soothing.

A recognizable voice caught his ear, punctuated by a pair of quick, sharp coughs. "Spare change?" the speaker said, shaking a rusted tin can held in a hand covered with torn glove remnants. The man wore pitiful rags, and his face was unshaven and dirty, but Torval recognized him at once—Hal Sommersby, the friend of Joe who'd nearly died the night before, until the demon brought him some soup. Hal stood slumped against the opposite side of the alcove, near a heavy, barred load-in door that bore a sign saying "No Entry."

Hal turned to Torval, shaking the tin cup. "Spare some change, sir?" he asked miserably, obviously making a great effort to look as pathetic as possible.

The demon momentarily hesitated. Hal had no idea who he was! Well, of course he didn't. After all, the body of Joe Sampson now wore clean clothes and had been washed and shaved. Hal saw only a stranger. Best to let it remain that way, thought Torval.

Before he could reply, though, Hal narrowed his eyes. "Wait a minute," he said suspiciously, coughing loudly as he stepped closer. "I know you, don't I? Oh, my God, it's you, Joe! What happened to you? How did you get like that?"

"Yes, it is I," replied Torval, sighing to himself. "I apologize for not explaining before, but you were ill last night, and I did not see you this morning. I have acquired a job."

"You…you what?" Hal shook his head in disbelief. "You? Joe Sampson? Got a job? You swore you'd never do that, Joe! You said you'd never go back. You didn't deserve it, you said. What happened?"

Torval sighed again. He'd been ordered to avoid this very situation—getting involved in his host body's old life. He ought to just move on and distance himself from any entanglements. He should just tell Hal to go away, but something wouldn't let him. He still had this recollection, left over from what he recalled of Joe's life, that Hal was his friend. Torval never had a friend before, and while he didn't really comprehend the meaning of that term, he knew friends were somehow desirable.

Ah, thought Torval, this is another opportunity to learn something about humans. I can discover what this curious thing called "friendship" is!

But how to do so without revealing his true nature? He'd used the story that he'd turned over a new leaf after nearly dying in the alley, so he fell back on that once more. "I was sick," he explained, "and I felt myself dying, but I survived. That was when I decided to change my ways."

Hal stared at him, raising both eyebrows simultaneously. "You had a near-death experience? Really?"

"To be truthful," embellished Torval, "I believe I actually did die. But then I found myself alive and recovering. When I reached the shelter, I knew what I had to do. I had to get out of the cold and snow, and to do that, I needed a job."

Hal shook his head, lowering the cup to his side. "That's amazing, Joe," he admitted. "I never thought you'd do it. Not you. You've turned your back on so many chances before."

"I suppose," suggested the demon, "that dying has finally changed me."

"For the better, it looks like. You look amazing, man! So this is what you're like all cleaned up, huh? Slick new clothes, and a fresh shave and everything! You must have some cash now. How about buyin' a buddy some lunch, and maybe a bottle or two?"

"I have no funds," said Torval regretfully, "as I have not yet earned any pay. Even if I did, I would not purchase alcohol. I will not consume that substance again."

Hal just stared at him, totally flabbergasted. After a moment he recovered and slapped his friend on the shoulder. "Sworn off the booze, too! And you're talking clear as a bell, like someone with an education or somethin'. This must be the real you, isn't it? I feel like I never even knew you, Joe. I didn't, did I?"

Torval was glad for that little leap of logic, as it let him effortlessly explain some of the incongruities Hal had already noticed. "No, you did not," he said smoothly. "This is the real me, Hal. What you saw in the streets and alleys was someone else. I hope we can still be friends."

"Don't worry, man, I still won't forget what you did for me. Friends it is. Wanna try to scavenge some pizza over by Linguini's? It's a nice enough day, so there should be some marks out front."

Torval knew pizza was some sort of food, and all at once his stomach growled, indicating hunger. The bagel from the morning's breakfast must be long since gone, and his efforts at Shelly's apartment left his body needing fuel. "Certainly," he agreed at once. "Lead the way."

* * *

As they walked, Hal shuffled along with a kind of limp, often stopping to let out a series of coughs. More than once, he spit out a thick yellowish glob onto the nearby curb, causing passersby to curse at him and shy away. The illness remained with him, obviously, but only its lingering remnants, fading as it had from Joe's body once Torval arrived within it.

In fact, thought the demon, might Hal himself now be possessed? What if another demon is on vacation even now in Hal's mortal shell? Highly unlikely, but still, Torval felt the need to know. He managed to arrange to brush against one of Hal's partially gloved hands while dodging pedestrians on the crowded streets. Their flesh touched for a moment, but nothing changed, so Hal clearly remained fully human.

After a few minutes of brisk walking, which involved crossing two streets by dodging cars and oil-coated puddles, the two arrived at Linguini's. The café-like restaurant had a patio front, with entrances on either end as well as a main double door. Guests came and went, some with briefcases or shopping bags in their hands, obviously enjoying the opportunity to grab a quick lunch while doing their business in this part of the city.

Torval hesitated, not sure what to do. He could surely enter, but he doubted very much that the dirty and malodorous Hal would be allowed passage. His friend didn't even try to go inside, however. Instead, he made a quick pass along the front of the building, carefully studying the patrons as they munched on triangle-shaped slivers of food, lost in their own conversations.

Hal stopped near the right-hand side of the patio, where a couple relaxed next to a circular table. The man wore a dark blue business suit and held a black, rectangular object in one hand, which he deftly manipulated using a series of buttons. Across from him sat a golden-haired woman in a plain gray coat studying a sheaf of black and white paper. Neither paid much attention to each other. A half-eaten disc of the same sort of yellow and red foodstuff sat on a tray before them, sliced into triangle patterns for reasons that eluded Torval.

Hal lingered near them and whispered to his companion, "These look ripe for the plucking, my friend. Better let me do it, 'cause you look too sharp to be beggin'."

Joe nodded, not exactly sure what was going on, and Hal stepped closer to the couple. "Pardon me," he asked, cradling his tin can in his hands like a priceless treasure, "do you think you kind folks could spare a slice for a guy who's down on his luck this fine afternoon?"

The businessman glanced up from his PDA and scowled, wrinkling up his nose as the smell of Hal pierced the more inviting scents wafting out from the restaurant. "Go away, before I call the cops!" he ordered gruffly. "And get a job!"

The woman nearby pushed her newspaper down and rolled her eyes. "Oh, come on, sweetie, just let him have some. It's not like we're gonna finish it anyways."

"Luann," replied the businessman with a sigh, "you can't just keep feeding these bums, or they never learn. They just keep leaching off everybody."

"Oh, so you're gonna change that by letting one poor guy starve? Jesus, Fred, have a goddamn heart!"

"Fine," Fred replied with an exasperated sigh. He held up the platter resignedly. "Knock yourself out."

"Bless you, sir," said Hal, eagerly snatching the remaining pizza without waiting for further approval. Stacking the four slices in an open hand, while still managing to hang onto the coin-filled cup, he turned and scurried off toward the nearest alley. Torval, a bit bemused by the exchange he'd just witnessed, followed a short distance behind.

As soon as they were out of sight of the patio, Hal set down his rusted tin can and began to cram some of the pizza into his mouth. Then he held out his hand to Torval, who took a slice for himself.

The pizza smelled wonderful, and Torval took a bite with some measure of anticipation. He wasn't disappointed, for the cheese and tomato flavor tasted just as amazing as its alluring odor promised. Chewing slowly, he closed his eyes and let the flavors flow through him. He'd thought the soups he'd already experienced were wonderful, but they didn't hold a candle to this savory delight.

For several minutes, Torval eagerly devoured the pizza, deliberately over-chewing and swishing the remnants around in his mouth to enjoy the taste as long as possible. After finishing the first slice, he took another from Hal, who himself proceeded to eat the final piece. The meal ended all too soon, leaving Torval's stomach satisfied, and yet he felt sad to be finished already. He wanted to eat more of this thing called pizza, as often and as frequently as possible.

He had no money yet, though, and as Hal had pointed out, he didn't much look like a beggar anymore. The only reason his friend got anywhere was that he looked pitiful and pathetic, so much so that the woman named Luann actually forced her companion to give some food to him. Torval had no doubt that if he tried to beg like Hal, he'd be laughed right off the patio.

"Damn," said Hal as he wiped his face with the back of a ratty old jacket sleeve, "I don't think I've ever seen anyone enjoy their lunch quite as much as you just did, buddy. I thought you were gonna come or somethin'."

Torval didn't quite understand that comment, but the meaning was clear. "As I said," he explained, continuing to enhance the deception of his recent personality change, "after getting so close to death, I wish to appreciate life."

Hal nodded. "Yeah, makes sense," he agreed. "Y'know, I almost died too. Maybe I should think about that myself. I don't know if I could go back to work like you're trying to do, though. Bills and taxes and responsibilities . . . no, I think I'm fine out here, thank you very much."

"I do not understand," admitted Torval. "Why do you choose to live this way? These things you mention, are they so bad that a life sleeping in alleys, begging for money and food, and depending on the kindness of strangers is preferable to the alternative?"

Once again, Hal just stared at his friend, a dumbfounded look on his grime-caked face. "What the hell has gotten into you, man?" he finally asked. "This just ain't like you, Joe! Two days ago you were drunk as a skunk in the gutter just like me, and perfectly happy to be there, and now it's like you've never even been around. Are you sure that's really you?"

"It is I," Torval replied hurriedly, worried that he'd said too much and blown his cover. "I am the same Joe Sampson you remember, but I have changed, Hal. I feel like I've awakened from a dream." Yes, that was a good analogy, thought Torval, recalling how the dream seemed to quickly slip away from him the night before. "I no longer want to be like I was. I want to sleep under a roof, in a warm room, and never go hungry again. If I must work for these things, that is a price I am willing to pay."

Hal picked up his can and stared at it, unwilling to meet Joe's eyes. There was a strange expression on his face, as if Torval's words had shamed him somehow. "I'm sorry, Joe," he said after a moment. "I can't do that. I just can't, and I can't see how you would want to either, but if that's your choice I won't try to talk you out of it."

"My mind is quite made up," agreed Torval.

"I can see I can't go with you," Hal went on. "I'll still be here, if you want to come talk to me, but they won't let someone like me into that world. Do you understand?"

"Yes, I believe I do." Something like sadness pierced Torval's thoughts, for he knew what Hal was doing. He was severing their ties. So much for finding out more about friendship!

"I'd better go," Hal said with a heavy sigh. He put his hand on Torval's shoulder for one lingering moment. "You'll always be my friend, Joe. Don't forget that. If this doesn't work out, and you need to talk to someone, you know where to find me. Goodbye."

Torval tried to think of something else to say, but he couldn't. He thought he saw something glistening on Hal's face, but before he could identify what it was, the bum had turned away and disappeared into the crowd.

"Goodbye," Torval finally managed, but Hal was already gone.

# Chapter 15

The encounter with Hal left Torval haunted by a strange emotion that left him feeling empty inside, similar to hunger or remorse but not quite the same. Even though he didn't really know the man who'd just wandered off into the streets, Torval still felt a sense of loss. The uneasy sensation that he suspected was "sadness" suggested that he'd once again failed somehow.

Apparently, succeeding as a human would be even harder than he ever imagined. There must be far more to mortal existence than just acquiring food and shelter. These foreign emotions, which assailed him from all sides despite his frequent attempts to deny their presence, were too ingrained in his human psyche to ignore.

As he wandered back on course for the shelter, returning once again to the main thoroughfare he knew would take him to his destination, Torval idly wondered just how much of this emotional overload would follow him back to Hell, once this blessed vacation finally ended. Surely he wouldn't have to dwell on these feelings once he returned to his route!

Again the unsettling possibility that he might be evolving reared its ugly head. What if he really did advance to Second Class, and part of that promotion involved the requirement to feel and remember human emotions? Some, perhaps, might be worth the trouble, but so far as he could tell, most were not. If he had to spend the rest of his demonic existence suffering from feelings of pity, remorse, sadness or embarrassment, that would be intolerable!

Again, he turned his thoughts to Prelz. The ex-Tempter would no doubt be able to fill him in on how all that worked. Perhaps Torval could simply refuse promotion, or maybe his new form would be somehow better suited to handling human emotions. There seemed to be little doubt that they would be a part of a Second Class existence—why send him here to Earth in human guise, except to train him to handle such things? The more Torval thought about it, the more it all made sense.

He came to a cross street he recognized, waited out the light, and headed down toward the entrance to the shelter. Upon arriving, he found a short line of haggard bums extending out the doorway. Prelz wasn't in the line, so Torval attempted to push past, only to be halted by a pair of dark, weathered hands wrapped in fingerless gloves. "Not so fast, fancy-pants," growled the gruff, thickly bearded man, who seemed a bit more threatening than the other transients. "No cuttin' in line!"

"I merely wish to see if someone is here," insisted Torval. "I am not hungry in the least."

"Don't matter," hissed the man, producing a sort of whistling sound when he spoke, primarily because he lacked any front teeth at all. "Get to the back if ya don't wanna get hurt!"

Now that Torval actually looked closely, he saw many scars and worn patches on the bum's skin, souvenirs from past back-alley fights. Despite his slight hunch and wiry build, he seemed capable of defending himself, and Torval already knew his own body had little in the way of stamina.

Sighing, the demon backed off and moved to the end of the line, another six people back. Best to not make trouble, he thought. If he wanted to survive here, he might as well follow the rules. Besides, he was in no hurry, and from this spot he could easily see if Prelz attempted to leave the shelter.

Perhaps ten minutes later he finally got inside the building, whereupon he abandoned the line and walked up and down the packed rows of homeless people. All had bowls of soup and thin, pitiful-looking sandwiches on metal plates before them, in various stages of consumption. Some talked quietly among themselves, while others simply ate in silence, alone with their thoughts. Torval felt that odd emotion called "pity" once again. With only a little effort, they could leave this place and dwell in homes of their own, yet they chose not to do so.

Torval began to understand why people like Christine, Lakisha, and the other workers at the shelter volunteered to help. The feeling of pity was quite compelling, and besides, he already owed many favors to others, so helping these poor souls would be one step toward repaying that debt. Yet what could he possibly do for them? He had no money, at least not yet. Perhaps later, when he had funds, he could aid in some way.

He didn't see Prelz, nor did he see anyone else he recognized at first. Actually, that wasn't quite true—some of the bums seemed familiar, but Joe's memories were gone and Torval couldn't recall their names. None seemed to recognize him, but considering his recent change of appearance, that wasn't surprising. He did, however, spot the abrasive Lakisha tending one of the soup pots in the back.

Sighing resignedly, Torval headed over to her, ignoring the sullen line of homeless people waiting their turn to eat. "I have a question," he stated as he reached the stove. "I am looking for Pr—I mean, Jake. Have you seen him?"

"Jake?" asked the middle-aged woman, idly stirring the bowl of white broth in front of her. "Who's askin'?"

"It is I, Joe Sampson," replied Torval.

She narrowed her eyes, and then her face lit up. "Well, I'll be damned! That is you, isn't it? I thought I recognized your voice! You mean you were actually serious about getting a job?"

"Yes, I was. Christine was kind enough to provide me with these clothes, and I was successful in acquiring employment this very morning."

"Well bless her little heart! I owe her an apology, don't I? Yes, I surely do! She was right about you, at least so far. You better keep that job, Joe! If you disappoint her—she's known way too many disappointments, y'know. If you get back on the bottle, I swear to Christ Almighty I'll never give you another drop of soup, and I mean it!"

"Do not worry," replied Torval, "I intend to remain employed for the duration of my stay—I mean, for as long as it takes. Now, please, if you have seen Jake, I would appreciate any information you have as to his present location."

She chuckled. "Now, look here, Joe, you've already impressed me enough, you don't need to throw all them big words around! Besides, I got no good news for you anyways. He hasn't been in at all, and I've been here since we opened this mornin'. If you want, I can tell him where to find you."

"No, I don't know where I will be." He paused, and then remembered what he was supposed to do in these situations. "Thank you for your help, Lakisha. I will try to return here from time to time and look for him."

"Good enough," she replied, patting him on the shoulder. "I sure hope I was wrong about you, Joe. Go out there and prove it, would ya? Good luck!"

* * *

Torval left the soup kitchen feeling that irritating sensation of failure once again. Without Prelz to talk to about what he'd experienced today, he was at a loss. He could always wait for their scheduled meeting at six o'clock that evening, but that was hours away. What was he to do in the interim?

He walked down the street and paused at the corner, gazing out at the vast expanse of city that surrounded him. The sun shone brightly out of a clear blue sky, causing most of the buildings to gleam and shimmer in the cool afternoon air. Vehicles splashed through melted snow in all directions, honking and dodging each other, while hordes of pedestrians made their way along on their own individual errands. Everything seemed to be flowing in a sea of chaos, yet there was a certain pace about it, as though this was the way things were supposed to be. The city hummed and throbbed with its own strange semblance of life, and despite being human, Torval knew he still didn't quite belong here. He wasn't a part of this world.

There was just too much he didn't understand. He'd hoped Prelz would answer his many questions, but that would have to wait. He'd eaten already, and secured employment and shelter. None of the few people he knew in this world were available to talk to, either. So he had nothing to do.

He stood on the corner for some time, just watching people and vehicles flow by, trying to think. A car screeched its tires and emitted a loud honk, narrowly avoiding collision. A trio of white and gray birds swooped down onto a sidewalk, fought over some crumb dropped by a man eating a hot dog as he walked, and swooped away, chasing the one lucky enough to secure the largest chunk of bread. A silver arrow-like craft, trailing four lines of white smoke in its wake, crossed the sky far above the buildings, and somehow Torval knew this was yet another creation of Man.

So many questions, and no answers to be had. If only...

The demon paused. Perhaps he might find answers after all, and he thought he might know where to look—a place Alan Ferrell called a "library." Torval's knowledge of human vocabulary suggested this was a place with books, but beyond that he didn't know what to expect. There were no libraries in Hell.

The concept of a library did remind him of one prisoner on his route, a woman named Clarissa Konani. Her cell consisted of a tiny, windowless room that sported several tall racks of books in various shapes and sizes. However, the numerous tomes contained nothing but anecdotes about her life, which hadn't been at all pleasant. A former teacher turned drug addict who spent her miserable existence stealing to support her habit, Clarissa's goal had always been to forget her troubles, but in Hell she had no choice but to remember them through the written word. For every minute spent not reading yet another passage about her pitiful life, white-hot lances of pain pierced her needle-scarred skin.

The rows of books in that cell resembled what would be found in a library, Torval knew, but that's about all he could recall about such places. The books on shelves in the Middle World would cover subjects other than Clarissa's life, obviously, but would they be of interest to a demon trapped on Earth? Alan's comments suggested that they would, so Torval decided at once to find a library and learn the truth for himself. If nothing else, that would give him something to do until six o'clock.

Now he just had to find one of these institutions. Previously, while dressed as a bum, getting information from humans proved difficult, but he looked more presentable now. He turned to a large man in a raincoat standing nearby, a wrinkled newspaper tucked underneath one beefy arm. "Do you know where I might find a library?" the demon inquired.

"What? Oh, sure," replied the man in a somewhat hoarse voice. He coughed and cleared his throat, then pointed down the street in the direction exactly opposite where Roxton Auto Parts could be found. "Three blocks that way, turn right, look for the big granite pillars. Can't miss it."

Torval nodded and said the phrase that had quickly become an essential part of his human vocabulary. "Thank you."

"You're quite welcome," replied the man, smiling in a friendly manner before crossing the street when the light finally changed. Torval turned and headed in the direction he'd been given, grateful for the assistance. How much easier this was, now that he looked like a typical human being! Furthermore, now that he was properly dressed and bathed, he could easily enter any of these buildings without any problems. In fact, now that he thought about it, entering the library as a bum probably wouldn't be allowed. Being employed already showed it had extra benefits above and beyond a simple paycheck.

Now he only had to worry about how to secure any of the books inside, assuming he could find one with the answers he sought. Torval had no money as yet, and begging for cash wasn't an option. Unless the books were somehow free, he'd never actually be able to acquire one. Because money seemed to be necessary for everything in this human world, he doubted very much if he could get a book without paying at least something for it.

Nonetheless, he kept going, for he had little to do otherwise, and besides, at least he could find out more about the library. Perhaps they would allow him to look over their selection of books until he found what he wanted, and then let him glance through it long enough to ensure it was the proper type. Then at least he would know how much he had to earn before he could make his purchase.

In due course he came to the library, a short gray building decorated with engraved stone pillars around a wide glass entryway. The words "Public Library" stood out beneath a strange red display made of something akin to bent pipes twisted in a tangled weave. What purpose this object served totally eluded Torval. Perhaps it was some kind of marker, or more likely the remnants of some failed structure left behind as a warning to others.

Looking further, he spotted a placard at the bottom of the warped length of pipes. "Modern Sculpture by Karl Foster," the words said. Torval stared at the object again for a moment, baffled. A sculpture suggested something artistic and pleasant to look upon, but this was neither. This Karl Foster person must've twisted some plumbing about, painted it, and declared it a sculpture, which made no sense at all. What was it doing here, in front of the library? Unless, as Torval surmised initially, it served as some sort of warning. Yes, that was it. This was a warning to other sculptors not to make this same sort of mistake.

Nodding to himself and somewhat pleased at having solved this mystery, Torval strode up the stairs to the front door and entered the stone-walled structure. Once inside, he stopped, staring in awe at what stood before him. Instead of just a couple of rows of books, as he'd expected, there were instead dozens, extending out around him as far as he could see. There were, in fact, more books than he could ever possibly count. Furthermore, as he let his astonished gaze travel upward, there were even more shelf-lined floors above him, accessed via spiral staircases. The selection of books seemed endless.

Staring about in wonder, Torval noticed several other humans wandering through the aisles, searching for something of interest, while others sat idly reading at desks or in chairs. To his left, an old woman in a plain white dress stood behind a desk, a magazine open before her. A nametag on her chest identified her as "Karen," though it didn't mention her last name. She glanced at Torval somewhat curiously, but didn't say anything. She looked as if she wanted to speak, but her mouth remained shut in a tight line.

Torval accepted the unspoken invitation and moved closer. Although the size of the place overwhelmed him, he felt determined to succeed. "I am looking for—" he began.

"Shh!" the woman whispered quickly.

Torval stopped and stared at her. The gesture's meaning seemed clear—he was not permitted to speak. But how could he communicate? He stood there in confusion, unsure of what to do.

The old woman smiled. "You can talk," she said in a low whisper. "Just keep your voice down. Never been in a library before?"

"No," admitted Torval, taking her advice and speaking quietly. "I had not expected it to be like this. So many books!"

Karen nodded and emitted a faint sigh. "I guess that's the way things are these days. Nobody comes to libraries anymore, with everything available on the Internet. Give me a quiet room and a real book, though, that's all I need!"

Torval looked around. There were indeed people here, were there not? "If nobody comes to libraries," he said in confusion, "what are all of these people doing here?"

The librarian emitted a low chuckle. "Oh, never you mind, I didn't mean to seem bitter. Just commenting on the times is all. It doesn't matter, I suppose. What can I do for you?"

Glad to be back on topic, Torval explained, "I am looking for books on subjects that interest me."

"Well, you've come to the right place," Karen told him. "I'm pretty sure if you name a subject, we've got a book about it."

"That is good," replied Torval eagerly. He stopped, considering for a moment what he wanted to know more about. So many questions... his mind immediately went back to the first thing that he tried to ask Alan about, the topic that had brought up mention of libraries in the first place. "I wish to know more about money. Can you show me which books discuss this subject?"

"Oh, no, not me," she replied with a laugh. "I couldn't possibly know where everything is in this place! Lucky for you we have a card catalog. Step over there to the cabinets." She pointed at a trio of tall shelves, each filled with small rectangular drawers made of a light brown wood. One cabinet was labeled "Author," another "Title," and a third "Subject." Torval stared at them, clearly at a loss.

"It's easy," said the librarian. "You want to know about money, you say, so go to the Subject row, and look it up. It's in alphabetical order, you see. So when you find one that sounds interesting, look at the numbers on the left side of the card, then go find that number using the signs. See?"

She pointed again, and Torval followed her finger to a spot above one of the many rows of books. There were indeed numbers there—"500–540.5," in fact. As he looked around, he saw a similar sign above each row, and the numbers were smaller to his left and larger to the right.

"I think I understand," he told the woman. "Thank you." That phrase was now virtually automatic.

He headed over to the cabinet and began to look through the drawers. Very quickly he discovered that the letters on the front indicated the starting letters on the cards inside, which led him to the one labeled "Mo-Mu." After a moment he found a selection with the subject of "money" and from here he began to study the many titles, looking for one that sounded closest to what he wanted to know.

Finally he found something that seemed correct, a card with the name "History of Money" by someone named Dr. Philip Azzerton. The phrase underneath read, "A discussion of how money came to be, and how it works today, by the noted historian Dr. Philip Azzerton, Professor of Economics at Harvard University from 1990–2004."

Withdrawing the card, Torval closed the drawer and moved purposefully through the library to the proper spot. The method used to order the books seemed quite straightforward, and that was something he could appreciate. Using a numerical system instead of an alphabetical one allowed there to be three separate ways to locate the desired writings, and also for new tomes to be inserted at leisure without having to reorder the existing sequence. Very convenient and proper.

Searching along the shelves for several minutes, he located the book he wanted and pulled it out. A thick, heavy hardback with a thin plastic sheet over the cover, *History of Money* looked like something he couldn't possibly read in one sitting. Just the thing to pass the time in my flop when I'm not working, Torval thought.

He took the book back to the front, where the librarian waited, studying her magazine through a pair of glasses that seemed to have only half-sized lenses. She glanced up at Torval's approach and let the spectacles drop down about her neck, where they hung on a simple silver chain. "Did you find what you were looking for?" she inquired curiously, as before keeping her voice low.

"I believe so," said Torval quietly, showing her the book. "Although I have no money at this time, I wish to purchase this one. Can you tell me how much it costs, so I know how much to bring when I wish to buy it?"

The woman chuckled. "Oh, we don't sell books here, silly," she told him. "Libraries aren't bookstores! You really don't know what this place is for?"

"I am afraid not," replied Torval. "If I cannot purchase the book, how may I read it?"

She gave him a bemused look. "Why, you just open it up and start reading! Find a chair someplace and have a seat. You can stay as long as you like, although we do close at seven. When you're done just leave it on one of the tables and someone will put it away for you."

Torval raised an eyebrow. "There is no fee?" he inquired, somewhat surprised by this. "I do not have to pay?"

"No, of course not," she answered, now grinning almost from ear to ear. "This is a public library. It's open to everyone, just like, say, a museum or park. You can read any of the books here, and if you have a library card, you can even check them out for up to two weeks."

Torval blinked a few times. The books were free! So, not everything in this world cost money! He could simply come here whenever he wished, and read any of the tomes on these endless shelves, at no cost whatsoever. Why was this place not packed with humans, then?

Well, the old woman did mention something about checking books out for use outside the library. Perhaps that's how it should be done, thought Torval. "So I must have some sort of card to check this out?" he asked curiously.

"Yes, but I'll need your address and phone number to make you a card," she replied. "And I'll have to make a copy of your driver's license and put it on file."

Torval sighed. "I have none of those things," he admitted sadly. "I suppose that means I cannot take the book from this place."

"I'm afraid not," Karen told him, sounding disappointed. "I can understand not driving in New York City, and maybe even not having a phone, but how can you not have an address?"

"I was homeless until this morning," Torval replied honestly. "I now possess a flop, but I do not know the address."

"Ah," she replied in a doubtful tone. "Well, when you find out what it is, and get yourself a phone, you can ask again. Maybe we can make an exception for the license, if you have a major credit card or some other form of ID."

"Very well," agreed Torval, choosing not to mention that he didn't have any of those things either, nor did he even know what a credit card was. "In the meantime, I suppose I will have to read this here. That is fine, as it will give me something to do. I must be somewhere at six o'clock, however. How may I tell the time?"

"Oh, there's a clock over there," the woman replied, pointing at a small round device hanging just above the desk to her left. "If you need to watch it, I suggest those chairs." She pointed at a batch of seats, made of simple wood frames with green upholstery, in a kind of half-circle around a short table. None of them were occupied.

"Thank you," said Torval once again, taking his leave and heading over to the waiting chairs. He selected one and sat, ensuring that he could see the time easily, and opened the book.

After flipping through a couple of pages of contents and titles, he came to the beginning of the text. "Money," wrote the esteemed Dr. Azzerton, "has been around nearly as long as civilization itself. The earliest forms of money are often attributed to the era of the well-known philosopher and early economist Hammurabi, but in fact, money actually predates his lifetime by several hundred years . . ."

In no time at all, Torval found himself lost in the words.

# Chapter 16

"Sir?"

Torval heard the voice in a detached way, as of someone calling to him from a great distance. The sound seemed to echo hollowly about inside his head.

He wasn't a demon at that particular moment, but rather a Greek trader named Antigonus on the island of Rhodes in ancient Greece. At present, he held a bagful of silver drachmas in a meaty hand, hoping to purchase wine for a coming feast. He continued arguing with a merchant over a clearly unfair price, considering a rival made a similar purchase for three-fourths the cost just the previous season. The swindler insisted the value of wine had increased, now that the grape crop had been harvested and fresh ones had to be imported from nearby islands. Preposterous! Why, Antigonus of Rhodes knows more about wine than—

"Sir! Wake up!"

Joe's body jerked itself awake. Torval blinked and looked around, surprised to find himself so suddenly back in the library. He was still reading...wasn't he? Apparently not. He must've dozed off right there in his seat, with the book still halfway open on his lap.

He'd been reading about money. He remembered that part, but he certainly hadn't intended to take a nap. The weakness of his frail shell simply reared its ugly head once again.

Torval realized, even as he unconsciously rubbed his throbbing temples, that the old woman named Karen stood over him. "What is it?" he asked reflexively. "Did I do something wrong?"

"No, not really," she replied, the crinkled lines of her mouth arching upwards in a half-smile. "I just remembered you said you had somewhere to be at six, and I thought you probably wouldn't want to be late."

She reached out with a bony finger, indicating the clock, and Torval saw the truth in her words—he had to leave, and quickly, if he wanted to be on time. He set the book on the table and stood, momentarily dizzy from his body's sudden transition from sleep to immediate activity. "Thank you," he said almost automatically. "I might well have missed my appointment. Apparently, I fell asleep."

"Yes, I saw that," she told him, her smile expanding on her aged face. "You'd better be going. Don't worry, I'll re-file the book for you, so next time you visit it'll be in the same place. Be sure to let me know if you need a library card!"

"I will," agreed Torval, heading woozily for the exit. He stepped outside to find the sun nearly gone for the day, and the formerly blue sky a faint pink. Traces of lavender clouds visible just between the buildings seemed painted there by an artist's hand. The endless lights were already turning on, but the impending change from day to night hadn't made New York City any less busy. Pedestrians still strode by in great numbers, and the progression of vehicles remained in full swing.

Torval started walking along the busy sidewalk, heading toward the shelter where he'd agreed to meet Prelz. The trip wouldn't take long, he thought, but because of the nap his gait was unsteady. His earlier exertions left him drained, so that sleep came without warning, and now he had a headache and felt exhausted. That didn't make sense, because as he understood things, sleeping was supposed to be refreshing—and until now, it had been just that.

Perhaps his rest shouldn't have been interrupted, or more likely, he shouldn't have napped at all. As near as he could tell, he'd been out for at least an hour. He remembered looking up at the clock shortly before five, even as he started reading the chapter on Greek developments in coinage. That's what reminded him of Antigonus of Rhodes, a prisoner he once visited on one of his rare trips outside of his own punishment route.

He recalled those early years of his career, shortly after his promotion to Third Class, with only a vague detachment—as if those events had happened to someone else. Back then, as part of his training, he had to occasionally visit other layers to see how other Punishers did their work. Such a trip took a considerable amount of time and effort, since he had to charter a ferryboat on the River Styx or one of the other winding waterways that meandered haphazardly through the Lower Realm. Nonetheless, much as Torval hated to admit it, he did learn many things on those visits.

Antigonus was one of the few memorable prisoners he encountered back then, and until now, that memory had remained buried deep in his subconscious. Through shrewd dealings and iron-fisted control of imports and exports throughout the Aegean Sea, the trader amassed a vast fortune that made him one of the richest men in ancient Greece. What few knew, however, was that he was also one of history's first counterfeiters, having turned many of his personal resources to the production of fake drachmas made of trace amounts of silver mixed with cheaper metals. He collected the silver used for his illicit work almost exclusively by "clipping" real coins, meaning he shaved small quantities off the edges in such a way as to mimic ordinary wear. As his punishment in Hell, Antigonus haggled constantly over trivial items, but instead of coins, he argued over how many brutal lashings he would receive as "payment."

In Torval's dream, he recalled one of the great marketplaces of Rhodes, and the coins he held were those same drachmas that seemed so very important to Antigonus. Torval didn't understand why the man would go so far out of his way to create false money when he already had the skill and talent to acquire plenty of the real thing. Furthermore, during his lifetime, the Greek trader would never have been able to spend all those funds, unless he emptied his coffers over the course of years of shameless hedonism. Instead, Antigonus died wealthy, killed by a seizure while counting his stacks of false coins in a dark and otherwise empty basement.

Torval had a much better understanding of money now. How the stuff came to exist made perfect sense. In the early days of civilization, barter was the primary method of trade—a fisherman who desired bread simply arranged a mutually agreeable swap with a needy baker. Unfortunately, this system worked only when the two traders both had items the other wanted. If the baker didn't want fish, but needed wine, then to get his bread the fisherman would have to find someone willing to trade wine for fish, then trade the wine for the bread. But what if the vintner didn't want fish either, but needed new baskets for his grapes? The chain of trades required for the poor fisherman to get his bread quickly became cumbersome and inefficient.

That's where money came in. Money didn't have to be coins or paper—it could be anything that the majority of citizens agreed had value. Early civilizations used shells, stones, alcohol, and other forms of currency as tokens that could later be traded to others for an accepted price. Thus, the fisherman could sell his fish to anyone for ten cowrie shells (an actual currency in some parts of the ancient world), and give those shells to the baker for some bread. The baker then had shells of his own to purchase the wine he wanted, when he was ready to acquire it.

There was more to the modern monetary scheme, of course. Torval only read a fraction of the book, so he only had a basic understanding of the process. Things like paper currency and governmental control of money's value still eluded him, although he felt sure the book (or any other similar one in the library) could explain those things. However, he had the distinct feeling, at least from the somewhat dry historical text he'd read, that he still had a long way to go before he understood why humans sinned so greatly over currency.

He came to the shelter at last, and this time there was no line, so he made his way inside. Prelz waited there, seated at a half-empty table while spooning some yellowish broth into his mouth. The ex-Tempter looked haggard and tired, even more so than usual, but Torval nonetheless felt his lips turning into a smile, a natural response to the much welcome sight of the former demon.

Quickly Torval moved over to one of the seats and sat down, not bothering to get a bowl of soup for himself as he wasn't quite hungry yet. Plus, he expected food later when he returned to the auto parts warehouse. "I am glad you are here," he said as he settled into place. "I have many things to ask you."

"Sorry, what?" asked a surprised Prelz. "Do I know you, friend?" There was a brief moment while he stared at Joe's recently shaven face and then his bushy eyebrows went up. "Oh, shit, it's you! Sorry, man, I didn't recognize you like that. Should've expected it, I guess, seeing as how you're all employed and everything."

"You know about that?" asked Torval curiously. He'd told Prelz about the trip to the employment office that morning, of course, but not about actually acquiring work. In fact, the ex-demon had been doubtful there'd be an offering so quickly, or so Torval recalled.

"Yeah, I overheard Christine and Lakisha talking about it," explained Prelz, pointing over at the counter. Torval glanced back to see the normally coarse black woman pouring soup into a waiting bum's bowl. In the back room, a slender, familiar female figure had her back to him, busily working on another batch of broth.

Torval let his gaze linger on Christine's distant form. She wore a simple light brown dress with an oversized black belt about her waist, as well as the boots she'd had on that morning, and her dark hair dangled behind her head in a bouncy ponytail. Something about her presence seemed strangely comforting, even at this distance. He very much wanted to get up and go talk to her, to share his experiences of the day, but he couldn't very well do that now that he'd finally tracked down Prelz.

"So you know where I am working?" asked Torval, his eyes never leaving the trim figure in the distance. "Christine told you?"

"No, not so many details," replied Prelz, scooping another mouthful of soup into his bewhiskered mouth. "Tell me all about it. Sounds like you must've had an interesting day."

"Yes, I should think so," Torval replied. "After I left you, I came here and Christine took me to get cleaned up. Thus my current appearance."

"Wait, Christine took you?" Prelz raised his graying eyebrows again. "Did she wash you herself?" He chuckled loudly, then coughed a couple of times, obviously mis-swallowing in his effort to make a joke.

"No, I took a shower alone," explained Torval, completely missing the insinuation. "She was quite helpful nonetheless, providing these clothes and arranging for a shave. After that we went to the employment agency, where she convinced a man named Simon Spencer to get me a job at a place called Roxton Auto Parts."

Prelz nodded, obviously recognizing the name. "Yeah, I've wandered by there before. Not too far away. There's something . . ." He paused, scrunching up his forehead as he tried to recall some forgotten detail. "Something about that place. I don't remember it now, but I'll ask around. Anyway, what are you doing? Selling car parts? You don't seem terribly qualified."

"No, I am a janitor," said Torval enthusiastically. "I will clean a bathroom in their basement, and in exchange, I am allowed to sleep in a hammock near a heating device. Furthermore, I will be given food in exchange for my labors. Is that not wonderful? I will not be sleeping on the cold streets any longer. I will have a place to stay for the remainder of this vacation."

"Good for you!" Prelz said in a congratulatory tone. "That's pretty good, getting a job right away. Better than I could've done. Now just don't screw it up and you'll be fine."

Torval found himself smiling again, and as he did, he felt a strange swelling sensation in his chest. Another emotion, he realized, and this one was "pride." He was proud of himself for pleasing Prelz, a superior in the demonic hierarchy—or at least, the closest thing to a superior in this bizarre mortal world. Torval hadn't felt pride before, perhaps because in Hell he could expect no reward for good work other than the lack of a disciplinary response from Landri or some other Second-Class demon.

Still, Torval sensed a veiled warning in Prelz's words. Don't screw it up, indeed. Torval had no intention of making any mistakes. He'd do the job as ordered and thereby ensure himself of twelve more days of peace and comfort before he could go back and return to his duties.

"I will be as effective as possible," he agreed. "I believe I will have little trouble pleasing my new masters."

Prelz grinned knowingly. "You know what? I bet you find after a couple of days that just having a roof over your head and some food in your belly isn't enough."

"But that is all I require," protested Torval. "I have no need for anything more."

"Really?" Prelz looked at him doubtfully. "There's absolutely nothing else you need? You don't owe anyone anything?"

"Well, perhaps—"

"And you're fine just eating what they give you? You don't want to try some other kinds of foods?"

Torval licked his lips. "I did try something called 'pizza' today, and it was—"

"What about entertainment? You'll get bored, you know. Trust me, when they say 'idle hands are the Devil's tools,' they aren't kidding."

"Oh, I will have no trouble in that area," said Torval quickly. "Today I visited the library, where they have a limitless supply of books. I could spend every remaining minute here in that place and I doubt I would finish even one shelf."

"Ah, you tried a library! Good, good." Prelz seemed pleased to hear that, again giving Torval a welcome twinge of pride. "Well, what about the ladies? You're only going to be here two weeks—you should at least try your hand at romance. I saw you eyeing Christine over there, and she helped you out, so she must like you. If you're going to put the moves on her, you'll need someplace to go besides some dark basement with a hammock."

Torval sighed, again glancing back at Christine's distant form as she meandered from stovetop to oven, occasionally washing a few dishes as well. The faint sound of whistling wafted out from the back room, reminding him how much she enjoyed helping others, that odd phenomenon that made her so enigmatic and intriguing.

"Ah, so I'm right," said Prelz, noticing his companion's wistful gaze. "You do like her, don't you?"

"Yes," admitted Torval, feeling strangely irritated at having this fact dragged out of him so directly. "I do not understand why, but I want to interact with Christine more. As much as possible, in fact."

Prelz grinned, showing a mouth filled with irregular, yellowed teeth. "So would damn near any man in this place, I imagine," he commented wryly. "I bet you got a chance, though, 'cause as it turns out, that face of yours ain't too bad to look at. You two are about the same age, too, I suspect. She's outta your league, though, that's the problem. Besides, you wouldn't know the first thing about women."

"Actually," Torval replied, "I did meet a woman today at the employment agency. Her name is Shelly Mendez. Her body was covered with the most intricate tattoos."

Prelz stared at him, the dark sockets of his eyes narrowed almost to slits. "How much of her body?"

"All of it."

"You saw all of her body?"

"Yes, I did. Just before we had sex."

Prelz dropped his spoon, which clattered loudly in the nearly empty soup bowl. "You had—" he started, sputtering. "You're not lying to me, are you? Making fun of poor ol' Prelz?"

Torval emitted a strange noise from deep within his throat. With a start, he realized this was a laugh—his first one, in fact. Something in the look on his companion's face, and the way he reacted to the news, amused Torval greatly, forcing his human body to react with that strange, cough-like sputter. Torval didn't know why Prelz's reaction seemed so funny, only that it was.

"No, no, of course you wouldn't lie," went on Prelz, "and I doubt you could tell a joke if your life depended on it. So you really did get it on! Less than twenty-four hours here and already you scored! I don't know if I should congratulate you or slap myself silly for taking so long myself. How'd you manage it? How'd you get somebody to sleep with you so easily?"

Pride, again! Torval could feel the swelling sensation welling up deep within, as if he would explode at any moment. He forced the alien feeling down as best he could and tried to explain himself. "To be truthful, Shelly made the offer, inviting me to her apartment. Christine told me she was a prostitute, which turned out to be true, but there was no exchange of funds, as I had none to give. I believe Shelly intended to rob me, and was rather disappointed."

"Oh, I see," said Prelz with a sharp laugh, nodding heartily. "Good! That explains it. I don't feel so bad now. You were her mark and she was gonna roll you. Guess you both got to enjoy yourselves for a bit, even if she didn't get paid. Nice job scorin' the freebie!"

"It did not feel right," went on Torval somewhat dejectedly. "She expected payment and I did not give her anything, so I feel as though I wronged her somehow."

"Well, you didn't, trust me. Besides, you both got lucky, so you're even. Any chance you can see her again? Sex only gets better the more you do it, you know."

"Unlikely. She, too, believed she was wronged, and ordered me away. I doubt I will copulate with her again."

Prelz winced and shook his head. "Okay, okay, look, we have to talk about how you speak, my friend. You can't use words like 'copulate' or nobody will understand you. Nobody talks like that! You sound like a walking dictionary half the time. Use more common terms, or abbreviate, or use slang. Instead of 'we had sex,' you say 'we got it on,' or 'we did the nasty,' or something like that. Your body's ingrained knowledge of language should have access to those sorts of phrases. Just mix them into your speech."

"I will try," agreed Torval, glad for this sort of advice. That's why he sought out Prelz in the first place, after all.

"That's another thing! Stop using full words when you don't have to. Use contractions as much as you can. It's not 'I will try,' it's 'I'll try.' Go on, do it. Practice right now, on me."

"I'll try," said Torval with uncertainty. The abbreviation seemed cheap and lazy, like someone taking a shortcut. He'd been conditioned throughout all of his existence not to take shortcuts, lest he be punished. "This will be difficult," he admitted. "However, I will—I mean, I'll attempt to do better."

"Good. Also, you can swear if you want. Most people swear every few sentences, or even more often. Does that human brain of yours remember Sean Martinez, the guy who likes to hang out down by the piers? He says 'fuck' every other word. You don't have to be that extreme, obviously, but cursing every now and then is totally normal. Go on, try it. Swear."

"Uh... shit," said Torval experimentally. "Shit this fuck."

Prelz rolled his eyes and put his hand momentarily against his forehead. "Oh, never mind, let's just forget I said anything. Now, getting back to the subject of women, how was this Shelly, anyways? Did she know her stuff?"

"I believe so," agreed Torval. "She removed her clothes, and I climbed onto the bed, and—"

"Skip the blow-by-blow!" interrupted Prelz. "I get the picture! What I mean is, was she any good in the sack?"

"Lacking anything to compare her with, I suppose she was," replied Torval with a shrug. "I must admit, the entire experience was quite overwhelming. It seemed to be over quickly, although from the pain in my muscles and my sudden inability to breathe, it must have lasted longer than I remember. I had little control over myself at the time. This human body I wear took over completely."

Prelz laughed and slapped him on the shoulder. "That's what happened to me the first time!" he admitted easily. "Don't worry, it gets better the more you try it. I wouldn't concern yourself too much, though. Since the only things you need in life are food and shelter, you won't have to worry about getting lucky again."

"Wait! I do wish to know more!" admitted Torval, feeling the sudden urge to explain himself. "When I return to Hell, I will need to describe what I have learned here to my foreman. If I do not—I mean, if I don't comprehend why humans commit evil acts in relation to sex, I will have failed in my mission here."

Prelz chuckled at that. "Right, sure, that's the only reason," he muttered sarcastically, almost to himself. "All right, fine, whatever you say, my friend. So there we have it, something else you gotta concern yourself with while you're here. We need to get you laid, but the right way this time."

"What do you mean, the right way?"

"Well," explained the more experienced demon, "what you performed today was what we humans call 'casual sex.' You met somebody, you got it on, you broke it off clean. No emotional involvement, no worries about disappointments, no need to ever see that person again. It's quick and easy and nobody gets hurt, assuming you used protection. You did... didn't you?"

"If you mean the strange implement that went over my—" Torval began.

"Okay, okay, good! One of you was thinking, anyway. Fine, moving right along. So yeah, nobody gets hurt. The thing is, casual sex is ultimately meaningless. It's not what doing the horizontal tango is supposed to be all about. Another term for it is 'making love,' and it means what it says. To really enjoy sex, you should do it with someone you love. Or at least care for, anyway. Anything else is at best inappropriate, and at worst, a sin punishable by any of the many judgments you've seen in Hell."

"I see," said Torval, nodding. "So what I did today was, as you say, wrong. I should find Shelly and apologize."

"No, no, don't worry about it," interrupted Prelz. "Inappropriate, maybe, like I said, but you both consented and you both got what you wanted. It wasn't like you raped her or anything. She invited you, and she seduced you. If anyone should apologize, it should be her."

"Somehow, I doubt that will be forthcoming," Torval remarked.

"Probably not. In any case, what we need to do, if you want to really understand what sex is all about, is get you involved with someone a little more important in your life. Right now, the only one I know about who meets that criteria is her." He pointed with a bent finger at the happily whistling Christine, at that moment busy drying dishes in the back room.

Torval nodded eagerly in agreement. "I will admit, the subject of an intimate encounter with Christine has crossed my mind. She intrigues me more than any human I have interacted with since my arrival in this city. When I met Shelly Mendez, she simply asked me if I would like to have s—er, to 'do the nasty,' as you called it. Is that what I should do with Christine? Simply ask?"

"Oh, no, hell no!" coughed Prelz. "Are you crazy? She'd slap you silly and never talk to you again! You can't just proposition someone like that!"

"But that is what Shelly did," protested Torval.

"Yes, but she was a hooker, wasn't she? And she was looking to rob you, as it turned out. Trust me, my friend, that's not the way it's done. You need to get to know her better, go on a couple of dates, kiss a few times . . . then maybe you could test the waters, carefully at first. Read the signals, send out some vibes, all that stuff."

Torval shook his head in confusion. "I do not—I mean, I don't know how to do those things. Can you teach me?"

"I can give you some advice," agreed Prelz, "but honestly, I'm really not a very good choice for helping the lovelorn. Tell you what, I'll tell you what I know, and then you're on your own. You like reading, so you can check out some romance books, and maybe after you have some money, you can go see a date movie or two."

"That sounds encouraging, whatever a movie might be," Torval agreed at once. "How long will this process take?"

"What, before you get into her pants? Oh, there's no way to tell. Depends on how easy she is. Someone like her, probably not so much, so I suspect it may be a while. Weeks, maybe."

"But I only have twelve more days!" protested Torval.

"Then you better get started, my friend. You'd better get started!"

# Chapter 17

Torval felt a strange tightness in his chest as he approached Christine, who continued whistling away in the back of the soup kitchen, keeping her back to him as she mopped a soiled corner of the floor. He didn't understand why he should be so anxious. Speaking to Christine, or any other human for that matter, shouldn't cause him any emotional reactions at all, but it did, and he had no way to control such feelings.

Still, he pressed on. Prelz, who'd moved outside as the shelter slowly filled up with patrons, had explained that the first step was to engage in conversation until Torval and Christine were comfortable together. Then, at some point in the future, when Torval could afford it, there would be a "date," whatever that might be.

His throat felt dry, so the worried demon forced a swallow before finally speaking. "Hello," he called out, not sure what else to say, but needing to get her attention nonetheless.

"What? Oh, hey, Joe!" she replied with another of those heart-warming smiles of hers. "Sorry, I didn't see you there. I spilled some gravy here and had to wipe it up. What can I do for you?"

Torval hesitated. What, indeed? He hadn't thought this far ahead. "Well," he replied slowly, "I suppose I wanted to inform you that I report to my new job at eight o'clock."

"Good for you!" She pushed the mop's dripping strands into some kind of plates mounted above a bucket, then pulled a lever attached to the handle. The resulting squeeze forced most of the water out into the can, where it collected into a grimy pool. "I'm glad you found something you like. That's not a very good job, but it'll do for a start. Once you're on your feet again, maybe I can help you find something better."

"I doubt that will be necessary," said Torval, "but I appreciate the offer. Thank you for everything you did for me today, Christine. Without your aid I would still be on the street."

She smiled again. "It's worth it, Joe, if it helps you change your life for the better. Please, whatever you do, don't start drinking again! You don't need booze. You may think it's a solution to your problems, but it's not. It's exactly the opposite."

"Don't concern yourself with that," the demon replied, purposely working a contraction into the conversation. "I have no intention of ever consuming alcohol again."

"Good, I hope you stick to that," said Christine with a noticeable twinge of doubtfulness in her tone. "Oh, I'm sorry if I sound cynical, Joe, but it's just that I've been disappointed so very many times. I honestly believe you may be different, though. Something about you makes me believe it. I can tell you've changed, really changed, and I like it."

Torval felt that pull on his mouth that indicated another smile, that strange depiction of pleasure that the human face seemed to do of its own accord. He didn't mind, though. The fact that she liked him was what he'd hoped very much to hear. "Thank you, Christine. I will endeavor to not disappoint you."

"I'm glad," she told him. "Did you get anything to eat, Joe? You have a job now, but that doesn't mean you aren't still hungry, and I know you probably won't get paid until at least Friday."

"I am not hungry yet," he answered, choosing not to remind her he didn't actually expect a paycheck, "and even if I were, I was told to expect a meal when I report to work."

"Oh, that's right, I forgot. That's such an unusual arrangement you have there. Pete told me all about it after you went in to get the tour, and it makes sense. You see, his grandfather grew up in the post-Depression era, and having workers live right on the premises was fairly common back then, so he sees nothing wrong with carrying on the tradition. Personally, I'd never do something like that, but to each his own, I suppose."

Torval nodded, even though he didn't quite understand what kind of era would follow depression. The terms didn't seem to go together at all. Something else to ask Prelz about, or possibly research in the library the next time he returned there.

"Anyway," went on Christine, "Pete said his grandfather hired a lot of different people to work that job before you came along, most of them homeless like yourself. So far they've all been disappointments. This is your chance to show them you're not like those others, Joe. If you do a good job, Pete said there'd be more opportunities for you later, too."

Torval didn't really want any more opportunities, as the food and living space would be sufficient for his purposes. However, that isn't what bothered him about Christine's words. Instead, he kept fixating on that name she kept using, that of Pete Roxton. Something about that bothered him. Apparently they spent some time conversing after Torval left their presence.

Without thinking about it, Torval inquired further. "What else did you talk to Pete about?"

She grinned sheepishly and looked away, pretending to focus her attention on mopping up the last remnants of the spill. "Oh, just a few other things," she said with a slightly different tone of voice that Torval didn't quite recognize. "He really likes you, you know. He said you looked attentive and had good eye contact, which I suppose is true."

She looked back at him then, and their eyes met directly. Torval had, as usual, been staring right at her, as he did automatically when interacting with humans. Now, for the first time, meeting someone's gaze felt strange and awkward, so he glanced reflexively down at his feet.

Christine, too, looked away shyly. "Anyhow," she went on with noticeable haste, "be that as it may, I have to get back to work, and you should probably get moving if you're going to walk all the way down to the warehouse on time. Best to be early on your first day, you know."

"Yes, and if I am on time, I receive my food," agreed Torval, glad for the change of subject. "There is, however, one more thing I must ask you, Christine. I have been contemplating this for some time, and you seem to be the best person to ask."

"What is it, Joe? You know you can ask me anything."

No, I didn't know that, but he filed that information away for future reference. "I've observed," he said carefully, "that you seem to enjoy helping others. In fact, for as long as I have known you, that is what seems to give you the most pleasure."

"That's true," she agreed. "I wouldn't be here if I didn't enjoy it. Why are you bringing this up again?"

Christine seemed slightly flushed, as if embarrassed to be confronted with this particular subject, but Torval pressed on. "I don't understand why you do the things you do. Why do you help people? Why did you help me today? A simple feeling of happiness does not seem to be sufficient to motivate you to sacrifice so much time and money for people like me."

She sighed, pushed the mop into the bucket, and leaned on it slightly, running her free hand through the wisps of dark brown hair that dangled haphazardly down over her forehead. "Sometimes I wonder that myself," she admitted, "but I feel like I have to do something, even if it's just volunteering in this kitchen. I just can't stand to watch people suffer, when I know there's something I could do about it."

"I still don't understand," Torval continued. "Why do you feel this responsibility toward others? I have not met many others who feel as you do. What is it about you that makes you so different?"

Christine shook her head. "I don't know," she replied, but something in her voice suggested she wasn't telling the whole truth. After being around so many sinners throughout his existence, who would tell any lie imaginable to try to get out of their punishment, Torval had developed an almost instinctive ability to detect falsehood. He started to confront her when she spoke again.

"When I first came to this city," she sighed, staring past him and obviously remembering some day long past, "I was amazed. Everything was so overwhelming, and there were so many people everywhere! The whole place seemed so alive. But then I started noticing there were a few, here and there, who didn't seem to belong. They fell through the cracks, I suppose you could say. They lived in alleys and begged for money and for the most part they were mistreated, or just ignored as if they didn't exist. But they did exist, Joe! You do exist, all of you. You're human beings and you all deserve so much more out of life than just slowly wasting away and dying on a bleak street corner! I couldn't just walk past people like you every day without doing something to help.

That's why I started volunteering here at the shelter. If a couple of hours of my life every day makes the world a better place, that's the least I can do."

Torval nodded slowly as she spoke, absorbing every word. What she said made a certain amount of sense, although she still hadn't revealed exactly what made her feel as she did. Again, he was about to inquire further when she pressed on after a short pause to catch her breath.

"It does get a little frustrating, you know," she admitted with a sigh, "especially when I see the same broken people shuffle through here every day, never improving or getting better. I go home sometimes and just lie in bed, unable to sleep, just wishing there were some way I could get through to you. That's why it was so wonderful to see you change, Joe! You're turning into the good man I always knew you could be. I don't know if it was something I did or said, but it doesn't really matter if I had anything to do with it at all. Just being able to watch you get off the streets makes everything worthwhile."

"That is what I want to understand," he insisted. "Why? Why does it make everything worthwhile? Why does it make you feel so good? What is it about helping me that pleases you so?"

She looked at him again and that ever-present smile seemed to fade, almost but not quite into a frown. He could tell she was displeased, but he couldn't very well take the questions back. "Does it really matter, Joe? It's the way I am. I like helping you, and that's all there is to it. Or do you think I have some kind of ulterior motive?"

"No, no, nothing like that," he insisted quickly, sensing that this conversation had just taken a wrong turn. "I apologize, Christine. I did not mean to offend."

She shook her head and waved a hand in a gesture of dismissal. "Oh, it doesn't matter anyway. Some people are more helpful than others, and I guess that's just the way I am."

"It's a shame there are not more like you," pointed out Torval, "or more homeless people might be motivated to improve themselves."

Her smile returned, perhaps a bit more brightly this time. "That is so very true, Joe. So very true! I know there are a lot of other good people out there, but volunteering at a place like this takes a lot of time. I guess I'm just fortunate I have a decent job that finishes promptly at five every day, and nothing else that occupies my time afterward. Although, if I'm lucky, that might be changing." She chuckled to herself at some personal joke. "Anyway, be that as it may, I really do have to get back to work. For a change, I have someplace to be a little later, so I want to get this place cleaned up before we finish the dinner rush."

"I see," said Torval. He added curiously, "Where exactly are you going?"

She smiled even wider. "That, Joe, is none of your business! Now go on, get out of here before Lakisha sees you wasting my time and kicks you out. Go on, go! You don't want to be late for work!"

"Very well," he agreed reluctantly, even as she poked the mop handle in his direction, shooing him out of the kitchen. "Have a good evening, Christine."

"You too!" she replied amiably, turning away to resume her labor.

The demon made his way to the exit, where Prelz waited impatiently, and as he did, Torval could hear Christine starting to whistle again. He risked a glance back, and for a fleeting moment he thought she might be watching him go. If so, however, she gave no outward sign, pushing the mop and bucket around a corner and out of sight.

Torval sighed as he left the shelter. Christine was such an enigma, a human who wanted to help others for no obvious reason, other than to feel good inside! Torval still had no idea what that involved, but he sensed its importance—perhaps such a thing might prove to be the key to understanding mortality itself. Even so, whatever that feeling was, it couldn't have been that motivating, or more humans would be volunteering in places like this one. There must be more to it, thought the demon, and her way of ducking the question suggested that there was indeed.

Plus, there was one other thing she avoided discussing, a mystery he had little chance of solving tonight. Where exactly was she going, anyway...

* * *

"You seem quiet," said Prelz as he shuffled along, accompanying Torval as they made their way through the brightly lit streets. "What are you thinking about? Usually all you want to do is talk."

Torval nodded, fidgeting as they waited for the proper crossing sign to illuminate, or at least for the endless stream of cars to lessen so they could proceed without being hit. As he'd already learned, he didn't actually have to wait for the green "Walk" sign—that was apparently just a recommendation, not a rule. Humans could cross the street whenever they wanted.

The sky above was dark now, but the lights around them were so bright it might as well be daytime. With the setting of the sun, the temperature dropped once more, and Torval felt chilly despite his new jacket. Shivering, he pushed his hands into his pockets and paced slightly.

"I have been trying to fathom the concept of goodness," he admitted after a moment. "I know that it is not something easily explained, as is the nature of evil. Nonetheless, I feel I must understand it, at least as best I can. If I do not, this vacation will have meant nothing, and I will be punished upon my return to Hell."

Prelz shrugged. The flow of vehicles came to an end, so they joined the other pedestrians in crossing the street. Nobody seemed to mind the presence of Joe among them, but Jake's ragged clothing and foul scent were repulsive enough that a kind of empty bubble formed around the two demons as they walked.

"I can't really explain it," said the former Tempter. "I don't think anybody can. Good acts get you to Heaven, and evil ones to Hell. That's how it works, and that's the best way to put it as far as I know."

"Yes, you mentioned that before," agreed Torval, "but I am convinced people do not do good acts simply to ensure their passage to Heaven upon death. There is more to it than that. Christine Anderson does not volunteer at a soup kitchen in order to be rewarded when she dies. That in and of itself is inherently selfish, and there is nothing whatsoever selfish about her."

"Ah, so this isn't about good or evil at all, is it?" Prelz chuckled loudly. "This is about Christine! You really have a thing for her, don't you?"

Torval looked away, lost in thought, paying little attention to his surroundings as he meandered down the cracked and broken sidewalk. "She baffles me," he admitted after a moment. "When I am around her, I experience confusing emotions and sensations that no other human evokes, not even Shelly Mendez. Initially I thought it was this body's attraction to Christine's, but that has proven itself to not be the case. At least, not entirely. Even now, I want to return to her side, to talk to her, to be near her . . . by Lucifer, it is maddening!"

Prelz slapped his companion on the back with a loud, barking laugh. "Ha! I do believe you're in love, Torval! Imagine that! A demon in love!"

"Love?" Torval shook his head in confusion. "What is this love?"

"Some say it's what makes the world go 'round, my friend," said Prelz wryly, "even more so than money. It's a feeling humans have when they want to be together, and they can't stop thinking about each other. When they care so much about one person that they matter more than themselves."

"But that does not describe me," argued Torval, a bit worried by that description. He did not want to be afflicted by an emotion quite that strong, one that sounded capable of overwhelming his conscious mind completely. "I only wish to be near Christine in order to learn more about humanity, in order to benefit myself when I return home."

"That's what you say, but I'm not so sure. You're certainly acting like a lovesick teenager!"

Torval found Prelz's comments somewhat irritating, so he tried to change the subject. "I do have more questions, about a great many things—" he began.

"Oh, no you don't, we're going to talk about Christine some more!" interrupted Prelz, grinning as he continued to dig for information from his increasingly uncomfortable-looking companion. "How did your little chat go? Anything I need to know about?"

Torval sighed resignedly. "We spoke of my job, and then I tried to find out more about why she was such a good person, but I learned little of interest."

"I'm not surprised. You can't just ask a human why they're good or evil. They won't be able to answer, and even if they could, they probably wouldn't want to."

"Yes, I believe I discerned that very fact," pointed out Torval. "There was another issue, however. Christine indicated that she was going somewhere this evening, and that this was different and unusual."

"So?"

"I was unable to ascertain what this journey of hers involved, but I would like to know more. I owe Christine a great deal, and seeing as how I will not have funds for some time, I would like to find out if I can repay her in some other manner. Perhaps some clue can be had from the nature of her trip this night."

"Oh, I get it," said Prelz, catching on at last. "Fine, I'll see if I can find out what she's up to. Hmm, here's a question for you. Why do you feel like you have to repay her at all? She didn't ask you for anything in return for those favors, did she?"

"No," admitted Torval, "and in fact, she refused to accept repayment, but nonetheless I feel it important to reciprocate. This has something to do with the nature of goodness. I am trying to understand, and perhaps by doing good, I can evoke those feelings in myself that Christine seems to find so important."

"Ah, gotcha. Makes sense. You know, come to think of it, there may be someone else you can talk to about this stuff. I'll see if he's willing to meet with you. What time are you done with work?"

"I am not certain," replied Torval. "Lincoln did not say precisely, but I believe I was to stay through the night."

"Fine, then I'll just hang out near the shelter around breakfast tomorrow. Come find me around eightish, and maybe I'll know more. Anyway, looks like we're here. Time for you to go get some work done."

Torval looked up as they finished crossing another street, and sure enough, he spotted the bright sign advertising Roxton Auto Parts. The place looked radically different at night, as the high-walled warehouse turned dark save for a few faintly glowing bulbs that shone with a pale reddish hue. The walkway to the front door was cloaked in shadow, although a gleam from within indicated someone remained inside. Probably Pete Roxton, waiting to lock him in for the evening, as Lincoln had explained so many hours ago.

Pete Roxton! Torval felt another wave of unease at that name. The way Christine spoke about him, and the expression on her face, unsettled Torval greatly. She liked Pete, obviously, and that bothered the demon, despite his desires to the contrary.

Still, Pete was now Torval's boss, or one of his bosses anyway. He'd have to put those strange, irritating feelings out of the way when dealing with the man. After all, he wanted to do a good job so he could keep his flop, get fed, and eventually earn enough money with which he could repay Christine.

"Very well," he said with a sigh, tugging absently on his coat as he pressed forward toward the warehouse door. "I will talk to you tomorrow."

"Good luck, Joe," said Prelz with a grin. "You're gonna need it."

# Chapter 18

Torval entered the warehouse and found himself in the same foyer he'd seen that same morning, except this time there were no customers. In fact, there was no one there at all. The desk, where the clerk took orders and answered the phone, stood vacant.

Not sure what to do, he glanced back out the windowed door, but Prelz could no longer be seen along the darkened street corner. He must've already departed, leaving Torval on his own.

Not wishing to proceed further into the building and offend his new employers, the demon occupied himself looking around the waiting room. There were some chairs, but he didn't use them. Instead he shuffled about, reading the various signs advertising automobile parts with meaningless names like "transmission" and "carburetor." Vaguely he recalled hearing Lincoln Roxton mention similar items that morning, but they held no more meaning now than they did then. Perhaps this would be another subject to research in the library.

In due course a man Torval didn't know emerged from the depths of the warehouse, speaking backward over his shoulder. "Well, I'm outta here," the short, burly human said to someone unseen. The new arrival wore a blue uniform shirt like the one Torval had observed on other employees of this place, and he sported a thick, bushy black mustache the same color as his long, greasy hair. "You have a good time tonight, and don't do anything I wouldn't do!"

With that the man laughed at some unknown joke and passed right by Torval without so much as a glance in his direction. Meanwhile, the person he'd spoken to appeared through the same passageway, grinning. "It's a first date, Chuck, there's no chance of that! Now get out of here before I fire your sorry ass."

Torval recognized the second man immediately as Pete Roxton, but he didn't seem to notice Joe standing off to one side. The demon, conditioned not to interrupt his superiors without cause, remained silent while the conversation continued.

"Ah, you're just jealous 'cause I got a wife and kids to go home to," responded Chuck, stopping at the exit with the door half open.

"Oh yeah, just what I need, somebody to tie me down, and kill my independent lifestyle! That's fine, you go back to the wife, and sleep well knowing I'm out on the town doing whatever I want tonight."

"You do that," the man named Chuck responded with a chuckle. "I wouldn't trade my life for yours, that's for sure. Have a good time!"

"See ya tomorrow," replied Pete, but there was no sign that the other had heard him, for he'd already gone out the door. Pete stood there shaking his head for a moment, still grinning, before turning to his new employee. Apparently he'd noticed Joe after all.

"Glad you made it," said Pete, glancing at his watch. "Good thing you're a few minutes early, 'cause I got a hot date, as I'm sure you heard. Come on, let's get you downstairs."

"Very well," agreed Torval, following his new boss as they headed for the staircase he remembered seeing that morning. The rest of the warehouse looked mostly dark, suggesting Pete was quite possibly the only other person here. Once he departed, Torval would be alone in this place, but that didn't bother him at all. For the most part, he'd been alone for his entire existence, unless the self-absorbed souls of punished mortals counted as companions.

As Torval followed his employer down into the dank and poorly lit basement, Pete turned the conversation to business. "Joe Sampson, that's your last name, right? I think that's what you said, but I'm not real good at names."

"Yes, it is," agreed Torval immediately.

"Well, Joe, here's the thing. Most of the time, an employee has to fill out all these forms, like W-4s and shit like that. You know?"

"Not really." Torval had no idea what Pete was talking about. Well, that wasn't entirely true. He knew what a form was—prisoners like Bob Collins had to fill out such things as part of their punishment, and of course Torval himself dealt with a form at the employment bureau that morning. What a W-4 might be, though, he had no clue.

"Good answer, my friend," replied Pete with another of those big grins that seemed quite common on his rugged, disconcertingly handsome face. "We're gonna get along real well, I can tell that already. Anyways, the employment people, they want forms so they can track what we pay you and how much you earn so you can get taxed, and so they can keep their eye on all of us, y'know? Well, this job you have here, it's not really like that. What we're doing here is sort of like adoption, if you get my drift. You've come to live with us, here on the premises, like a long lost son of my grandpa's, and that means when we give you money, it's kinda like a gift, you see?"

"Yes, I am familiar with gifts," replied Torval. He didn't understand quite what was going on here, but he knew deception when he heard it. Pete's explanation suggested he wanted to bypass the proper procedures, whatever those were. Torval would never have attempted such a thing back home, as something like that would've earned him a severe punishment, or worse. Here, though, exploiting loopholes may well be commonplace and ordinary. He resolved to inquire with Prelz later, but for now he just allowed Pete to continue talking.

"Good, I was hoping you were." Pete stopped walking, having arrived in the storage room Torval visited earlier in the day. The place looked exactly the same, although perhaps a few things had been moved around—he couldn't be sure. "Now, what that means is there ain't gonna be any stupid forms, and you ain't gonna go tellin' anybody you got this job. Understand?"

"Well, I've already told a few people," admitted Torval worriedly. "I told a few . . . friends."

"Oh, that's cool, that's cool," replied Pete, slapping the demon on the shoulder reassuringly. "You can tell friends. I mean, don't tell no officials, got it? Don't worry, this works out great for all of us. You don't have to pay taxes, and neither do we. It's all under the table."

Torval looked around for a table, but didn't see one. Would his pay actually be handed to him underneath a piece of furniture? Probably not—just another human euphemism, he realized. "I understand," he lied smoothly. "I do not wish to pay taxes in any case."

Actually, the more he thought about this arrangement, the better it sounded. He'd been instructed not to draw any attention to himself or the old life his body once led. If the name "Joe Sampson" started appearing on official documents, that could create complications. Better to stay unnoticed.

This job sounded better and better all the time!

Pete nodded, pleased to see his new subordinate in such total agreement. "Good, now that we got that settled, here's the deal. See the fridge over there? We got a box of fried chicken for you, and I even grabbed a couple sodas for ya. The Colonel himself provided your meal tonight." He opened the door to the small mini-fridge, indicating a red and white package bearing the stylized image of an old man with a pointed beard. Torval caught a whiff of the scent coming out of the box and felt himself salivating already. He felt hungry again, the empty feeling in his gut striking suddenly and without warning.

"Now," went on Pete, closing the refrigerator and moving to the open door opposite, "as to work, I'm sure my grandpa explained you had to clean this here bathroom. There's some cleaning stuff in the box here." He kicked at a cardboard container on the floor, beneath the sink. "Give it your best shot. I don't care if you eat, sleep, then work, or work then sleep then eat, or whatever order you want. Just get as much of the bathroom clean as you can before I get in tomorrow morning. Although, if I'm lucky, maybe I'll be late." He chuckled to himself. "Any questions?"

Torval stepped across the basement and poked his head in the bathroom. Turning on the light, he beheld a chamber that clearly hadn't been cleansed in years. His earlier distant look at the room didn't really do it justice. The sink, urinal and toilets were soiled with rings of dark brown or black stains, and the floor was coated with dust and grime as well as patches of oil and grease. The entire area reeked, even worse than the bums he knew, or he himself when he first arrived on this world. A curtain in the back of the room concealed a small shower like the one in Christine's apartment, but Torval didn't feel the need to look there yet, figuring it would probably be just as unclean as the rest of the place.

After that, he looked down into the box of supplies. He first noticed several bottles of liquids in various colors, from blue and yellow to a kind of sickly brown. Another cylindrical container all but glowed in neon green, with blue powder scattered about its flat metal top. In between these items lay a number of brushes of various shapes and sizes, as well as several tools and a trio of long wires with short fuzzy bristles sticking out in all directions.

Torval shut his eyes and tried to remember the cell in which one of his prisoners, a small Oriental man named Haji Chou, endured his torture. In life, Haji was a ruthless leader of a criminal organization that thought itself above the law. Those who crossed him were often killed by having their faces shoved into toilets until they drowned. As punishment, Haji cleaned an endlessly dirty lavatory for all eternity, and in a subtle irony, the toilet often filled itself with blood. If he didn't clean that out quickly, it would congeal, wracking his body with acidic burns.

Torval could remember some of the procedures the unfortunate Haji had to employ. The bottled chemicals were unfamiliar to the demon, but he understood the basic idea. They would be poured on various surfaces where they would dissolve the dirt and grime, whereupon the stains could be easily wiped away.

Wiped away... that could be a problem. Torval turned to Pete. "I do have a few questions. First, what will I wipe the dirt with? I see no towels or rags here."

Pete grinned yet again. "Sharp-eyed, too, I like that. I was wondering if you'd notice. Here you go." He stepped across the room and picked up a closed box Torval hadn't noticed until that moment. "There's some rags in here. Use whatever you need and toss the dirty ones back in the box. What's your next question?"

"What happens if I run out of any of these supplies?" inquired Torval. "Are there replacements elsewhere?"

"Oh, you shouldn't run out," replied Pete, kicking at the box again. "All those bottles are full, or mostly full anyway. We never really used them much ourselves, y'know? I know this room is pretty bad, but you shouldn't need more than what you have. If you do run out—no, wait, strike that. Don't run out. If you run out, you did something wrong, got it?"

"Understood," said Torval immediately. "I have one final question. What happens if I finish?"

"Heh, that's a good one! You ain't gonna finish, my friend. This room will take more than one night to clean. Just do the best you can. When I come in tomorrow, we'll discuss your performance."

"Very well. However, in the off chance that something does go wrong, or that I believe I can do no more on this task tonight, what else shall I do? Is there anything else?"

"No, no, just go to sleep when you're done," sighed Pete. "Oh yeah, one last thing before I forget. These files here, they're all private, right? And the door over there, the one that says keep out—well, don't go in. I think you got told that already, but just in case, I'm warning you now. Got it?"

"Yes, sir," said Torval, glancing over at the closed door with the conspicuous "Keep Out" sign. They didn't want him seeing what was back there, did they? "I believe I have no further questions," the demon concluded.

"Good." Pete glanced at the watch on his wrist and became suddenly anxious. "Oh, geez, I'm gonna be late! I gotta head out, so you have a good night, Joe. I'll lock the door up top so you won't be getting out of here again until tomorrow morning, okay?"

"Yes, I am prepared," stated Torval. He figured he should say something else then, although the usual "thank you" didn't seem quite appropriate in this case. Remembering what Chuck had said earlier, Torval repeated the words. "Have a good time," he said flatly.

"Oh, I intend to! You too, Joe. You too."

* * *

Once the banging sounds of Pete's departure finally faded, Torval decided to eat his dinner before commencing work. For one thing, the smell of the fried chicken awakened his appetite, and for another, handling food after cleaning the disgusting bathroom sounded quite unappealing.

He took the box out of the refrigerator and inspected the contents. There were strange oblong shapes covered with a kind of rough brown coating, as well as a yellowish, round cake and two small containers similar to the ones that held the soup he took to Hal the night before. Torval had no idea what this food might be, but the aroma assaulting his nose suggested it must be quite tasty indeed.

Nor was he disappointed. Unsure of what to do, he simply picked up one of the brown objects, this one shaped roughly like a small club, and took a bite. Savory juices flowed into the corners of his mouth, bringing with them an amazing flavor like nothing he'd ever experienced before. He tore off a chunk of chicken and chewed it voraciously, enjoying every moment. Even the pizza he'd had for lunch paled in comparison to this incredible taste sensation.

For the next several minutes he rapaciously devoured the three pieces of chicken in the box. Each had a different shape and consistency, but was basically the same: chewy, savory meat locked within a spicy, crunchy exterior, all of it clinging to skeletal remnants that were themselves inedible. Torval found himself going over and over the bones with his fingers and teeth, seeking out and consuming every tiny fragment of meat he could find.

When he finished cleaning off the last of the thigh, he worked on the biscuit and then moved on to the mashed potatoes and green beans in the plastic containers. These foods were interesting in their own way, and quite satisfying, but didn't hold a candle to the chicken.

When he finally completed his meal, Torval sighed happily, patted his full stomach a couple of times, and looked once again at the red and white box with the old man's face on the side. Whoever this Colonel was who donated the food, he certainly owed the man a favor! If nothing else, he should seek him out and tell him how much he enjoyed the meal.

Torval did, however, find his mouth somewhat dry, and recalled Pete saying something about "sodas" to drink. There were two cans inside the refrigerator, near where the box had been sitting. Each of the red cylinders had the name "Coca-Cola" printed on the side in sweeping calligraphy. Torval picked one up, finding it cold to the touch, but not so much that he couldn't handle the can. Now he just had to figure out how to open it.

The top looked like it might come off, so he pulled on it a bit and twisted a few times, but got no results. The remainder of the metal had no seams whatsoever. Was he supposed to cut it open somehow?

After a minute or so of study, he noticed the odd tab resting flat against the top, next to an oval-shaped inscription on the surface. He tried turning this device from one side to the other, but nothing happened. Then he lifted it, figuring it might be some sort of lever, and found only one side moved. In fact, as he pulled upwards, the opposing tip pressed into the inscribed area, and a satisfying hiss resulted. Torval lifted harder and was rewarded with the oval section popping into the can, revealing a brown liquid that bubbled and fizzed as if boiling, despite its coldness.

Happy to have solved this puzzle, Torval sipped at the beverage and found himself surprised by the sweet yet bitter taste, and the way the bubbles frothed within his mouth. The chilled liquid, sugary taste, and fizzing sensation on his tongue combined in a most intriguing and enjoyable way. He drank down another swallow, and then another. The more he drank, the more intense the pleasurable burning sensation in his throat.

Suddenly he realized the can was empty. Without even realizing it, he'd guzzled the entire contents! Was he really that thirsty or did he just enjoy the taste that much? Perhaps a little of both.

Torval reached for the second can, but stopped himself short. Something about this liquid concerned him—the way he found himself wanting more, so suddenly and unexpectedly. He felt a sinking sensation in his chest as he suddenly realized he might've just consumed alcohol. What if he became drunk, as Joe would've wanted so badly to do? What if the chemical addled his brain and made him fail to perform his assigned tasks? He would fail, and be back on the street, and worse yet he'd disappoint Christine to the point where she'd never speak to him again!

He looked at the empty can fearfully. There were smaller words printed on it and he read these with great concern. Some of the words explained what the liquid contained, including things like caramel colors, sugar and caffeine, as well as other words Torval doubted he could pronounce—but, thankfully, none of these were "alcohol."

Breathing a sigh of relief, he considered drinking the other soda, but in the end chose not to. He would be here a long time tonight and that other can seemed to be the only beverage available. In fact, come to think of it, he probably shouldn't have eaten all the food in one sitting, but it was just so good he couldn't help himself.

He closed the refrigerator door, set the bone- and trash-filled box aside, and moved to the bathroom. His fingers were sticky, so he used the sink to clean them, only to find the water didn't go out the drain. Well, that wasn't completely true—it drained, just not very quickly. Torval frowned. That would just make the cleaning process all the harder.

He looked around for something to use to dry his hands and decided to use one of the clean rags. As he moved to pick up the cardboard box, his eyes chanced to fall on the forbidden door. The words "KEEP OUT" seemed to scream at him in giant red letters. What could possibly be back there that the Roxtons didn't want him to see?

For a moment, Torval considered finding out the answer for himself. Nobody could see him, so he could just take a peek without harming anything. There didn't seem to be a lock, either, as far as he could tell—

just a somewhat rusty-looking doorknob that practically begged to be turned.

He was about to take a step toward the door when he stopped himself, shaking his head at his own foolishness. Why did he care what that portal concealed? Nothing back there could possibly interest him, and besides, he'd been specifically ordered not to look. So why would he want so badly to defy his employers?

All at once he realized this was another human weakness—curiosity. In fact, he'd just experienced nothing less than pure temptation. So, Prelz was right about that! Humans didn't need demons to tempt them. The seeds of that particular flaw were inherent in their psyches.

Torval turned away from the door. He was no weak human to fall victim to such a simple thing as curiosity! Best to get started working and put that door's tempting secrets out of his mind, where they belonged.

The cleaning products in the box were unfamiliar, but the names and descriptions on the sides explained their purpose. The brown liquid would clean water stains; the yellow, porcelain surfaces; the blue, windows and mirrors; and, finally, the lavender substance would remove clogs. The cylinder of powder advertised itself for use specifically in toilets.

The brushes were another matter, as they had no convenient labels to describe their uses. He found one shaped like a kind of ring on the end of a stick, and several others of various sizes, with bristles ranging from soft to rigid. One of the implements was very small, and with a start Torval recognized it as a well-worn toothbrush, like the one he'd used that morning in Christine's apartment. Was he expected to brush his teeth as well? Surely not, considering that the bristles were coated with dark gray stains. Ah, he realized, this particular item must be used to clean small spaces.

How interesting that a device as simple as a toothbrush could be used for cleaning more than just teeth! He doubted he would've considered that option if he hadn't seen one sitting here in this box.

Torval sighed, figuring he might as well begin with the sink. In order to get the water to drain, he would have to use the clog remover first. He followed the instructions, only to find he had to wait a while to see results. Fine, there were plenty of other things he could be doing in the meantime.

He moved on to the first of the two toilets and reached for the green powder. After scrubbing for a few minutes, he'd seen almost no change at all. The thick grime barely budged, so he noticed only a slight lightening of the color in some spots. The more he worked, though, the better it looked, but his arm quickly became sore as well. He changed hands and continued his task, switching off every time his muscles got weary.

After half an hour, he could tell he'd made slow but steady progress. Clearly this wouldn't be a job he could finish quickly. Pete Roxton's assessment that this task would take quite a while appeared to be correct.

Whether he could finish it tonight, Torval didn't know, but he was determined to try. He knew from what he'd been told that his performance would be evaluated, and if he didn't do well, he might lose this job. Besides, he told himself, think of the rewards! His own place to sleep, with a roof over his head and warm air all around. And, if he did well, actual money, without any taxes to complicate things. He could finally begin to repay all the debts he'd incurred so far, and any new ones as well.

With all of that in mind, he soldiered on well into the night.

# Chapter 19

Vaguely, Torval became aware of voices speaking somewhere nearby. They seemed to be distant, almost like echoes. He blinked and opened his eyes, wincing at the light shining down from the bulbs in the cracked ceiling above. The glow wasn't very bright, but it stung nonetheless.

He'd fallen asleep. He remembered lying down, intending to take a break to ease his weary body. This followed a failed attempt to figure out how to use the hammock, which seemed impossible to climb into. Every time he attempted to lift a foot off the ground, the accursed netting swung and flipped over, tossing him out onto the hard concrete floor. In the end, he decided to simply stay put, closing his eyes for a brief nap.

Not so brief, it seemed. The room's only clock, hanging slightly askew on the wall next to the stairs, told him he'd slept until a quarter past six—almost five hours!

Cursing his frail human body for what must've been the hundredth time, Torval sat up and stretched, yawning widely. His back and shoulders ached, probably from lying on the uncomfortable floor all night long, but that hardly bothered him. What really hurt were the muscles of his arms and neck, which he'd stressed beyond their usual tolerances by his efforts to scrub the bathroom clean. Some of the stains and rings proved quite stubborn, but Torval was a persistent demon, and he refused to let the weaknesses of his human form stop him if at all possible.

He regretted not finishing, though. At the point where he decided he finally needed a break, he'd already completed his second pass through all of the fixtures in the bathroom. He felt fairly confident the toilets would pass inspection, as they'd been his primary focus. The sink, now unclogged after several applications of the blue liquid (which surprised him by the strange way in which it foamed upon contact with water), should function sufficiently for Pete's purposes.

Torval regretted failing to complete his work on the shower. The basin began the evening coated with a variety of different layers of greasy muck that proved quite resistant to the chemicals at his command. Furthermore, the flat, rectangular brush that had the most luck scrubbing away the offending dirt quickly became caked over with a white soapy residue that wouldn't come off easily. He found himself spending more time cleaning that sponge than he did the shower.

Worse yet, most of the cracks between the tiles in the shower's wall were blackened with a foul-smelling stain that only very fine bristles would remove. He spent well over an hour going over the horizontal and vertical lines with the toothbrush, doing the best he could to whiten the surface underneath. Even so, when he finally became so tired he could barely keep his eyes open, he hadn't completed the task to his satisfaction. Some of the cracks remained slightly less bright than the others, and he felt certain that would be counted against him at his evaluation.

If only he'd been able to stay up longer! But his body failed him, as it had so many times already. For a while he was fine, toiling away at a measured pace, shifting from task to task as one muscle group or another complained too much at this cruel treatment. After a while, though, he grew thirsty, and consumed the remaining soft drink, and then his eyelids seemed to grow steadily heavier. Then there came a brief period when he felt refreshed, and threw himself back into his labors, but a short while later he could feel his pitiful body collapsing. Sleep was the only answer, and so he succumbed.

Now it was too late to attempt to perform any further labors. He could hear voices from upstairs, and judging by the clock, the morning shift had already arrived. In fact, as he stood and paced about, shaking off the last vestiges of a strangely dreamless rest, he noticed light coming in from the stairwell. The door up top was open.

Curiously, the voices he heard weren't coming from the stairs. Instead, they emanated from another part of the basement. He moved toward the sound, thinking at first that there might be people behind the forbidden door, but in fact the noise came from somewhere near the heating system. Stepping closer, Torval noted that the electric heater was off at the moment, but that wasn't unusual. He'd observed during the course of the evening that the device switched itself on and off at regular intervals, perhaps regulating the level of temperature in the building through some means beyond his comprehension.

With the heater off, the hollow spaces beyond conducted sounds from upstairs. Torval found, by placing his ear close by, that he could actually make out the words. In fact, he could even identify the speakers by the sound of their voices, even though they were somewhat muffled and distorted by echoes.

One of the speakers, quite clearly Pete Roxton, seemed overly eager about something, so Torval listened in. "...wasn't bad at all," the distant voice explained. "We went to a little Chinese place, you know the one on the corner by the little art house? She said she wanted something spicy, and they've got the hottest Szechuan stuff I know."

"Did she like it?" asked the other voice, the one belonging to Lincoln Roxton.

"Yeah, I think so. She ate all of it, anyway. I tried to pay for hers, but she wouldn't hear any of it. Y'know, I bet she would've paid for mine too if I'da let her."

A hollow-sounding chuckle echoed down the vent. "That sounds about right. You gonna see her again?"

"I hope so," said Pete. "We didn't really have time to do anything but eat and talk, although I have to admit I did suggest a bit more, but she didn't really like the idea. Probably 'cause we both had work in the morning, but I'm gonna ask if she wants to do something tonight, since it's Friday."

"Good for you. See if you can take it a little slower this time, my boy. This isn't the usual kind of woman you go out with. She probably doesn't want to rush right into the sack."

"Yeah, well, I can tell that already, but don't worry, it's not like this is the only thing I've got going on right now."

"Son, I don't know where you learned to play the field like you do, but it sure as hell wasn't from me." Torval thought he caught a distant air of disapproval in the elder Roxton's words, although it was hard to tell through the vent's echoing distortion. "Anyway, enough about your dating habits. What can you tell me about our new employee?"

There was a pause, and Torval felt his chest tightening. Some part of him suggested that perhaps listening in on this conversation wasn't entirely proper, but it wasn't his fault they weren't doing enough to keep their words to themselves. Besides, he really wanted to hear Pete's honest evaluation as quickly as possible.

"Well," said Pete after a moment, "I don't really think you'll believe it until you see it. Seriously."

"That bad, huh?" inquired Lincoln.

"No . . . that good! The bathroom is spotless, and I ain't kidding, either! I've never seen porcelain glow like that! I think he must've worked all through the night until he just dropped. He even fell out of the hammock and didn't even notice! When I went down there, he was curled up on the floor, and he was so out of it he didn't even wake up when I checked his work. I bet he didn't get more than an hour of sleep, if that."

"Hmm, sounds promising," Lincoln went on. "He really did that good a job, eh?"

"Well, it wasn't one hundred percent perfect, but pretty damn close," Pete answered. "He didn't clean up the brushes afterward and didn't put anything away, but that's about the only thing I could even hope to complain about. I'm serious, Pops, that's the most amazing feat of cleaning I think I've ever seen! If you ain't impressed, I don't know if impressing you is even possible."

Torval took a deep breath. That feeling of swelling in his chest came over him again. Pride, he knew. There was something very satisfying about listening to Pete's words. In all his hundreds of years of existence as a demon, he'd never heard praise like this.

Actually, he'd never heard praise at all. Compliments, especially like Pete's, were just as savory as the chicken he'd consumed for dinner, if not more so.

Even as he puffed himself up, Lincoln Roxton continued to speak. "Well, good, glad to hear he's a hard worker. He certainly seemed eager enough after our interview yesterday. What about the other thing, though?"

"Oh, the door?" Pete paused again, and Torval realized he had to be talking about the forbidden portal. "Yeah, that's the best part. He didn't open it."

"And the files?"

"Didn't look in those either, near as I can tell."

Lincoln didn't say anything for a moment, and Torval wondered if perhaps somehow he'd made a mistake. Was he actually supposed to look inside the secret room after all? Was telling him not to look actually some sort of bizarre human code to do it anyway?

The answer came after a couple more seconds. "Amazing," said Lincoln, sounding rather surprised. "An actual honest man, here in our city! Who would've thought?"

Pete laughed heartily. "Not me, that's for sure. I'm damn sure if someone locked me in a room and told me not to look at something, I'd take a peek the first chance I got. Not this guy."

"Well," said Lincoln, "I suppose that means he's passed the first test. Didn't really think we'd find anybody trustworthy so quickly, or ever for that matter, but there he is. Want to go on to the next step?"

"Sure, if you don't mind the risk."

"Well, I don't really like that part, but we already agreed this was the best way to go about it, didn't we?"

"Yeah."

"Well then, let's—"

That was the moment when the heater decided, for whatever reason, to reactivate, overwhelming the conversation with a hissing rush of air. Surprised by the sudden sound, Torval jerked his head away and banged his temple against the side of the vent. The brief pain dazed him for a second, but he shook it off. Unfortunately, he could no longer hear the conversation from upstairs, but that didn't matter. He'd heard what he needed to hear.

So, he'd done well! The pride in Torval's heart felt like a kind of mild euphoria, making him feel light and buoyant. Furthermore, because he'd been so productive, he'd earned the right to go on to "the next step," whatever that meant. Perhaps a promotion or some other sort of new opportunity—and maybe the chance to earn some actual money!

Well, he'd find out soon enough, but for now Torval had another task. Pete just mentioned a failing that would be easy to correct, so the demon moved over to the bathroom and started picking up the cleaning supplies and brushes. Most of the latter were quite soiled, so he spent a few minutes cleaning them off as best he could in the sink. Once finished, he used the last remaining clean rag to wipe out the leftover debris, leaving the porcelain surface absolutely spotless. As a final step, he piled everything into its original boxes and placed these where he'd initially seen them when he'd arrived the previous night.

Just as he finished, he heard footsteps on the stairs. Standing almost at attention in the doorway, he awaited the approach of the two Roxtons. They spoke in low voices, but stopped as soon as they reached the basement floor.

"Ah, there you are," said the older man. "My grandson here has been raving about your work, Joe. Let's take a look."

He pushed past Torval and stared for a moment at the demon's handiwork. The room was, indeed, all but spotless. Torval's fears of disappointing his boss by not finishing were completely unfounded. His many years as a Third-Class demon made him something of a perfectionist, something that surprised the Roxtons. In fact, there were few people in the world who would've been disappointed by what they saw in that shining little room.

Lincoln turned to Torval. "My boy, this is without a doubt the cleanest bathroom I have ever seen in my entire life. This is some amazing work. How the hell did you do this, anyway?"

"I scrubbed," explained Torval. "I scrubbed very hard. I apologize if I used too much of the cleaning supplies in the process, but some of the stains were quite stubborn."

"I don't care about that! I can't imagine how anyone could've done this in one night. Are you sure you're human?"

Torval almost gasped with shock. Had he unwittingly blown his cover by doing too good a job? But no, the question was merely rhetorical. Lincoln Roxton had no idea he was talking to anything other than a man. "Yes, I am human," Torval reassured him quickly. "I simply wished to do an effective job. I did not want to disappoint you."

"You didn't, my boy. You sure didn't! In fact, since you did such a wonderful job, you've earned a special bonus assignment. That is, if you're up to it."

"I would definitely be interested," said Torval at once, happy to have thrown the old man back on track. "What is the nature of this assignment?"

"Pete'll explain it," Lincoln answered. "I need to get upstairs and get started on some accounting work before the rest of the crew shows up. Don't worry, though, it won't be a problem for someone with your obvious attention to detail. Once again, good work, Joe. You're gonna work out great around this place."

"Thank you, sir," replied Torval, even as Lincoln departed and headed back up the stairs.

Once he was gone, Pete put on another one of his affable grins. "You've done the impossible, man. You impressed my grandpa. Didn't think I'd ever see that happen."

"I only wished to do the best job I could," replied Torval honestly. "Is that so unusual?"

"Hell yes it is!" insisted Pete. "Especially the kind of people we get around here. Buncha slackers, I tell ya. Every one of 'em. Not you, though. I've never seen anybody work so hard for a job, especially not like this."

"As I said, I wish to get off the streets and live in a place of my own. I did not want to lose that opportunity by performing poorly on my first day."

"Well, you keep up this kind of work, and you can stay here as long as you want, my friend. Anyway, now let's get on with it, shall we? Let's go upstairs—I have something to show you."

"Yes, sir," replied Torval, following in Pete's footsteps as he headed upstairs, walking briskly down a hall and into an office. The small compartment was horribly cluttered, especially the desktop, which looked all but invisible underneath piles of scattered papers. Ironically, the stacked-together inbox and outbox stood empty.

"All right," said Pete, reaching underneath the desk, "here's what we need you to do." Reaching behind the desk, he withdrew a small black attaché case, the kind with a built-in combination lock set underneath the handle. "A certain customer of ours is expecting a delivery fairly soon. Normally we, um, hire some extra help to make the arrangements, but with you working out so well, we're going to let you do it for us today. All you have to do is take this briefcase to an address I'll give you, hand it over to the man waiting inside, and bring what he gives you back to me. There's more to this that will come later, but for now that's how you'll get started. Sound good?"

Torval nodded, seeing nothing unusual whatsoever with this arrangement. Instead of being a janitor, he would now make deliveries. Back home, there were Fourth-Class demons assigned to such tasks, ferrying messages here and there throughout Hell's many crevices and layers. Although this job fell beneath Torval's demonic classification, it certainly seemed to be a step up in the ranks of the human hierarchy.

"Yes, sir, I believe I understand the task," he said readily.

"Well, there's a nice bonus in it for you," went on Pete. "If you bring me back the package my associate is holding, safely and without opening it, there's a hundred bucks in it for you. Cash. How does that strike ya?"

Torval almost gasped. A hundred dollars! That was more money than he'd ever seen, and far more than he ever expected. That much cash would buy him meals for days, perhaps even for the rest of his time here on Earth. Or, even better, he could spend some of it repaying his debts to Christine.

The possibility that the extra pay might be anything other than an honest wage for his work didn't occur to Torval at all. Instead, he agreed readily to Pete's proposal. "I will do it. When do I begin, and where do I go?"

Pete grinned and stood up, leaving the briefcase on his desk. "I knew I could count on you, Joe! I'll leave this here while you go freshen up a bit. You can even take a shower if you want—you've certainly earned the right, since you're the one who cleaned it out! Anyway, a couple of my workers bring in donuts in the morning, so by the time you get back here, you can have breakfast too. Then I'll give you the details on where to go and all that."

"Very well," agreed Torval. "I will return shortly."

As he turned to leave, he saw a different sort of expression on Pete's face, a kind of sly smirk instead of his usual friendly smile. There was more to this arrangement than he'd just explained, Torval knew at once, but whatever that might be, he supposed he'd learn about it in time. After all, Pete did say this was just the beginning.

Torval dismissed Pete's odd expression as just another of his employer's quirks and headed downstairs to enjoy a much-needed shower.

# Chapter 20

Torval's third day on Earth began even better than the last. The day was sunny once again, and the arctic chill of his first night on the planet had been replaced by a warm breeze that made his jacket entirely unnecessary. At present, he had the garment folded in half and balanced across the top of Pete's briefcase, which he held carefully and firmly in his right hand as he strode down the crowded street.

The shower he'd just enjoyed left him feeling refreshed and wide awake. However, after cleansing himself thoroughly, Torval found to his dismay that he had no clean clothing to wear. Putting on yesterday's outfit felt decidedly uncomfortable, but he did it anyway. After all, he literally had no other choice.

He also found he had no way to brush his teeth, which was unfortunate because over the course of several hours of sleep, they became coated with a distasteful residue probably left over from his second soft drink the night before. He wasn't about to use the grime-coated brush from the cleaning supplies, so he had to settle for just swishing water around in his mouth and using his tongue as best he could.

Not that it would've mattered much anyway, for as soon as Torval went upstairs, Pete handed him a donut. The disc-shaped cake, covered in a coating of sweet glaze, contained a sticky purple goo with a tart, tangy flavor. As with most of the foods he'd tried, Torval found himself amazed by the taste, devouring the donut quickly and then digging into a second one. While Pete jokingly remarked that Joe "looked like a man who'd never had breakfast before," Torval simply lost himself in the incredible sensations coming from his mouth.

He wanted another, but Pete closed the box before he could reach in and turned the discussion to business. He explained that Torval should deliver the briefcase to a man in a certain apartment in a place called the "Lower East Side," at an address written on a card now in Torval's possession. Seemed simple enough, the demon thought at the time.

There were additional rules, of course, as he quickly learned. The briefcase could only be handed over to a specific person at the given address, not to anyone else. Torval must then return by lunchtime with "the package," whatever that might be. He wasn't to look inside either item or allow them to fall into anyone else's hands but those who they were intended for. Finally, he wasn't to discuss the nature of this task with anyone other than the Roxtons.

As soon as Torval indicated that he understood these requirements, Pete ushered him out of the building. Once outside, his boss handed Torval a plastic rectangular card, the purpose of which wasn't stated, and gave him his final instructions. "You'll probably want to take the subway, 'cause the Lower East Side is pretty far. Here, take my spare MetroCard, which I'll want back later. I'd suggest heading over to Rockefeller Center and taking the F south to the Second Avenue station, or maybe Delancey Street. After that you'll have to look around, but I'm sure you'll find it. You strike me as a pretty resourceful guy. Good luck!"

Torval started to protest that he had no idea what Pete was talking about, but hesitated, unsure whether he should profess ignorance when in fact, as a native of this city, he may well be expected to understand those directions. In the brief moment he stood there, trying to make up his mind, Pete waved goodbye and went back inside, presumably to begin his work for the day.

That left Torval with two choices: Go back in and ask for more information, or proceed with his task and figure things out as he went. He chose not to bother Pete and instead started walking, heading in the general direction of the shelter. Once at the next block, out of sight of the warehouse amidst the seething crowds, he stepped into an alcove and caught his breath.

If anything, the city seemed even busier than the day before. The snow had by now melted almost completely, leaving the roads and sidewalks dry. The warmer air changed the way people dressed, allowing them to go coatless, and now the outfits they wore seemed brighter and more expressive. In fact, everything about the streets seemed to glitter and gleam in the morning sunlight, as if some shadow had lifted and everything turned bright and shiny.

Torval, too, felt buoyed by the good weather and comfortable temperature, but also by his opportunity to complete a bonus task for his employers. When he first arrived here, he had a simple goal to acquire food and shelter for himself. Now, with those things secured, it felt good to have another purpose. Now he just had to complete his task, and all would be well.

He looked again at the address on the business card Pete provided. He'd found a street address, as with Shelly Mendez's note, but he had no idea where this location might be. The street had a name, "Bowery," but that meant nothing to him. Perhaps it would have had meaning for Joe Sampson, but those memories were no longer accessible. He would have to find his way there on his own.

Pete did mention using something called a "subway," and indicated Torval needed the "MetroCard" for this procedure. Torval removed the plastic rectangular object from his pocket and looked it over. From the instructions printed on the surface, he needed to slide this device into some sort of machine in a certain way. Where this might be and what purpose it served, Torval had no idea.

There were other instructions, the most critical of which involved finding a place called "Rockefeller Center" where this mysterious "subway" could be accessed. Torval looked around, studying the many signs posted on the buildings around him, but saw nothing that indicated any of them had anything to do with Rockefeller Center.

He thought about asking some random passerby for information, but it crossed his mind that he'd arranged to meet Prelz at breakfast time this morning. Certainly the other demon would know where to find this mysterious place.

The walk to the shelter seemed to go faster than last time, perhaps because the weather was better. As he hurried along, keeping pace with the endless flow of humans on their way to work, he passed the street where he'd turned to visit Shelly Mendez the previous day. For a moment he thought about going there again, and a certain part of him wanted to do so very much, but he forced himself to continue on. He could speak with Shelly again when he wasn't on a mission for his new employers.

In due course he came to the shelter, already open with a short line waiting outside. One of those in the line, or rather leaning against the wall close by, was Prelz. The ex-demon spotted Torval at once, gave a short wave, and came over to meet him.

"Mornin'," said Prelz amiably. "How'd it go last night?"

"Very well," replied Torval. "Very well indeed. I was given a kind of human food called 'fried chicken,' which was quite enjoyable. Also a beverage called a 'soda' named 'Coca-Cola.'"

"Heh. I bet you liked that. I remember the first time I tried that stuff. Felt like it was biting into my tongue."

"Yes, that is an accurate description," agreed Torval. "After eating, I proceeded to clean a bathroom. This was much more difficult and time-consuming than I anticipated, but I proceeded in the manner I have seen certain prisoners in Hell accomplishing this task. Fortunately, here on Earth the dirt did not reappear. Nonetheless, I felt my job was incomplete when my body finally failed me. My employers, the Roxtons, did not share my concerns. They felt my performance was above expectations. They were pleased, and for that I was rewarded with a new task."

Prelz nodded. "Good for you. Does that have something to do with that briefcase you're carrying?"

Torval didn't look at the black, hard-shelled case still firmly clenched in his hand. "This? I am sorry, but I am not permitted to speak of it."

"Excuse me?" Prelz cocked his head sideways. "Not permitted by who?"

"My employers. I was given this container with explicit orders not to discuss its purpose with anyone." That much was true, but Pete hadn't told Torval not to talk about the existence of the job itself. "If I complete my bonus assignment, I will be paid one hundred dollars."

Prelz nodded, almost to himself. "I think I'm getting the picture now. You Third-Class types, always so anal-retentive!"

"What does that mean?" inquired Torval, recognizing this as another one of those strange human sayings that seemed to make no sense on its own.

"What I mean is, you have to follow orders exactly, don't you? Fine, you have a secret mission, I guess I can buy that. A hundred bucks, eh? What's in there, anyway? Drugs?"

"I do not know," replied Torval honestly, "and I was also ordered not to find out. I therefore will not do so. As it turns out, I was given this assignment specifically because I did not look inside a secret room. Because of this, the Roxtons feel I can be trusted."

"Funny how a demon is someone they think they can trust," said Prelz, chuckling. "Demons aren't exactly seen as paragons of honesty in human mythology, y'know. If he knew what you really were, you wouldn't be carrying that thing right now."

"Nonetheless, despite my true nature, I will obey my orders." Torval decided to change the subject before Prelz argued the matter further. "Now, I have a question for you that is totally unrelated to this issue. I need to find a particular place, and I was told that to get there, I had to take a subway which could be found at Rockefeller Center. Do you know where that is?"

"Of course I do," replied Prelz, grinning. "Okay, I get it, you have to deliver the briefcase to somebody. You really shouldn't practice deception, my friend—you really aren't very good at it."

Torval sighed in frustration. He did very much want to be more open with Prelz, but felt hamstrung by the command from Pete Roxton. "I am sorry, I cannot discuss the nature of my assignment."

Prelz threw up his hands. "Yeah, yeah, I get it! Fine, look, you and I both know you're a delivery boy for the day, all right? Don't worry, I won't tell anybody. Rockefeller Center is a couple blocks that way, you can't miss it. Look for the subway entrances along the wide parts of the sidewalks nearby. They have signs and staircases heading down underground. Do you know what line you need?"

"Line?"

"Yeah, subway trains have routes, or lines. They're usually letters or numbers."

"Oh. Letters. Yes, I was told I needed to take the 'F.' I did not understand what that meant until now. So, subways are trains?"

"Yeah, underground trains. You'll love 'em."

Torval nodded in understanding. He knew what a train was. There were several prisoners along his route whose cells had something to do with trains. One, a grizzled old man by the name of J. Richard Getz, was in life obsessed with punctuality, demanding it of himself and everyone he knew, including his employees at the railroad yard he owned and operated. Being late by even a minute was grounds for termination. As his punishment, Mr. Getz had to ride an empty train in an endless circle, passing through ever-changing terrain without ever reaching a station.

Of course, that sort of train rode above ground, unlike these mysterious 'subways' that operated beneath the surface. "I see," Torval remarked, thinking once again how innovative these human beings could be. Not content with building vehicles that cut through vast areas of land, they had to build them underneath it as well!

"That look on your face tells me you're clueless," snickered Prelz, "but that's nothing unusual. Ah well, you'll experience it for yourself soon enough. What stop are you getting off at?"

"I was told Second Avenue. Or something called Delany Street."

"Delancey. Got it. Yeah, make sure you take the F line south. Don't go north or you'll wind up in fucking Queens."

Torval didn't know what intercourse with royalty had to do with subway trains, but clearly going north was a mistake he wanted to avoid. "South, then. Very well, that is where I shall go."

"You can't take the subway for free, y'know," cautioned Prelz. "You need some cash for a card?"

"You mean this?" Torval showed the MetroCard, the purpose of which still eluded him. "Is this some sort of alternative type of money with which I will purchase passage on the train?"

"Not exactly," said Prelz, looking rather pleased that he didn't have to hand over any of his hard-earned coins. "The card has a strip on it, see?" He pointed at a brown stripe running along its edge, the same edge that was supposed to be inserted into the as yet unseen scanning device. "There's magnetically encoded bits of info there that tell the computers you've already paid for a ride. That way you don't need cash."

"What is a computer?" inquired Torval, studying the plastic rectangle in his hand. "Where are these 'bits of info' you describe? What does it mean to be magnetically encoded? How does this stripe tell anything to anyone?"

Prelz shrugged, with an expression that suggested he'd known all of those questions were coming. "Hell if I know! Computers are everywhere, man. They're human devices that do some of their thinking for 'em, I guess is the best way to describe it. It's all about automation."

"You are confusing me," admitted Torval. "Why is automation so important?"

"Because it makes things easier and cheaper," explained the other demon. "The subway used to use tokens, but they switched over to this system a few years ago to cut costs. Good move for them, bad for us bums. Used to be we could find tokens all the time and sell 'em to tourists for a lot more than they were worth. Not anymore. 'Course, I do find a card every now and then, which is good too. Better, sometimes, depending on what's on it."

"I believe I understand," Torval interrupted, before Prelz could turn this into another of his long-winded stories. The subject of computers and automation would have to wait for another time. "Thank you for the information, but I must now proceed with my mission." He started to turn away.

"Wait, wait, not so fast," Prelz cut in. "Don't you want to know what I found out last night?"

"About what?"

"You know," said a grinning Prelz. "Her."

"Oh. Christine." Torval turned back to the older demon, amazed that he'd managed to briefly forget the maddeningly lovely social worker. Apparently he'd focused his attentions a bit too tightly on his new assignment. "Yes, of course. Were you able to discover something?"

"You could say that. Look, you probably aren't going to like what I'm about to tell you, I'm just warning you now."

"What is it?" demanded Torval, impatient to hear the news.

"Well," Prelz answered, "I came back here last night like I told you I would. I thought she might be gone by then, but she was still here, just gettin' ready to head out. I watched from the alleyway over here, and she was out by the street, waitin' for somebody. After a few minutes some guy drove up, in some kind of fancy Buick or something. He got out and talked to her for a few seconds, then he opened up the door all gentlemanly-like. Imagine that, somebody who owns their own car in New York! Why not just take a damned taxi?"

As Prelz told his story, Torval felt his chest tightening with irritation. Some man had picked her up, then. That's what she'd been so excited about after she finished serving soup yesterday. A man was taking her out!

Why did he feel such a surge of emotion at that thought? Rationally he knew he shouldn't feel that way, but there was no denying the reaction. Something about Christine made him want her for himself, so much so that the thought of another human spending time with her made him feel . . . what? Not anger, at least as he understood it. Some other petty emotion.

Jealousy, again. He'd felt it before, only far more mildly, when she first exchanged smiles with Pete Roxton, back when Torval first met the man. The emotion seemed so much stronger now, though. He was jealous of this person, whoever it was—this unknown interloper who came and took Christine away at precisely the moment Torval began his work shift.

In fact, that was something of a coincidence, wasn't it? Pete seemed quite eager to leave the warehouse last night, because he was going out on something called a "date" that clearly involved meeting a woman. In fact, come to think of it, he left at just about the same time that—

Torval felt a sudden chill as a horrible thought occurred to him. "Prelz," he asked worriedly, "did you see this man closely? Was he tall, with black hair, and prominent musculature? The features a human female would consider handsome?"

"Yeah, that's about right," agreed Prelz, "but I did better than just get a look at him. I was close enough to hear his name. She said it when she thanked him for helping her into the car."

Torval swallowed hard. "What was it?"

"Pete," replied Prelz, and Torval's heart seemed to sink right through the pavement.

# Chapter 21

Pete Roxton! Torval couldn't get the man out of his head. As the demon walked down the narrow sidewalk, through an area of construction where people could only pass by each other in single file, he tried very hard to focus on his mission, but his thoughts kept going back to his boss, and how he'd "put the moves" on Christine. At least, that's how Prelz described it, just before he and Torval parted ways just a few minutes before.

In addition to his frustration with Pete, Torval also found himself mildly annoyed with Prelz. Instead of trying to be supportive, the other demon actually laughed at Torval's difficulties. "The best thing about this is that you introduced them!" Prelz chuckled, apparently finding the irony greatly amusing. In the end, Torval simply said a flat goodbye and turned away, struggling to control the seething anger and frustration rising in his gut.

Those emotions were mostly contained now, and he knew he shouldn't blame Prelz anyway. None of this was his fault, and although he could've been more tactful about it, the ex-demon seemed naturally spiteful. Was he not once a Tempter, after all, doing his best to prod humans into doing evil? He certainly does seem to be good at it, mused Torval, even if he doesn't do it on purpose.

Besides which, Torval reminded himself, Prelz did do me a favor by discovering some important information. If the former Tempter hadn't reported the connection between Pete and Christine, Torval might never have figured it out on his own. Looking back on it now, it all seemed so obvious, especially the timing of their uncharacteristic activities, but he was so intent on the details of his new job that he hadn't thought about what anyone else might be up to.

Actually, the more he thought about it, the more Torval realized he should've been able to figure all of that out. He'd spent his entire existence keeping track of what human souls were up to in their cells. He thought they were predictable and easy to manage, but now that he'd lived a while amongst them, he knew this wasn't really true at all. Alone, in their programmed illusions, humans could be understood. Here, among others of their kind, constantly interacting with each other in new and unexpected ways, they were impossible to comprehend.

And that's what bothered Torval most. He felt the need to understand humanity, at least partially, in order to succeed in his mission here in the Middle Realm. Yet with every passing hour, the mystery of Man only deepened.

Christine was a perfect example. He'd already spoken with her on several occasions, yet he felt no closer to comprehending her than when he arrived. Furthermore, he wished to get to know her better, but he didn't know how. The phenomenon of romance was unknown to him, and confusing to even contemplate, yet according to Prelz he would have little choice but to try. Obviously, Torval needed more information if he wanted to pursue that path.

Pete Roxton, who already had a head start by virtue of the "date" last night, complicated matters immensely. Pete, having spent his life as a human, already knew the proper way to commence romancing Christine, and in fact started doing so immediately—apparently within mere moments of their first meeting. Torval would need to learn quickly in order to overtake his new rival.

*Rival.* In all his hundreds of years in Hell, he'd never had a rival. There weren't exactly hordes of demons lining up waiting to become Torturers. Those among the Third-Class rank were given specific assignments depending on their nature, and to fill openings created by demons who either had progressed to the next level, or failed in some way and were consigned to demotion or Oblivion. Only when a demon approached the next step in his evolution would he begin to develop aspirations and cravings of power—something Torval had yet to experience for himself.

Prelz was right in pointing out the irony inherent in the situation. Pete wouldn't have met Christine if not for Joe Sampson. In fact, come to think of it, that meant Torval had directly interfered in their lives by being here in Joe's body well after the pitiful wretch died. Yet how could Torval have known? It wasn't as though he arranged the meeting on purpose. Maybe Pete and Christine would've met anyway, for all he knew. Pete already admitted noticing her presence on one of her earlier visits to the warehouse—perhaps their eventual interaction was inevitable.

All of this didn't excuse the terrible emotion he now felt—the awful, heart-wrenching jealousy of Pete Roxton. How did he do it, anyway? How did Pete manage to convince Christine so easily to accept a date that evening? Torval tried to imagine the scenario, but with himself doing the asking, and couldn't. What would he say? "Please come to dinner with me, Christine?" She wouldn't see Torval the demon, she'd see Joe Sampson the bum, with no money and nothing to offer, while waiting in the wings stood Pete, the successful businessman with his ruggedly handsome good looks, his own vehicle, and an apparently charming personality that already intrigued Christine. How could someone like Joe Sampson compete with that?

For some reason, the thought of her rejection chilled Torval to the bone, causing him to involuntarily shudder for a reason other than cold air against his skin. Torval realized then that this was "fear," another decidedly loathsome human emotion. He was a demon—he had no need to fear anything, as not even death mattered to him on this world. Yet here he was, afraid nonetheless.

Afraid of a woman...a human woman who intrigued him by virtue of her very goodness, a concept so foreign that the mere thought of pursuing her left him shaking and weak in the knees. Curse this blessed humanity anyway!

Fortunately, he found something else to think about, for as he turned a corner, following the instructions given to him by Prelz, he found himself staring at Rockefeller Center. The collection of buildings, striking in their art deco design, stood out magnificently against the rest of the skyline. Colorful flags flew from seemingly every terrace, and some of the towers possessed overflowing gardens on various levels. A few of the structures were constructed in unusual shapes, or possessed attractively angular arrangements of windows. Many appeared specialized, such as the one with the eye-catching "Radio City" signs in orange neon.

So, that's the name of this place: Radio City. Until this point, Torval hadn't known that, and although Joe probably did, Torval no longer had access to those memories. The name seemed somewhat short and simple for such an impressive place, but then, humans still made little sense.

Rockefeller Center, it seemed, wasn't just a simple square or region but rather a collection of similarly designed buildings, with a few specialty ones thrown into the mix. In fact, in the midst of the cluster of towers, he found a plaza surrounded by trees and rows of red and white flags. Large numbers of humans meandered about this area, some with odd devices in their hands that they occasionally held up to their faces. From the glass lenses and the way they were pointed at distant objects, Torval guessed these were cameras.

One of the prisoners on his route, a man named Kevin Steele, had in life been a freelance photographer. In order to produce the disturbing images that seemed so in demand, he would sometimes commit horrific crimes and take pictures of the aftermath. The bloody shots would inevitably fetch a high price from various publications, but eventually the authorities caught up with him. After Kevin died in prison, he wound up in Hell, forced to reproduce the same photographs he took in life. Each time he captured a new image, the painful injuries he inflicted on his subjects would be mirrored on himself.

From this particular prisoner, Torval knew about cameras, but Kevin's was much larger, with a long cylindrical lens extending out the front. The tourists in the plaza used much smaller versions, some of them barely larger than the plastic MetroCard Torval carried safely tucked away in his pocket.

As he walked along, he saw several people photographing a bronze plate attached to a marble structure. He spotted writing there, so he moved closer to read it. The initial phrase, arranged in a circle about some sort of seal, identified the area as an official landmark of New York City, although the significance of an "official landmark" eluded him. However, the name of the city caused Torval to raise an eyebrow. Did this place have two names, or was one of them incorrect? Most likely New York was right, because it was "official." Perhaps Radio City was just a nickname.

He continued on, reading the rest of the plaque:

**Rockefeller Center**
is one of the foremost architectural projects undertaken in America in terms of scope, urban planning and integration of architecture, art and landscaping. It was developed by John D. Rockefeller, Jr. The Center's original architects were: Reinhard & Hofmeister; Hood, Godley & Fouilhoux; and Corbett, Harrison & MacMurray. The original complex of fourteen buildings was constructed between 1931 and 1939, and provided jobs for thousands of laborers in the building industries throughout the Depression.

New York Landmarks Preservation Foundation
1989

Most of the words were meaningless to Torval, but he did glean a few useful nuggets of information. For one, Rockefeller Center was somehow significant and vital, and as a resident of this city he was expected to know that. Second, the name "Rockefeller" came from someone important who had built the place, although the numbers that designated years didn't really tell him much (since he had no idea what year it was at the moment). However, by the date under the Landmark Preservation Foundation notice, he could tell these buildings had been here for at least fifty years.

Also, there was mention of a "depression" again. That was the second time he'd heard a word for an emotional state used in that particular context. Obviously it was a euphemism for some period in history which he would have to research.

There were other items of note within the area, such as a variety of pieces of art—including one statue of a flying man inside a ring that appeared to be made of gold—and a curious white rectangular area in which people seemed to be gliding along rather than walking. However, Torval forced himself to press on with his task. He had no time to explore at the moment, although perhaps after he finished, he could come back here and familiarize himself with his surroundings. There certainly seemed to be enough interesting things to see, especially the way the people in the walled arena managed to balance themselves while apparently sliding along on thin blades of metal attached to their feet. Perhaps this was a human method of personal transport he simply hadn't encountered yet, but needed to be aware of.

In due course he came across a sign pointing out the subway entrance, which was indeed located underground. People seemed to come and go via the stairs with some regularity, so he followed a couple as they headed downward. Nobody took any notice of him as he went—using the subway was clearly commonplace.

At the bottom of the stairs Torval discovered the purpose of the MetroCard that Pete Roxton let him borrow. The demon found himself stymied by a strange blocking contraption with an immobile bar across his path, and while he stood there wondering whether he should simply step over it, a man in a gray business suit pushed past him with a muffled complaint. "Damn tourists, holding up the line! Move it!" he muttered, sliding one of the plastic cards through a slot before pushing the metal bar out of his way. Before Torval could respond, the man was out of earshot, heading further down the underground passage.

Torval repeated what the hurried commuter had done, using the card in his pocket, and found that now the bar had unlocked. He stepped through, and that was that. Simple enough, he thought, putting the MetroCard back in his pocket without any further thought on the matter.

Now he had to get on the F train, so he started walking again, following the flow of human beings who all seemed to be going in one direction only. In due course he came to an open area, well lit, with numerous signs behind glass lining the walls and standing on their own platforms. The ceiling hovered low overhead, making the crowds seem even more claustrophobic than usual. Beyond the milling humans, two sets of tracks extended off to the sides, into dark caverns and out of sight. Most of the people, probably close to a hundred of them, faced toward the tracks, either waiting silently or speaking to companions in low voices. A distant rumbling and occasional hiss sounded, reminding Torval of the darker corners of the Fire Pits.

As he stood there, unsure whether he should be doing something, he heard another sound: a distant strumming punctuated by occasional verses of song. A beat pounded along as well, a repeating thump-thump that accompanied the music and seemed to divide the singer's words.

The overall effect was quite pleasing to the ear, and Torval thought, so this is what music is supposed to sound like.

Along his route in Hell, there were two musicians, a bald black man named Paul Krees, whose instrument of choice was the saxophone, and the long-haired, freckled Vern "Morning Glory" Stevenson, who played guitar. In life, Paul played with a jazz band, but by day also happened to be a prominent member of the New Orleans criminal underground. Vern, by contrast, was a drifter and self-proclaimed hippie who sold drugs and practiced the occasional date rape before moving on to the next town. Both men were punished in Hell by being forced to play bad music with broken instruments until their ears and fingers quite literally bled. Every time Torval had to visit their cells, he found it best to tune out the horrendous noises they produced, for even his demonic ears couldn't stand such tones for long.

Now, for the first time, he could actually hear music as it was meant to be: melodious and pleasing to the ear. In fact, save for the occasional snippet from a passing car radio or other source, these were the first such sounds he'd heard since arriving on Earth. Unless he wanted to count the equally pleasurable, happy whistling produced by Christine in the soup kitchen, which, while certainly nice enough, wasn't quite the same thing.

Without even realizing it, Torval found himself moving closer to the music, and found it coming from a young man seated on the floor, leaning back on one of the many pillars spaced here and there throughout the subway platform. Like Vern Stevenson, this youth was long-haired and shabbily dressed, and held a guitar, but he also kept two small cans between his legs. The larger of these sat upside-down and he struck it regularly with his elbow, producing the regular thumping sound that accompanied his playing. The other can waited open side up, and while Torval watched, a couple of passersby stepped over and dropped a coin or two inside. The singer nodded and smiled at them without missing a beat.

The demon continued to listen, enjoying the song, which told a story about a man and a woman who passed each other on the subway every day but never spoke to each other. Eventually, one day, the man decided to finally ask her name, only that day she wasn't there, nor was she the next, or the next. Finally, at the end of the song, he learned she'd perished in an automobile accident the very morning he'd finally worked up his courage. The music ended there, with no further explanation of what happened later.

Several of the onlookers clapped in appreciation of the story, but Torval didn't, and in fact wasn't even really sure what the hand-slapping gesture meant. Did they appreciate the song or were they, like himself, frustrated by the sudden ending? He wanted to ask, but before he could step forward, the musician began to sing again, this time with a different tune and faster beat. Almost simultaneously, the rumbling and rushing noises he'd been hearing, but hadn't been paying attention to, grew louder and louder, completely drowning out the music.

All at once, a flash of gray announced the arrival of a train, and the commuters began to gather up near the doors even before they opened. The young man went silent at this and picked up his cup, looked through the coins inside, and smiled to himself.

Was guitar-playing the musician's job, or was he just another beggar like Joe used to be? Torval didn't know, and didn't really have the opportunity to ask. The train awaited, and people were already boarding, so he followed them inside. He was still thinking about the singer, now sitting idle while he waited for his next audience, when it occurred to Torval that this might not be the correct train, but before he could verify anything the doors slid shut in his face.

* * *

There was nothing to do but wait it out, so Torval waited. Many of the other passengers had by now taken seats, but others remained standing, holding onto loops dangling from the ceiling. As he had nowhere to sit, Torval reached up and took hold of one of these. Just in time, too, as the train lurched forward without warning, and he surely would've been thrown to the ground without the handhold to steady himself.

The train hadn't been moving long before it began to slow, and a voice from somewhere overhead announced "Seventh Avenue." A moment later the vehicle ground roughly to a stop. Some of the others on the train departed while new ones entered, and within moments the subway started rolling again.

This process repeated itself several times, but now a pattern emerged: beginning with Fifty-Ninth Street, the numbers began to climb quickly. Seventy-Second Street, Eighty-First Street, Eighty-Sixth Street . . . how high would they go before Torval reached his destination? He had no idea. If the city was truly as endless as he thought, he might never get off, just like poor J. Richard Getz in his endless loop down in Hell.

Even as he became more and more worried with every passing moment, a female voice suddenly startled him. "You look lost," she said, and Torval turned to see who might be talking. The speaker turned out to be a middle-aged woman wearing a crimson scarf that accentuated a dark blue blouse and sharply pressed knee-length skirt of the same color. An odd wing-like piece of jewelry decorated her lapel, and her free hand hung onto a black case attached to a pair of plastic wheels. She smiled and stared at Torval with an expectant look, waiting for his reply.

"You startled me," admitted Torval after a moment. "I am sorry. You are correct, it seems. I believe I am lost, and am not sure what to do."

"Yeah, I could tell." She grinned at him. "Don't worry, everybody has that look the first time they get on a subway. Been in New York long? I'm Tracy Cullen, by the way."

"I am Joe Sampson," said Torval reflexively, "and I have been here two days. This is my first time on a subway, at least as far as I can recall."

"As far as you can recall?" She flashed him a curious glance. "I've had too much to drink myself on occasion, but I think I'd remember being on the subway."

"Oh, I have not been drinking," replied Torval. "I no longer drink in that manner. I am simply lost. I expected to have encountered the station I was looking for by now."

"Well, where are you going?" Tracy asked helpfully. "I know the lines pretty well. When you don't own your own car, this is the best way to get around, and after a long week of flying it's a whole lot better than getting caught in traffic anyway."

"Flying?"

"Yep, I racked up twenty thousand miles this week," said the woman proudly. "Just got back this morning on the Tokyo redeye." She pointed down at her clothing as if that should mean something to Torval, but seemed to notice his confusion. "Oh, sorry, I thought you'd understand. I'm a stewardess."

That also meant nothing to the demon. "Stewardess?"

"Oh, wow, you don't get out of the city much, do you? I work on board airplanes, making sure the passengers are comfortable."

That, at least, made some sense. Torval could recall, from his recollection of illusions involving trains and boats of various sorts, that some humans were required to travel about, meeting the needs of the passengers. Perhaps an airplane was just another form of conveyance, but he got the impression that asking for more information would be far too great an admission of ignorance than he could afford.

Instead, Torval returned to her original question. "I am attempting to locate the Second Avenue exit," he told her. "Failing that, I can use Delancey Street, or so I was told. However, I was not to go north or I would end up in fucking Queens."

She giggled at that. "Oh, you poor dear! You are going north, but not to Queens! This is the D train to Brooklyn!"

Torval felt as though a large stone had materialized within his stomach. "But I require the F south," he protested.

"Well, somebody put you on the wrong platform, then. Get off at the next stop, follow the signs rerouting you south, and get off anywhere below Fiftieth. Then just wait there and make sure you get on the F train. The letters are in the window, or on the front panel as the train arrives. Don't worry, if you get lost, you can always just ask anybody, or look at one of the subway maps."

Joe's eyebrows went up. "There is a map?"

She laughed again. "Oh, my, you're just a babe lost in the woods, aren't you? Just remember not to be intimidated, Joe. It's not as scary as you think. Back when I was growing up, yeah, the subways were pretty crime-ridden, but not anymore. It's safer down here than up top, I think. Anyway, we're stopping. Better get off here or you'll end up across the river, unless you've got a real hankering to see Yankee Stadium."

"No, I do not," he replied, again resisting the urge to admit he didn't know what that was. "Thank you for your aid, Tracy Cullen. I wish I had some way to repay you."

"Oh, you don't need to repay me," she replied. "Just glad to be of help. Now go on, before the doors close!"

He took her advice and let go of the handhold, stepping forward and off the train just before the doors shut. Turning, he caught a final glimpse of the stewardess, who gave him a quick wave before the train moved on.

Torval returned the gesture, not really sure why, and looked around. As before, he stood on a waiting platform, but this time there were far fewer people, and there seemed to be several potential exits. As Tracy had pointed out, though, there were signs indicating which tunnel led where. One of them, he saw, led to southbound trains. Too bad I didn't notice those before, Torval thought to himself with a sigh.

He followed the path that led around and over to another platform on the opposite side. As he arrived, he noticed several people clustered around one of the many colorful placards mounted on posts within the station. Moving closer to investigate, he saw numerous red, blue, yellow, and green lines meandering about amidst brown clumps on a field of blue. Circles, labeled with words and numbers, were scattered about the lines in apparently haphazard fashion.

Torval leaned closer. Many of the words he saw were unfamiliar, but then he caught sight of one he recognized: Rockefeller Center. So, this was the map Tracy talked about! He studied the orange lines radiating out from it and saw, after a few moments of study, that the one running upwards crossed over circles marked with numbered streets. In fact, those were the same streets he'd heard announced as station stops while riding on the train. At the one marked "145th Street," a red arrow proclaimed, "You are here."

Quickly everything fell into place. He saw now that he'd indeed gone north (recognizing, though he wasn't sure how, that the top of the map represented that direction) and the little D in the circle next to the orange line was the route indicator. Tracing backward down the page, the D merged with several others, one of which was the F. Following that one, he saw with satisfaction that it did indeed cross little circles labeled "2nd Avenue" and "Delancey." All he had to do, then, was get from the D south onto the F south, which he could do at Rockefeller or any of several stations south of it—exactly as Tracy Cullen had described.

She did, indeed, know her subway routes! Furthermore, Torval realized, she'd just done him a favor. She had helped him, and he'd incurred yet another debt that he'd have to repay, somehow.

Every time he interacted with a human, it seemed, he added to his growing list of debts. How was he ever supposed to cover them all? The hundred dollars he would earn from his extra work today wouldn't even come close to doing so.

Torval sighed. Perhaps he just didn't understand this whole helpfulness concept at all. What if Tracy wasn't giving him directions because she expected some reward? What if she just did it because that's how humans did things? Was it simply human nature to be helpful?

He shook his head doubtfully. If people were naturally kind to each other, why did they wind up in Hell? Did punishment only apply to those who went against their nature? Or was it, in fact, human nature to be evil and self-centered, thereby earning a just punishment, while the few who fought against their flaws gained access to Heaven?

So many questions, and still no answers! He had so many things to ask Prelz—the poor ex-demon would most certainly be overwhelmed.

The sound of an arriving train broke his attention away from the map, and Torval studied the vehicle, looking for the letter Tracy told him to watch for. He found it after a moment, a large orange "D" in one of the windows. That was the one he needed, so he moved quickly to the entrance and stepped inside. This time, there were fewer travelers, so he could sit down. The hard bench-like seat provided little comfort, but it was better than standing, or so his feet insisted.

The train began to move, and Torval watched the walls speed by outside, glad to be heading once more in the right direction.

# *Chapter 22*

Transferring trains proved to be a relatively easy process. Torval simply exited at the Rockefeller Center stop, ironically where he'd begun his journey, then waited patiently for an F train to show up, which it did about five minutes later.

There were no musicians to entertain him this time, but he did get to overhear a couple of nearby conversations. A tall, well-groomed man spoke into a small hand-held device, referring to something called "stocks" that were apparently up several points, and therefore needed to be sold. Once the broker moved out of hearing range, Torval found himself listening to two women discussing the events of the previous evening in detail, where they apparently attended a party and acquired some substance that made them "high." This subject produced quite a bit of bubbly laughter. Why someone would become so amused by moving upward left Torval baffled, but he thought better of inquiring further.

This time, armed with his knowledge of the subway map, Torval didn't feel as worried when he boarded the next train. He knew now that the subway would stop several more times, and turn east before reaching the exit he desired. Knowing this, he was prepared to exit at Second Avenue and did so promptly, a little bit proud of himself for finally comprehending how the subway worked.

The lesson from all this, he told himself as he pushed through the exit turnstile and headed up the stairs to the street, is that proper research has its rewards. If he'd bothered to investigate the subway more completely, he wouldn't have had any difficulties at all. In fact, if he'd just seen the map in the first place, he probably would've understood everything on his own, without requiring help from Tracy Cullen or some other random citizen of the city.

With that in mind, he now had to locate his final destination on his own. Emerging from the stairs, he found himself on a street corner, and he already knew to look for signs in specific locations advertising which street was which. Unfortunately, these gave him no clue whatsoever to where the one named "Bowery" might be.

He glanced around, looking for another map like the one for the subway, but saw nothing of the kind. All he saw were buildings in all directions, traffic rushing by on the roads, and the seemingly endless flow of humans streaming by all around him.

Bowery must be close by, thought Torval, and in fact, he'd been told he could use either the Second Avenue or Delancey Street exits. That meant Bowery was probably between the two. Since the train went that way, he thought, remembering his direction changes as he'd come up the stairs, then I should go that way as well.

His reasoning proved correct, for within a couple of short blocks he came to Bowery Street. Now to find the numbered address. This proved no trouble at all, as the proper location was only a block and a half away. He located the apartment complex by following street numbers, as he'd done when he sought out Shelly Mendez.

This time, however, the entrance didn't open right into an apartment, but rather into a corridor lined with doors. This reminded him of Christine's apartment building, so he knew exactly what to do. The number he'd been given, 205, wasn't among those Torval passed as he headed down the corridor. Instead, he came to a stairwell, which he forced himself to climb, despite the fact that he'd all but worn himself out from all this walking and climbing. At the top, he paused to catch his breath, but saw the door he wanted just a short distance away.

He knocked, and received an almost immediate response from within. "Yeah?" came a gruff, barked reply.

For a moment Torval hesitated. The voice inside sounded upset, as if the man didn't want to be bothered. The address was correct, though, as a quick check of the note confirmed. "It is I, Joe Sampson," said the demon. "I was told to bring you something."

"You're who?" demanded the man from the other side, sounding even angrier this time. "I don't know any Joe Sampson!"

"I apologize," said Torval quickly, worried that the door might burst open with a vengeful human on the other side. "I was sent here by Pete Roxton with a briefcase. If I am at the wrong apartment, I—"

"Oh, you're from the warehouse!" the man interrupted, and his voice immediately sounded happier, almost as though relieved at this news. "Sorry, I was expecting somebody else. Get your ass in here!"

Something inside clicked and shifted, and the door suddenly swept open, revealing a large, overweight man seated in a metallic chair atop large, gray wheels. In one hand he held the doorknob, and in the other a large, smoothly carved stick obviously intended for use as a weapon. The man's head was almost completely bald, with prominent jowls surrounding a wide mouth nearly bereft of teeth. Several long, white scars crawled up and down his body, easily noticeable considering his lack of a shirt.

The room's occupant seemed to be alone. Furtively, he rolled his chair forward slightly, glancing to and fro to make sure nobody else lurked within the hall. Satisfied, he let go of the door and waved Torval inside. "Come on, hurry, before someone sees you!" he urged.

"Very well," agreed the demon, scuttling in swiftly and moving far enough away that the stick couldn't reach him. Although the wheeled contraption didn't seem particularly mobile, Torval wasn't taking any chances. He moved over toward a nearby table that seemed covered in scattered papers, and made sure he could escape around the furniture if something went wrong.

"Sorry 'bout that," said the overweight man, who, Torval noted, seemed to be sweating profusely. In fact, the room felt rather warm, a lot more so than some of the other places he'd visited. "My phone's on the fritz, so if Pete called to tell me he was sending a new guy, I didn't get the message. Nice to meet you. The name's Brent. Brent Maclure."

He set the club down, leaning it against the wall near the door, and reached out a flabby hand. Torval took it and shook warily. Brent bore a slight resemblance to Foreman Landri in that he didn't seem willing to stand up or walk around, although he had a long way to go before he reached the Second-Class demon's incredible girth. Brent also seemed a lot friendlier, at least now that he'd introduced himself.

Torval didn't know what to say at this point, so he remained silent, resulting in an awkward lull in the burgeoning conversation. Under normal circumstances, if he understood human greetings, Torval was to identify himself at this point, but he'd already done so. Repeating his human name would seem out of place. Furthermore, he'd already explained why he was here, so what else could he possibly say?

Finally Brent shrugged and rolled the chair back a bit, wiping his perspiration-soaked face with a moist handkerchief. "Heater's on the fritz too," he muttered, almost to himself. "Lazy-ass super! Two days I gotta live like this, and I can't open the damn windows either. Painted shut. My apologies, but it's not like someone in my condition can move somewhere else real easy, y'know?"

"Your condition?" inquired Torval reflexively. Other than being somewhat plump and overheated, Brent didn't appear injured in any way. There were certainly fatter people walking about the streets of the city.

Brent narrowed his eyes. "Yeah, you think I'm in this wheelchair 'cause I'm lazy? I'm paralyzed below the waist. Geez, didn't Pete tell you nothin'?"

"Not really," admitted Torval. "I was not given very much information at all." Now, at least, he understood what the mobile seating was for. Something like that, if built large enough, might even enable Foreman Landri to move outside of his office for the first time in ages. Torval resolved to at least suggest it when he returned to Hell. He didn't know a thing about building a wheelchair, of course, but that wasn't his problem. Surely someone there could figure it out, as they had with the steam-powered ship that sailed across the Styx.

Brent rubbed his chin between thumb and forefinger, studying Joe carefully for a moment. "Hmm, well, maybe that's not a bad idea. They're getting a lot more paranoid over there after those collectors beat me up. Doesn't pay to lose too many bets in this town. Good thing I had somethin' socked away for a rainy day."

Torval lifted up the briefcase. "Regardless of your situation," he said evenly, returning the focus of the conversation to his mission here, "I was ordered to bring you this. In return you were to give me an item to take back to the Roxtons."

"That's it? That's really all they told you?"

"I was also instructed not to examine either item, or to discuss my task with anyone. I have lived up to these rules to the best of my ability."

"You're a strange one," observed Brent. "I never heard any errand boy talk like that before. Let me see the briefcase."

Torval handed it over without delay or complaint. Apparently unconcerned with the volume of sweat coating the exterior, Brent set it on his lap and began fiddling with the latches. "Nope, hasn't been opened," he pronounced after a moment. "Now let's see what we got."

He worked the combination lock for a moment, smiled at his success, and popped the switches simultaneously. Lifting the lid, he began to rummage about inside. From his vantage point, Torval could see a couple of file folders containing layers of paper that seemed to be connected together, like one very long contiguous sheet folded and stacked as a unit. Some sort of writing scrawled its way across the first page, but he couldn't make out what it said.

"Ah, good, very good," Brent went on. "Looks like a sweet-ass coupla weeks! The lieutenant's gonna be pleased as punch. Tell Pete and the old man they're doin' a bang-up job over there."

"I will tell them," agreed Torval, presuming, from the phrasing's context, that "bang-up" was a good thing.

The wheelchair-bound man closed the briefcase, reapplied the latches and set the container down on the floor. "Now, I've got somethin' for you to take back to them. You've been trustworthy so far, and careful enough to not attract attention on your way here, but what's in this box is far more important than what you brought to me. Don't lose it, and don't look inside, and don't show it to anyone. Got it?"

"Yes, sir," Torval replied at once. Those were the same instructions he'd already received from Pete, so there was no contradiction. Actually, if there had been, he wouldn't have known what to do. Presumably follow Pete's orders first, as he was Torval's direct supervisor, and that took precedence over anything else.

Brent rolled his wheelchair over to the little apartment's kitchen, disappeared from sight for a few moments, and then returned, pushing a two-foot-high brown cardboard box with his big, meaty hands. Clear strapping tape covered the container from top to bottom, leaving almost none of its normal surface exposed to the air. On top, a half-torn shipping label was all that marked it as anything other than a featureless package. Torval noticed a brown logo there, and the words "Next Day Air," but the shipping address was missing.

Torval leaned over and picked up the box, not sure what to expect. The weight didn't seem overwhelming, but the square container was bulky and difficult to support correctly. Unlike the briefcase, there were no convenient handles to use, so he could only wrap his arms around the back side and clutch it to his chest.

"Sorry I don't got nothin' better," apologized Brent, "but this just came in this morning, and I ain't exactly mobile, y'know. Now get it back to them right away. Don't stop for nothin', got it?"

"Yes, sir."

Brent nodded. "You seem like a pretty straightforward guy. I think I like you, Joe. You're going to fit in real well round here."

That wasn't the first time he'd heard that, and Torval felt the same feeling of pride as before. "Thank you, sir. I will endeavor to do my job to the best of my ability."

"Good for you. Now go on, get the hell out of here! I got shit to do! Don't make me get out the whuppin' stick!"

He feigned a move toward the club he'd left nearby, and Torval wasted no time rushing past and out the exit. Brent's low chuckling followed him out into the hallway, only to be cut off by a loud slam from the door a few seconds later.

* * *

Thinking back as he left the building, Torval could recall seeing at least a couple of wheelchairs out on the various sidewalks during one or another of his errands. He'd simply assumed that these were some other form of human conveyance, similar to the skinny wheeled frames some people rode on the streets. Because there were several prisoners on similar devices along his route, Torval knew these contraptions were called "bicycles," although how they remained stable while moving was beyond his ability to comprehend. There were, however, no wheelchairs in Hell, as far as he knew.

Such a simple device, thought the demon, once again amazed at the human ability to adapt objects to their own purposes. He wondered why no demon had ever considered using wheels attached to a chair, but then, there would be no reason to do so. No demon ever became permanently injured, and even if they did, there would be no one to help them. Kindness and service to others were unknown in the Lower World.

On his way back to the subway, Torval stopped to look around at the many vehicles on the streets. So many different ones, of all shapes and sizes. As he stood there, a man zipped by on a bicycle, wearing a waterproof jacket and carrying a large bag strapped to his back. Despite its smaller size and simple construction, the bike had one thing in common with every other conveyance, including the one Brent was using: wheels.

What made that chair mobile were its wheels—the round, spoked devices that turned and rolled, propelling the occupant forward or backward. There were few wheels in Hell, with so little need for them, but here in this human city, they were everywhere. In fact, every mobile device the humans used to travel possessed wheels of some sort. Cars, buses, bicycles, trains, and even the strange flat boards several youths skated upon down a nearby sidewalk—they all used wheels.

Such a simple connection, but one that until that moment he'd never really grasped. Wheels were the key component in human vehicles! That explained how they could move around so easily, at speeds faster than their legs could normally propel them. Wheels made high-speed movement possible.

Had any demon ever noted this before? Surely someone had, back in Hell. Something so simple couldn't have been missed for so many centuries. Could it?

Unfortunately, Prelz probably wouldn't know the answer to that. Torval intended to ask anyway, but he doubted a Tempter would have any further information on such innovations. He'd have to bring up the subject when he returned home after the vacation was over. At least he'd learned something potentially new and useful that he could report to his boss. Maybe this insipid holiday wouldn't be a complete waste of time after all.

Returning to the Roxton warehouse proved to be more difficult than the initial trip. Finding the subway again, taking the proper route to Rockefeller Center, and navigating back through the streets were actually relatively easy tasks. The problem was the box.

While it initially didn't seem all that heavy, the box proved very bulky and difficult to manage, for it didn't easily fit in Joe's skinny arms. After walking just a block, his muscles started straining, and he had to set the container down to rest. He wound up trying several other positions, such as resting it on a shoulder, or even on his back as some of his more physically tortured prisoners used when carrying their burdens. Nothing really helped, so Torval could only lug the blessed thing a few steps at a time before setting it down to catch his breath.

Nonetheless, he persevered, and after what seemed like hours he reached the door to Roxton Auto Parts. Before he could get inside, Pete spotted him through the glass and rushed out to help. "Sorry, man, that's a lot bigger than I thought it would be," he offered immediately, hoisting the box up onto one of his thick shoulders as if it weighed nothing at all. "Didn't think about that, and Brent wasn't answering his goddamn phone. Sorry to put ya through that."

"I am fine," lied Torval, actually quite sore and exhausted from the journey. The final two blocks were the worst, as he could only haul the box a couple of steps at a time. "The container was indeed inconvenient, but my task is complete. Is there anything else you wish of me?"

"Nope, not right now," said Pete with a cheerful smile. He carried the box inside, easily opening the door with his free hand, and waited there for Torval to follow. The demon found himself wishing, not for the first time, that his human body had a bit more strength and stamina.

"Ya did good," said the younger Roxton as he set the box down behind the front counter. "Didn't open it, either, I see. How anyone can be that immune to temptation, I have no idea, but damn, I admire you! Anyways, I suppose you're ready for your payment, right?"

"Yes, I am," agreed Torval. In fact, thinking about the money helped keep him moving throughout the whole arduous trip back to the warehouse.

"I thought you might be." Pete stepped over to a device on the counter, one that Torval knew from cell illusions as a cash register, and worked a few of the buttons there. A bell rang and the drawer below popped open, allowing Pete to withdraw a stack of bills, which he began to count out in front of him. "Twenty, forty, sixty, eighty, there's your hundred," he said, slapping down five green slips of paper with prominent 20s marked in their corners. "And, since you followed all of the instructions exactly, and got back here early, here's a bonus." With that, he added a sixth bill, before returning the rest to their slot in the drawer.

Torval reached out and gingerly picked up the twenties, holding them reverently in his hands. The bills were crisp and new, without even a trace of wear. He'd never held that much money before, and hadn't expected to ever do so. The feeling was overwhelming.

With this much cash, he could do so many things...

"Thank you, sir," he managed to blurt out. "I appreciate the extra money as well, even though I did nothing special to earn it."

"You did plenty," replied Pete with a grin. "Look, Joe, good men like you are hard to find in this city. Most people would've at least looked into that room downstairs, or the box, or tried to get inside the briefcase. Or they would've grilled me for more information, or any of a hundred other stupid things. Not you, though. You just took what I told you, did it exactly as I said, and came back here without any complaints. That's more than I ever expected out of anyone. A lot more. And that's why I felt like you deserved a little extra. Just keep on doing what you're doing, and there's more where that came from."

"More?" replied Torval eagerly. "You mean I could earn this amount of money again?"

"At least that much," said Pete, grinning even more widely. "Maybe not right away, 'cause I don't have another delivery scheduled, but soon. I'll let y'know. In the meantime, come back here tonight for your regular shift, same time and everything. That's all we need from you for right now. Oh, and if you want to use the bathroom for a shave or something, feel free. You cleaned it, you get to use it whenever you want."

"Very well," replied Torval, still staring wide-eyed at the bright green twenties in his hands. For the first time, he thought he understood the overwhelming appeal of money. "I will return again tonight at eight o'clock."

"See you then."

Pete reached down, lifted up the box, and carried it off deeper into the warehouse, not bothering to say goodbye. Torval knew he'd been dismissed, though, so he headed for the door, departing automatically just as he always did after Foreman Landri finished one of his lectures. Torval's attention remained on the cash, though, until he bumped painfully into the glass door. That impact jarred him back to his senses.

Shaking his head, he folded up the bills gingerly and pushed them into his pocket. Money! He had money, finally, for the first time since he'd begged a few dollars from passersby on his first night on Earth. He was miserable back then, but now, he felt empowered. Money gave him options, and the ability to acquire things that would make his remaining days in this place a little more comfortable. What's more, he could expect additional opportunities in the near future.

The more he earned, the more things he could do. He could buy different clothes, so he didn't have to wear the same ones every day. He could purchase his own razor, to shave the stubble that already tickled at his bare chin. He could ride in cabs instead of walking all the way to the shelter and back every day. He could even repay Christine, once he'd taken care of his own needs.

Christine... he owed her so much! All of this, everything he'd done to improve his lot, he owed to her. But how to repay those debts? As Prelz had suggested, he probably couldn't just hand her a wad of cash. She'd just refuse it. That's just the way she was. She honestly did him all those favors without expecting anything in return.

No, he had to do something else. Something that would refund at least some of the money, and in a way she would appreciate.

After a few moments, standing there on the street corner, right hand still in his pocket wrapped around those comforting bills, it came to him. Something he could do that would repay his debt, and also bring him a step closer to understanding the baffling enigma that was Christine Anderson.

He would ask her out on a date.

# Chapter 23

So what did he really know about dating? Torval turned over the concept in his mind as he walked in the general direction of the soup kitchen, not in any particular hurry.

Prelz had already explained that dating was one of the early stages of the human romantic ritual, but hadn't given any other details. Presumably, or so Torval imagined, he and Christine would go out for a meal together, and possibly enjoy some other form of entertainment, but that was as far as his understanding went. The rest remained a mystery.

Sometimes, sex would be involved, but according to Prelz, that came later, after a variety of preliminaries. From what Torval now knew, "making love" was different than "casual sex," which could happen anytime and lacked any real meaning. These were two different things, and Torval intended to figure out what that difference might be.

He had no idea how to proceed, but he could remedy that through research. He had learned just how important research could be, as his experience on the subway suggested. The other problem would be a bit more difficult to overcome—that being his rival and current supervisor, Pete Roxton. The insufferably handsome man had already taken Christine out on a date, which gave him a head start in the romance ritual. What if he'd already arranged another such event for tonight?

Torval thought back to the conversation he overheard that morning through the quiescent heater vent. He didn't realize it at the time, but Pete referred to Christine when he discussed his trip to the Chinese restaurant. What was it he said . . . ? Ah, yes. He intended to ask her out again tonight because it was Friday.

Torval's knowledge of human language told him that Friday was a day of the week, which encompassed seven days. Torval vaguely remembered something about God creating the world in seven days, although that might've just been a legend, like the Tree of Knowledge story Prelz already referenced once before. Regardless of the truth of things, humans clearly arranged their weeks in groups of seven days, almost certainly in deference to the world creation story.

In any event, since Pete said today was Friday, that meant tomorrow would be Saturday. That much Torval knew from his ingrained education. However, the significance of those days of the week eluded him. Why one should be of any more importance than another, he had no idea. Friday, though, certainly possessed some kind of significance, at least as far as Pete was concerned.

Regardless of that, Pete clearly intended to ask Christine out tonight. However, the more Torval thought about it, the more he realized how little influence he had on the situation. He had to work tonight anyway, so there could be no date with Christine, regardless of what Pete intended to do with her.

Actually, the scheduling of work presented a serious challenge. Torval already knew Christine worked during the day, volunteered at the shelter at night, and then had some free time after approximately eight o'clock to attend a date. That meant he would have no window of opportunity, unless she made some sort of exception for him, or he somehow avoided working at some point.

He could think of only one way to possibly discover such an exception, and that was to ask her directly about her schedule. Somehow, though, asking Christine about dating made him feel uneasy. In fact, the more he contemplated how such a meeting would proceed, the more his chest tightened. He started sweating noticeably, and felt colder than the cool air might otherwise suggest.

Nervousness—that's what this was. He was nervous! The thought of asking Christine on a date made him queasy. Bless it all, why did Christine affect him so?

With a frustrated sigh, Torval wrung out his slippery hands and tried to think about something else. The money in his pocket came to mind immediately. With so much in the way of funds, he must carefully consider how to spend it. Yes, that would definitely help get his mind off the annoyingly intriguing Christine Anderson.

So what did he need? Thinking back over the events of the day, Torval knew one thing was fresh clothing. The undergarments under his shirt and pants were already chafing uncomfortably, so at a minimum they needed replacing. Additionally, he had some stains on the outside of his clothes as well, most of those from kneeling and scrubbing at the bathroom the night before. Sleeping hadn't helped his appearance either, as his trousers were now rumpled and wrinkled. Only the turtleneck sweater seemed undamaged, save for darkened patches around the elbows.

Torval figured he could keep the same shirt, as he wore it out of sight underneath the sweater anyway, and the shoes and socks were probably fine. The belt, too, didn't need replacing. So he needed to find a sweater, pants, and underclothes. That should be easy enough, as he'd remembered seeing several shops advertising clothing, at least one of which was just a few blocks ahead.

He began to walk in the general direction of the clothing shops, still mulling over in his mind what he could buy, when he came to a gathering of humans near a marked area called a "bus stop." Torval had passed similar locations many times without much thought, but on this occasion there seemed to be something happening, because the people there had formed into a ring and seemed intent on watching some activity. Seeing as how he was in no hurry, Torval joined with the others to have a look.

In the middle of the ring, a young black man sat on a wooden crate in front of a short table made out of a simple cardboard box. He wore a long-sleeved T-shirt and a blue cap with its brim pointed backward, and in his hands he held what looked like a little white ball. Several long braids of hair protruded out from under the cap, which had a curious combination of the letters "N" and "Y" emblazoned upon it. Torval had seen this particular symbol on humans here and there, but had no idea what it meant.

There were three small plastic cups on the table, upside-down. While Torval watched, the youth covered the ball with one of these, slid them about randomly on the tabletop several times, and then asked the audience to point at the correct cup. Someone near the front of the ring reached out with a confident finger, and the man revealed that the guess was correct.

"There ya go, mon," he said in a curiously thick accent. "That was easy, wuzzn't it? Now all y'have ta do is guess it right and double yer money! Put yer bet on da table and have a go, mon!"

He waited expectantly, and there were mutters through the crowd, some suggesting it was indeed easy and others saying it must be some kind of trick. One of the bolder members of the audience reached out and planted a ten-dollar bill on the table, and the black man smiled.

"Alrighty then, here we goes! Where she stops, only I knows!"

He swirled the cups about the makeshift table for several seconds. Everyone, including Torval, had their eyes on those containers, but even so, the demon knew he'd lost track. The better seemed confident, however, and pointed quickly at one spot when the shifting finished. With a frown, the black man revealed the ball.

"Good eyes, mon," he complimented with a nod, reaching into his pocket and paying the winner. "You has done dis before, I betcha! Someone else wanna try, hey?"

The winner took his money and melted away, and some of the crowd followed, leaving gaps in the audience. Torval slid closer, intrigued by the game, and the possibility of perhaps increasing the amount of money he already possessed. He felt certain that if he'd been closer, with a better field of view, he could've followed the cups correctly. All he had to do was fix his eyes on the proper container and not flinch for any reason.

Another person took a turn, and also won, doubling his money to the consternation of the black man with the strangely braided hair. This time, Torval felt he too would've won if he'd only put down some cash. The victor was again shooed away, and several other eager betters were already stepping up to the table. Torval would have to wait his turn.

He watched again, keeping his eye carefully on the cup, which shifted smoothly about without ever leaving the surface of the table. This time, though, he must've lost track, for the ball was under a different cup. The player, too, had thought the same, and seemed honestly shocked to see he was mistaken.

At this there were some more murmurs in the crowd, but another player won after that, and then another. Torval found himself moving ever closer to the front when someone spoke behind him. "Don't do it, dude," a man's voice warned quietly. "It's a trick."

Torval thought at first the warning wasn't directed at him, but he glanced back to see a young man in a long gray jacket looking directly his way. "I'm serious," he went on, nodding in the direction of the game. "It's all a scam. Trust me."

Torval stepped back from the crowd, studying the speaker, who seemed to be rather heavily dressed. Most of the other people in the vicinity didn't even have coats, or if so, theirs, like Torval's, were slung over one arm. The man had stringy brown hair that draped around his face, as if needing desperately to be cut, yet at the crown he was partially balding, giving him a ragged, wild look. He also seemed somewhat nervous, shifting back and forth in his muddy tennis shoes and glancing to and fro furtively.

"What do you mean, a scam?" inquired Torval curiously, wondering if this man, too, might be attempting to perform a good deed, as had so many other representatives of this city.

"It's a con," came the reply. The man stuck out a shaky hand, apparently in greeting. "Name's Zac. I can tell you're a tourist, like some of these others. You got the look."

"I am Joe," replied Torval, shaking hands reflexively. "Yes, I believe you might refer to me as a tourist. I have never seen a game like this. The rules appear quite simple, so I do not understand how it could be a scam."

"Well," replied Zac in a comfortably friendly manner, "I been around these parts a long time and I seen it all. Three-card monte, shell games, you name it. Plus I recognize a lot of those guys, anyway. They come and go 'round here, hopin' to find a mark just like you."

"I still do not understand," went on Torval, focusing once more on the game that had commenced again. Apparently the operator, having decided that not enough people were playing, had changed the rules slightly—now prospective players could place bets after he'd moved the ball around. That way there was no risk at all of losing sight of the correct cup. If Torval wasn't sure he was correct, he simply wouldn't bother betting. It all seemed like easy money, except for Zac's warning.

"Well," said his informant, "you see those guys there, all around the table? The one in the jacket, and those two in the white shirts, and the construction lookin' guy? Those are all shills."

"Shills?" Torval didn't recognize that word.

"Yeah," explained Zac, "they all know Lucky there, the guy runnin' the game. We call him Lucky 'cause he ain't never been caught. Anyways, some of them other guys there, too, they're all muscle or lookouts.

Everybody who's played so far is in on the trick. Now when they get somebody who's not with their group, like that Jappy dude there who looks real interested, see the one?"

Torval followed the shaky finger to an Asian man in black glasses who seemed quite intrigued by the proceedings. He stood close by the cardboard box, but not yet near enough to contemplate putting any money down. Nearby, a frail-looking woman of similar ancestry kept whispering in his ear.

"Once they got a mark like him," went on Zac, "some of the shills there, they'll try to pretend like they figgered out some big secret, right? Then they'll say it loud enough for Jap-boy there to hear, and he'll think he's got it made. Only when he puts down his cash, he'll lose every time. I ain't never seen nobody able to make that ball disappear and reappear like ol' Lucky can!"

Torval nodded in understanding. So, this was a con! He recalled several con men in cells along his route, including Jacob Spencer, a swindler who used telephone scams to convince people to reveal bank information, so that he could empty out their accounts. For his punishment, Jacob—an aquatic aficionado in life—had to swim repeatedly across a wide river containing sharp-toothed fish that nibbled his flesh from his bones at each crossing. Torval had never encountered an act quite like this "shell game," but he suspected Mr. Spencer would've been quite capable of conducting it, had he chosen to do so.

The volume of people involved in the con surprised Torval. Jacob, as he recalled, always acted alone. From Zac's explanation, there were at least a dozen people working together, none of whom seemed to show the slightest bit of knowledge of the other. Most even appeared to be from different walks of life, as well as different races and even genders. Nonetheless, as he watched, events did unfold exactly as Torval's benefactor predicted. After a few minutes, the Japanese businessman stepped forward and eagerly bet, only to discover he was incorrect, losing his money.

Zac smiled. "Now they'll meet up later and split the cash," he explained. "Any second now, they'll—yep, there they go."

As he spoke, the man named Lucky gathered up his cups and ball, picked up the crate he'd been sitting on, and scurried away, leaving the upturned cardboard box behind. The other onlookers also seemed to vanish into the crowd, none of them following Lucky or even glancing in his direction. Apparently getting the money off the foreign tourist was all they needed.

"Thank you," said Torval after a moment. "Had you not warned me, I may well have fallen into that trap, and I do not have much in the way of funds."

"That's weird," Zac replied, stepping off the curb and toward a nearby wall, out of the flow of pedestrian traffic. "I would've thought someone visiting New York would have plenty to spend."

Torval followed the young man, actually glad to be out of the crushing nearness of the crowd. "I do wish I had more," he admitted. "However, I only just today earned enough money to begin making purchases."

"Oh yeah? Good fer you," said Zac with a smile. Several of his teeth were noticeably crooked, giving his otherwise amiable expression a broken, distorted look. "Lookin' to get a souvenir, maybe? I might have some stuff you'd be interested in."

"You?" inquired Torval. "I had expected to find such things in stores—"

"Nah, no need to go indoors!" Zac went on hurriedly, his voice swelling with sudden enthusiasm. "Why pay all that sales tax and overhead? No, no, look to the streets, my friend. Besides, I just saved ya a bunch of cash, don't forget! Here, come back in this alleyway and have a look at good ol' Zac's travelin' storefront!"

So saying, he moved past the bus stop and into a narrow alley not unlike the one Torval found himself in upon arriving on Earth. Garbage cans, puddles of melted snow, and a locked chain-link fence at the end completed the scene, just like any of dozens of other alleys Torval's body knew by heart. The only thing missing was a cardboard-covered bum sleeping off the booze.

"Anyways, have a look," said Zac, opening up his coat with his right hand and pointing with the left. There, strapped to the interior of the lining, were at least a dozen watches, all looking shiny and new. Below these hung two rows of jewelry, all different types, from necklaces to earrings and more. "All one hundred percent real, my friend, and at a fraction of the price you'd pay in any shop!"

Torval moved forward, staring. He'd never heard of anyone selling merchandise in this way, but then, he didn't know a lot about this strange world, so perhaps this was normal. Besides, Zac had indeed done him a favor, so buying some of his wares might be a good way to repay his kindness. For once, thought the demon, he might actually be able to reciprocate a good act!

What's more, he actually did need a watch. On many occasions, he'd found himself wondering what time it was, putting him at the mercy of others. If he ever found himself in some location without a public clock, or someone to ask the time, he'd have no way of knowing. Since he now had reason to be certain places at specific times, a watch would be a good thing to have.

Still, they all looked quite expensive. Most were made of what looked to be gold, and some were decorated in glittering jewels. A few seemed incredibly intricate, far more complex than he really wanted. "While I do require a watch, I fear I could not afford these," Torval said after a moment. "My funds are, as I said, quite limited."

"Yeah, I saw you didn't have a watch," admitted Zac with another jagged-toothed grin. "Tell you what, though, you can have any of 'em for fifty bucks."

"Fifty?" Torval was surprised. From what he understood of the value of gemstones and gold, these would have to be far more valuable than that!

"Okay, forty," Zac countered. "Just 'cause I like you, man. Just think, no sales tax! You know ya want one. Get two, in fact. These here—" he said, pointing at a couple of the skinnier ones, "—look good on any lady's arm. Ya got somebody special?"

"Not yet," replied Torval, "although I am attempting to remedy that. Again, your offer is intriguing, but—"

He'd intended to add that he didn't really want to spend one-third of his cash on a single item, but Zac didn't let him finish. "Thirty then," the increasingly shaky-looking man haggled. "Or two for fifty. C'mon, man, you gotta know this is a great deal!"

Torval hesitated. As he continued to haggle, Zac looked ever-increasingly nervous, glancing over Torval's shoulder on multiple occasions. Something about this whole arrangement made the demon decidedly uneasy. Perhaps it was the seller's worriedness or the way he so quickly lowered the price, but Torval got the distinct impression that this must be some kind of deception.

Was that what was happening? Did Zac befriend him solely for the purpose of enticing him into making an ill-advised purchase? Perhaps the watches were broken, or possibly counterfeit, like the coins created by the long-dead trader Antigonus of Rhodes. On the other hand, perhaps they were indeed genuine, and Zac had acquired them illegally.

The last possibility seemed the most worrisome—and the most likely, the more he thought about it. Torval didn't want to be caught with stolen property. He'd only just begun to fit in on this world, so breaking the rules was unacceptable. Spending the last of his time here in a jail cell didn't strike him as particularly pleasant. Best to avoid the risk, he decided.

"I do not think making a purchase would be wise at this time," he said, stepping toward the street. "I apologize, Zac, but that is the way it must be."

Zac closed his coat and sighed, looking dejected. "Fine, if that's the way ya want it, Joe, but think about one more thing. I got somethin' real special here in my other pocket. Let me show it to ya, and I bet you can't say no."

"Very well," agreed Torval, deciding to humor the man. He'd already decided not to spend his money, so he might as well have a look. Heedless to the danger, he stepped further into the alleyway, right up alongside Zac, who shifted so his back was toward the street, effectively shielding them both from being seen by passersby.

Zac opened his coat and grasped a handle on some sort of metallic object lodged in a sort of bandolier. Torval's eyes widened as he realized that the black and gray device was, in fact, a gun.

Of course, he knew what guns were. There were guns all over the place in cell illusions back in Hell. Normally, such weapons were used to torture prisoners who'd employed them for various crimes during their lives. Although he didn't understand exactly how a pistol functioned, Torval knew exactly what one could do. With a simple flick of his wrist, and a twisting of his finger, Zac could bring Joe Sampson's time on Earth to a swift and bloody end.

So far, during his time in the city, Torval hadn't concerned himself much about dying. The possibility had occurred to him on several occasions, such as when he took his first cab ride, but since he knew all that would happen was he'd return to Hell, this gave him little cause for concern. Now, though, he had things he wished to do first. He wanted to spend his money, learn from Prelz, enjoy more food, read books, and above all, romance Christine. He couldn't do those things if Joe Sampson died.

There did exist a chance, however slight, that he might somehow be misinterpreting this situation. Seizing on this slim possibility, Torval said blithely, "Does that mean you want me to purchase a gun?"

Zac chuckled at that. "Wow, you gotta real sensa humor there, dude," he offered, now no longer looking quite as jittery as before. "No, you had your chance ta buy somethin', now you're just gonna pay me. Empty out yer pockets, or I'll blow yer head clean off."

"You are robbing me, then," said Torval flatly.

"Well, duhhh," hissed Zac, rolling his eyes. "Come on, man, hand it over! My trigger finger's gettin' pretty shaky here."

A lance of cold passed through Torval as he realized he would have to give up his hard-earned cash to this stranger. All those labors this morning, and all the possibilities his earnings afforded—all of that ruined by a chance encounter on the street! Also, so far he'd encountered mostly good humans during his travels here, and now he found himself facing one who was—

*Evil.* The man was doing evil! An evil act, perpetrated right here in front of him—that was something new! So far during his time in the Middle World, Torval had seen plenty of evidence of goodness, but not evil—at least not until now. He couldn't resist trying to learn more.

"You are committing a crime," the demon went on, as if the gun a few inches from him meant nothing. "You are deliberately committing an evil act. I must know, why are you doing this? What motivates you to be this way? Are you not aware that this is wrong? What is it that allows you to bypass your human morals and—"

"Shut up!" yelled Zac suddenly, starting to draw the pistol from the shoulder holster. "Just shut the fuck up and hand over your money now, or I'll—!"

"What's going on back here?" interrupted a man's voice—a voice that held a deep note of authority. "Zac Turillo, is that you, harassing somebody into buying one of your cheap knockoffs?"

As the newcomer spoke, Zac's anger vanished and his face turned pale. He took a step backward, whipped his hands down to his sides and closed his coat swiftly. "No, no, officer, we're just talkin'," he protested weakly. "Can't a decent, law-abiding citizen give a poor lost tourist some helpful advice anymore?"

Torval turned to see a uniformed policeman standing at the entrance to the street. The man looked tall and solidly built, without a trace of fat anywhere on him. His face was craggy and rough, and the grim expression there, right down to the neatly trimmed mustache, suggested he meant business.

"Oh, you can," said the cop, "but that's all you better be doin' on my beat. Is this gentleman harassing you, sir?"

Joe considered his response carefully. With a word, he could reveal the presence of the gun, and declare that Zac had threatened him with death. Yet if he did those things, the policeman would involve Joe in some sort of prosecution proceedings that would disrupt everything he was trying to do in the city. From the sheer number of lawyers and similar people in Hell, Torval knew he wanted little to do with such people while he remained on Earth.

Furthermore, he had questions he wanted answered, and he wouldn't get those if he turned Zac in. Instead he faced the quivering man and replied, "I was simply asking some questions, and if they are answered to my satisfaction, there will be no trouble."

"Fine," said the policeman, apparently satisfied with that answer. "Now, I heard there were some scammers here earlier, runnin' a street game. Any of you see anything?"

"Nope, not me," said a suddenly less worried Zac. "Did you, buddy?"

"There was a game played with cups and a ball," replied Torval, "but the men involved departed some minutes ago."

"All right, I'll keep an eye out. Now, you two, if you're gonna talk, do it out here on the street, not in some dark alley. You never know what sort of things might happen down there. Come on, out. Out!"

Torval agreed, and moved to a position out on the open sidewalk. Zac followed and watched nervously as the beat cop sauntered off, occasionally chatting with pedestrians, and all the while keeping a careful eye on what was going on around him. Perhaps his approach is what caused the shell game to break up so swiftly, thought the demon.

"You coulda turned me in," said Zac quietly after a moment. "I wasn't gonna shoot you, y'know."

"I did not think you would," replied Torval with a shrug. "The weapon would've drawn attention to yourself, and you had no easy route by which to escape from that location. Besides, you do not strike me as a hardened criminal. You appeared too afraid. That is why I asked you those questions."

"What questions? Oh, yeah, right," replied Zac, who now seemed to have deflated, as if winded by heavy exertion. "Dude . . . I dunno . . . I been sellin' shit like this for months, tryin' to squeeze a few bucks out of tourists and stuff, but I barely make enough ta live on. That's why I got me this gun, see? It's like insurance. I'd never use it, though, never! I may be a crook but I ain't no murderer, not me."

"Why do you do it?" asked Torval directly. "Why do you steal? Is there no better way to earn money?"

"Not for me," Zac complained. "Dude, I tried, but there ain't no jobs, and I don't wanna be no bum! I'm too shaky for Lucky's crew, but I found this guy, he works for one of the pawn shops, who gets all this fake shit and sells it to me for peanuts. All I gotta do is sell a few every day and I can keep my place. It's harder and harder every day, though. Nobody buys and there's so many cops, and just one bust and I gotta start all over."

"But surely you know what you do is wrong," put in Torval. "You are doing evil, are you not? You know that if you are caught you will be punished. Is that not so?"

"Yeah, yeah, of course it is," Zac admitted. "Sure, it's wrong, but you know what, man? I don't really care. These people, they're so rich, they come here to the Big Apple and they eat hundred-dollar meals, and they don't give a shit that people like me can't get real jobs, so why shouldn't I take some of their money? They don't need it, do they? And I do. So why shouldn't I just take it?"

Torval frowned. He had no good answer to that, and yet, he'd heard this very same excuse many times back in Hell. Those rich people, his prisoners explained, were born into money, or had things easy for one reason or another—why should the poor be punished for an accident of birth, or some other crippling defect? Why shouldn't they be entitled to their share of the wealth?

"You did not earn my money," said Torval after a moment, "whereas I did earn it. I was given a task, I performed it, and I was rewarded for my efforts. You did not participate in this endeavor, and therefore, you are not entitled to any of my reward. Why should you be allowed to simply take it, simply because you possess a gun and I do not? Surely even you must know that this is unfair."

Zac stared at him, contemplating the words. "Yeah," he said after a short wait, "yeah, I hear ya man, and I'm sorry I tried anythin', but I thought you were just like them others. I didn't know you."

"It does not matter who I am," Torval went on. "The point is, you did nothing to earn a share of anyone else's money. Taking it from them under such circumstances is wrong and will earn you a just punishment, sooner or later. Are you not aware of this?"

Zac's shoulders sagged. "Yeah, yeah, I guess I am," he sighed wearily. "It's just that it's so hard, y'know, and this is such easy money—"

"That is why you do it, then?" Torval pressed, sensing he might finally be getting to the heart of the matter. "Because it is easy?"

"It's the easiest thing I know," admitted Zac after another delay. "It's easier than payin' taxes and workin' long hours, that's fer sure."

Torval nodded. Things were beginning to make sense. This man could probably find a proper job, but he chose instead to commit crimes because of simple laziness. In his own words, robbery was easier than working for a living. Perhaps he'd finally learned one of the basic tenets of evil—that it promised a quick and easy route, without regard to the consequences.

"Thank you," the demon said after a moment. "You have answered my questions, Zac, and I have learned something, which is all I could have asked for. In addition, I owe certain debts, which I can now begin to pay. For helping me, I will give you this."

Reaching into his pocket, he pulled out one of his twenty-dollar bills—the extra one he'd received as a bonus. Even as his face twisted into one of those enjoyable, reflexive smiles, he handed the money over to a stunned Zac, who took it in a shuddering hand.

"Y-you're actually going to give me money?" stammered the man. "I tried to rob you at gunpoint and you—you're paying me?"

"Since I arrived here," explained Torval nonchalantly, "I have been the focus of several acts of kindness, which I feel obliged to repay through others. This is the first of those payments. Thank you for your help, Zac."

The man just looked at him, almost through him, and for a second Torval thought maybe Zac could see past his human disguise. Just as the demon turned to leave, though, Zac suddenly moved again. He reached into his coat and withdrew one of the watches, one with a wide band of gold links and a white face studded with gems. "Take this," he said, shoving it toward Torval. "Go on, man, at least let me give you this one! It didn't cost me anything, since I—oh, never mind, just take it! You need a watch anyway, and this one actually works!"

"Very well," agreed Torval, taking the item and sliding it on his wrist, where it dangled limply. Apparently the band was a bit wide for someone as thin as himself, but he could work around that. At least he had a timepiece now. "Thank you once again."

"You too, man," Zac replied. "I got some thinkin' to do, now, I guess. See ya 'round."

He turned and departed, disappearing into the crowd. Torval watched him go, thinking inwardly that those parting words seemed improbable at best. He doubted very much that he'd ever see Zac again. Not that it mattered, anyway.

Now to get some fresh clothing, he told himself, setting off once again down the crowded street.

# Chapter 24

As he walked along, thinking about the encounter with Zac, Torval absently fiddled with the watch. The band was far too wide, so that if he didn't hold the timepiece in place constantly, it would fall off. The same problem didn't seem to be afflicting any other nearby humans, most of whom wore watches securely attached to their wrists.

At the next light he stopped and studied the band. Most of it consisted of silver and gold links, like pieces of chain braided together, but one section resembled a pair of slightly curved flaps. These had a joint between them that could be folded, and after a moment of fiddling Torval figured out the trick of it. Once pushed together, the flaps snapped in place, securing the band tightly. By lifting up on a small tab, he could pop the clasp open again whenever he wished.

Glad to have made that connection, he pushed the watch under his sweater, where it settled in comfortably enough that he quickly forgot it was there. Continuing on across the street, he contemplated what he'd just learned from the street vendor and would-be mugger. Torval now knew one reason why humans committed acts of evil—because they were easier than doing things honestly.

In fact, thinking more about the experience, Torval understood just how easy robbery really was. He'd spent that entire morning running an errand for Pete Roxton, and lugging that obnoxious container back to the warehouse, not even counting the previous night's labors that had earned him that very opportunity. Yet Zac Turillo, lurking in the shadows with his gun, could've taken every one of those six twenty-dollar bills with a simple threat (assuming, of course, that Joe Sampson wasn't presently possessed by a demon with motives other than survival). So instead of many hours of work, all Zac had to do was point a gun at people and take their hard-earned funds.

Yes, it did seem easy, until Torval factored in the risk. The police officer who happened upon the scene could've put a quick end to the crime if he'd actually seen the weapon. Zac could've been arrested and imprisoned, or perhaps even shot. So yes, the mugging would've taken only minutes, but the penalty for failure was far more severe.

Torval could understand that risk. Back in Hell, First-Class demons frequently involved themselves in intrigue and power struggles as the more advanced among them strove to one day achieve the elusive ranks of the elite—baron, duke, and so forth. The rank of Duke of Hell, for example, brought with it status and power, and the ability to do nearly anything within the demon's own layer. Yet the penalties for failure were harsh and sometimes very final. Just as Zac potentially faced death under a police officer's gun, a demon that lost a power play faced the great blackness of Oblivion.

Torval wanted nothing to do with such games, one of the many reasons he hoped this vacation wouldn't lead to a promotion. He didn't know if he could advance to Second Class without also acquiring a taste for power, nor did he have much desire to find out. So, for similar reasons, he also rejected the possibility of breaking the law to earn money while on Earth. He would follow the rules, exactly as he did back home, and that's all there was to it.

At length he reached a building where he knew he could purchase clothing. The department store, as its name proclaimed, showed off numerous male and female outfits in picture windows. Why it should be known as a "department store" baffled Torval, but humans used many names that made little sense. Shrugging, he went inside.

The racks he encountered first contained clothing made for ladies, although for some reason a few men shopped among the rows. Perhaps purchasing gifts for others, he deduced, moving along the main pathway deeper into the store. Many of the outfits he saw on display did indeed seem elegant. He tried to imagine what they might look like on Christine, but couldn't quite put together the mental picture properly. When he thought of her, he could only visualize that happily smiling face and those penetrating blue eyes.

Perhaps I could purchase something like this for her, he thought, wondering if that might begin to repay his debts. However, he didn't know if she would even like these things. He hadn't seen her wearing anything quite like these garments. What if he spent a considerable sum of money on a dress that she despised?

Forgetting that idea, he moved on further into the store, toward the signs directing him to men's clothes. Once there, he perused the various rows and shelves, looking first for a replacement set of trousers. He found quite a collection of possibilities, apparently known as "slacks," arranged with some sort of numbering system Torval assumed meant the price. There were some numbered in the 40s, while others went as low as 30. Torval couldn't see any differences that would explain why one pair cost 48 dollars while another seemingly identical set cost 32, but since he had only a limited amount of money, he selected the cheapest and moved along.

Now, he supposed, he had to purchase the slacks, so he looked around for some means to do this. After a moment he spotted a cash register, which he recognized from examples found in cell illusions. As Torval moved toward the machine, a freckle-faced young woman greeted him immediately. She wore a light green collared shirt that bore a nametag identifying her as "Sarah." As he stepped up to the counter, she made a curious gesture with her head, tossing her long blonde hair back over her shoulders and smiling at him. "Find everything you need, sir?" she inquired graciously.

"So far," replied Torval, bemused by the fact that she referred to him as "sir." No one ever referred to a Third-Class demon in that manner back home. "I wish to purchase these."

Sarah took the pants and swiftly removed the hanger, tossing it onto a pile hidden half-concealed behind her post. Then she found a tag Torval hadn't noticed before, pointed a disconcertingly gun-like device at it, and produced a "beep" from her machine. At once a series of numbers appeared on a display above the register. Torval's eyes jumped at once from the mysterious tag to the numbers, which displayed a price of $78.50.

Before he could protest, Sarah spoke up. "Buying a gift, I see," she said amiably. "Will that be cash or credit?"

"Um, it is not a gift," replied Torval worriedly, for he now realized he'd completely misunderstood the clothing labels. The numbers on little wheels amidst the racks didn't indicate the price at all! Too late now, though—he'd already committed to buying.

"It's not?" Sarah asked, a wrinkle of surprise crossing her freckled forehead. "You mean it's for you?"

"Yes, that was my intent," replied the frustrated demon, "but I also had not understood the price."

Sarah chuckled at him. "Don't worry, I see this all the time with people visiting from overseas. Here in the States, I'm guessing you'd be about a size 38, not a 30. If you tried to put these on, you'd see the top of your socks!"

"Then that number refers to . . . sizes?"

"Yep. You might want to try some on before you check out next time. You can use the changing rooms in the back if you like."

Torval followed her pointing finger and immediately spotted a doorway in the back marked "Fitting Rooms." So, it he could simply put the pants on here in the store! That was useful information, indeed.

"In the meantime, want me to cancel this purchase for you?" Sarah went on. "I'll hang them back up, if you don't want them."

"Certainly," agreed Torval, breathing a sigh of relief that he wasn't about to waste four-fifths of his remaining money on ill-fitting pants. "Thank you," he added after a moment, barely remembering the proper ritual.

"Sure, anytime," said Sarah with a smile. "Where are you visiting from, if you don't mind my asking? Your English is pretty good."

Torval hesitated. He couldn't tell her the truth, obviously, and yet he didn't really know any other places. Wait—there was another place name he knew, from the book about money. "I am from Rhodes," he replied, using the city the ancient trader Antigonus hailed from, and hoping it was still there after all these years.

"Roads?" she asked curiously. "What roads?"

"It is a city in Greece," explained Torval.

"Oh, Greece! Wow, that's cool! I'd love to go there someday and see all those ruins, like the Coliseum! I saw some pictures in my art history class last semester, and I thought they were really neat."

Torval sighed. So, the country was in ruins! Well, even so, the lie seemed to have fooled Sarah. Still, best to not allow this conversation to continue, lest he reveal through some other error that showed he really knew very little about Greece. "In any event," he said hastily, "I thank you for your help, Sarah. I must be going now."

"Sure," she replied, looking a little disappointed, as if she'd hoped to continue talking. Humans certainly did seem to enjoy doing that, if given a chance, didn't they? "If there's anything else I can do for you, just let me know!"

* * *

Now that he understood the numbers on the racks indicated sizes, and the prices were on the little tags dangling from each article, Torval had an easier time of it. Taking Sarah's suggestion that he might be a size 38, he moved through the men's department looking for something affordable. Unfortunately, most of what he found turned out to be at least fifty dollars or more, which seemed excessive. Torval had no idea how much pants were supposed to cost, but he only had a hundred dollars available, and if he spent more than half of that on one item, he doubted he could afford the other things he needed.

Fortunately, after exploring the store further, he discovered some cheaper items known as "jeans." In addition to thicker and heavier construction, they were advertised as being designed for laborers. Just the thing to wear while working at the Roxton warehouse!

Exploring further, Torval located a section where the jeans were "on sale," which apparently meant they were cheaper than normal—twenty percent off the listed thirty dollar price, in fact. Satisfied with this, and pleased at discovering such a bargain, Torval picked some jeans and went to try them on.

Torval had little trouble figuring out the fitting rooms. He went inside, selected one of the empty chambers, changed his pants, and inspected the result. The jeans were indeed comfortable, not binding at all, and the multiple mirrors showed they looked adequate, at least as far as he could tell. Lacking any means to identify whether they were properly sized or fashionable, all he could do was judge them on the basis of comfort. Since they weren't falling down about his ankles, or constricting his breathing, he judged they would suffice.

As he moved to put his original pants back on, his eyes fell upon a small tag which he hadn't really looked at before. Hidden amidst the small writing there, he found the number 38. Now that he knew this referred to a size code, he realized he'd chosen correctly. Well, Sarah had, actually—good thing for him she had a good eye for sizes!

With the selection made, he headed back out to the same register he'd used before. Sarah was still there, but had another customer at the moment. He stood in line, observing the purchase procedure. The man there used some sort of card instead of cash, one very much like the MetroCard that allowed access to the subway. Just like that device, the blue rectangle operated by sliding through a slot, where it apparently secured the purchase for the buyer somehow.

Torval remembered that Prelz earlier referred to this process as "automation." The card had something magnetic on it that a "computer" was able to read. In some way Torval didn't fathom, this entire process totally replaced money. Had the humans come up with something better than cash? Would souls no longer come to Hell for money-related crimes? If so, that would reduce the population considerably.

He doubted that, though. As Prelz told him, humans had plenty of evil within their souls. They would just find other ways to sin. Perhaps there were methods available to cheat or defraud these mysterious "computers," whatever they were. Torval felt sure that if stealing from them was easier than earning a living, there would always be some humans who would take advantage of that fact to do evil.

"Find what you needed, then?" asked Sarah, breaking into his thoughts. Torval realized the other customer had departed without his noticing. Stepping into the man's spot, the demon handed over his selection. "Size 38," she went on, grinning. "Told you!"

"Yes, you were correct," Torval agreed. "That was very helpful, Sarah."

"I aim to please," she replied, ringing up the sale with a satisfied grin on her face.

Torval watched the numbers on the screen, which were higher than he expected. Instead of twenty-four dollars, the supposed price after the twenty percent discount, the cost climbed over twenty-five dollars. Apparently, something called "sales tax" got added on at the end. Yes, he remembered encountering sales tax once before, back when he purchased the bagel and coffee the previous morning.

Torval knew a little bit about taxes. Taxation caused plenty of crimes that landed sinners in Hell. Some of these unfortunates were tax collectors, intent on following the letter of the law without regard to anything else, while others were cheaters who ducked taxes, or used them as a basis for other illicit activities. Taxes were fees, collected by societies or governments for some reason or other, but that's about as far as his knowledge went.

He knew he didn't want to pay the tax, but on the other hand, he felt pretty sure that refusing to pay would be a mistake. Instead, he simply withdrew two twenty-dollar bills from his pocket and handed them over, hoping that he didn't need one of those little cards to actually make a purchase.

Fortunately, he didn't. Sarah took the cash, slid it into the drawer, and counted out his change, a little over thirteen dollars. After that, she deposited his jeans into a plastic bag and set it on the counter. "Thank you, sir. Will there be anything else today?"

"Not at this time," replied Torval, pocketing the change and holding out one of the five-dollar notes. "Here is your tip."

"Tip?" She gave him a befuddled look. "Oh, no, you don't have to tip me! I appreciate the thought, but—"

"But you have provided me with a service," he answered. "I was told that when someone provides a service, they are to receive a tip."

"Well, yeah, I guess," Sarah answered with a giggle, "but that's for, like, food service and stuff. Not department stores. Sorry, I guess you didn't get the full explanation."

Torval nodded. So, he hadn't quite understood that particular custom properly. He should tip when served a meal, not for other types of service. Good to know.

"Very well," he replied, "but still, you did help me avoid a mistaken purchase, and for that I believe you deserve a tip."

Sarah hesitated, glancing around and running one hand through her wavy blonde locks. "I don't know," she said worriedly. "I don't think I'm really supposed to accept tips. I've only been working here three weeks, and this is the first time anyone's done anything like this."

Torval nodded. "I do not wish to get you in trouble, Sarah. Perhaps if I simply left the bill here on the counter." He set it down next to the register and looked back at her. "Thank you for your help today."

He departed without glancing back, so he never knew if she actually took the five dollars or not. As he moved toward the exit, he felt another smile growing on his face, and realized, not for the first time, how much he liked it.

* * *

Was that a good act? Torval wondered about that as he left the store. He gave Sarah money that she wasn't expecting, and doing so did indeed make him feel happy inside. Giving twenty dollars to Zac also evoked a similar feeling, although not nearly as pronounced, primarily because of the watch.

Torval pulled up his sleeve and looked at the timepiece, which ticked away dutifully, displaying the time exactly as it was supposed to. He'd intended to simply give Zac money, which would've repaid one of his many debts, but instead he effectively bought a watch. Providing Sarah with five dollars, despite her attempt to refuse it, felt good, and yet that wasn't a gift, but a payment for her earlier service.

At least, thought Torval, he hadn't allowed either human to give him something—information—and not be paid for it. Still, he hadn't managed to truly do good, at least as he understood the concept. If he had, he would've given them something without receiving anything at all in return, except perhaps the pleasant feeling of warmth that, even now, made him smile.

Did doing good feel that way all the time? Was it even more pronounced when he did it properly? Is that why Christine did the things she did, in order to feel this way? If so, that would explain much, indeed. Perhaps goodness brought on sensations of euphoria. Yet if so, why would anyone do evil? Wouldn't people like Zac prefer to do good deeds instead, to feel this way all the time?

Torval sighed. He still didn't think he was on the right track. He didn't think doing good involved feeling some sort of pleasurable sensation. Otherwise, evil would bring an opposite, painful response. Things just wouldn't be that easy.

He continued on down the street, thinking ahead to his next purchase. He'd already decided not to buy a new sweater, at least for now. The jeans cost more than he'd expected, despite being less than half the price of the slacks, and he didn't want to drain all his money. Instead he would find some undergarments, as well as a couple of other items that had crossed his mind while he shopped. He expected to find these in the approaching corner shop, described by its name as a "drugstore."

Another of those strange human names, thought Torval. There may well be drugs available there, but that wasn't what any of the signs and displays in the windows suggested. Many of the advertisements suggested low prices, for which he was grateful.

Shopping for a while, he located some cheap underwear, which apparently came three to a pack, and were in the correct range of sizes. Three should suffice for now, he decided, continuing down the rows.

He also knew he needed a way to shave, for his chin itched with stubble. After some searching, he discovered a selection of razors as well as cans of shaving cream. The razors looked nothing like the ones Ross the barber employed, but then, Torval didn't fancy the idea of using something so sharp and dangerous without being able to see his own face directly. The plastic-handled razors on the wall racks were advertised as safe, and cost only a few dollars. Perfect.

Torval also recalled needing some shampoo. The shower at the Roxton warehouse had soap, but no shampoo, so he'd used some lathered-up soap earlier, but the effect wasn't the same. The drugstore, fortunately, had quite a selection. Lacking any way of judging one brand from another, and knowing he only needed enough for less than two weeks, Torval simply selected the cheapest and smallest one.

He couldn't think of anything else, so he went to the cash register near the front of the store and made his purchase. There were no unexpected issues this time, so he left after a few minutes of waiting, toting another shopping bag under his arm.

* * *

The soup kitchen was fairly close now, but he headed there via a different route this time. He knew the way, instinctively, but the stores weren't what he was used to. In fact, as he came to the spot he knew he needed to turn, Torval spotted a familiar image—a red and white, stylized image of a bespectacled old man with a white beard. Below the icon, at an angle, were the distinctive letters "KFC."

So, this is where the Colonel lived, the one who'd provided the amazing meal the previous night! Torval knew he needed to stop there at once and thank the man. After waiting for a break in traffic, he quickly scurried across the street, despite the fact that he wasn't at an intersection. This seemed to be a common enough practice, so Torval saw nothing wrong with doing so.

Once he entered the restaurant, he saw at last what the letters stood for—"Kentucky Fried Chicken." So, that the official name of the food he ate the previous night! By far one of his best experiences on Earth so far, as the smell wafting through the place reminded him at once. In fact, he was already getting hungry again just from the scent of it. Perhaps he might purchase another meal during his visit.

But first, to business. He stepped up to the counter, where a dark-skinned young man of Hispanic descent stood waiting, dressed in a uniform of similar colors to the KFC logo. "May I help you?" he asked with a faint hint of a Spanish accent.

"Yes," replied Torval. "I wish to speak to the Colonel. I need to thank him for the meal he provided me last night."

The man behind the register glanced from one side to another. "Is this some kinda gag?"

"No, I do not believe so," replied the demon, somewhat surprised by this reaction. "I was provided with a container of chicken for dinner last night, and was told the Colonel himself donated it. I must thank him for this personally."

"Uh, right. Let me get the manager." The confused-looking youth headed back deeper into the store, where he found someone else and conversed briefly with him. After a moment, the manager approached, a very tall, thin man of advancing years, with only the barest hint of hair remaining on his otherwise bald and bony head. He wore a nametag that read, "Dale Stevens, Manager."

"Step over here," asked Dale, looking about as confused as the Hispanic man. Torval moved over to one side of the counter, allowing another waiting customer to place his order. "Now what's this about wanting to talk to the Colonel?"

Torval repeated what he'd told the other man. "All I wish to do is express my gratitude," he insisted.

"Well," said Dale with a grin of understanding, "I think someone's putting you on, my friend. He's talking about Colonel Sanders, who founded the first Kentucky Fried Chicken years ago. That's his face up there on our sign, but he's long since passed on. Whoever told you that was just speaking metaphorically, I bet."

"Oh," replied Torval, somewhat crestfallen. "I see. Pete must've meant that he purchased dinner from this place. I misunderstood."

"That's okay," said Dale. "Actually, it's really nice of you to stop by. Did you really like it that much?"

"Yes. Yes, very much so. I had not thought anything could evoke such a sensation in my mouth."

"Wait, so that was your first time eating fried chicken? Ever?"

"Yes," admitted Torval. "Until recently my diet has been very . . . limited."

"Well, glad you liked it," Dale replied, looking a bit bemused by the idea that someone could be Joe's age without sampling fried chicken at least once in his life. "There's a lot of chicken places out there, but I always thought KFC's the best. You should try some of the other kinds on the menu. I don't know if you had crispy or regular or what last night, but you might like one of the others even more."

"I shall do that," said Torval. "In fact, I believe I will have some right now. The smell of it is making me very hungry."

"Good for you. Have a nice day, then."

"I will try." Torval started to ask another question, but it was too late. Dale had turned away and was already heading back into the store. There was nothing to do but save the queries for another time. Now that he knew where this place was, Torval expected to return here often.

He returned to his place in line, studying the menu. He wasn't entirely sure precisely what he'd eaten the night before, but like Dale suggested, there were plenty of options. Any one of them would do. Furthermore, according to the display, if he purchased a "value meal" he would also acquire a drink, and one of those drinks was Coca-Cola—the same thing he'd enjoyed in the cans the night before. Another perfect choice.

The lunch cost him a little over six dollars, but as far as Torval was concerned, it was money well spent.

# Chapter 25

"There you are!"

Torval glanced around for the sound of the voice, which had erupted the instant he entered the nearly empty soup kitchen. The immediately identifiable figure of Prelz waved at him from the back.

"I was starting to wonder if you'd ever show up," Prelz said as his fellow demon approached. "Been checking in here all day."

Torval sat down at the otherwise unoccupied table. The few workers at the kitchen were in the back, performing various cleaning duties instead of serving food. Apparently lunchtime had passed, so with no handouts available, the bums were all out on the streets.

"I apologize for the delay," said Torval, setting his bags down next to him and flexing his somewhat sore arm muscles. Carrying the box earlier, and now his purchased goods, had taken its toll. "I earned some money and went, as I believe the humans say, on a shopping trip."

Prelz grinned. "I can see that. I'm surprised you got paid so early, but then, knowing what I know now, I guess it's not too shocking."

Torval's eyebrows went up. "You have information? What is it?"

The ex-Tempter nodded. "Yeah, I did some checking around. I thought I'd heard something about that warehouse, but I wasn't sure, but from what I'm hearing, they do more than just sell car parts."

"Oh?" inquired Torval, a bit irritated by the delay. Prelz seemed to enjoy drawing this out. "What do they do?"

"You didn't hear this from me," came the reply, "but I think they're a front for a chop shop."

Torval stared at him. The phrase made no sense whatsoever. Yet another one of those odd human euphemisms, apparently.

"I figured you wouldn't know what that was," replied the continuously grinning Prelz. "A chop shop is where they take stolen cars and break them down into their components, then sell off the parts individually. The full car can be tracked, you see, but most of the parts can't. Plus, depending on the car, the bits might be worth more than the whole."

"You are suggesting the Roxtons are involved in illegal activity?" asked Torval doubtfully. "That they are committing crimes on a regular basis?"

"Yes, that's exactly what I'm saying."

Torval blinked a few times and looked down at the tabletop. Somehow, what Prelz just explained didn't seem possible. Lincoln Roxton had been running that business for a very long time, or so his stories led Torval to believe. How could they do anything illegal for so long and not be caught? And how could Prelz know about it, and not the police?

"You don't believe me," the Tempter stated, interrupting Torval's thoughts. "Well, I admit I don't have any proof, just some stories from a few people I know. Cars being driven into the place late at night, or on weekends, and never coming out. Rumors of investigations, too. Then there's what just happened with you."

"What do you mean?"

"Think about it," his companion went on. "You get an ordinary janitorial job, and the next day, they're having you deliver some secret briefcase to somebody, and you get paid in cash for the trip. That's not how things are normally done in this world, my friend! People don't get paid under the table unless there's some reason to hide the transaction."

"He did use that odd expression," admitted Torval, "and it did seem unusual, despite my lack of experience in this city. Nonetheless, I have seen no evidence of any wrongdoing. The briefcase contained only papers."

"Oh, is that so?" inquired Prelz. "Ah, so you got a look inside."

Torval cringed. He wasn't supposed to reveal that information, according to his instructions. Yet, he felt certain he could trust Prelz—if not, well, who on this strange world could he possibly trust?

"Well, it doesn't matter," the other demon continued, rubbing at his forehead absently. He looked a little weary. "Look, I could be wrong about this, I guess. Like I said, I've got no direct evidence, but what info

I do have points that way. It's not natural to hire some random guy on the street, have him make some secret delivery, and then pay him off with cash. The only reason they would do that is if they were up to something."

"But what purpose would it serve?" asked Torval, mind whirling from these accusations. "Why would they trust someone like me to deliver something incriminating, if that is what you are suggesting? That would be a greater risk than simply doing it themselves, would it not?"

"Depends on what was on those papers," said Prelz, continuing to rub his forehead, as if to ward off a headache, "but yeah, I guess I see your point. Why not just send out one of their other employees to do it? Or this Pete guy could just take it himself? Well, I don't know all the answers, my friend. I'm just warning you, you might be getting involved in something illegal."

"I have broken no laws," Torval assured him. "Unless taking money 'under the table' is itself a crime."

Prelz shook his head and took a couple of deep breaths before responding. "No, not really, as long as you don't exceed a certain amount, I suppose it isn't. People pay for things in cash all the time, if it's not excessive. Besides, theoretically you'd be expected to report it on your taxes, but since you aren't going to be around long enough to worry about that, nobody's gonna care."

"Then I am not worried." Torval forced a shrug. "What the Roxtons are doing in their warehouse does not concern me. I will be careful to obey the rules of this world, and perform my tasks as directed. If I do not break any laws, I have nothing to be concerned with."

"That's true," agreed Prelz. "Actually, I'm kind of surprised by your reaction, y'know. I wasn't expecting you to have such a crisis of conscience there."

"What do you mean?"

"Well, I saw that look on your face, and I'm pretty good about reading stuff like that, after so many years in my business. I was a Tempter, you know."

"I still do not understand what you mean."

"It bothered you," explained Prelz, "that you thought you might be doing something wrong. You didn't like the thought that you might be committing a crime, did you?"

"I suppose not," admitted Torval sheepishly.

"That makes some sense, coming from your structured, regimented background," Prelz mused. "Your life's always been very orderly, hasn't it? You've never broken any rules or disobeyed any commands. It's not in your nature. So while you're here, you want to do the same thing. It terrifies you to think you might get into trouble, doesn't it?"

"I do not think 'terrifies' is the proper term," argued Torval, actually feeling a bit irritated by this line of questioning. "It does bother me, however. I admit that freely. This world is different from my home, and yet I feel bound by its rules, just as I do by my foreman's commands, and the orders of any greater demon."

"That's natural, I guess, but it's more than that, I can tell." Prelz ran his fingers through his thick, stringy beard for a few moments, contemplating his younger associate. "This has to do with your trying to figure out the nature of good and evil, doesn't it?"

"Yes, of course," admitted Torval with a sigh. "I have been attempting to understand the nature of good, and in doing so, I have tried to be what others consider a good person, in the hopes of gaining some measure of enlightenment. In fact, earlier today I committed what I believe to be at least two good acts."

"And?"

"And what?"

"And how did it make you feel?"

Torval started to reply, but hesitated, trying to find the words. After a moment, he realized he couldn't really explain it. "I do not know," he finally admitted. "It was . . . pleasurable. I suppose it was a form of happiness, because it made my human face smile."

"You felt good about yourself, then. It warmed your heart, didn't it?"

"Is that the way it is described? I suppose, then, that is what I felt. A fleeting emotion, but no less enjoyable. Yet I cannot accept that humans do good deeds simply for such sensations."

"No, of course not," agreed Prelz. "There's plenty of reasons, but mostly, they do good because it's the right thing to do. That's why you like it, and that's why it bothered you to think you were doing something wrong when I told you about the chop shop. Not because you're afraid of getting caught, but because you're in a human body now and you have a conscience."

"A what?" The look on Torval's face was one of complete befuddlement. "What is that? I am not familiar with the term."

"A conscience," explained Prelz, "is that little inner voice that tells you when you're doing something wrong. It's not a real voice, mind you, just a kind of sense of worry or dread, a sort of subconscious warning signal to your conscious mind."

"I admit I did feel something like that when you told me what a chop shop was." Torval thought back to that moment, recalling the sensation as best he could. "A sort of hollowness in my stomach, not unlike hunger, but also with a sort of chill."

"That," said Prelz, "is the opposite to that feeling of pleasure and happiness you got when you did something good. Remember when I told you about the Tree of Knowledge, that the first humans supposedly ate from, and learned what was good and what was evil? If that legend is true, then that's where they got the ability to feel those sensations. They're sort of a warning and a reward, to lead people to choose the proper path. But a lot of people don't feel them, or don't care. They just do whatever they want."

"I am beginning to understand why some people do evil," said Torval. "Today I encountered a man who attempted to rob me, and he explained that it was easier to take my money than to earn his own. Do you think he felt that same hollowness?"

"Probably," answered Prelz. "I can't wait to hear all about that particular escapade of yours, but you can tell me on the way."

"On the way where?"

"Remember when I told you I had someone I wanted you to talk to?"

"Vaguely..."

"Well, I went to his place today and checked his schedule, and he'll be in his office this afternoon, if you want to go. This is just the sort of person you can talk to about good and evil, if that's what you want, or anything else for that matter."

"Really?" inquired Torval. "What sort of man is this, that can answer such questions?"

Prelz grinned. "You'll understand more when we get there," the ex-demon explained. "He's a priest."

* * *

The building on the street corner ahead didn't look like most of the others Torval had seen in his journeys through New York City. With an angled roof, multicolored windows, and fenced-in grass yard, it looked out of place among its steel and asphalt surroundings. In fact, the stone-walled church might have been from another age entirely, transported somehow to this modern city through unknown means.

Before the structure stood a low sign, encased in glass, which announced some sort of services being held on certain numbered days. Prelz paid these no heed as he led Torval up the cracked, crumbling stone steps to the arching wooden doors. He looked anxious to get inside, and a bit pale, as if the brief walk to the church had exhausted him.

The vacationing demon hesitated at the entrance, unsure if a bum like Jake would be allowed inside such an imposing structure, but Prelz went inside without stopping. Within, the two demons entered a small atrium that opened into a wide-open cathedral topped by a domed roof covered in fanciful paintings. Torval gasped aloud. The church didn't seem this big from the outside! Was it some sort of illusion, or something more . . . ?

Most of the open area was lined with rows of seats, all facing toward a large, ornately carved table on a raised dais. Behind this, a ten-foot-high statue of a man hung on a cross, his head lolling to the side, ringed with a crown of thorns. To Torval's horror, the man's arms and feet appeared to have been nailed to the cross. The sight was so totally unexpected, especially in what he'd expected to be a sacred place, that he thought it must be some sort of mirage.

Prelz watched him with some amusement, actually chuckling aloud, despite the fact that he looked spent and sweated noticeably from the exertion of walking just a few short blocks. "Surprising, isn't it?" he said in a low, quiet voice. "Didn't expect to see that, did you?"

"N-no," admitted Torval shakily. "This is a church, is it not? Why would they portray such a—a grotesque image?"

"Let me explain, before I take you in to see Father Michaels," said Prelz, sitting down in the front row of pews to catch his breath. "Remember I told you there was another human legend, that the Creator Himself came to Earth in a man's body, to live a life as one of these people?"

"Yes, I remember you saying something about that, but what possible relevance could that have?"

"That's Him," explained Prelz, pointing at the horrifying statue.

Actually, Torval had seen much worse tortures in cell illusions, but what bothered him wasn't the physical abuse, but the fact that such a thing would be prominently displayed in a supposedly holy place. "What do you mean, that's Him?"

"That's the man God supposedly became," Prelz went on, wiping the perspiration off his forehead. "He was called Jesus Christ, and He was born about two thousand years ago, give or take. The people back then couldn't accept that some random unknown guy was actually their Creator, you see. They thought He was a blasphemer, so they tortured Him like this, until He died on that cross. That's how people were executed back then—by crucifixion. Then, supposedly, He rose from the dead, forgave them their sins and returned to Heaven, after which He hasn't much gotten involved in human affairs."

"So that is why they make a statue of Him like that?"

"Yes, exactly so. They say it's because this Jesus died for their sins, but I suspect it's also to remind people of their own foolishness. I mean, seriously, if a man can lay His hands on somebody and cure their illness, doesn't that mean He's something more than just a man? I'd think that would be kinda obvious, don't you? Back then, though, people led simpler lives, and something like that scared the hell out of them—if you'll forgive the expression. Plus, Jesus was a threat to the establishment, too, because He preached tolerance and understanding, and challenged those in power, so of course they wanted Him dead too. It wasn't until many years later that those who remembered Him began to understand who and what He truly was."

"Do you believe this story?" asked Torval. "You speak as if it is just a legend, and yet you sound at least partly convinced."

"Who can say?" shrugged Prelz. "It's been two millennia, y'know. They didn't write down any of that stuff for years after He died, so I'm sure the stories grew in the telling. What's important, though, is that a lot of humans today believe it. There's a collection of religions called 'Christianity' that revolve around this Jesus Christ person, and although they have some slight differences between them, they all agree that Jesus was God in human form."

"Yes, I have heard of Christianity," said Torval. "There was a man in one of my cells who prayed regularly to Christ for deliverance from his punishment, and I have heard the name from others as well. Now that I understand the background, I know who they were referring to, and some of what they said makes more sense."

Prelz studied him for a moment, again scratching at his beard. "Why didn't you ask them about it back then?" he wondered.

"In the cells?" Torval cocked his head. "I don't know. I suppose it never mattered before. I didn't care."

"But you care now."

"Only insofar as it aids me in understanding good and evil," explained Torval. "Speaking of which, when will I meet this priest?"

"Fine, enough history lessons, I suppose. Damn, I'm still winded! I usually don't mind walking around too much, but I'm exhausted." Prelz shrugged and pulled himself to his feet, wobbling back and forth as he gathered his strength. "Anyway, he's in his office, probably preparing his next sermon. I dropped by earlier and he told me he'd be here all afternoon, until the evening service. Come this way."

Torval followed as Prelz led him past the altar and toward a doorway on the far back side of the church. This led into a hall containing a coat rack, small closet, and several doors. One of these stood open, and clearly visible beyond a man in black clothing waited, seated at a desk. He wore an out-of-place white collar fastened securely about his neck. He seemed busy with some papers, but glanced up at the sound of approaching footsteps. "Ah, it's you, Jake!" he said immediately, standing up. "And you brought the friend you told me about. Good, good."

"Yep, this is Joe Sampson," said Prelz. "Joe, this is Father Thomas Michaels."

The priest nodded, but didn't leave his office, which was extremely small—just big enough for a single, simple desk and accompanying chair. The tall, lanky man was dressed entirely in black except for the white collar underneath his lapels. He had a narrow, square sort of head, with closely cropped black hair showing only a bare hint of lightening about the sideburns. "Nice to meet you," he said in a friendly voice. "Jake told me all about you earlier today. He said you were confused, and could use some counseling."

"Yes, I suppose that is so," agreed Torval. "I am, um, new to this city, and I seek to understand why people act as they do."

"You want to understand good and evil," offered Father Michaels.

"Yes, just so."

"Very well, then. Take my hand, Joe. Go ahead. No need to be afraid."

Thomas extended his hand. Torval, having experienced this greeting already numerous times, thought nothing of it and shook. For a moment, he thought perhaps Father Michaels would be revealed as a demon in human form, but nothing happened. He seemed completely human, to Torval's relief.

However, the priest's face betrayed a completely different reaction. He held onto his guest's hand for several seconds, not letting go, studying the man before him with something akin to wonder.

Finally, Father Michaels released his grip, shook his head, and took a long, deep breath. For a moment, he seemed afraid, as if looking for someplace to flee. The moment passed, though, and he wiped his suddenly moist brow and tried very hard to look unconcerned.

"What is it?" asked Torval finally, starting to become a little concerned. "What's wrong?"

"Nothing," replied Thomas, glancing over at Prelz with a resigned look on his face. "It's just that I hadn't expected to ever meet another demon in my lifetime. Having one around is plenty, thank you very much."

# Chapter 26

"Wait," said Torval, confused. "You can see me as I truly am? You see my demon form?"

"When I touched you, yes," admitted Father Michaels. "I must admit, I was surprised. You don't look anything like Jake here. In fact, you look a lot more like what demons are supposed to look like, at least how they're usually thought of. That's why I reacted like that. You scared me, there for a moment."

"I apologize," said Torval hastily. "I did not mean to frighten you. I was under the assumption that humans couldn't perceive my demonic state."

"Normally they can't," put in Prelz, "but there are some who can, apparently. I must admit, it was as much a surprise to me as it was to Thomas here, when it first happened. I suppose it's because he's so devout, or something, although I've never really figured it out."

"I like to think of it as a sign from God," suggested Thomas dismissively. "He gave me this ability for a reason, just as He has plans for everyone. In any event, please, come with me. There's a conference room in the back where we can all be seated more comfortably, if you want to talk further."

"Sure," agreed Prelz. The priest led on, down the hallway, to another door in the back. This opened into a narrow room containing a simple table with a half-dozen chairs arranged haphazardly about.

"Forgive the accommodations," said Father Michaels, "but we don't have a lot of space here. This is the best I can do, unless you want to talk out there in the open, where someone might walk in or overhear us."

"I'd rather not," Prelz replied, sitting down as best he could in the cramped little room. The priest also took a seat, and motioned for Torval to do the same, which he did with some difficulty.

The fact that a human could see him as a demon felt strange to Torval, but it didn't really bother him all that much. As far as he was concerned, it was just another strange anomaly in a bizarre world filled with anomalies. For whatever reason, this human priest could see demons for what they were, so that was that.

"Let me tell you something about Father Michaels here," Prelz began once he'd gotten as comfortable as he could on his rickety folding chair. "Back when I was having my crisis of conscience, all those years ago, he was here for me. He heard my confessions—these Catholics, you see, have a ritual of confession where they can admit their sins and be forgiven. The priest, of course, is bound by his oath to the Church never to reveal what he hears in the confessional to anyone—not even another priest."

"It's a burden," noted Thomas with a smile, "but you get used to it."

"Anyway," Prelz continued, "it took a while, but I eventually confided to Thomas that I was a demon. He didn't believe me, I'm sure."

"Not at first," the priest agreed, "but I believed that you believed it, and that's how I approach things."

Prelz nodded. "I still remember what you told me back then, when you thought I was really just a man—a confused man, obviously, or maybe crazy. You said I shouldn't think like a demon, but as a human being, and do what a man would do. To follow my conscience. That's what got me started thinking about renouncing demonhood. And then there was that one day I shook your hand to thank you for all your advice, and you saw me as I truly was."

"Yeah." Father Michaels chuckled. "That was a real eye-opener, I can tell you! I spent a lot of time praying after that, but then I realized you weren't any different than any other soul, just trying to find redemption."

"You helped me," pointed out Prelz, "and I appreciate that. I know that's why you're here, and that's what made me think to bring Joe here to see you. He's not like me, stuck on Earth on some unnecessary assignment. He's here on vacation, so he can find out what it means to be human."

Thomas nodded. "So you said earlier, but why? Why would a demon need to understand humanity?"

"We aren't sure, but we think it's because he's facing an impending promotion, and he needs to know this stuff so he can take on his new job. Well, that's just a theory, of course. Anyway, sorry, I shouldn't be talking for Joe—I know I like to talk too much sometimes. Go ahead, Joe, ask him whatever you want."

"Yes, please," said Father Michaels. "Just remember, Joe, I'm bound by my oath in this room just as I am in the confessional. Anything you say to me will be held in the strictest confidence. I'm not even permitted to reveal to anyone else that I know you're a demon. Not that I ever would," he added with a shrug. "I'm pretty sure no one would believe me."

"Very well," said Torval hesitatingly. "Since I arrived on this world, there is one specific facet of human life that interests me the most. I wish to understand the nature of good and evil."

Thomas sighed, looking up at the ceiling with arms thrust outward as if in supplication. "Something simple!" he said with a certain amount of sarcasm. "That's kind of hard to explain, isn't it? Well, I suppose the best way to put it is that good is helpful, positive, and constructive, while evil is selfish, harmful, and destructive. That's the nutshell version, as best I can put into words."

"Very well," replied Torval with a nod. "That is what I needed to know. Thank you for your time, Father Michaels." He started to stand, intending to leave, but couldn't quite make it out of the chair right away.

"Wait, that's it?" Prelz gaped at him. "All this work getting this meeting set up, and you ask one question, and that's it?"

Still trying to escape the chair, Torval shrugged. "I found out what I needed to know."

"You don't have any other questions?"

"I have many," replied Torval, realizing now that he wasn't going to escape this place quite so easily, "but I had intended to ask you, not a human. Nonetheless, if you like, I can do so here. Perhaps Father Michaels can help answer them as well."

"Sure," agreed the priest. "I'm here to listen, and provide answers and advice. That's what people like me do."

"All right, then." Torval paused, thinking about the many things he'd wondered about during the course of the day, and one item in particular jumped to mind. "I would like to take a woman out on a date. How may this be accomplished?"

Thomas hung his head. "And then there are some things I really can't help with," he said with a resigned sigh.

Prelz laughed uproariously, slapping at the tabletop in sudden mirth. Torval stared at him, confused by this reaction, until the other demon composed himself enough to explain. "Sorry, Joe, but Catholic priests aren't allowed to frolic with the opposite sex. You actually have more experience than Father Michaels on that particular subject. How about you ask something else?"

"You aren't... allowed?" inquired Torval doubtfully.

Thomas nodded. "Yes, it's one of the vows we take, when we receive the Sacrament of Holy Orders—when we're ordained as priests, I mean. Being chaste keeps us pure, supposedly, although I must admit it doesn't make me immune to temptation." He flashed an accusing glance at Prelz, who rolled his eyes and grinned.

"Very well, I can see you would not be able to help explain the difference between sex and love, either," noted Torval.

"Afraid not," agreed the priest. "There are some subjects I'm just not an expert in."

"All right, I will proceed to another query," said Torval, moving along to the next item on the mental list he'd compiled. "Several times today, in my travels about the city, I have encountered items referred to as 'automation' or 'computers.' From what I have been able to discern, they are devices of some sort that perform specialized tasks. For example, I was given a card that I slid into one of these computers, and I was permitted access to the subway. How do these machines work? We have nothing like them in Hell."

"You don't?" asked Father Michaels, sounding surprised by this. "Well, I mean, I suppose you wouldn't, would you? I guess it's not a very modern place, is it? Just fire and brimstone all about?"

"Now, now, none of that," warned Prelz. "You know we're not supposed to discuss what Hell is really like. It's against the Compact."

"Yes, well, you can't fault a man for trying." Thomas chuckled. "I hope I never have to see the place firsthand, after all, but that doesn't stop me from being curious."

Torval was silent for a moment. He hadn't realized he shouldn't talk about Hell with humans, although perhaps that fell under the "no interference" command from Geezon. Actually, the possibility of such a discussion had simply never occurred to him. No one had, until now, shown any interest in his origins, but then, how could they? He was supposed to be a human, not a demon.

"Anyway," the priest went on, "I'm really not a good source of information about computers, either. I don't really understand exactly how they work, but they're machines, just like cars and cell phones. Somehow they use electricity to make calculations, and depending on how they're built, they can perform certain tasks, just like a car can carry passengers around the city."

"Actually," remarked Prelz, "when I first got here twenty or thirty years ago, or however long it was, there weren't very many computers at all. Remember how I told you they used to use subway tokens and now they have card readers? That's what I'm talking about. Seems like there's always some new device coming along."

Torval nodded. "Yes, a great many things in the city are strange to me. You are saying many are relatively new?"

"Depending on the machine, yes," explained Prelz. "Ever see someone talking into a little box in their hand? That's a cell phone, and they've only been around for a decade or so. They're like telephones that you see in homes, but mobile, you see?"

"I don't know how those work either," Thomas remarked. "Something about towers around the city that pick up and relay signals to the phones themselves. They say that someday soon there won't even be wired phones anymore—everything will be cellular. I don't have one myself, but then, I don't have any family to call, and besides, can you imagine what would happen if it rang in the middle of the Eucharist?" He chuckled at that, although Torval had no idea what he was talking about.

"So, if I am to understand this," Torval asked, "the humans create new inventions on a regular basis? Every few years, or even faster?"

"There's new things coming out all the time," Father Michaels confirmed. "Every day, it seems like. I guess with six billion people on the planet, that's a lot of new ideas."

"Six . . . billion?" Torval was flabbergasted. "There are that many humans alive at this moment?"

"Yep."

Torval leaned back in the chair, totally dumbfounded. Six billion people! If they all died tomorrow, and even half of them were judged evil, would that many souls even fit in Hell?

Thinking about it, he remembered that once, long ago, he recalled hearing a promise, possibly from one of Lucifer's grand speeches, that there would be some kind of final judgment, or Apocalypse, in which the world would be scoured clean. Perhaps that hadn't happened simply because humanity was simply too numerous, and there would be nowhere to put them all.

Then again, perhaps it didn't matter. There were hundreds of layers in Hell, and Torval had no idea how deep most of them went. His own route had close to a thousand imprisoned souls, and over the centuries he'd changed that route many times, always at the orders of the foreman. If he'd actually cared to count, how many souls could he remember? Ten thousand? More? And how many other demons were there like him, walking similar routes? There may well be billions of souls already in Hell, for all he knew.

He couldn't quite wrap his mind around such immense numbers, so he shifted his thoughts back to the original matter, that of human technology. He knew about some of Man's creations, such as trains and typewriters and desktop telephones—not these new mobile devices, though. His knowledge of these came from seeing them in cell illusions, and while in a cell, he had the ability to interact with them in a way that his prisoner expected, because that too was driven by the illusion created by the soul itself. However, the souls he regularly visited had been in Hell for decades or even centuries. The older they were, the fewer machines and devices they had accompanying them.

In fact, come to think of it, when Torval first began his career as a Torturer, the most complex devices he encountered were farming tools and barrels of wine. Over the years he'd seen a gradual improvement in human technology, a little bit at a time, but he'd never really cared to notice before. So what Prelz and Thomas just told him made a certain amount of sense.

"Are you all right, Joe?" asked the priest, interrupting Torval's thoughts. "Your face went blank there for a moment."

"Yes, I am fine," replied the demon. "I was just . . . thinking. I have been doing my job for a long time, and yet, it seems as though I was never really paying attention at all."

"I know exactly what you mean," agreed Prelz. "You're starting to wake up, Tor—I mean, Joe. You're starting to think you were just going through the motions, and now, you're waking up from a dream."

Torval just stared at him, unsure of what to say.

"Yes, my friend," said Prelz, slapping him on the shoulder. "A very, very long and boring dream."

* * *

"So, what did you think?" inquired Prelz as he exited the spacious church, this time passing several humans on their way inside. Several of the passersby glanced back at the demon dressed as a bum, shaking their heads, one going so far as to hold her nose and mutter a half-formed curse at the scent wafting out from Jake's ruined garments.

"About what?" replied Torval, still trying to assimilate everything Father Michaels told him over the last hour and a half. The explanations and stories seemed to flit haphazardly about within his mind, unable to find a place to land.

"About Father Michaels, who else?" Prelz snorted, slapping his companion on the back. "Who else would I be talking about?"

"Oh. Well, I suppose he was informative," considered Torval weakly. "He answered many of my questions, and explained many things I had not previously understood."

Prelz waited at the edge of the street, watching for a good time to cross, and finally made his way hurriedly to the other side. Torval followed, shuffling quickly to avoid the next oncoming line of traffic, which already seemed to choke the roads as the hour grew late.

"You don't seem all that excited," said Prelz with a sigh. He already looked completely recovered from his earlier exertions, and strode along with renewed vigor. "And here I thought I was doing you a big favor."

"It was helpful, I assure you," Torval told him reassuringly. "I now know far more about good and evil than I did before. I also believe I have an understanding of the nature of religion. Or, at least, the foundation of such. Nonetheless, there are many questions Father Michaels was unable to answer, and in fact, for each thing he told me, I felt more questions arising. Furthermore, I am still struggling to make sense of much of what he did explain."

"That's natural." Prelz chuckled as the two headed back in the general direction of the shelter, in no particular hurry. "That was a lot of information he spewed out. Did you like the extended version of the Christ story?"

"Yes, it was very intriguing," admitted Torval. "Even if this Jesus person was not truly the Creator in human form, He certainly had a lot of useful lessons for humanity. His powers, too, were formidable, yet were used wisely, and in a way I believe would be called 'good.' Yet, had He so chosen, He could have wreaked much destruction with those same abilities. I can understand why those in power feared Him so."

"Good, good, I can see you were listening. Christianity is just one of the religions on this world, though. There are dozens, maybe hundreds, of others, and they all have equally compelling stories. I should find a rabbi for you to talk to, I guess, because they could tell you the Christ stuff from a totally different angle."

"What is a rabbi?" inquired Torval.

"Never mind, never mind. You and your damn curiosity! Anyway, you were still disappointed with Father Michaels, I can tell. Was it because he didn't answer a lot of your other questions?"

"Yes." Torval took a moment to emit a pronounced sigh. "He could not provide the information I most desired. Therefore, I will inquire again of you: How may I ask a woman out on a date?"

Prelz threw back his head and laughed. "I knew it!" he managed after a few moments. "You can't get Christine out of your mind, can you? You keep thinking about her all the time, right?"

Torval felt his face heating up, an altogether unsettling sensation. The emotion of embarrassment, he knew, and one that made his chest tighten and his fists clench of their own accord. He struggled to control these alien feelings and in the process found himself unable to speak.

"Sorry, sorry," went on Prelz, managing to control himself after a moment. "Sorry, my friend, I didn't mean to make fun of you. It's just that it's kind of amusing to see you having your first crush. You're like a teenager who just discovered for the first time that he likes girls."

Torval forced himself to nod. "I cannot explain it," he stated through gritted teeth, willing the unpleasant sensation away. "As a demon, I have no interest in such relationships, and yet here, in this human body, I cannot help myself. I do indeed find myself constantly thinking of Christine. I want to talk to her, to go out on a date, and much more than just that. I find myself wondering what it would be like to kiss her, or to copu—no, wait, what was the expression you used before? Ah, yes. To do the nasty with her."

Prelz rubbed his temples, sighing sadly. "You're never going to get slang right, I fear," he commented with a bemused shake of his head.

"Nonetheless," went on Torval, "as much as I try to fight it, that is what my human body wants. Since I am here to see what it is like to be human, I feel I must at least try to accommodate it."

"Really?" inquired Prelz with a raised eyebrow. "That's really all you want? Just to get it on with her, and that's it?"

"No, that is not all," protested Torval at once. "I want to understand more of who she is, and why she is good. I want to know her, as a person. If our bodies prove to be compatible, and that aids in this process, so much the better."

Prelz nodded, grinning knowingly. "Now you're just telling me what you think I want to hear. Let me ask you something, Torval. Did you ever ask yourself why you arrived on Earth in the body of a man? As opposed to a woman, I mean."

"Well, no," admitted the demon, somewhat surprised by the abrupt change in Prelz's line of questioning. "Why does it matter?"

"Humanity is almost exactly half male and half female," explained Prelz. "At least, in most societies today. It wasn't always like that, but nowadays it's almost exactly fifty-fifty. So do you think it was random chance you became a man when you went on vacation?"

"With the numbers you just described, I would guess so, but I believe you would not have offered the question if that were the correct answer."

"Insightful as always." Prelz chuckled. "No, you had a one hundred percent chance of arriving as a male, because you, my friend, are a male demon."

"What?" Torval found himself completely befuddled. "Demons are neither male nor female," he argued. "We do not reproduce as humans do. There is no point to our having gender."

"Nonetheless," went on Prelz, "it's quite true. When you climbed out of the Deep Pits, as a Fourth Class, you were sexless, but when you advanced, you gravitated toward one of the genders automatically. No one really knows how the choice is made, but it's probably related to whoever your handler was, or possibly toward the current male/female demon population. Whatever or however it works, you shifted toward the male. Haven't you ever noticed how your fellow Third-Class demons have vaguely male or female appearances? How the female ones have a different, curvier shape, and vestigial breasts? Certainly nothing that would ever function, and yet there they are. And on Second-Class demons and above, the genitalia actually work. It's said that First-Class demons are even capable of bearing children—maybe the creatures that spawn from the Pits come from such lofty origins, although if so, the exact method is kept pretty secret."

Torval shook his head in wonderment. How could it be that he had never heard such things before, or even contemplated them? Yet Prelz's words had the ring of truth. There were, indeed, male and female traits on every Third-Class demon and above. Furthermore, he had always thought of himself in the male sense, without even realizing it. In fact, that explained something else, something that now occurred to him for the first time.

"So," he went on slowly, finally beginning to understand, "that is why whenever I pass into a cell illusion, I always take a male form! Even if my prisoner was female, I still appear as a male every time."

"Yep," agreed Prelz at once. "Exactly so. You're male, Torval, and always have been, at least ever since you achieved self-awareness. Now, for the first time in your life, you've met an interesting female, and you can't stop thinking about her. This thing you're going through is entirely natural, my friend, and it's nothing to be ashamed or afraid of."

"What do you mean?" inquired Torval worriedly. "What exactly am I going through?"

Prelz laughed again and clapped him on the shoulder. "You, my friend," he replied with a knowing grin, "are experiencing puberty!"

# Chapter 27

Torval stared across the room, trying very hard to compose himself. His hands were clammy and cold, and felt moist beneath his fingers as he rubbed them together nervously. A thin sheen of sweat covered his forehead and he wiped it away without thinking about it.

"I do not think I like puberty much," he remarked sullenly, not taking his eyes off the trim form in the distance. Christine stood there, serving soup to the next homeless person in line, a smile on her face and a whistle on her lips. The attraction he felt was palpable. He could almost feel her drawing him toward her, like a magnet in human form.

"No one really does," replied Prelz, slurping at the creamy mixture steaming on the tip of his spoon. "Look, there's nothing to be scared about, my friend. Just talk to her like you would anybody else."

The odor wafting out of the soup bowl should've set Torval's taste buds to tingling with anticipation, but he wasn't really hungry, and he could only really think about Christine. Why should this be so hard? All he had to do was go up and ask if she wanted to have dinner with him. And yet he all but shook with fear and doubt. What if she refused? What if she laughed at him? He was only a bum, after all. He'd be nothing if she hadn't helped him out numerous times already. She'd see him only as a worthless shell of a man, the man she thought of as Joe Sampson.

If only she knew he was a demon—but no, that wasn't really an option. If he tried to explain, she wouldn't believe him. Unless she had the same ability as Father Michaels, and could see him as he truly was, there'd be no way to prove he was anything other than a bum. Besides, what if she did have those unlikely powers of observation? Did he really want her to see what surely must seem, to her, a repulsive, grotesque shape? A form every human learned in childhood to loathe and fear? No, far better to maintain the human disguise, for whatever it might be worth.

Prelz already tried to explain what asking someone on a date was all about. If Torval understood the process correctly, he should simply propose that he meet Christine for a meal and perhaps a "movie," or some other form of mutually agreed upon entertainment. After some discussion between the two demons, Prelz suggested something called a "romantic comedy," a film called *Queen Takes Pawn* currently showing at a nearby theater. After Prelz's explanations, Torval felt he at least comprehended what one of these movies must be, although he still wasn't entirely sure what to expect. Nonetheless, Prelz seemed certain Christine would enjoy it, and that would have to do.

In addition, either before or after the movie, Torval intended to take her to an Asian restaurant called the China Cottage. Torval already knew, from what he'd overheard through the heater vent, that Christine like Chinese food. Furthermore, the price of both dinner and movie should, at least according to Prelz, almost exactly use up the rest of Torval's funds. The entire process should take approximately four hours or so, depending on how busy the restaurant was, and afterward it would be close to bedtime. If anything else happened after that, well . . . that was a bonus.

That last part confused Torval the most. The date would end when the last of these events concluded. At that point, there'd be some sort of mutual evaluation of the date itself, probably just as they were about to part for the evening. If both he and Christine had a "good time," however that might be defined, then she might, if she felt so inclined, ask him back to "her place." After that, anything could happen, including but not limited to drinks, further conversation, and quite possibly copulation.

In the event she did not feel so inclined, the date would simply end and both would go their separate ways. Torval could then attempt another date later or give up pursuing her, if he felt he had no chance to continue the relationship. The thought of this particular result worried him greatly, so he intended to work very hard to make the date work out correctly. Yet, as Prelz so concisely pointed out, he had no reason to worry about that if he couldn't arrange a date in the first place.

So, all of this ran through Torval's mind as he sat there in his uncomfortable chair watching Christine serving dinner to the homeless, a cheerful smile emblazoned across her lovely face. She seemed not to have noticed him, and yet more than once he'd seen her glance casually in his direction, letting those lovely blue eyes survey the room, and linger ever so tantalizingly on his own. Perhaps she even enlarged her smile at the sight of him, but then that might've just been his imagination. Did she really see him there or was he just another lost person in this sea of broken humanity?

He didn't look like these others, he realized, glancing down at the clothes she'd bought for him, and then at the rags on the bums nearby. Surely she must've noticed his presence there, for he stood out quite clearly from the rest. Nor had he attempted to get any soup for himself, for he could afford his own. At least, until he spent the last of the funds he'd earned this morning.

As he sat there watching her, the last of the line finally filtered through the door. Christine served the final bowl of soup and put her ladle down, heading over to collect the first tray of dirty dishes from the empty table in the corner. Still whistling, she carried her burden to the back of the open chamber, out of sight.

"Okay, time to go for it," said Prelz, in between slurps of thick white broth. "Remember what I said. Just be yourself! No reason to be nervous."

Torval turned to look at him. "Did you feel this way?" he inquired. "The first time you asked a woman out, I mean."

"Worse, I suspect," Prelz replied with a shrug. "My first girlfriend was a demon, you know."

"What?" Torval gaped at him.

"Yep, you heard me," replied his friend, grinning at the reaction. "Oh, that's right, I haven't told you this one, have I? Okay, fine, you deserve to know, I guess. I'd been at the post office about a month, and I was feeling the same things you're feeling now. Because I was Second Class, I was better able to control my emotions, but they were still there."

"But... a demon?" Torval remained confused. "But you couldn't—oh, wait, that's right, you did say that Second Class have fully functional—"

"It's not that!" interrupted Prelz swiftly. "We were both here on Earth, in human bodies, don't forget! I'm not talking about attraction between demons, I'm talking about humans. She was reasonably pretty, too, with long dark hair, and even longer legs that—oh, never mind, you wouldn't be impressed! Anyway, I got the hots for her, and so I got up the nerve to ask her out, and even though we weren't supposed to—being fellow postal employees and all—we went out a few times. The sex was pretty good, too. Even though we could see each other as our true forms, in the dark we were still both human. Plus, she was a whole lot more experienced in human... well... copulation, if you want to use that word you like so much. She taught me a lot, you know. An awful lot."

"What happened then?" Torval inquired, truly interested in the answer. He'd thought as far ahead as dating Christine, and perhaps the night to follow, but that was all. What came next was a complete mystery.

"I thought I loved her," sighed Prelz, staring at a point somewhere behind Torval's head. "Maybe I did. Yeah, yeah, I'm pretty sure I fell in love. The crazy kind, though—the kind that makes you stupid, so you don't realize what you're doing. It didn't last long. They found out and transferred her away, and I got slapped on the wrist for consorting with a fellow demon. 'Not on the job,' they said. I could have whatever human I wanted, but not another Tempter.

"So that's what I did after that, y'know. I dated humans, and each time I did, it got easier and easier, but I never really found love. Not the kind they talk about in all those romance novels, or in those movies. Every now and then I think about Maliza, and I wonder where she is now, but it doesn't really matter, y'know? We never had a chance. Not a chance in Hell."

Torval started to reply, but paused. Prelz kept on staring past him, completely lost in thought. This wasn't the time to interrupt. Whatever might be passing through the older demon's mind seemed very personal and private.

*Love.* So far the emotion had eluded Torval. He felt he'd managed to form a basic comprehension of the concept, but its complexity eluded him. Yet here sat Prelz, lost in thought, caught up in his recollection of a brief, distant, all but forgotten taste of love.

There must be something important about that emotion, thought Torval suddenly. In fact, something about his friend's story felt incomplete. Did this affair with the demon called Maliza have something to do with Prelz's decision to become human? Torval suspected it did, though he didn't really know why. There was just a feeling, almost a kind of intuition, that led him to that conclusion. Something in Prelz's story, or the wistful expression on his aging face, only made sense if considered from that angle.

All at once, Torval knew what he had to do. He needed to experience love. Even without a true understanding of that emotion, he felt the weight of its importance. Love was somehow crucial to his comprehension of the true nature of humanity—something a demon simply couldn't understand.

Until he knew love, he would be incomplete.

What he felt for Christine wasn't love, at least not yet. That much he understood. Yet he could sense the potential there. The attraction he felt to her was like a seed that had been planted and even now struggled toward the light. He had to try to nurture it, to coax it into growing. The only way that could happen was if he could conquer this accursed fear and nervousness and do what must be done.

Suddenly filled with resolve, he stood up from his seat and walked away from the table. He didn't look back to see if Prelz had even noticed his departure. His only thoughts were of Christine, whose happy whistling came to him like a beacon, a lighthouse guiding him safely to shore.

"Oh, hi, Joe," she said as he approached, flashing yet another smile in his direction. She now wore a body-length apron as she worked at the sink, rinsing and washing dishes one after the other. No one else lingered nearby, the other volunteers apparently busy with other tasks.

"Hello, Christine," he replied, swallowing with difficulty in his cotton-dry mouth. "I have something—I mean, there is something I would very much like to ask you."

"Oh?" she replied curiously, setting down one of the plates and starting to dry it with a quilt-patterned rag. "What is it, Joe? You seem concerned—I saw you earlier, and you looked pretty worried. You know you can ask me anything. I'm here to help."

"I know that," he replied nervously. For some reason his feet shuffled about on the floor, and he fought to control himself. "You have done so much for me these past days. The job you helped me acquire was more than I could have hoped for. That is why I feel I need to—"

"Oh, Joe, you don't have to repay me!" she interjected quickly. "Just seeing you like this, standing up straight, with some pride in yourself—this is all I could've hoped for! You don't owe me anything!"

"No, no, it's not that," he stammered. This conversation wasn't working out the way he'd planned, but then, he wasn't really surprised—they rarely did, after all. "I understand that. You are a good person, Christine, and you need no reward."

"Why, thank you, Joe." She was positively beaming. "That's the nicest thing you've ever said to me."

A hopeful sign, Torval thought. The way she smiled at him made him feel as though he might melt. Gritting his teeth, he pressed on as best he could, but all he could do was fumble for the words. "I would like to—not repay you, no, but something else. I want to—bless it all, why is this so hard to say?"

"Just say it, Joe! Whatever you want to say, I'm listening." The look on her face looked like a cross between hopefulness and concern.

"Very well," he agreed, clenching his fists tightly. "I would like to—I mean, I would very much want to—take you out on a date."

She stared at him, blinking. The light blue of her eyes seemed to pierce into his brain, but she didn't reply for several long moments.

"There, I said it," he gasped, trying to compose himself. "That is what I want. I want to take you on a date, Christine. I like you very much, and I think I always have, but until now, I could not ask you. If you do not want to go, I will understand. I will simply—"

"No, no!" she insisted suddenly, herself stumbling over her words as she tried to reassure him. "No, that's not what I mean! I mean, no, you don't have to go! Oh, let me try this again." She paused and took a breath. "All right, here goes. Yes, Joe, I'll go on a date with you!"

"Really?" Torval blurted, a sudden feeling of relief washing through him. He felt suddenly elated, as if ready to leap into the air and fly away. "You will? Really?"

"Sure," she replied with a giggle. "In fact, I thought you'd never ask!"

* * *

The rest of that night passed in a rapid blur. Torval had only the vaguest recollection of the rest of the conversation with Christine. He somehow sputtered out his proposal to take her to the movies and to dinner, and she accepted. He would now meet her tomorrow afternoon, which was Saturday, meaning she didn't have to work during the day. They would see something called the "matinee" showing, and then have an early meal, giving her time to make it to the shelter for her regular volunteer shift. That would leave Torval able to go to work that night if the Roxtons needed him.

He had a fleeting memory of all of that, but didn't recall exactly who said what or when, or how long the rest of the conversation actually lasted. Usually he could remember most of the details of his interactions with humans, but not this time. Instead he distinctly recalled the sensation of floating on air as he stumbled giddily out of the soup kitchen and off to the warehouse for another night of hard labor.

He barely paid attention as Pete Roxton hurried through his explanation of the night's assignment, which was to straighten up the innumerable boxes lining the basement floor. Torval followed the instructions exactly and without thought, dwelling only on the Saturday to come.

He had a date! He'd offered and she accepted, and thus the stage was set. He would go out and experience the first step in establishing a human relationship, and possibly ignite a spark of what might one day turn into love. The very possibility left him grinning like a fool, filled with a bouncy energy that he didn't fully comprehend, but didn't mind one bit.

After about an hour he finally came down from the clouds and started to focus on his work. The assignment was relatively simple, but rapidly exhausted his frail human form. Most of the boxes contained heavy papers or books of some sort, although he didn't look in any of them intentionally, only when a lid popped open or fell askew. Arranging the containers in the proper order, sorted alphabetically and lining the walls, proved simple in concept but difficult in practice. More than once he found himself with a box out of place, forcing him to move an entire stack to correct his error.

As a result he quickly became hungry, so he moved on to this evening's meal. In the refrigerator he found a bag with a prominent label suggesting the food inside had been somehow crafted by royalty. Torval doubted this, however, thinking that just like the mysterious Colonel from the night before, this King of Burgers was just an icon of sorts.

Inside the sack he discovered a disc-shaped item in a wrapper, a container with yellow sticks coming out of it, and several small white packets called "ketchup." He also found a note that read as follows:

> Joe: Sorry this is cold, but I had to pick it up on the way in to work. Nuke it in the microwave for a minute or two when you're ready to eat it. In case you don't know or remember what a microwave is, it's that machine on top of the fridge. Just put the bag inside, punch the start button a couple times, and take it out. Enjoy! —Pete.

Torval appreciated the extra instructions, for he surely wouldn't have understood the meaning of the otherwise incomprehensible phrase "nuke it in the microwave" without the explanation. After some fiddling he figured out how to open the door, inserted all of the food, and pushed the buttons accordingly. They didn't do anything, though, until he realized he had to shut the door first.

Just as the note described, the food warmed up within a couple of minutes—almost too hot to touch, in fact. He had to wait for it to cool, but as he did so, he sampled some of the yellow sticks. They were soft and salty, reminding him of some of the soup he'd tried earlier, but without the liquid consistency. He couldn't figure out the purpose of the white and red packets, which he suspected should be cut open, but lacking any kind of knife or sharp object, he couldn't get them to tear. Besides, they were almost boiling hot, so he left them where they were.

The larger item inside the wrapper proved to be a sandwich made up of two discs of dark brown meat surrounded by green and red vegetables as well as layers of melted golden cheese. Unsure of what to expect, he tentatively nibbled at the hot burger, only to discover a brand new flavor at least the equal of, if not superior to, the taste of chicken or pizza. In fact, the more he gobbled down this amazing sandwich, the more of it he wanted. He almost wept when it was gone.

He consoled himself by finishing off the rest of the fries, enjoying another soft drink to wash it all down. This left him more than sated, for the burger had been a double and therefore quite filling.

Was there no end to the incredible tastes these humans could create? If only he could eat all the time—but no, that was a sin he knew well, the sin of gluttony. No wonder the obese prisoner Juan Candual, his body overwhelmed with fat, had to sit in his cell near tantalizing foods, never quite able to reach them. Or poor Clarise O'Reilly had to eat constantly, but only a thick greasy paste that tasted like bile. In life these souls were slaves to the sense of taste, and a passion for eating that overwhelmed all else. With foods such as hamburgers and pizza available so readily, Torval could almost understand such temptations.

Regardless of that, he'd consumed his meal in its entirety, so he pressed on with his labors. After another hour, he completed his task, having moved and dusted off every box and sorted them according to the directions. Pete explained earlier that the cardboard cases contained records of some sort, and had at one time been properly arranged, but casual movements left them scattered all over, so that locating the proper item now took far too long. By placing them in order, Torval allowed the Roxtons to locate what they were looking for at a moment's notice. A worthy goal, indeed.

The entire task took perhaps three hours, if that, leaving Torval with a vast amount of free time. He occupied some of this by double- and triple-checking his alphabetization efforts. Assured that it was correct, he then opened one of the boxes, just to ensure the contents were indeed in the proper order. Perhaps the documents inside were also mixed up, which would add to the difficulty of the task considerably. That might explain why he had so much time left over.

The papers seemed correct, however. The box labeled "Aa-Ar" did indeed start with receipts attributed to names beginning with those letters. The pages, arranged in folders by name, seemed to indicate numerical transactions attributed to those individuals. In fact, the pages themselves looked similar to something he'd seen before. They were attached together in a kind of folding joint, just like—what?

A few moments' thought brought the memory to the fore. These were like the pages he'd seen in the briefcase delivered to Brent Maclure earlier in the day. In fact, except for the exact information on these particular sheets, they might well be identical.

Suddenly Torval felt a chill run through him and he shoved the folder back in its place. This was private information! In fact, now that he remembered, Pete had asked him not to look inside. Yes, he definitely recalled that specific command. In his excitement over securing the date with Christine, Torval forgot to pay close enough attention, and now he'd made a mistake. He'd failed in his assignment, and failed the Roxtons!

He replaced the box quickly in its place, moving away as if it might be poisoned, but it was too late. He'd screwed up, and he had no way to undo what he'd done. He'd seen the secret pages. There would be no bonus for him this time, no extra assignment for additional cash. He might even be fired!

He glanced around. There was no one to see him, was there? So how could they know? If he didn't say anything, they'd have no idea he'd ever looked at the contents of the folder. Besides which, even though he knew he'd seen some sort of receipt for a man with the name of Carl Aaronson, Torval still had no idea what the receipt was for. He hadn't looked that closely at the paper. So where was the harm?

Nowhere, except that Torval knew he'd violated the rules. That knowledge gnawed at him. If he were back in Hell, he would've been punished for his transgression. That was what he deserved now. The Roxtons would have to punish him, and if that punishment meant no extra pay, that would be sufficient.

But what if they went further? What if they felt they could no longer trust him, and put him back on the street? What then? How could he take Christine on a date, knowing that the next day he'd be begging again? He couldn't fail her like that. She expected him to keep this job, and stay out of the soup kitchen. How could he continue to build a relationship with her, if he let her down this way?

He remembered how happy she'd been when he cleaned himself up, got the job, and seemed to be pulling his life—well, Joe's life—out of the gutters. To tell her he'd been fired would sadden her greatly. How could he allow that to happen? The thought of making Christine feel bad made Torval's stomach hurt, in a way he couldn't explain. He didn't want her to be sad—he liked it better when she was happy.

What a strange sensation, he realized after a moment, taking a step back and detaching himself from the situation at hand. Here he was, worried about someone else's feelings! Why should that be? Did he want her to be happy so that he'd feel better about himself? Or did he genuinely care about her emotions?

Care... about her? That was the crux of the matter. Did he care about her, about someone else besides himself? In all his ages of existence, in all his watching over tortured souls, he couldn't remember thinking about anyone that way. He'd watched people go through all manner of punishment without ever feeling an ounce of pity or remorse, or trying to put himself in their place. And now here he was, after just a couple of days on Earth in a human shell, worrying about the feelings of another!

He pushed those thoughts away. What Christine feels shouldn't matter, Torval told himself. He'd deal with this issue of violating the Roxtons' trust in his own way. They would surely want to punish him, so he'd take it on himself to do something else, something extra, to possibly mollify them. But what could he do?

Casting about the basement, he noticed the bathroom, still immaculately clean from the previous night. Come to think of it, Torval recalled, there were a couple of places he hadn't quite finished cleaning. Yes, that'll do it, he decided at once. He'd take some extra time to finish off the tiles, and the rest of the floor around the toilet area. When they saw he was willing to do some extra work, it would reinforce their faith in him. They might come up with some other punishment as well, but at least this would blunt the blow.

Even if they do fire me, he told himself, I'll find some way to explain it to Christine. She'd just have to understand that he did his best, even gone out of his way to punish himself. Besides, even if she became unhappy, that wouldn't matter. Her feelings didn't matter, he insisted to himself, not really believing his own thoughts, but trying very hard anyway. They don't matter at all.

Sometime later, after the bathroom was spotless and his fingers sore from scrubbing, and as he finally collapsed and fell asleep on the hard floor beneath the hammock, he kept right on denying what he felt deep down inside. Her feelings didn't matter. They just couldn't.

But they did.

# Chapter 28

"Good Lord, Joe," came the voice above him. "Are you some kinda machine, or what?"

Torval shook himself awake. In a glimpse in his mind, he remembered a boat, somewhere on a gray ocean, sailing . . . where? And a woman on the railing . . . was it Christine? He couldn't see . . .

The image faded away. He stood weakly, suddenly aware of several sharp pains in the muscles of his back and arms. His fingers, especially one of his thumbnails, ached tremendously. "I apologize," he managed drowsily. "I was . . . I do not understand. If I have offended—"

"Not at all," replied Pete Roxton, looking somewhat red-eyed and tired compared to the previous day, when he seemed filled with energy. "I just mean, wow, you really worked hard! Everything's exactly where it's supposed to be, and the bathroom—why did you do that? It was already as close to perfect as it needed to be! You didn't have to scrape every little mote of dust out of every crack!"

"Again, I apologize," went on Torval, rapidly regaining his senses. "I was—well, perhaps I should explain to both you and Lincoln."

"What, to Grandpa? What's he got to do with it?" There seemed to be a significant note of irritation in Pete's voice, and Torval practically cringed at the reaction.

"I have failed you," admitted the demon after a moment, hanging his head in shame. "I must apologize and beg forgiveness."

"For what? For beating your head against the wall cleaning this place? No shame in that, Joe! Sorry if I gave you the wrong idea—I'm not mad at you! I'm just a bit tired this morning—I always stay up too late on Friday nights, dancing and partying, you know?"

Another stab poked at Torval's stomach. What if he'd gone out with Christine again, and they stayed out late? What if she—

No, that doesn't matter, he insisted to himself. She'd accepted his offer for a date today, and that was enough for now. If Pete Roxton truly proved to be a rival for her affections, Torval would simply deal with that later. For now, he had another issue to resolve, and afterward perhaps none of that would matter.

Without any remark regarding the "partying" comment, Torval started up the stairs. Shaking his head at his employee's reticence, Pete followed, eventually taking the lead and heading toward the front counter. Lincoln waited there, straightening out some items in the front window display.

"I think Joe here wants to say something," commented Pete at once. "He has to apologize for working way too hard, and doing way too good a job."

Lincoln laughed at that. "No reason to be sorry for somethin' like that, my boy," he replied, setting down the sign he was fiddling with. "You can be as much a perfectionist as you want 'round here. Maybe teach my grandson here a thing or two while you're at it!"

"That is not the nature of my apology," admitted Torval with a resigned sigh. "I have failed your trust, I fear. You ordered me not to look inside the boxes I was moving, but my mind was elsewhere, and I looked at one of the folders by mistake. I regret doing this with every fiber of my being, and stand ready for any punishment you see fit to level upon me."

Pete and Lincoln glanced at each other, and both stifled a collective snicker. Torval stared at the floor in between them, as if awaiting a blow to the head or a stern whipping.

"Well," replied Lincoln, still trying to avoid chuckling, seeing as how Torval appeared completely serious, "what exactly did you see?"

"A receipt," replied the penitent demon, "for a man named Carl Aaronson. I did not see the amount or the reason for the purchase. As soon as I realized I was breaking your commandment, I ceased looking and put the file away. Then, as my penance, I cleaned the remainder of the bathroom, the parts I failed to reach the night before. If that is not sufficient, I can—"

At that, Pete could no longer stifle his laughter and had to turn away, holding his gut, hand firmly emplaced over his mouth. Lincoln stepped over to the confused-looking Torval and clapped a hand about his shoulder. "My boy, my boy, you are way too honest for your own good. Those things in those boxes—those are sales records from sixty-plus years of auto parts sales! That receipt you saw was probably decades old. There's nothing to it at all."

"Yeah," agreed Pete, now in control of himself again. "The only reason I told you not to look in there is because I didn't want you wasting your time. In fact, why don't you come with me right now, will ya? I wanna show you something."

He led the way back to the basement, followed by a still shaken but much relieved Torval, with Lincoln taking up the rear. As the demon watched, wide-eyed, Pete went over to the locked door with the big "Keep Out" sign on it and reached for the handle. "I think we can trust you well enough now," said Pete, opening the door and flipping on a light switch on the inside wall. "This is why we didn't want you coming in here, Joe. This is the big secret."

The room beyond was small—smaller than the bathroom, actually little more than a modified storage closet. Inside, on a very narrow desk, sat a machine that resembled the device the woman named Sarah used to ring up his purchase in the department store the previous afternoon. This one was considerably larger, however, and more complex, with several additional parts. There was a screen, presently blank, atop a thick metal casing, and before that sat a keyboard and a curious oval-shaped black object attached to the main body with a thin wire.

"What is it?" asked Torval curiously.

"Our office computer," replied Pete proudly. "It's a Pentium—oh, never mind, you probably won't know what all that means, anyway. We're going to be converting to computerized records, which is one of the reasons we want this place down here cleaned up and sorted. In fact, I was rather hoping we could train you on how to do it, Joe. You probably don't know a thing about computers, which is exactly as much as Grandpa and I both know."

"I do not understand," replied Torval in complete stupefaction. "I do not know anything about this device. What is it you would have me do? And why would you trust me after I broke the rule you presented me?"

"Because it means you're human." Lincoln chuckled. "I must admit, we were starting to wonder. You didn't even try to come in here, and you're the most efficient guy I've ever known. That's what makes me think you'd be perfect for working on this thing."

"I have never so much as touched such a device," protested Torval. "I would not even know where to begin!"

"That's all right, we all have to start somewhere," replied Lincoln, obviously unconcerned with Joe's excuses. "Look, here's the deal. Right now you're working for basically nothing, but we'll pay you fifteen bucks an hour for data entry, starting as soon as you're ready. We've waited years to get started, mostly 'cause I'm too much of an old curmudgeon to change my ways, so we can wait a bit longer while you get up to speed. Plus in the meantime we can still send you on other errands for extra cash. Sound good?"

"Fifteen dollars an hour?" Torval considered that. If he worked for five hours a day, he would earn another seventy-five dollars, in addition to the other bonuses. Why, at that rate he would soon be awash in cash! "Of course—that sounds perfectly reasonable," he managed to say.

"Good, then here's what I want you to do when you come back tonight," said Lincoln. "See this manual?" He picked up a large book, sitting on a shelf below and to the right of the desk, until then unnoticed in the shadows. "Sit down here, read it, and get familiar with the computer. Play around with it as much as you want, but don't break it. When you think you understand, read this." He lifted out another, smaller book. "This is the manual for our data entry software. Run it, and practice with it. Enter a few of the records from those folders you saw into the computer, as practice. We're not open Sunday, but I'll pop in that morning to see how you've done, and to let you out. Pete'll be here at the usual time that evening so you can get some sleep. If you're ready, you can start entering stuff on Monday night and we'll get you on the payroll for real."

"That is—that is more than I could have hoped for," sputtered the completely overwhelmed demon. "I hope that I can comprehend this device and do as you say. I will do my best."

"I'm sure you will, my boy," agreed Lincoln with another clap on the shoulder. "I'm sure you will."

* * *

Torval left the Roxton warehouse with a feeling of detachment, as if he might somehow still be dreaming and hadn't quite awakened. When he went to sleep the previous night, he'd expected punishment and perhaps even termination for his error. Instead, they effectively promoted him, and in fact seemed to trust him all the more.

Humans! Torval still had no idea what truly motivated them, or why they did what they did. He thought he'd made some progress toward that goal, but now, despite their energetic forgiveness, he still felt as though he'd failed.

He made his way to the shelter slowly, breathing in the cool morning air, which helped his head to clear. The sky held a few scattered clouds, but the sun still shone down through the blue, making the glass and steel of the nearby buildings glisten in the early light. The streets, now dry and far cleaner than they seemed the previous day, seemed only lightly traveled, and the usual crush of pedestrian movement was subdued. The city, by comparison with earlier in the week, looked quiet and calm.

Of course, that's because it was Saturday, Torval now knew. Prelz had explained the days of the week to him yesterday, when they were discussing the possibilities involved in scheduling the date with Christine. Humans worked five days out of the week—usually—and on Saturday and Sunday they were free to act as they wanted. So traffic would be lighter on a Saturday simply because so few people were actually working, the rest sleeping in or simply staying home.

The ease of the morning stroll helped Torval gather his thoughts. Apparently, by confessing his crime, he'd absolved himself to the Roxtons. They had reacted with amazement and mirth, as if confession were not normal human behavior. Nonetheless, by admitting his guilt, he'd reassured them that he was, in fact, trustworthy. Somehow that seemed like a contradiction, and yet, it made a certain amount of sense.

Torval shook his head in surprise at that. Perhaps he'd made some progress understanding humans after all...

He checked his watch. It was still morning, and he wasn't supposed to meet Christine for many more hours. What should he do with the rest of the morning? He realized at once that he still didn't know exactly what he should do during the upcoming date—at least, not the specific details—so he felt he should find out more information from Prelz. With that in mind, he proceeded apace to the soup kitchen.

The shelter was open, but Prelz was nowhere to be found. Probably out begging for coins, thought Torval, glancing inside the doors. He thought he recognized some of the bums there, but no one even remotely resembled the older demon. He'd have to search elsewhere, perhaps on nearby street corners.

As he stood there, one of the kitchen workers happened to notice him. The man was black, and fairly tall, with a raggedly unshaven salt-and-pepper beard and neatly trimmed hair. He wore one of the ubiquitous aprons and a white paper hat that sat slightly askew. "Joe Sampson?" asked the volunteer, his mouth opening to reveal several missing teeth.

"I am he," replied Torval curiously. He supposed he should've known this person, probably from Joe's time lingering here, but couldn't recall the name. Perhaps it was Marley, or Marvie. Yes, that was it. He liked to be called "Marv."

"Oh, yeah, sorry, almost didn't recognize ya dressed like that, and all shaven and stuff," came the reply. "Hey, there was a phone call for ya earlier. I know, seems weird, ya gettin' a call here, but I think it was Harry or sump'n like that. Anyways, here's the number."

With that, Marv reached down and pulled a scrap of paper from his apron pocket. He handed this to Torval, who looked at the seven digits there uncomprehendingly.

"If ya wanna use the phone," said Marv, "ya can use t'one in t'back. G'on, nobody's lookin, I won't tell nobody."

"All right," agreed Torval, heading into the back room. There were no other workers there, and Marv didn't follow. Without thinking about it, Torval walked over to the telephone on the wall, able to identify the device well enough but not quite comprehending how to use it.

He picked up the receiver, expecting Joe's body to go about the business of using this strange machine, but nothing happened. A faint buzzing sound came to his ears and he held up the handle to his head, and he noticed the tone came from one of the two cups at either end. In fact, holding it there, he realized it was supposed to sort of wrap around his face, an arrangement that seemed somehow natural.

Now what? He looked at the digits on the paper and then the numbers on the keypad by his fingers. A sequence, like the numbers in an address, he thought to himself, pressing the first three numerals one after the other. In response, a tone in his ear indicated he'd done something right, although each beep sounded slightly different.

Now he paused. There was a dash on the paper, but nowhere on the keypad did he see a dash symbol. Staring at it in confusion, he hesitated several seconds and suddenly an insistent beeping began in his ear. Confused, and aware he'd done something wrong, he put the receiver back where it started and the annoying sound shut off.

What was he supposed to do about the dash? There were letters under some of the digits on the keypad, and there were also other symbols, a "*" and a "#," whatever those meant. Plus there were other buttons such as "Mute" and "Hook" which he didn't understand. Perhaps he was supposed to press one of those? Or maybe the dash meant zero, or one of the other buttons?

After a moment of consideration he realized he must be overthinking the problem. The dash didn't correspond to anything on the keypad—it didn't indicate any buttons at all, only a reminder to pause, so that the machine could process what he'd already pushed in. That's what the loud beeping meant—that he could proceed with the other numbers.

Of course! That had to be it, because nothing else made sense. With that in mind, he lifted the receiver again, and entered the first three digits. Then he waited until the loud, pulsing sound returned, and typed in the other four. Nothing happened, except that the repeated beeping continued.

Bless this heavenly thing! He replaced the receiver, somewhat frustrated, and studied it some more. This cannot be that complicated, he told himself. Humans use these things all the time. What if the dash simply means to pause momentarily, but proceed before the angry beeping can commence?

He tried that, waiting only a couple of heartbeats before entering the rest of the numbers, and this time silence followed, for a few moments at least. Then, he heard a distant ring like a jangling of bells. For an instant he thought he'd messed things up again, like before, but the sound was different this time, so he waited.

After a second ring, there came a click, and a voice sounded in his ear. "Hello?" it said simply. Something seemed familiar about that voice. "Hello? Is someone there?" it repeated after a moment.

Torval suddenly realized he recognized who it was. "Hal?" he said aloud, unconsciously speaking into the mouthpiece. "Is that you?"

"Joe!" came the reply. "Oh, good, I was hoping you'd call! Listen, I have to talk to you! Can you come meet me? Right now, I mean?"

"I believe so," answered Torval reflexively. After all, he had no other pressing matters to attend to, at least not for several hours.

"Good, good! Remember the pizza place where I saw you last? I'll see you there in about fifteen minutes, okay?"

"Yes," Torval replied. "I am not far from there now."

"Great! See ya then. Bye!"

A click followed, and then the irritating droning sound from earlier began to play in Torval's ear. He put the receiver back down until the noise went away, then turned and left the shelter.

* * *

So, Torval thought as he walked, that's what using a telephone is like. So simple and easy . . . what a remarkable device!

When the voice came through the receiver, Torval recognized it as that of Hal Sommersby. However, he didn't even know where Hal was. His friend could've been anywhere in the city, anywhere at all, and all Torval had to do was pick up the phone, dial seven digits, and they could have a conversation, just like that.

The more he thought about it, the more Torval recognized the utility of such a machine. In Hell, if one demon needed to talk to another, they had to meet face to face. If that other demon happened to be on another circle, that meant a lengthy trip along the Styx in one of the Charon steamships, followed by another journey down one of the canals that connected the layers. If the demon wasn't there upon arrival, a wait would ensue—sometimes lasting days or longer until he returned from whatever errand he might be on. In some places, where the demons were powerful enough, private messengers could be used, but even so the process seemed excruciatingly primitive.

With such a thing as a telephone, if someone like Geezon needed to contact a demon like Torval, he wouldn't have to travel for hours from the circle hub all the way down to Layer Four Hundred Twelve, and then wait for Torval's shift to end. All he'd have to do is pick up a phone, dial the number for that layer, and speak to him directly. Or, lacking that, he could contact Torval's superior or someone else who could pass on the message. The entire process would only take minutes.

But how did telephones work? Torval had no clue. They used some sort of curly wire, and he already knew that wires had something to do with the way most of these human devices functioned. Perhaps Prelz would know more, or maybe one of the books in the vast public library held the answer.

As he walked, contemplating the miraculous telephones and their possible utility in Hell, Torval's mind returned to the conversation itself. He hadn't spoken with Hal Sommersby since—when? Two days ago? Or was it yesterday? He couldn't remember exactly. Hal had recovered from his sickness and treated Torval to some pizza slices begged from a kind couple at the restaurant just now coming into view on the street corner ahead. Their discussion hadn't ended all that well, as Torval recalled, and in fact the whole episode left a kind of bad taste in his mouth (if he understood the human euphemism correctly). So why did Hal's voice seem so animated? Did the telephone amplify the sounds somehow?

Torval supposed he'd find out soon enough. He came to the restaurant and looked around, but saw no one at first. Then he noticed a car sitting along the side of the road, next to a sign that said "No Parking – Tow Away Zone." This was one of those bright yellow, ubiquitous vehicles that roamed every street—the kind with a sign on top that clearly marked it as a taxicab. Almost as soon as Torval noticed the cab, its doors opened and Hal exited, accompanied by a joyful-looking girl in her twenties, with brown hair tied up in loose ponytail. She wore a tan coat with an unusually wide black belt, and a bright orange scarf fluttered about her neck.

Torval's eyes lingered on her only a moment before being drawn to

Hal, who looked far different than before. Instead of rags and a shredded coat, the man wore clean clothes and what looked like a brand-new jacket. His beard and mustache were neatly trimmed, and he leaned upon a cane that also looked new. His eyes shone brightly and he wore thin, almost invisible glasses. A huge grin swept across his face as he approached.

"Joe," called out Hal excitedly, reaching out to clasp Torval's hand, which he shook vigorously. "I just had to see you one more time before I left! I wanted to thank you—thank you from the bottom of my heart."

"For what?" asked Torval. "What did I do? And what happened to you? You look as I did the day I got my job."

"Yes, yes, that's exactly it," gushed Hal. "I thought about what you said, Joe. How you were cleaning up your life—getting off the booze, getting a job and all that. I couldn't get it out of my head, you see. I took some of the money I begged that afternoon to the liquor store, but I couldn't seem to make myself buy anything. That's when I did it, I finally did it."

"Did what?" asked the demon, glancing briefly at the young lady standing nearby. She grinned at Hal's words and put her arm around his waist, hugging him, even as he returned the gesture.

"Ever since I gave up on the world," explained Hal, pulling a faded rectangular piece of gray paper from his pocket, "I've had this card with me. I told myself I'd never call, but I never quite seemed to lose it, either. In a way, it was sort of a symbol. If I ever lost it, it would be the end of my last hope—the end of my life, such as it was. Is that crazy, or what?"

"Not crazy," said the young woman by his side. "Not crazy at all, Daddy. It's the sanest thing I've ever heard."

He leaned down and kissed her on the forehead. "Oh, I forgot, I haven't introduced my daughter. Tina, this is Joe Sampson. The man who saved me in the end."

She rushed forward and wrapped her arms around Torval, hugging him tightly. "Thank you, Joe Sampson," she all but cried. "Thank you for being an inspiration to my father! I thought I'd never see him again. You don't know how long I searched—"

"That's all over now, honey," he told her. "I'll never leave you again. I only hope someday you can forgive me."

"Oh, Daddy, I already do. I already do."

She was back in his arms now, and Torval saw that both were indeed crying, wiping the tears away without even realizing what they were doing.

"Anyway," Hal went on after a moment, "this card had my ex-wife's number on it. Instead of buying booze, I bought a prepaid phone card and dialed the number, figuring after all this time it would've been disconnected. But Tina here never gave up on me. She kept the number all that time, even after Hannah moved back to Idaho. She waited for me, Joe. She waited here in Manhattan, just on the faint hope I'd come back someday. How could I have been so blind? How could I have ever turned my back on them? Just because I lost my job—"

"Daddy, forget about it," Tina urged him. "That's all in the past. You're back now. You can stay with me till you're back on your feet. You'll find another job, I just know it, and everything will be fine. I have some money saved up—an account Mommy set up for me, that I never—"

"We'll talk about that all in good time, baby," said Hal quickly. "Look, Joe, I don't think I can ever repay you for making me see the light, but I want you to have this." He reached out his hand, the one with the faded business card. "Take this. If you ever need anything—anything at all—just call this number and ask for me. If it's within my power, I'll do it, whatever it is."

"Hal," said Torval, still a bit overwhelmed by what he was seeing, "you owe me nothing."

"No, I do! I wouldn't have—if it weren't for you, I mean, I wouldn't—"

"I did nothing," insisted Torval forcefully. "You were sick, as I was. When you awoke, you simply realized, as I did, that we both nearly perished, and that there was more to life than sleeping in the street. That was all you experienced, and nothing more. You would still have understood, as I did, what you had to do."

"No, I wouldn't have. You don't get it, do you? After I got better, all I could think about was getting food and booze, until I saw you. You changed everything for me, Joe. You showed me it was possible to get back on my feet. I'll never forget that. Never."

Tina glanced back at the cab, and Hal noticed the gesture. "Oh, right, the meter's running! Sorry, baby, I'm eating up all your money already, aren't I? Come on, let's go before I drain your wallet dry." He reached out and shook Joe's hand one last time. "Thanks again, man. Like I said before, I owe you big, and I mean it! If you need anything, just call!"

"Nice to meet you, Joe!" called out Tina as the two of them scooted back in the cab. "Bye-bye!"

The doors slammed shut and the vehicle drove away. Joe watched it go, still trying to wrap his mind around what he'd just witnessed, until the car was lost amidst a sea of other taxicabs. Only then did he look down at the faded card in his hand.

Folded neatly beneath the scrap of paper, obscured from view when Hal handed it over, was a crisp new hundred-dollar bill.

# *Chapter 29*

Torval stared for a few long moments at the folded scrap of green paper in his hand. Even though he could only see the denomination, he knew immediately what it was.

A hundred dollars! Right there, in his palm, given to him for no reason whatsoever, as far as he could tell.

He continued to stare stupidly at the money, unfolding it carefully in something akin to total confusion. Why had he been given this gift? Why did Hal choose to slip it to him in secret, without telling him? Was he afraid Torval might refuse it? Or did he wish to hide the transaction from his daughter? Furthermore, what had Torval done to earn such a reward? Hal seemed different, completely unlike what Joe would've expected; and yet their hands had touched briefly, and he wasn't a demon. So the real Hal Sommersby had somehow changed.

Torval remained baffled by the claim that he'd somehow done something to influence this, apparently without even realizing it. Thinking back over both conversations, both during the pizza-begging lunch and just now, Torval still couldn't quite recall what he might've said to change Hal's mind about being a bum. All the decision-making had been Hal's. So why did he choose to give the credit to someone else?

Because, realized the demon after a moment, Hal found inspiration in what he'd seen. Joe, having put aside that old, wasted life, and committing to change, thereby encouraged Hal to do the same. In his own words, he never would've done it had he not followed the example of his longtime friend, Joe Sampson.

Yet even so, as the demon unfolded the magical hundred dollar note between his shaking fingers, he still felt he hadn't really done anything. Hal could've changed himself and his ways at any time. He clearly must've been close to doing so, and by keeping his family's phone number on his person, he definitely wanted to. Yet he'd never done it, in all those many years of being on the street. He may never have, had he not chosen to interpret Joe's actions as some kind of sign.

Even so, mused the demon, sitting down somewhat dazedly on the sidewalk, even if someone else deserves some measure of credit, it surely isn't me! In fact, he reflected, Christine made all of this possible. The clothes, the job, the food and shelter—she's the one who should've been thanked. This money should be hers!

Nonetheless, Torval knew, without even thinking about it, that she'd never accept such a gift. Taking money wasn't in her nature. She was too...too good to take it from him. She would insist he keep it, to spend on himself. Yes, that's what a good person would do, inasmuch as Torval understood the concept so far.

If she wouldn't accept it as cash, thought the demon, he'd just have to do something else for her instead. Something that cost money, but that she couldn't possibly refuse. But what?

He got to his feet and pushed the bill, as well as the faded business card, into his pocket, where they joined the remaining cash he still had from his other expenditures. Some of his purchases from the previous day, as well as his dirty clothes, had been left behind in a box in the Roxtons' basement. The brand new blue jeans, while comfortable, were tighter than the trousers he'd worn previously, and getting the money into his pockets wasn't nearly as easy as before. This suggested something else he needed to acquire, so as he continued to think about how to repay Christine, he made his way toward the drugstore he'd visited yesterday.

Entering, he found himself wandering, lost in thought as he searched for the item he wanted. Eventually he found it—a small folded object made of something called "faux leather," whatever that was. Just the thing he needed to contain his cash—a wallet. This one cost eight dollars, which seemed like a reasonable sum.

Once he had the wallet, he left the store, studying the pockets and flaps in the little container. The cash, obviously, went in the large folded area down the center, but he didn't know what the other, clear plastic slots were for until he remembered the MetroCard. He'd returned that item to the Roxtons, but as near as he could recall, it should fit neatly into one of those pockets. Perfect—now the next time they loaned him that item, he would be less likely to lose it.

The wallet pressed against the seat of his pants as he walked, a comfortable reminder of its presence. Now that he'd acquired what he wanted, he still had to figure out what to get Christine. He owed her so much—so many debts he felt he could never possibly repay. What could he buy that would at least start the process?

Clothing wasn't an option—he'd ruled that out the previous day, when he realized he didn't know what she might like. Furthermore, thinking about it further, if he did try to purchase an article of clothing, how would he know what size to acquire? His own adventure in determining his size was proof he couldn't try that again, at least not without knowing her dimensions, and if he asked, that would spoil the surprise.

For some reason, he felt like whatever he got for her should be a surprise. That much he knew for sure. If he asked her for advice, or if she knew what he was up to, she'd certainly refuse his gift.

Therein lay the heart of the matter, he realized as he wandered along the streets, looking to and fro at various storefronts for potential ideas. He could certainly enter a jewelry shop, for example, and purchase something there, or perhaps an item from a hardware store, whatever "hardware" might be. Yet how was he to know what she would want? And what could stop her from refusing it?

After a few more minutes of walking, he decided to give up on this line of reasoning. He was getting nowhere. Without Prelz around to ask, he'd be unable to proceed. With that in mind, he headed back toward the soup kitchen, keeping his eyes open for his fellow demon.

Unfortunately, Prelz remained absent. Since no appointment had been made, as Torval recalled, the ex-Tempter could be anywhere at all. If only he could use one of those amazing telephone devices—but Torval didn't know the number to dial. He was on his own, it seemed.

He could think of one other way to gain the information he sought, so Torval headed that way, picking up the pace a little. Surely somewhere in the massive collection of books in the library, he could find some sort of answer to his problem.

When he arrived, the place was open, and in fact seemed noticeably more crowded than two days ago. Perhaps because it's Saturday, thought Torval. The woman he spoke to the other day, the older lady named Karen, wasn't present, her post taken by a slightly younger-looking black man who seemed busy with something behind his desk. Torval reminded himself that he didn't really need help, since he already knew how to use the card catalog.

But what could he look up? The cards in the racks were labeled by subject, usually a single word. "Gift" came to mind, but upon flipping through those possibilities, none of the titles seemed to work. He hesitated, at a loss.

Perhaps it would be best, thought the demon, to step back a bit and better define what I'm doing. I'm attempting to find out how to repay Christine, which I'll do during the date this afternoon. I'll give her something, but it must be disguised so that it doesn't appear as a gift at all. Perhaps a part of the date itself?

He looked up "date," but the selections there seemed to be related to some sort of fruit that apparently grew on a type of palm tree. Continuing along in some frustration, he finally came to a single entry: *Dating in the 21st Century*, a book about "the perils and pitfalls of finding one's mate in the modern age."

That seemed like a good choice, so Torval noted the code number and moved to the appropriate shelf. He found the book immediately, a rather tall and thin volume compared to the others, coated in the same plastic sheath that protected most of the tomes surrounding him. He sat down in an open seat and began to read eagerly.

* * *

Some time later, he finally turned the last page, glad to have found this particular book. So, that is what dating is all about, he thought inwardly. A private social event, designed to let male and female humans meet each other, interact, share experiences, ask and answer questions, and enjoy each other's company. Often awkward, fraught with all manner of potential humiliations, sometimes even outright dangerous. No wonder he felt so nervous about the prospect—he had every right to be!

There were so many little things, so many nuances of the experience. The way he was supposed to open doors, and order food, and even pay.

What he could and couldn't talk about, such as why he shouldn't bring up her previous relationships, or discuss his own. To avoid comparing her to other people he'd known, or bring up any faults he noticed. Torval felt sure, now that he'd seen this book, that he'd have little trouble with the date this afternoon.

Unfortunately, though an excellent source of advice, *Dating in the 21st Century* didn't get him any closer to finding a worthy gift. The book did suggest one possible item—a flower or flowers of some sort, possibly in the form of a corsage—although that sort of thing was intended for use only on certain occasions. Torval recalled that back on his route in Hell, a woman named Yolande had to relive a school dance event called the "prom" for all eternity. In that particular illusion, she wore a very fancy dress with a large, somewhat wilted flower pinned to her chest. That, Torval surmised, must be the corsage the book talked about. Since he had no intention of taking Christine to a prom, he probably wouldn't need such a thing, although some other kind of flower might indeed be appropriate. Roses, so the book claimed, were always a winning choice.

Even so, that wouldn't nearly be sufficient to repay Christine for all she'd done for him. Torval continued to mull over the possibilities as he set the book aside. In addition to not discussing possible gifts, or at least not any he could be certain she'd like, the book made no mention of what happened after the date was over.

He still had some worries about that. Clearly what happened afterward would be something both he and Christine agreed to. He certainly knew he wanted more to happen—but what if it did? What exactly would he do? Would he grab her fiercely, as Shelly Mendez did when he visited her home, and engage in that peculiar tongue-wrestling ritual? Would the sex be as wild and urgent as it had been with Shelly?

Prelz had already cautioned his younger associate that "casual sex" wasn't the same thing as "making love," and that was part of the problem. Torval wanted to experience love, and if that required a different form of copulation, he had to know what that was all about. Clearly a human should understand such things, and if Torval didn't know the rules, he could ruin everything.

He returned to the card catalog and looked up "making love," but found nothing except a couple of references to song lyrics. "Sex," too, proved to be of little help, although there were a few books on human anatomy that might be enlightening. Those could be investigated later, he decided, after he'd learned more about the process in question.

He continued to search, trying other phrases he'd heard, like "doing the nasty," "getting it on," and even "copulation," but got nowhere. Perhaps the problem was that he just didn't know what to look for.

He proceeded to the desk, where the dark-skinned man waited, a bored look on his face. Thin glasses sat atop a rather large, flat nose, the surface of each lens bisected by a noticeable crease or seam of some kind. The attendant absently flipped through a magazine and only half glanced up at Torval. "Can I help you?" he asked in a quiet voice.

Torval nodded, taking note of the man's name, Carter, printed in block letters on the tag attached to the lone pocket on his neatly buttoned shirt. "I hope so," replied the demon, also keeping his voice low, as seemed to be the custom in this place. "I wish to know more about making love to a woman."

For a second the librarian didn't reply, instead just staring at the visitor with wide, curious eyes. Then he began to chuckle, glancing about at the other patrons as if searching for something. "Oh, ho ho, that's a good one," he chortled. "The others put you up to this, did they? Very funny, guys."

"I am not jesting," insisted Torval. "I have great need of this information. I am taking a woman on a date later today, and if things proceed as I hope, I will need to understand the proper procedures."

"Dude, seriously, you're cracking me up!" Carter laughed, struggling to keep his voice quiet, despite the fact that he could barely avoid breaking into more laughter. A couple of people nearby flashed him curious or cautionary glances, so he took a moment to control himself. "I get it, man, I get it. Okay, fine, I'll play along. I think what you need comes from another kind of bookstore, y'know?"

"Other kind?" inquired the demon eagerly. "What other kind?"

"Never mind," replied Carter, managing to become serious. "Look, man, we got nothing like that here. This ain't no porn shop. You want sex books, try one of the adult places downtown. Just don't tell 'em where you got the idea, you catch my drift?"

Torval frowned. He knew what "porn" was. There were plenty of people imprisoned in Hell for such things. Obviously the librarian had the wrong idea. "I believe you misunderstand," the demon explained. "I do not want porn, and I am not looking for information on sex. I want to know the proper steps involved in making love."

Carter sighed. "Wouldn't we all," he remarked, almost to himself. He began to grow noticeably irritated. "Okay, fine, I get you. Dude, it ain't like you think," he tried to explain. "It ain't no different, y'see? Sex is sex, and there ain't no book gonna explain it to you. You just gotta do it, y'know? Surely someone like you oughta have some hot chick somewhere you can bang. Just go for it, man! Now that's all I got to say. Unless you got some real question that ain't no joke, let me be."

Torval started to protest further, but stopped. The man's body language and expression told him any additional questions would just meet with more and more resistance. He was getting nowhere. The library would be of no further help, it seemed.

"Very well," he said, turning away. "Thank you anyway."

"Anytime, man," came the reply. Torval glanced back to see Carter shaking his head slowly and sadly as he returned to his magazine. With a frustrated sigh, the demon headed for the exit.

So, he thought, libraries are good sources of information, but not for every subject. There are still things that only experience can teach. Which meant, obviously, that even Prelz would be of little use, even if Torval could find the ex-Tempter on this particular morning.

As he stood there looking out at the street, a chill wind swept along, slashing at his face and arms. The day seemed colder, but the skies were still clear. Winter might be fading from the city, but it hadn't quite left completely. He pushed his hands into his jacket pockets, shuddering slightly, and started to head back toward the shelter. Maybe if he found Prelz, he could still provide some hint as to where to go from here.

As he strode along, the vacationing demon found himself thinking back to what Carter had suggested, if a little crudely. He should find, or so the librarian said, a "hot chick"—obviously a euphemism for a beautiful woman—that Torval could "bang"—yet another slang term for sex. These humans certainly had plenty of colorful ways to describe that particular act, didn't they?

In fact, Torval did know of one "hot chick" in the vicinity. In fact, as soon as he remembered her, a complete plan of action snapped immediately into place. Yes, it was perfect—exactly what he was looking for.

Furthermore, if everything went as planned, this could even be considered a proper way of repaying Christine.

Suddenly suffused with purpose, he turned on his heels and headed briskly toward the home of Shelly Mendez.

* * *

"What the hell d'ya want?" came the loud, angry shout from inside the partially open door. "Ya hard of hearin'? I said go 'way!"

"I must speak with you, Shelly," insisted Torval as forcefully as he could. "I have a proposal for you."

"Ya got lotsa nerve comin' back here," she complained, her tattooed face and shoulders just visible beneath the chain that kept the door from popping completely open. She wore a scoop-neck cutoff T-shirt, a rather short skirt, and very little else, save an angry scowl. Without waiting for any further explanation, she rudely concluded, "Now fuck off!"

With that, the door slammed ignominiously shut. Torval frowned and knocked again. On the way here, he hoped she'd perhaps forgotten her anger toward him, but obviously not.

"You learnin' impaired?" her voice called out, muffled through the thick wood. "I'm gonna call the cops if ya don't scram!"

"Please listen," implored Torval hastily, while she was still near the door. "I have money. I wish to hire you."

There was a pause, and then the door popped partially open again. "You what?" she demanded. "Look, asswipe, I may walk the streets when I has ta, but this ain't no fuckin' brothel! What we did last time, that was a one time thing, ya get it?"

"But you do not understand," argued Torval swiftly. "I do not wish to retain your services as a prostitute."

She seemed taken aback. "Okay, what then?" she demanded. "And this better be hella good, or this door's slammin' in yer face!"

"I want you to train me," the demon replied, explaining as best he could without giving her a chance to shut the door again. "Teach me how to make love to a woman. I must know how this is done, and you are the only one I know who can provide the proper instruction."

There was a long pause. For a moment, Torval thought perhaps Shelly had forgotten to breathe. Then she burst into laughter. "Oh, ha-ha, that's great!" she sputtered wildly. "That's just great! You want me to teach ya how ta fuck? Like some kinda sexual schoolmarm? Phaaa-ha-haa!"

Her reaction reminded Torval of the one he'd received at the library, when he asked for more information about this subject. He simply sighed and waited it out. When she seemed a bit more collected, he proceeded with his pitch.

"I am serious, Shelly," he told her, honestly and firmly. "I am woefully uneducated on such matters. I require instruction, and you seem to have more experience in this area than any woman I have yet met."

"Okay, okay," she managed after catching her breath, "fine, mister fancy-talkin' man, lemme pretend like I really give a shit. What exactly do I gotta do?"

Torval thought about it for a moment before replying. "The last time we met," he told her, "we had sex. I am told this is referred to as 'casual sex' and was therefore meaningless."

"Yeah, sez you, but okay, fair 'nuff. Since I didn't get nothin' out of it on account of you suckin' ass, it's as good a phrasin' as any."

"That," he pointed out, "is exactly my problem. If I was indeed as bad as you say, this must be remedied by training. Furthermore, I do not simply desire sex. What I want to do is make love to a woman. There is a difference, clearly a more subtle one than I had originally thought, but that is what I must learn to do."

"So what yer sayin," Shelly concluded after a moment, "is you got yerself some honey you wanna impress, and ya wanna do it to her right. Not 'wham bam thanky ma'am' like we did the other day, fun as it was 'n' all."

"Yes, I suppose that is accurate," agreed the demon with a quick nod. "I cannot afford to be as terrible as you say I am. I do not care about my own gratification—I must make love to this woman in a way that pleases her. It is as simple as that."

Her eyebrows went up as she started to realize exactly what Torval had proposed, and the idea clearly appealed to her, as he hoped it would. "You wanna satisfy her, izzat it?" she went on. "This woman you got, whoever it is. You wanna know how to make her scream, and you don't care nothin' about yerself?"

"That is correct," Torval replied succinctly.

A smile began to appear on her face as she considered the possibilities, but even so, she wasn't quite done with the questioning. After a few long moments, she asked the final query, and one Torval was already well prepared to answer.

"All right, let's say I agree," Shelly inquired with a suggestive smile. "What's in it fer me?"

He reached into his pocket and withdrew the answer from his wallet—a single slip of green paper, crisp and new, which he unfolded with a snap. The words "one hundred dollars" were clearly visible there, along with three-digit numbers on every corner. He had no reason to speak—the bill did all the talking for him.

The door shut momentarily. There was a rattling as the chain came off, and then Shelly frantically jerked the door open all the way, as if afraid her visitor might be already gone.

"Well, don't just stand there!" she insisted eagerly. "Get that tight li'l ass of yours inside!"

# Chapter 30

"Okay," said Shelly somewhat eagerly, "first rule is I get paid in advance. No trickin' me or hidin' the cash, and it better be a real bill or you'll be sorry, you got me?"

"I assure you it is not counterfeit," replied Torval with confidence, never even considering the possibility that the note might somehow have been forged. Certainly Hal lacked the ability to do so, or else he wouldn't have bothered begging for coins on the street. Nonetheless, Shelly examined the bill carefully, holding it up to the light as if looking for some telltale detail Torval didn't know about. She seemed satisfied after a moment, smiled, and shoved the money into a nearby desk drawer.

"Okay," she announced, turning back to him, "Perfesser Shelly's School-o-Luvin' is now in session. Have yerself a seat."

Torval looked around at the messy, unclean apartment. The only chairs were two noticeably bent folding types leaning against a dining table some distance away, and a torn recliner with an open cardboard box lying across it. Within the box sprawled a half-eaten pizza, a type of food Torval recognized immediately. However, unlike the hot and fresh slices he'd tried the day before, this one looked dried out, cold, and unappealing. Certainly he had no interest in attempting to eat such a thing, even had he been hungry.

He pushed the box out of the way and sat down in the chair as Shelly had directed, keeping his attention focused on her. He had, after all, paid good money for this lesson, so he didn't want to miss a moment of it.

"Okay," she began, pacing back and forth, obviously considering what to say. "I gotta admit, I ain't never done nothin' like this before, so this may be rough at first. Lemme think."

"Take your time," he told her. "I am in no hurry."

"Okay, fine, neither am I. Not like I got anywhere ta go." Shelly hesitated, continuing to pace back and forth, occasionally rubbing her chin with her fingers, or absently playing with a lock of her hair.

Finally, after a few more seconds, she went on hesitatingly. "See, it's been awhile since I got made love to, y'know? Sex, yeah, I get that a lot, you found that out yourself, dintcha? Ha-ha, yeah, but that ain't what you want now. See, the other day, neither of us, we didn't care nothin' 'bout each other, see? We just wanted ta do the wild thang, and that's okay I guess, for what it's worth. But makin' love, 'tween two peeps who care 'bout each other... hmm..."

She stopped, staring off into space, lost in thought for a moment. "Yeah," she finally went on, "it's been awhile. Damn, that long... even Ricardo, damn his worthless ass, he didn't really make love ta me. For him it was kinda like a race, I think, but boy did he ever have some en-err-geee..."

A half-smile of recollection crossed her face, and just as quickly vanished. She ran a hand through her long black hair, letting it flop back down briefly across her eyes, and for an instant the demon noticed an expression very much like those he saw regularly on the bums down at the shelter. A sort of forlorn hopelessness, or possibly regret, as if something desirable had gone away, now forever lost.

Shelly snapped out of her reverie after a moment. "Well, forget that!" she said loudly. "Screw Ricardo anyway! He was always chasin' any other chick that came along anyways. Never cared 'bout me. The last boy who really cared was Geraldo Cordilla. I was sixteen, see, which is too young, or so they say, y'know? But Geraldo, he was older, and in college, and he treated me like I was a real woman. Yeah... yeah, he knew how ta make love ta me. He cared 'bout me, I know he did. He was the last one ta... ta actually kiss me like he meant it."

She turned away for a moment, putting one hand to her face. Perhaps she had something in her eye? Torval felt that perhaps he should make a comment, in the awkward silence that followed, but couldn't think of any kind of response.

"It don't matter," Shelly went on after a moment, wiping off her cheek. "His family, they moved away that summer, and he had ta go with 'em. We was gonna write, but then I moved here, and that was that. Don't matter anyways. What I'm gonna do, I guess, is show ya what he useta do. The things I liked. Your girl whatshername, she oughta like 'em too. Can't imagine why she wouldn't, bein' a fellow woman 'n' all. That good enough fer ya?"

"Certainly," agreed Torval. "I am anxious to get started."

"I just betcha are." She managed a wan smile. "Now here's the thing. You men, see, you think we chicks like the rough stuff. Well, that's true some a the time, when we's in the right mood. But makin' love, well, it ain't like that, not at first. Ya needs ta start out slow, see? It's all about the anticipatin'. We both know where we're gonna end up, right? But ya take yer time gettin' there."

Torval nodded. "I see. So I should make you wait? Is that it? Simply sit here and let you think about what is to come?"

"No, no, that ain't what I mean! Sheesh, this is gonna be harder than I thought, ain't it? Okay, look, we ladies also like bein' touched, and caressed, and all that happy stuff. 'Member how I kissed ya all hard and rough when ya first came here? Sorta like that, only with some carin'. Ya gotta do it slower, with passion, y'know? Tell ya what, stand up."

Torval stood, facing her. He was just slightly taller than she was, so he had to look down slightly at her darkly tanned face. She was indeed attractive, as he'd noticed when he first met her, and yet all he could think of was Christine. He wanted it to be her shining blue eyes he stared into, not Shelly's dark brown ones.

Shelly kept right on going with the instruction, not really looking at him directly. "Okay, now, take me in yer arms," she explained. "No, not like that! Slowly, like I'm real delicate-like. Here. Put yer hand here, and another one there, yeah, just like that. Now just slowly pull yourself to me and then..."

He did as she asked, and as she drew close, his body just sort of naturally took over on its own. He bent his head slightly and drew her face closer, and as he did, his eyes shut automatically and their lips met. For a long moment he simply held her there, enjoying the feeling, making no attempt whatsoever to slip his tongue into her mouth. She, too, did nothing of the kind, instead simply clutching him, and then finally relaxing in his arms.

After a few seconds they separated, almost as if by reflex. Shelly stared at him with obvious amusement. "Ya don't need no instructin' there, Joey boy," she told him. "Ya got it right straight off. Now that's what I'm callin' a kiss! God, why don't men kiss me like that no more? I gotta knock off this whorin' shit and find me a real man like you."

"I appreciate the compliment," replied Torval honestly, feeling a slight twinge of pride at her words. "However, all I did was what you showed me to do. It seemed natural and correct."

"Well, it was, it was. God, I miss that... anyways, let's move on. Ya gots the kissin' down pat. Now, like I said, us chicks like bein' touched in all the right places, so come on back here to the bedroom, and I'll show ya where ta start..."

* * *

Torval panted from lack of breath. A few ragged sheets stuck to his frail body, soaked in sweat. The heat radiating from Shelly, one arm draped across his heaving chest, felt oppressively intense. She gave a kind of happy sigh and snuggled against him, running her fingers up and down his quivering shoulder, sending chills along his spine.

"Gratz, Joey boy," she whispered softly in his ear. "Ya passed Perfesser Shelly's final 'xam. Now ya knows how ta do it right. That's what I call makin' love right there."

Torval nodded weakly. He couldn't possibly reply with words; he was too out of breath. Unlike the sex during their previous encounter, this intense session lasted far longer and drained him utterly. His human body was completely exhausted. How he remained conscious at all remained a mystery.

Staying in control, or so he'd just learned, turned out to be the key to making love. Last time, he gave in to the weak desires of the flesh, allowing his pre-conditioned muscular responses to take over. But as Shelly explained, what the male desired from copulation wasn't always the same thing the woman wanted. He had to find the middle ground that would satisfy both participants. So instead of shutting down his conscious mind, he listened to her frantic instructions—gasped ever so urgently in the throes of passion—until after what seemed like forever she made a sort of choking scream, convulsing as if in pain, and Torval could stand no more. After that, he too climaxed, and after those few brief moments of frantic pleasure, only fire in his chest and burning muscles remained.

Clearly this is something that can only get better with practice, he told himself. His body simply wasn't used to it, and after a while, he hoped, things would improve.

He'd succeeded, at least, in pleasing Shelly. The way she held him now, caressing his skin and sighing in satisfaction, showed that he'd been a good learner. Still, there was no guarantee that Christine would react in the same manner. All Torval could do was try to follow Shelly's instructions, modifying the procedure as needed, until Christine, too, lay beside him as Shelly did now, awash in the welcome afterglow.

There was something quite pleasing about these post-coital moments, he realized as he caught his breath and the pain gradually subsided at last. Having a woman rest against him like this, feeling her pulse against his skin, her breath tickling the whiskers on his cheek... this seemed right somehow, as if this was the way things were supposed to be.

Perhaps that's the whole point, Torval considered after a moment. Human beings needed to reproduce. That's how the species propagated itself, and how new souls came to be. As he understood things, raising a child was a long and difficult process, usually undertaken by a couple who stayed together for the benefit of their offspring. So it would be to their advantage to be in love, to feel sensations like these. Such emotions would help to keep the pair together, especially if they could feel this way all the time, throughout their entire lives.

So did that mean love existed solely to help humans reproduce? Was it at heart that simple? Or did the emotion hide something even more complex, something he could only begin to touch the surface of?

The perplexing puzzle must've shown on his face, for Shelly took note and sat up slightly. The loss of heat from her naked body caused a wash of air across his skin, and Torval shivered involuntarily.

"What's wrong?" she asked quietly. "Ya not get what you was lookin' for? Sorry if it weren't what you were 'spectin'."

"It is not that," he interrupted. "Your instruction was exactly what I needed, Shelly. I feel I now understand the process completely."

"But . . . ?" she went on. "There's always a 'but,' y'see. I knows that look on yer face. What izzit?"

"Well," he continued, "if I am to understand this correctly, we have just made love, is that right?"

"Oh, did we ever!" she cooed happily. "I ain't come like that in prolly ten years or more. Usually the men I'm with, they just bang away, not carin' bout me, and I gots ta pretend, y'know? Make noises, and all that, while they're thrustin' and pushin', till they're done and gone. Then I finish meself off with . . . well, y'know what I mean. Anyways, forget about that, I still don't know what's up. If I did good, what's the problem?"

"We made love," Torval explained, "but I still do not fully comprehend what love is. Is it merely a means to ensure propagation of the species, or is it a binding force that links two humans together?"

She stared at him for a moment, obviously confused. "Dude," she finally said, "I gots no idea what you just said, but I get that ya don't get love. Nobody does, really, and surely not me! Maybe Geraldo, he and I, maybe we was in love, I don't know. Too young to be sure, I guess. But my momma, she always told me, when I find love, I'd know it. Y'see? So if this chick yer datin', if she's the one, you'll know. Ya just will."

"And I must make love to her, as we just did, to discern this?"

"Not necessar'ly," Shelly said with a chuckle, "but man, it sure wouldn't hurt none! Ya do ta her what ya just did ta me, and at least yer gonna buy yerself plenty a time ta find out."

Torval nodded. "Very well, then. I believe I have accomplished what I set out to do, at least for now. You have been an excellent instructor, Shelly, but now I must depart. I have many more things to accomplish before my date begins."

She sighed with obvious disappointment. "So yer just gonna up 'n 'leave, just like that, then?" She ran her hand up and down his arm suggestively. "Not gonna wait a bit, so we can try somethin' like that again?"

Torval felt a faint stirring within his body, down below his waist, but he knew without a doubt he wouldn't have the stamina for another attempt. "I am afraid not," he told her, not without allowing some of his own disappointment to slip into his voice. "I do admit, that was most pleasurable, but this weak frame I wear cannot stand such exertion. I must rest and recover should events proceed appropriately."

"Aw, dammit!" Shelly complained, sitting up in bed and crossing her arms petulantly. "I finally find a guy who's good in the sack and he don't care nothin' about me! Just usin' me like all the rest." There was a pause as she hung her head sadly. "I almost forgot, didn't I? Almost forgot what I was, there for a minnit. Dammit all. God dammit, I'm fuckin' pathetic, ain't I? So goddamn pathetic..."

She wiped at her eyes again, and Torval realized those were tears forming there. That must've been what was happening earlier, when she began the instruction. She was upset and distressed, clearly, but why? Had he not explained at the forefront that she was to teach him, and nothing more? Where did she get the idea that anything else was involved?

Despite his confusion at Shelly's unexpected emotions, he felt the immediate need to comfort her somehow. Without understanding why, he sat up and put an arm around her torso. "You are not pathetic," he told her firmly. "I am sorry I cannot be more than what I am, but I made it clear this was just a business arrangement between us. I required instruction from you and you provided it, as we agreed. Nothing else was stated or implied. Furthermore, I could not be more satisfied with your services. You were a truly excellent teacher."

"Services," she repeated with a sigh. "Seems like that's all I ever do, service people! There's gotta be more ta life than this, dammit! But I can't find no good jobs, and hookin' is the only way I can—"

Suddenly she froze, and her eyes stopped watering as she began to stare into space ahead of herself. One hand came up and hovered in front of her chest, rotating slightly. Torval watched in silence, wondering what was going on, and if perhaps she'd suddenly become ill, or some new emotion he knew nothing of would now bring itself to the fore.

Finally she turned to him, those brown orbs of hers wide and sparkling in the faint bedroom light. All traces of sadness were gone, just like that, and in their place shone newfound excitement.

"That's it!" she blurted out. "I gots it! I know what I'm gonna do!"

"What?" Torval asked in confusion. He had no idea what she could possibly be talking about.

"I'm gonna do what I just did!" she went on quickly. "I'm gonna teach people like you! It ain't whorin', not really, is it? And there's gotta be lotsa men like you who wanna know how to have sex—no, make love, yeah, that's right! Perfesser Shelly, that's me! Ha-ha! Oh, man, if this works—it'll be perfect!"

"I do not understand," Torval insisted. "What are you talking about?"

"What you said, man, what you said!" she continued, babbling excitedly. "Ya said this was a 'business 'rangement!' So that's what I'm gonna do, Joey-boy. I'm gonna make this a business, plain and simple. I'm gonna hang out a shingle, or whatever ya wanna call it."

"Hang out a what?"

"A shingle—oh, never mind! I'm gonna start a business, don't ya get it? I'm gonna teach people how ta make love!"

# Chapter 31

"You about done in there?" called out Shelly, somewhat breathlessly. "C'mon, you, hurry it up! I got things ta see, places ta go, people ta do . . . catch my drift? Ha-ha-ha!"

"I'm dressing as quickly as I can," Torval protested, looking around for his socks, which lay crumpled up in a pile next to where he'd kicked his shoes earlier. Earlier in the session, Shelly instructed him on the art of stripping slowly and enticingly, as opposed to simply ripping his garments off haphazardly, as they'd done during their first tryst. Apparently removing one's clothes was something of an art, one of many procedures called "foreplay" that served to lengthen the anticipation of the pre-intercourse interval. As near as Torval could tell, making love comprised a ritual of indeterminate length, but with a definite beginning, middle and end.

Even more followed—something Shelly called "pillow talk," which in this case resulted in her sudden and inexplicable brainstorm that now had her all excited. After coming up with this new idea, she raced about the apartment, chattering to herself, apparently making plans that mostly made little sense to her demonic guest. She had to make phone calls, and arrange certain purchases, as well as research, and possibly acquire some kind of certification or license—although listening to her debate with herself, she had her own doubts that such a thing would even be possible.

Actually, the idea wasn't a bad one, as far as Torval could tell. Being a prostitute was inherently wrong—selling one's body was one of the earliest known sins, in fact. Yet what she talked about now wasn't merely simple prostitution. She instead intended to be an instructor in the ways and means of sex. According to her, there were plenty of men out there who had no idea how to please a woman, but wanted to know—and she'd be more than happy to teach them, for a fee of course.

So was that against the law? Listening to her prattling, he knew she wasn't sure, and Torval had no idea either. Wishing to help others sounded "good," at least as far as he understood that particular concept. Furthermore, if someone needed instruction, Shelly clearly had the qualifications to provide it. Torval had definitely learned a great deal, just in the last hour or so. If he could please Christine using his newfound skills, it would be money well spent.

The morality of the issue still eluded Torval, however, even as he pulled on his socks and shoes. What she intended was still, at its core, taking money in exchange for sex. Whether this comprised actual prostitution wasn't for him to say. Had he been a Judge, perhaps he could've rendered a decision, but he wasn't, and had no desire to be. Human laws, too, might know the answer, but he had no access to those at present. In fact, checking his watch, he doubted he had time to investigate. He would be meeting with Christine fairly soon.

He stood, producing a loud creaking from the rickety bed, and immediately staggered against the nearby wall, catching himself with a free hand. His legs were wobbly and painfully sore, and he fought back a wave of sudden dizziness. The lesson exhausted him, and recovering would take some time. Plus, he realized after a moment, his stomach required filling. He would have to stop for lunch on the way back to the shelter.

Yes, food will help, he thought to himself as he moved back through the messy apartment. Shelly paced back and forth near the door, holding a small black object close to her head, speaking in its direction with some urgency. Hesitating, Torval realized this was most likely a kind of telephone, albeit much smaller than the one he'd used at the shelter, and this one used none of the wires that seemed to make most human technology function.

"C'mon, Frankie, ya gots ta hear me out on this one," Shelly said into the device. "I'm tellin' ya, it's gonna work! I had this mark—" She glanced up at Torval and then turned away quickly. "Er, customer, I mean—and he paid me to—yeah, of course we did, but it ain't the same, that's what I'm sayin'!"

Torval wanted to move toward the door, for she'd urged him to hurry and depart, but she blocked his way. Glancing up at him, she raised a single finger, as if to order him to halt. So he halted, listening curiously to the remainder of what sounded, to him, like a one-sided conversation.

"He paid me," Shelly said forcefully, "to teach 'im how ta do it right! Not ta just bang me, like some kinda guerilla, but ta care 'bout what I was wantin'. And it worked—it was some a the best ever! I'm tellin' ya, Frankie-boy, I'm good at this. I can do this! Ya gots ta give it a chance!"

She listened eagerly, but seemed somewhat crestfallen by whatever the unseen Frankie said in reply. "Okay, then just gimme one chance," she pleaded after a moment. "Find some guy ya know wants a lesson. I'll give a free sample if I gots to, if that's what it takes!" There was another pause. "Okay, okay. Good. That's fine. Call me, then. I'll be waitin'. Sheesh!"

She pulled the black device back from her head and poked at the front of it. "It's hard ta find a good pimp nowadays," she sighed, apparently done with that other conversation and once again able to focus on her guest. "Him and me, we parted company couple months back, when I tried ta go legit. He wants me back on the streets, but I ain't gonna do that, not again! I'm gonna run with this idea of yours, Joey, and that's that, whether it's with Frankie or somebody else. I'm tellin' ya, this is perfect!"

She stepped over and kissed him on the cheek, smiling at him. "What was that for?" Torval inquired, rubbing the slightly moist spot curiously. Did she wish to resume some sort of romantic procedure, or was that just another custom of which he was, until now, unaware?

"For bein' you," she replied with a grin. "You and yer big words! You gots no idea how sexy that is, y'know. And ya came back to me, after I dissed ya, and gave me a chance, one I don't really deserve... I'm gonna make this work, I swear it. I'm done with whorin', thanks ta you!"

"I am glad of that," replied Torval. "That profession only leads down one possible path, and to one destination."

"Yeah." She nodded in agreement, shaking her head sadly. "I think I knew it, but I couldn't stop, y'know? Too easy, and it ain't like I gots other choices. Anyways, it's all done with now. I hate to rush ya, but I gots things ta do round here, and places ta go, like I said. Out ya go!"

She opened the door, and Torval exited the building, still a little woozy and feeling pain in his knees and thighs as he started down the stairs. He looked back at Shelly, who gave a little wave. "Farewell, and good luck in your new endeavor," he told her sincerely.

"Thanks," she replied happily. "You too, man. Good luck with yer girl. She don't know how lucky she is!"

With that, she stepped back inside, disappearing from sight as she shut the door swiftly. Torval continued down the stairs, shivering as a bitterly cold gust of wind swept over him. The jacket, seemingly sufficient to protect him the day before, now seemed incapable of stopping the wintry air from penetrating to his skin. The fact that he remained somewhat sweaty from the earlier exertion didn't help matters.

In fact, he realized, he probably couldn't be considered clean any longer. That morning, he'd showered and cleansed himself before dressing, but Shelly hurried him out just now, leaving him no chance to repeat that process. That meant his sweat, mingled with hers, would dry on his body, leaving him malodorous—something the book he'd read at the library warned him most stridently against.

Fortunately, the warehouse wasn't far away. He walked in that direction, and as he did, his eyes immediately fell upon a small bistro-style restaurant called Rozelli's Italian Oven. The smell emanating from the vicinity immediately set his stomach to rumbling even more strongly than it already was.

There was no avoiding the place. His feet seemed to steer him inside of their own accord. One customer waited in line ahead of him, looking up at a menu over a prominent counter, so Torval perused the possibilities. Unfortunately, other than the fact that many of the choices were sandwiches, with which he was already familiar, he had no idea what any of these things were.

Well, almost. Nestled in amongst things like "spaghetti and meatballs," "seven-layer lasagna" and "twice-baked ziti" was something he knew about: pizza. Just thinking about the meat-and-cheese-covered slices made his mouth water. Unfortunately, pizza seemed to come in several sizes—small, medium, large, and king—and Torval had no way to judge which one he wanted.

The customer ahead of him finished his order and moved away, making it Torval's turn. "What can I get for you today?" asked the young man behind the counter. He wore a kind of oval-shaped paper cap over blonde hair, and his face was covered in freckles. Like so many other food servers Torval had seen, he wore a nametag, this one identifying him as someone named "Chuck."

"I would like a pizza," answered Torval, "but I do not know the size. How big are they?"

"Small's six inches," replied the youth, holding up his hands so that they were slightly spread apart. "Personal size, y'know? Medium's nine inches, large's twelve, and king size is sixteen. Unless you're orderin' for somebody else, you probably want a small."

"Very well," agreed Torval, noting that the prices quoted on the menu for a small pizza were, without a doubt, the most affordable. His supply of funds wasn't unlimited, after all. "That is what I shall have."

"Okay, what kind?"

"A pizza," replied Torval. "I thought I had made that clear."

Chuck sighed and shuffled his feet uncomfortably. "No, I mean, what do you want on your pizza?" He pointed with a heavily freckled arm at a spot on the menu Torval hadn't noticed before. "It comes with one ingredient. Each additional one is seventy-five cents extra."

Torval followed the pointing finger. There were at least twelve different words listed there, most of them unfamiliar to him. What, for example, were "anchovies"? And "pepperoni" didn't sound terribly appetizing, whatever it might be. Most likely these were types of meat, but he couldn't be sure. In the end, he went with the only selection he was sure of, because he already knew he liked that taste. "I will take extra cheese," he answered after a long delay.

"Good call," came the reply. "Something to drink?"

"Yes. A soft drink. Coca-cola."

"Righto." The man pushed a few buttons on the device Torval now knew as a kind of computer. "That'll be nine-fifty-five."

Torval withdrew his wallet, which until that point he'd almost completely forgotten about. The last time he visited Shelly, she tried to steal his money—what if she'd done the same this time? Fortunately, she hadn't, for all his cash remained safely tucked inside. He withdrew ten dollars and handed it over, taking the time to note that he still had several bills remaining in the convenient little pocket. The meal seemed a bit expensive, compared to what he'd had before, but he could afford it.

"Here you go." Chuck handed over Torval's change, along with a scrap of paper with a variety of barely readable figures printed on it. "Have a seat, and I'll call your number when it's ready."

"Very well." Torval took the receipt, expecting to see a large number like the ones he remembered from waiting rooms in cell illusions, but he could barely read the faded print. He found an empty seat and sat down, studying the scrap, noting that most of the numbers there were currency amounts. One three-digit figure seemed out of place, larger and off by itself. That must be the correct one, or at least he hoped so.

As he waited, he took stock of the aches and pains still suffusing his human flesh. His legs, and in particular his knees, were noticeably sore, as were his buttocks, a somewhat disconcerting place to have such discomfort. There was a faint pounding in his temples, and of course his stomach growled with hunger. The dizziness had faded by now, mostly, replaced by a strong anticipation of the food to come. And, of course, another body part ached, though that one somewhat pleasurably.

Sex is indeed exhausting, thought the demon, and yet enjoyable, as well as extremely important to the male-female relationship. Torval congratulated himself on coming up with the idea to visit Shelly before his date with Christine. Had he not done so, he surely would've embarrassed himself with clumsy, ill-advised attempts to emulate their first wild encounter. Christine deserved better than that. He still had much to learn, of course, but perhaps she'd be as good a teacher as Shelly.

Hopefully his body would recover from this exertion soon. Fortunately, this thing called a "movie" would apparently take about two hours, and dinner afterward would also require some time. That would give Torval a nice long break before the physical activity that followed.

Of course, he reminded himself, there was always the chance nothing would happen. The date might go poorly, although he'd do everything in his power to prevent that. Perhaps she simply wouldn't like the movie, or the food, which would be unfortunate. Maybe Torval wouldn't attract her, like she attracted him. There wasn't much he could do about that, except try his best.

In due course, Chuck called out his number, and Torval enjoyed another meal in silence, thinking eagerly about the afternoon to come.

* * *

Tasting food, thought the demon, is definitely one of the better human experiences I've enjoyed so far. Lovemaking, too, ranked high on his list of favorites. At this particular moment, though, a hot shower seemed by far the best.

The water struck him square in the back, between the shoulder blades, making his skin tingle all over. The sensation of liquid heat rolling down his bare body, wrapping around his legs, swirling about his feet—this was something akin to nirvana. If such a place as Heaven truly existed, perhaps the souls there felt such sensations all the time. He hoped so—that would be a worthy reward for those who'd led good and just lives. Especially considering the terrible fates that awaited those who failed to do so. Somehow, that possibility seemed appropriate, as if such things kept the universe in balance.

Awash in personal ecstasy, his mind began to drift. These humans, they had no idea what fate might await them. They lived their lives however they wanted, with the same sort of free will Geezon imparted on Torval before the transitioning. Lacking any evidence of an afterlife, they made decisions for themselves as the mood struck them. Choose the easy path, like Zac Turillo, and descend into evil, and they would go to Hell, where torment awaited. Or be a good person, like Christine Anderson, and they would reach Heaven, which must be wonderful indeed. The system made complete sense, as far as Torval understood it.

Still drifting along in a haze of pleasure, he started to wonder about the other humans he'd met since arriving here. What of Shelly, for example? Or Pete Roxton, Joe Sampson, or Hal Sommersby? Or even Prelz, now fully human by his own choice? All had done questionable things in their lives. Shelly, an admitted prostitute; Pete, a womanizer, or at least so it seemed from the brief conversation Torval had overheard; Joe, who fled from responsibility, much as Hal ran out on his family; and Prelz, of course, once a Tempter, deliberately leading others down the path of evil. Would the fact that Prelz chose to give up that life absolve him of those earlier sins? Torval doubted it very much.

How would he sentence these people, wondered Torval idly, if he had the ability? What fate would he choose for Shelly Mendez if her soul arrived in Hell? Would he make her suffer with painful, burning tattoos? Or would she be forced to service one terrible lover after another, enduring bad sex throughout eternity?

He shuddered at the thought. Shelly had good in her still, at least as far as he'd been able to understand the concept. She wanted to escape the life of prostitution that, for whatever reason, entrapped her. Would that desire be enough to avoid a fate like one of those he imagined? Only time would tell, and Torval doubted he would ever know. Her fate was in her own hands, her destiny hers to decide.

Exactly as it should be.

The water began to cool, and Torval knew he'd reached the end of the limit of heat in the shower. For whatever reason, these amazing liquid-spewing devices eventually ran out of the warmer stuff. He started to lather up, a bit late in the game, but the heat seemed so enjoyable he had simply lost himself in it.

Free will. That's what Geezon told him was the key to understanding humanity. Shelly had to make her own choices. Yet Torval felt as though he'd influenced her somewhat, without intending to do so. Did that mean he'd performed a good act, without realizing it? Or simply a serendipitous one? Did being good require conscious thought, and deliberately good intentions? Or could one simply do good by accident? If so, would that count toward getting into Heaven?

Those were questions for Prelz, or perhaps that priest, Father Michaels. Torval made a mental note to ask whichever of them he encountered next, even as he hurriedly rinsed himself off and deactivated the flow of now-chilly water.

He dried himself and removed another pair of clean underwear from the bag, which was already half empty. He needed more clothes, especially shirts, but had no choice at this point but to put on the same ones he'd been wearing. Since the library book told him to dress nicely for a date, he put on the best outfit he had, the turtleneck and slacks Christine gave him the day she took him to the employment office.

He finished by combing his hair and brushing his teeth, for once again the book's wisdom informed him that hygiene was of high importance. She'd appreciate fresh, minty-smelling breath, as opposed to the odors of whatever food he'd eaten recently. The book also recommended a product called "mouthwash," but Torval had none of this available. He should also use something called "deodorant," but again, he'd failed to plan that far ahead.

He checked his watch. He still had time—he could simply stop at the drugstore again and purchase the required items. As he started to leave, he checked himself, realizing he'd almost forgotten to take the wallet out of his jeans. Leaving that behind would've been a disaster!

After putting away his other clothes, he climbed the stairs out of the basement and looked about for one of the Roxtons, but didn't see either of them. He didn't recognize the man behind the sales register, which wasn't surprising—the Roxtons employed a number of workers, and hadn't taken the time to introduce him to any of them.

Torval decided finding Lincoln or Pete wasn't all that important. They'd given him free access to the basement and shower any time he needed them, after all. He walked outside, pulling the jacket tightly around himself, grateful for the thick turtleneck sweater's protection against the cold. A few wispy clouds hovered in the sky above the buildings, and the wind whipping down the street, if anything, felt even colder than before.

His body felt much better now. The hot shower, like a massage, eased his pain and soothed his sore muscles. Of course, he still had some residual soreness, but he could feel that fading away. In addition, the tasty pizza adequately sated him, and the last vestiges of dizziness and hunger headache were already gone.

In fact, he reflected as he stopped at the corner to wait for the streetlight, the little bit of soreness still suffusing his muscles actually felt rather enjoyable. Something seemed satisfying, at least, and he didn't really understand why. Was this his body's way of rewarding him? Was this the feeling every human strove daily to achieve? If so, it was a worthy goal, indeed.

The light changed, and he started to cross, but suddenly a car pulled up directly in front of him, screeching to a quick halt. The vehicle was of moderate size, painted a dull gray, with a kind of blocky, angular shape much like the taxicabs, but without the bright yellow color. The front doors opened and two men popped out, dressed in slacks, pressed white shirts, and solid black ties. Both wore sunglasses and were clean-shaven. The nearest was white and stocky, with short brown hair, a wide face and a distinctive scowl, while the other had black skin and a clean-shaven head that seemed to shine in the early afternoon sunlight.

They seemed fixated on Torval, approaching him directly. The demon froze for a moment, confused. He had no idea who these people were—he knew he hadn't seen them before, at least not since arriving on Earth. Yet they seemed to know him. The light-skinned one stopped directly in front of the demon, towering over him by a good six inches, and outweighing him by at least fifty pounds—all of it muscle. The other took up a position just behind and to Torval's right, between him and the main entrance to the Roxton warehouse. Neither said anything, but seemed to be staring at him, though it was impossible to tell through the dark glasses they wore.

Torval wasn't sure what to do. They wanted something, clearly. Was this a robbery? If so, he stood on a busy street corner—surely one of these other nearby humans would intervene, if that's what this was. Or had he chanced upon some other strange custom Torval didn't know about? Maybe he should say something—but what?

Fortunately, one of them saved him the trouble. The white one lifted up his arm, causing Torval to jerk back involuntarily. Clutched in a meaty hand, the still-unidentified man held a wallet half open, displaying a large, gold-colored medallion with a star motif. Torval saw, in the brief glimpse he had of the badge, a single word that made his heart sink and the breath catch in his throat.

The man spoke at last. "Police," he snapped in a clipped, businesslike voice. "Would you come with us, please?"

* * *

Torval endured the ride in the back of the unmarked cruiser with a mixture of worry and fear. His body felt cold, far colder than the weather might suggest. He shivered occasionally, casting his eyes about with the trepidation of a caged beast.

What had he done? The police were arresting him—that much he knew. He'd broken the law, and was going to prison. There would be no date with Christine. He'd spend the rest of his vacation rotting in some dark cell, like one of the sinners back on his route. Only this time he wouldn't be able to simply walk through the walls to escape.

The mysterious plainclothes police officers hadn't said anything since asking Torval, in their direct and forceful manner, to get into the vehicle. The demon acquiesced without a word, his voice apparently gone, lost between the heavy swallows of worry that followed. He felt afraid, more frightened than at any time since arriving here, and the impulse to flee was overwhelming. He couldn't escape, though. He couldn't even open the doors or roll down the windows when the vehicle stopped—there were no handles to permit flight, and a heavy metal grille blocked access to the front seats. He was trapped!

The black man turned to look at him through the fence, and Torval recoiled slightly. The policeman had a very thin mustache, the only hair anywhere on his head. The sunglasses made him look all the more enigmatic, since there was no way to read his eyes. The man studied his prisoner for a moment, then grinned and let loose with a gruff chuckle.

"Seems mighty scared, don't he, Vince?" remarked the driver, the white man with the thick body who looked quite capable of ripping Torval's arms off if he so chose.

"Yeah," agreed the other one. "Seems awfully guilty to me. I bet he's ready to confess. You ready to confess, pal?"

Torval gulped and tried to find his voice. "I—I do not know what you are referring to," he managed, almost choking. He realized how dry his throat was and swallowed a few more times before continuing. "I assure you, I have done nothing wrong."

"Yeah, yeah, that's what they all say," replied Vince with a hearty laugh. "Say, Marty, you think he don't know we know what he's been up to?"

"Probably not," replied Marty with a quick laugh. "Look, son, first off, why don't you tell us what your name is? I don't wanna call you 'perp' or 'scumbag' the rest of the day."

"My name is..." Torval paused, swallowing again. He'd almost used his demon name by mistake. "Joe. Joe Sampson."

"You sure?" asked the black man curiously. "You don't sound too sure. Joe Sampson, eh? Guess it's better than John Smith, amirite?"

"Yeah, well, we'll just have to see," agreed the driver. "All right, fine, Joe, if that's your real name, we're just havin' a little fun with you. You ain't under arrest or anything like that."

"I—I am not under arrest?" replied Torval, suddenly feeling lightheaded and very, very relieved. "Does that mean I can go? Will you release me?"

"Sure, in a bit," replied Marty, pausing briefly as the car turned a corner. He honked once at a slow-moving pedestrian, and then continued on. Torval realized, in that brief moment, that he had no idea whatsoever where he was—the car had turned several times already during its journey through the traffic-choked streets. If his captors did, in fact, let him out, how would he find his way back to the shelter?

"Listen, you ain't under arrest," continued Vince, "but the lieutenant, he wants to ask you some questions, y'see? We've been, well, keepin' an eye on the Roxtons for a while now, and we saw you goin' in and out of there a couple of times, so we picked you up. Nothin' personal, no arrest or anything, just want to have a little chat, if that's okay."

"I suppose," agreed Torval, "if you return me to the warehouse when we are finished. There are things I must do in that part of the city."

"Sure, sure," agreed Marty immediately. "We're all friends here, right? No reason we can't let you out where we found you. Ain't that right, Vince?"

"Yeah, sure, whatever," replied the other with a half-hearted shrug. "Anyways, like Marty says, this is just an interview, you see? We ain't holdin' you, but it'll be in your interest to cooperate. You do want to cooperate with the police, right? You look like a good citizen to me."

"I will cooperate," agreed Torval, feeling immensely relieved that he hadn't been arrested. He felt his body warming up, his pulse returning to normal. "Cooperating with law enforcement is the right thing to do, as I understand it."

"That's what I'm always sayin'," agreed the driver with a chuckle. "I think I'm gonna like you, Joe Sampson. Now just be sure you answer all the lieutenant's questions and don't hold nothin' back, okay?"

"Yeah," agreed Vince. "After all, we'd hate to have to bring up your little visit to the home of a known prostitute, wouldn't we? Yeah, we'll just keep that to ourselves."

"For now," put in a widely grinning Marty.

The two began to laugh, and Torval once again felt very, very cold.

* * *

"Lieutenant," said Vince, sticking his head through the open doorway of the glass-walled office, "here's that guy you told us to pick up. Name's Joe Sampson."

The man seated at the desk slowly stood. Unlike the plainclothes officers, he wore a blue uniform, spotless and crisply pressed. He wasn't nearly as heavily built as Marty, but he stood at least as tall and appeared quite fit. He kept his hair cut short, in an almost military style, and had steel-gray eyes that seemed to bore into Torval, even from all the way across the little room.

"Good," replied the lieutenant, motioning for Torval to enter. "Welcome, Mr. Sampson. Name's McCord, Lieutenant McCord. Call me by my rank, if you please. I prefer it that way."

"Yes, sir," replied Torval deferentially, shuffling inside the doorway with Vince and Marty blocking any retreat behind him. The demon felt much as he did when forced to report to Foreman Landri for some sort of discipline, only this time it would be of the human variety. The lieutenant's voice held a tone of immediate and powerful authority, and Torval knew it would take a distinct force of will to do anything but obey his every command without question.

"Have a seat," McCord went on, pointing briefly at a small, uncushioned wooden chair sitting against the wall near the door. Torval sat immediately, without a word, still glancing worriedly about the small office. A long table dominated the room, supporting a computer monitor not unlike the one in the once-forbidden room in the Roxtons' basement. Behind the lieutenant were several rows of gray file cabinets almost as tall as the ceiling. Other than a few pieces of paper on the desk and a couple of manila folders in an inbox, the place looked spotless.

Vince stepped forward, another folder in his hand. "Here's the report from the database," he announced, handing the item over. "Turns out he was in there after all. Didn't see that coming."

"Yeah, you owe me ten bucks," commented Marty.

Vince sighed and his shoulders slumped. "Yeah, yeah. Can you break a twenty?"

"Don't think so."

McCord, after giving the file a brief once-over while his associates spoke, sat down in a quick motion and waved backhandedly at them. "That'll be all for now. You two wait outside. I don't think this'll take very long."

"You got it, boss," agreed Marty, turning away. The door closed behind them, cutting off their continued discussion about their little side bet.

The lieutenant looked down at the file, reading more carefully now, occasionally glancing up at Torval, who now sweated noticeably. The air in the room seemed stale and uncomfortably warm, perhaps intentionally.

Torval still didn't know what was happening. He wasn't under arrest, so why should he be so afraid? The lieutenant only wanted to ask him questions. That's what the others told him, after all. So why be so concerned?

They mentioned Shelly Mendez earlier. They knew she was a prostitute, and that he'd been in her home. They'd followed him, it seemed.

They were watching him, and for how long? What did they know of him, of his actions on this world? Were they demons, who had discovered his existence here? Had he broken the rules?

No, they couldn't be demons, Torval reminded himself. The one called Vince had searched him carefully, resulting in physical contact, if only briefly. Then Marty held Torval's wrists, rolling his fingers in that strange black ink, pressing them onto paper to display a kind of imprint. To his surprise, the ink spots held faintly visible patterns, made by his fingertips, and after washing, Torval studied them closely. There were indeed tiny lines and grooves there, so small he'd never noticed them before. "Fingerprints," Marty called them.

All this time, he'd had such intricate details right there on his human flesh, and hadn't noticed! What other features hadn't he taken the time to discover on his body? These men weren't demons, but if he'd professed ignorance about something so obvious as fingerprints, Torval knew he might've given himself away.

He remained silent, brooding worriedly, until finally McCord sat back in his chair, flexing his fingertips together against each other. "Joseph Ryan Sampson," said the police officer after a protracted moment. "Your driver's license expired eight years ago, your commercial license two years after that. You have no credit cards, no home, nothing else in your report. No criminal record, although you were cited, and later cleared, for a truck accident nine and a half years ago. It seems as if after that, you just decided to just drop off the face of the Earth."

Torval nodded. "That is true," he agreed, for the information matched what he knew of Joe's faded identity. "I did not wish to bother anyone."

"Are you on the run, Joe?" inquired the lieutenant, leaning forward slightly. "Maybe you thought there was an arrest warrant out for you after that accident? If so, you're mistaken. According to what I have here, they found a structural fault in your air brake system that would've prevented you from stopping in time. You couldn't have saved those people."

"I am not on the run," replied the demon. Perhaps Joe would've been heartened to hear that information, but it meant nothing to Torval. He knew he had to explain his situation further, though, and let the officer continue to pry. "I am . . . rather, I feel . . . guilty about what happened. I left that life behind."

McCord shut the folder with a loud slap. "Fine," he responded in a tone that suggested Joe's past no longer mattered. "Whatever. Let's forget about that, shall we? Let's talk about the present."

"Very well," agreed Torval worriedly. "Why am I here? What is it you want from me?"

"Straight to the point, good, good. You might be someone I can work with, Mr. Sampson. Tell you what, if you want to get right to the heart of the matter, then so will I. Listen up."

Torval nodded. The sooner he got this over with, the sooner he could get back to what he needed to do—preparing for his date with Christine.

"The Roxtons," explained McCord with a very brief smile, "are dealers in car parts. I'm sure you know that already. What you don't know, or at least I'm assuming you don't know, is that some of these parts are stolen. We don't know exactly how many, or where they get them all, because so far they've been pretty good at hiding their tracks."

Torval nodded, but said nothing, eager for the man to continue. However, the lieutenant, obviously skilled at his job, didn't miss the body language clue.

"You don't seem surprised," he interjected. "Do you know something you aren't telling me?"

Torval shuddered. The man's piercing gaze seemed able to see right into his mind! "N-not exactly," he stammered, trying to come up with a believable response on the fly. "I apologize, sir, if I seem to have little useful information. I am, or was, a street bum. I have heard many things in my years out there, and one of those rumors was that the Roxton warehouse was a—" What was the strange euphemism Prelz had used? Ah, yes. "A chop shop."

McCord nodded slowly. "Yes, that's what we used to think, too," he remarked, "but you see, we've never been able to catch them at it. Every car that's ever gone in there for work, as far as we can tell, has always come out again. So unless they're taking out valuable parts and replacing them with junk, we're at a loss. If they are doing that, which seems unlikely, the only way we'd ever find out is if we had access to their records—and we can't get those without a warrant."

"I do not understand—" replied Torval, intending to add that he didn't know anything about warrants, but he didn't get the chance. The lieutenant interrupted before he could continue.

"We can't get a warrant because we have no evidence," sighed

McCord, "and without a warrant, we can't get to the evidence. You see my problem, then, don't you?"

Torval nodded vigorously. "Yes, sir, I do."

"So now you're probably wondering, what does this have to do with you, am I right?"

"Yes, sir," the demon repeated.

"Well," said McCord, "Vince and Marty suggested to me that you were more than willing to do your duty as a citizen, correct?"

"Yes, sir."

"And that you might have had a little side visit to a prostitute by the name of Shelly Mendez."

Torval sighed. "I did not—"

"Save it!" barked the lieutenant, raising his voice so suddenly that Torval literally jumped in his chair. "I don't care about whatever little story you might have cooked up that helps you sleep at night, and I don't give a rat's ass about what you do on your own time! What I care about is you can get into that warehouse pretty much anytime you want, as near as I can tell!"

"That is true," admitted Torval shakily. "I do have that ability."

"Good!" The lieutenant stood up, slowly and deliberately. "What I want you to do is try to get a look at their records, wherever they might have them, and tell me if you see anything out of the ordinary. Anything at all. You got it?"

"Yes, sir," replied Torval, swallowing heavily. The way the man stared at him was positively frightening. He had power, the power of his uniform and badge—the power to do pretty much anything to Torval that he wanted. Without even understanding how, the demon knew that Lieutenant McCord would use that power without a second thought.

"Good, good." The lieutenant leaned back slightly, seeming to relax, and all of a sudden the threatening posture and demeanor faded as if turned off by a switch. "I'm glad we can be friends, Joe. You seem like a good guy to me. If the Roxtons really are doing anything illegal, you wouldn't want them to get away with it, now would you?"

"No, sir, of course not," he agreed readily, although inwardly he wasn't so sure. If they were breaking the law, then yes, he would want to see justice be done, but somehow the thought of the kindly Lincoln

Roxton being a criminal just didn't sit right. Pete, though—well, that was a thought for another time.

"Plus," went on the lieutenant, "if they are doing something illegal, and you don't tell me about it, then you're an accessory, aren't you? Like I said, you seem like a good guy—I'd hate to have to throw you in prison. Now come on, let's get you back where they found you, okay?"

He stepped out from behind the desk, motioning for Torval to rise. The demon did so, somewhat eagerly, and followed McCord out into the main body of the police station. There were desks and computers everywhere, and policemen wandering to and fro, sometimes with other prisoners behind them. Waiting nearby, apparently still arguing, were Vince and Marty, both of whom quieted down and stood upon seeing the lieutenant in his office doorway.

"We're done here," said McCord. "See to it he gets back safely, boys. Oh, and one more thing, Mr. Sampson."

"Yes?" inquired the demon.

"Don't mention a word of this to the Roxtons, whatever you do. If they find out you're watching them, you'll never be able to get anywhere. Besides which, they'll probably fire you—and you'll be right back on the streets."

# Chapter 32

Torval felt an immense sense of relief as the gray sedan drove away, disappearing swiftly into a sea of yellow cabs and other random vehicles. The air remained cold and the wind still bit at him through his jacket, but somehow none of that chilled him quite as much as the encounter with the police.

Back in Hell, whenever he visited Foreman Landri, he knew what to expect. The foreman's manner of discipline was always harsh and, as far as Torval recalled, completely justified. He couldn't make up excuses to explain why he should be late with his rounds, or forgot a change in his route, or failed to properly chastise a prisoner. These were Torval's responsibility, and no one was to blame for his mistakes but himself. The foreman simply had a duty, as an overseer, to enforce discipline in the ranks.

Here on Earth, things worked differently. No longer was Torval simply walking a route and visiting sinners, as he had on nearly every day he could remember. Now, in the Middle World, he could do anything he wanted, just like all these other humans that surrounded him as far as the eye could see. They could do whatever they wanted, too. None of them had a foreman to keep them in line . . . or, at least, he hadn't thought so until now.

The police were the foremen of Earth, Torval realized. They enforced the laws that kept society in order. As long as men followed these laws, they had nothing to fear. If someone broke the rules, like Zac Turillo, he'd be arrested and his freedom would be taken away. Such was the price of evil in this world.

Torval never felt afraid or anxious in Hell. If he failed to do his job properly, he accepted his punishment without complaint. Yet here, in this place, he'd tried to do good, as he understood the concept. He had tried very hard to avoid evil, so there should be no reason to punish him. When the police captured him, and took him away . . . well, he felt like everything he'd tried to build was lost. Hence those alien emotions of fright and anxiety that made him feel so hollow inside.

Now that they were gone, he felt better. Much better, in fact. All would be well. The police hadn't arrested him after all. They simply needed his help. All he had to do to placate them was...

Spy on the Roxtons.

He felt uneasy again, thinking about the uncomfortable duty the lieutenant had assigned him. While trying to focus on this new directive, he began to walk, ambling slowly in the direction of the drugstore. According to his watch, he still had enough time to collect the hygiene products he needed before the date. He would've liked to have another shower, considering how much he had sweated during the interview with Lieutenant McCord, but that would take far too long.

Making his way along through the crowds, which had grown in number since morning, Torval considered what he'd been asked to do. The police wanted him to sneak a peek at the Roxtons' records. That should be easy to arrange. The records were right there, in files in the very basement where he worked in solitude. Furthermore, once he learned the proper procedures, he'd be using a computer to record that same data. He could hardly fail to look at the information. What harm would it be, to report what he saw to the police? To agents of the law—the enforcers of goodness in the human world?

No harm at all, his rational mind told him, but he still felt a strange kind of disgust at the thought. This felt like a betrayal, the same sort of sin that landed many a prisoner in Hell. The Roxtons had helped him. They gave him money, and a job, and food, and a place to sleep. What more could men do for one another? Was Torval supposed to forget all of that simply because the Roxtons might be breaking some law? For dealing in stolen automotive parts?

The whole situation confused him greatly. The more Torval tried to focus on finding an answer, the more muddled his thoughts became. He only broke out of the resulting stupor when a pedestrian bumped him crossing the street. The demon shook his head, clearing it, and realizing suddenly that he was standing at a corner, looking at a green "Walk" sign. He'd completely lost track of what he was doing, there for a moment.

He pressed on, looking at the problem from a more detached angle. This must be what the humans call a "moral dilemma," he decided. Many times, prisoners in his cells tried arguing that they didn't deserve punishment. According to them, they'd been placed in situations where there were no right choices. Torval, mocking them with responses provided by their own guilty subconscious, simply replied that there was always a right choice—they just didn't look hard enough.

So what was the right choice here—the good thing to do? Spy on the Roxtons without their knowledge, at the request of the police? Refuse to do so, and suffer their wrath? Or inform the Roxtons of his subterfuge, enabling them to hide whatever illicit activities they might be involved in from the eyes of the law?

Torval sighed. He had no idea. There seemed to be no right answer. Perhaps there could be times when that was the case. Did that mean that even now there were souls trapped in Hell that never had a chance to choose the path of good?

He shuddered at the thought. Surely that couldn't be true! Evaluators would judge a soul on its entire life, not on any single incident. The punishment a soul suffered often took the form of some aspect of their personality, often focusing on a specific place and time, but that was all. No one faced torture for just one single choice they made.

Did they . . . ?

He didn't know, and that was the problem. Prelz probably wouldn't know either. Or maybe he did, and that was yet another reason he chose to forego demonhood.

Torval frowned. So many questions! So many ways things might work differently than he ever knew. He'd lived his life for so long without ever concerning himself with such details. Now they seemed important, even vital, for reasons he didn't understand.

Looking up, he saw that he'd arrived at the drugstore. He had to put such matters aside, and focus on this moment—what he had to do now. The rest would have to come later.

Stepping inside, he made his way to the aisles and started looking for the deodorant.

* * *

"There you are!"

Torval glanced around, surprised to hear Prelz's voice. He'd almost given up on finding the other demon today. As he entered the shelter, he looked around for Christine, wondering if she'd be here as early as he was. He felt a mounting sense of excitement over the possibilities offered by the date, so much so that he'd forgotten totally about Prelz.

"Oh, hello," he managed, a bit surprised by the anxious way the bearded human face glanced worriedly about. "Where have you been? I attempted to locate you earlier."

"Hiding," answered Prelz. "Are those two still watching you? The ones in the Continental?"

"Who?" Torval looked around. He didn't see anyone except other bums, and a couple of volunteers getting the soup line started. "What is a 'Continental'?"

"Never mind. Come over here, into this corner, where we can talk."

Prelz half-dragged Torval to the far side of the room, almost making him lose his grip on the plastic bag containing his recently purchased hygiene products. "What is going on?" asked the vacationing demon, still at a loss.

Prelz almost pushed him down into a chair, then sat down next to him anxiously. "Those men. The ones in the suits. They've had their eyes on you for a while now. I was about to yell at you earlier today as you walked up to the door, when I noticed them in that gray car, shadowing you."

"The gray car." Torval nodded, understanding at last. "Oh, I see. That must be what a Continental is. Yes, I know those men."

"You know them?" gasped Prelz. "Is it a hunt team? You can tell me—please, tell me! If they are, I gotta split, and fast! If any of their hounds catch my scent—"

"They are not a hunt team," replied Torval reassuringly. "They are policemen."

"Is that all?" demanded Prelz. "Are you sure? Did you physically touch them?"

"Yes. They took my fingerprints. I can confirm that both are, in fact, human. They are named Vince and Marty."

Prelz sighed and seemed to collapse a little, obviously relieved at this news. "Good to know you're on a first-name basis," he remarked sarcastically. "Why'd they arrest you? What did you do now? Does this have something to do with the chop shop I told you about?"

"In a way. They were aware I am employed at Roxton Auto Parts, and want me to gather financial information from within. They believe the Roxtons are dealing in stolen goods, as you mentioned to me before. My help will enable them to determine the truth of this."

"Okay, fine, so they want you to be their inside man," said Prelz, having by now calmed down noticeably. He wiped a thin layer of sweat away from his wrinkled forehead and continued. "Why don't they just get a warrant and search the place?"

"The man who explained this to me, Lieutenant McCord, said they could not get a warrant for lack of evidence. What exactly is a warrant?"

"Uh, well, it's . . . um . . ." Prelz had to think about that one for a moment. "You know, I'm not really sure precisely what one looks like. Funny, you hear about crap like that but never actually see it. Anyway, far as I know, it's like permission to violate your privacy, y'know? A legal document that lets the police enter your home or business and search it."

"You mean they cannot do this normally?" Torval was surprised. "The police are those who enforce the law, are they not? Why can they not simply enter any structure they wish, in the pursuit of justice? If those inside are doing no wrong, they are in no danger."

"Well, in some places in the world, they can do just that," answered Prelz. "Not in this country, though. They value personal freedom here a lot more than some other places. The people here have a right to privacy, and that means 'no unlawful searches or seizures.' Anyway, just don't worry about that right now, take my word for it. So okay, I get it, the cops have a nice catch-22, don't they? So are you gonna help 'em or what?"

Torval didn't know what catching the number "22" had to do with anything, but he chose not to inquire. "That is something I have wondered about since they returned me to the street," he admitted. "I do not wish to betray the trust of the Roxtons, and yet, I do not wish to interfere with justice, or the laws of this world. I was told when I was sent here that making the right choices would make this vacation more enjoyable. So far, this has proven to be the case, yet in this particular situation, I cannot determine the right choice."

"Well, just so you know, you aren't actually required to help the police, if you don't want to," explained Prelz. "In fact, if you do give them any information, and it wasn't acquired with one of these warrants I was talking about, it's not admissible in court. All you'll do is confirm or deny their suspicions."

"More importantly," continued Torval, "if the Roxtons are not breaking any laws, by providing this information to the police, I am in fact doing my employers a favor. Furthermore, if they are doing evil, then if I am to do good, I must report them. Is that not so?"

"In theory, yes," agreed Prelz with a nod, "but what if they're running a chop shop because they're being forced to? What if they have no other choice? Getting them arrested might be the worst thing you could do. You have no real idea if you don't know the whole story."

Torval's shoulders slumped. "Yes, I had not considered that possibility," he admitted. "Bless it all—I mean, damn it all! I thought I had almost solved my problem."

Prelz grinned. "There aren't always easy answers, are there? Good, now you're getting an inside track on some of the problems these humans face every day. No good choices, just the best ones, or maybe compromises. Now you see what I was up against, when I was a Tempter. We're supposed to tempt them further? Seriously, why bother?"

"I am beginning to understand why you chose to act as you did," commented Torval. "I am asking similar questions of myself, and seeing things from points of view I never imagined."

The other demon nodded. "Yeah, I figured you might. Being human does that to you. You're not even sounding like a Third Class anymore. Hmm, that reminds me—give me your hand."

"Why?"

"Just do it."

Torval stretched out his arm. The other demon took his hand, as if to shake it, and shifted into his true form. The slitted eyes went up and his horned head cocked sideways, as if studying his younger charge. Then, after a few moments, he let go, returning to the aged bum shape Torval was more familiar with.

"You're changing," Prelz announced. "Your form is starting to shift. You don't look like a simple Punisher anymore. Your horns are longer and starting to curve, and you're standing up straighter, without that terrible slouch of yours. I didn't see your tail at all, either—I bet it fell off somewhere along the way."

Torval shook his head slowly. He didn't want to believe Prelz, but inside, he knew it must be true. He felt different—the only way to describe it, really. Though he didn't want it to, he could feel the change. He could feel himself advancing, slowly but surely.

"I want to see," he said eventually. "I want to see myself. Is this possible?"

"No, 'fraid not," replied Prelz. "You only see yourself as a human, and even if I grab you near a mirror, you'll never see your real self as long as you're here. Y'know, without that tail, you may have to learn to walk all over again when you get back."

"Perhaps so," agreed Torval with a sad sigh. "I did not want to advance, Prelz. I just wanted to return to my route. Now I sense this is not to be. Things will never be as they were, will they?"

"Don't worry about it," replied the other demon reassuringly. "Life—existence—is about change, Torval. For people and demons both. Humans are born, grow old, and die. We demons spawn, do our jobs, and advance when the time is right. We don't die, as far as I know, but we meet our ends one way or another, eventually. That's how things are, my friend. That's the way it works. We can't change it, so we may as well accept it."

"Do you suppose," wondered Torval, "that my foreman knew this would happen when he sent me here? That my replacement is already walking my route, back in Hell?"

"Probably," said Prelz with a shrug. "I'm sure, after hundreds of years in his office, he probably knows the signs of someone ready to advance. I wouldn't have thought you'd have been sent to Earth, though. Maybe you can ask him when you go back, if you ever see him again. Well, it probably won't matter anyway. Besides which, don't we have something else to talk about? You have a date coming up, don't you?"

"Yes, yes, of course," agreed Torval readily, snapping back to the present. "In just a few minutes, if my watch is accurate. That reminds me. I purchased these products. How are they used?"

"Let me see." Prelz looked into the bag. "Oh, okay, well, the deodorant is easy, you just pop the top off like this, and then run it along under your arms, here and here, to mask your smells. Simple stuff. The mouthwash, you gargle with it, then spit it out. Don't swallow it."

"Gargle...?"

"Yeah, you kinda lean your head back, and let it settle in the back of your throat, and then breathe out so the liquid gets all over in there and overwhelms any bad breath you might have."

"Very well, I will try it." He started to open the container, struggling for a moment against the tight cellophane wrap, until finally the cap came loose.

"No, no, not here, you need a sink to spit into," insisted Prelz. "See if you can go back there—uh-oh, there she is!"

Torval glanced up, following Prelz's gaze. Sure enough, there was Christine, standing in the entrance to the shelter. She spotted him at once and waved, heading in his direction. Meanwhile Prelz swiftly grabbed the hygiene products, shoved them in the bag, and hid it from sight.

"Hey, Joe," she called out as she walked up. She wore a heavy tan overcoat, thin leather gloves, and a familiar-looking pair of black boots that made her seem tall and elegant. Her hair was wrapped about itself in a series of attractive folds held together with a piece of barely visible plastic. She smiled, in that friendly and affable way of hers, and Torval felt his body warming at the sight.

"Hello, Christine," he replied, standing up automatically. "I am pleased to see you."

"And I, you," she answered, smiling even more brightly than before. "Hello to you too, Jake."

"Hey," he replied, shuffling a bit as he sought to keep Christine from noticing the plastic bag on his lap. "What's up?"

"Oh, nothing much. Joe here is taking me out to dinner and a movie," she answered, tapping him on the shoulder as she spoke. "Isn't that nice of him?"

"It's the least I can do," said Torval, carefully using a contraction to appear more at ease. "She has done so much for me."

"You should take an example from your friend, Jake," remarked Christine, not missing an opportunity to be as encouraging as possible. "Doesn't he look wonderful? Just amazing, what he's done for himself in so short a time. Although he could probably stand another shave." She reached up and ran a gloved fingertip across Torval's thin stubble.

Torval felt a shiver run up and down his spine. Her faintest touch seemed to set his skin on fire. Struggling to take his mind off the alien emotions that threatened to overwhelm him, he focused his thoughts on remembering to shave again once this date was over.

"Yeah, well, good for him," replied Jake, shrugging. "Joe here, he always did whatever he wanted. You better watch out, though. You got him lookin' so good, the other ladies are all after him now!"

Christine giggled at that. "I'll just bet they are," she remarked with a sly wink. "They can wait in line, for all I care. Now come on, Joe, or we'll be late for the movie."

She led him out of the building, to the chilly streets beyond, and just like that the date was underway.

# Chapter 33

The theater's exterior reminded Torval of the Radio City display he'd noticed during his visit to Rockefeller Center while searching for the subway. A large sign hung overhead, identifying the place, as well as a white marquee with unevenly placed black letters spelling out titles. One of these read Queen Takes Pawn, the name of the movie he intended to watch, so he was in the right place.

Christine led him inside, joining a line of patrons waiting at a small window for something. "I do like this place a lot more than the big megaplexes," his date remarked casually. "So quaint, and not so many crowds. Plus, it doesn't have that mass-produced feel. You know what I mean?"

Torval hesitated, trying to decide what to say. He had very little idea what she was talking about. Quite honestly, he didn't even really understand what this "movie" thing was supposed to be, other than a vague description given to him by Prelz. He said it was "like TV, only bigger." Just another of the many things Torval never quite got around to asking about.

"I apologize," he finally admitted, taking a chance that he wouldn't make a mistake by revealing his ignorance. "I do not know what a 'megaplex' is."

"Oh, right, sorry about that," Christine replied with a smile. "I forgot, Joe, you've been out of touch for so long. You've missed so many things. Let me see if I can fill you in. Years ago, a lot of the small movie houses started getting replaced by giant theater complexes with sixteen, twenty, even more screens. They were so big, you could see any movie there, anything that was out, even the lesser known films that usually showed up only in the art-house places. People started flocking to the megaplexes, and a lot of the smaller theaters had to close, unless they turned into second-run places like this one. The movies are cheaper here, but they've also been out for a while, so fewer people come. It's better that than close down, I guess."

"I see," replied Torval, thinking about what this might mean, and recognizing the similarity to his own current dilemma regarding the Roxtons. "So what you are saying is the business owners were forced to make a choice, and they wound up finding a way to compromise?"

"Yes, that's exactly it," agreed Christine. "That's very insightful, Joe. You catch on quickly. I think that's what I like most about the new you. You're so open-minded."

"I do feel like a new person," replied Torval, pleased she'd drawn a conclusion he could work with so easily. Best of all, he wasn't even forced to lie. The words he spoke were completely true, not just for Joe Sampson, but for the demon within. "I've kept myself locked away for so long, and now it is as though I'm seeing things for the first time."

"I'm so glad," she replied, hooking her arm around his and hugging against him tightly. "I spend so much time at the shelter, watching men and women like you waste away—it's so sad, because any of you, anyone really, can do better with your lives, if only you put your minds to it."

Torval nodded, enjoying the feeling of her warmth pressing against him. Hopefully there would be more of that later, and with less clothing in the way, but for now he had to carry through with the date ritual. In fact, he'd almost reached the head of the line now—what was he supposed to do, exactly? He should've paid attention to the previous patrons, but missed his chance, as they were already moving away, clutching scraps of paper in their hands.

"What can I do for you?" asked the young woman behind the counter. She wore a long-sleeved white shirt over which hung a maroon vest trimmed in black. Her dark hair dangled loosely about her head, framing a face that looked rather wide, along with the rest of her noticeably overweight body. She is unattractive, realized Torval immediately, in a way his human self-understood but his demon side did not.

"Uh," stammered Torval, "I, um, wish to buy a movie. It is called *Queen Takes Pawn.*"

"Buy?" she asked with raised eyebrows. "It's not exactly for sale yet, you know."

"I apologize," Torval replied. "I misspoke. I wish to see the movie, and that is all."

"Okay, fine. Just you?" asked the woman, glancing at Christine, who seemed oddly amused by her date's difficulties.

"No, both of us," he replied with some exasperation, reaching for his wallet. "What is the price?"

"Seven dollars," she answered with a smile, working with her fingers on some controls, until finally two tickets printed out. She handed these to Torval as he passed her one of the bills with a large "20" in the corner. She returned his change, saying, "Thanks, and enjoy the show. It's in the theater on the left. Next, please!"

Torval moved along, putting his smaller bills away even as Christine giggled beside him. "What is so funny?" he inquired curiously.

"You," she answered. "It's been so long, you don't even remember how to see a movie!"

"That is true. In fact, I cannot recall ever seeing one, at least not in a place like this." Again, an easy response to make, for it was completely true, and he didn't like the idea of lying to Christine any more than he had to.

"How long has it been, Joe?" she asked. "Ten years? Fifteen? Surely not longer than that."

Actually, he knew the answer to that question, thanks to the information provided by the police just a short time ago. "Nine and a half years," he informed her honestly.

"You were keeping track." She looked at him now with a curious expression, as if in wonder. "After all this time, you know exactly how long it was since—well, whatever it was that made you give up."

"Yes." He sighed, wondering how much he should reveal. He wasn't supposed to get involved in his host body's old life, yet she deserved an answer, and as true a one as he could provide. That seemed like the very least he could do for her.

"I don't like to think of it," he replied after a moment, looking away from Christine's piercing gaze, pretending to survey the theater's interior. A large glass-enclosed display area, containing various food items, dominated the center of the atrium. As Torval considered what to say, they moved toward the concession area, following a small line of people waiting to make additional purchases. Though Torval didn't feel very hungry, and intended to buy Christine dinner after the movie, he went along with the flow, seeing no reason to risk betraying his naiveté any more than he already had.

"It's all right, Joe, if you don't want to say anything," Christine insisted, noticing his hesitation. "You never have before."

"You have earned a reply," he went on. "I will tell you, Christine. You will recall that when I met with Simon Spencer at the employment office, I said that I had been a prison guard. While there is some truth to this, in fact my actual occupation was that of truck driver. Then there was an accident."

"An accident?" she asked curiously, looking noticeably startled to actually be hearing this story after so long. She'd obviously tried to get this information many times before, and never had any success—until now.

"Yes," admitted Torval, trying to imagine himself as the human Joe, not his true demonic self. "Innocents were killed because of my failure. I couldn't live with the guilt, so I fled from it. That is what led me here, to this city, after many years of wandering. I feel as though I was lost. I did not know what my life was truly about."

He began to slip out of the story of Joe Sampson, and into his own tale, without even realizing what he was doing. "I don't think I ever knew. I did so many things just because that was the way they were done, without asking myself why. Now the why has become important. I need to know why things are the way they are. Can you possibly understand?"

"I think so," she replied, smiling in a way that soothed him, her very expression reassuring him that everything would be all right. "Thank you for opening up to me, just a little bit, Joe. I think I always knew something terrible happened to you, and I can see it hurt you, deep down inside. I don't need to know any more details right now, but if you ever want to talk about it, you can. You can always talk to me, anytime. That's what I'm here for."

"That is good to know," he replied honestly. Perhaps she might, in fact, be someone he could safely discuss human issues with. He resolved to remember that in the future, but this certainly wasn't the time for such things. "However, we are almost at the front of this line. Is there something else we need to purchase?"

"Well, we couldn't very well see a movie without popcorn and drinks," she replied. "Let me get this, if that's okay."

She reached for her purse, obviously intent on buying something else for him, and Torval couldn't allow that. Already she'd spent too much money on his behalf. Besides, he knew from the dating book how he should handle this situation.

"Please," he interjected smoothly, "I am taking you on a date tonight, and you are not permitted to purchase anything. I will pay."

"Oh come on, Joe," she argued coyly. "I know you can't have earned very much from that job of yours, and concessions are always expensive at the movies. Won't you let me?"

"I insist," he responded, employing the simple phrase the book advised him to use. "You must allow me this."

"Such a gentleman!" She chuckled, poking him softly in the chest, but not so hard as to move him at all. "I never dreamed a real man lay buried under all those rags and dirt. Go ahead, then, Mr. Chivalry. I'll take a Diet Coke, and we can share the popcorn."

They were at the front of the line now, and Torval placed the order as she instructed, ordering a Coke for himself as well. He already knew that particular beverage by name, even if he didn't know why there should be a dieting version. He also didn't know what popcorn was, but the smell of it seemed enticing enough.

To his surprise, however, the food and drinks cost twelve dollars! That was more than the tickets themselves, and more than he'd spent on lunch. Well, I'm buying for two people, he told himself as he used up most of the change he'd received earlier. Perhaps this "popcorn" food is particularly expensive to manufacture.

She picked up the bag of yellow-white puffy things, with that peculiarly alluring smell, as well as her own soda cup. He took his own, and they proceeded along, deeper into the theater. Following the instructions given by the ticket vendor, they went left, passing under a sign saying "Queen Takes Pawn" and into a very dark chamber.

Torval was surprised to see how wide-open the place was, once his eyes adjusted. There were dozens, maybe hundreds of seats here, all lined up facing a large, white rectangular wall that seemed otherwise blank. Only a few of the chairs were occupied, mostly by couples, with a smattering of larger groups scattered about here and there.

Christine led him up to an open row, and then across to

approximately the center, where she sat down after manipulating the folding seat in a certain way. Torval realized after a moment that one could simply press down on the flap to make the seat extend outward, and, glad that he didn't have to ask for instructions, sat down carefully.

"Sorry about the price," she replied, sipping at her drink and casually munching on the popcorn. "I did warn you, though. These places have to charge high snack prices to stay in business. They make most of their money on food and drinks these days, it seems."

"I don't care," he replied smoothly, speaking only a half-truth. His supply of money was actually dwindling rapidly. "It's worth it, to bring you here and see you happy."

"That's sweet of you, Joe, but I want you to understand something," she replied in a serious tone. "You don't owe me anything. I don't want you feeling like you have to pay me back. Everything I did for you was a gift, freely given, without any debt attached. If you think you owe me, you're dead wrong."

"I do owe you," he informed her, "but I know now this is something I can never repay. Let us not speak of such things any further. I am here with you tonight because I wish to be. Is that not enough?"

She smiled again, looking at him with her head slightly askew. "You never cease to amaze me, Joe," she said after a moment. "At the risk of sounding pitifully lame, where have you been all my life?"

Torval shrugged, not sure how to respond to that. Something about those words warmed him greatly. She liked him, it seemed. Liked him as a person, as a human being, and possibly as a potential mate. He'd said the right things, it seemed, just by being himself.

Exactly as the book told him to do.

As he considered how to respond further, an unexpected blast of light startled him. The entire facing wall, which until now stood featureless and blank, suddenly lit up with giant words that seemed to fill his vision:

THE FOLLOWING PREVIEW HAS BEEN RATED (G) BY THE MOTION PICTURE ASSOCIATION OF AMERICA.

THE FILM ADVERTISED HAS BEEN RATED (R) FOR VIOLENCE, STRONG LANGUAGE, AND SEXUAL SITUATIONS.

Immediately thereafter, Torval's vision and hearing came under assault by the incredible wall of images before him. Faces, vehicles, explosions, amazing vistas...all flew past in a confusing, overwhelming array. The sound, too, blared in his ears, shrieking, assailing him with a cacophony of shouts, music, gunfire, and over it all a deep-voiced narration describing an adventure, a tantalizing hint of a story that promised to enthrall him greatly.

Just as quickly as it began, the preview ended, followed up by a title screen and hundreds of words and names that flashed by far too quickly to read. Torval suddenly realized he'd barely been breathing. He gulped in air, found his throat dry, and swallowed a few drops of Coke to quench his surprising thirst.

"That looked pretty good," whispered Christine from nearby, as if nothing unusual had happened. "Too much violence for me, though. Oh, this next one looks interesting..."

Before Torval could respond, the screen launched into another fast-paced series of sights and sounds. He watched, totally absorbed, quickly losing himself again in the impossibly huge images and loud, blaring music. The previous tale suggested warfare, killing and robbery, and of some heroic man trying to stand up for justice. This one advertised a love story, of two people caught up in some sort of historical drama, destined to be kept apart. Would they ever be reconciled? Torval wanted to know—but the teaser ended, again with just a title and dozens of names that meant nothing whatsoever. What was going on?

"You can take me to see that one if you like," said Christine from nearby. He'd almost forgotten about her, he was so caught up in the possibilities the unfinished story offered.

"I will," he heard himself saying. Then he understood—the fragmentary tale merely advertised another movie, whetting his appetite for the drama to come. "Like a TV show, only bigger," Prelz said earlier—an accurate assessment, at least as far as the size was concerned. Torval understood now—movies were stories, told on this giant magical screen, through some means of projecting other people's lives that, until now, Torval knew nothing about.

No wonder Prelz laughed when Torval said he was going to the movies. "You have no idea what you're in for," the ex-Tempter remarked. So very true, thought Torval. He, and everyone else in this room, would soon bear witness to an entire adventure playing out on this massive, malleable wall. Amazing, truly amazing! Was there anything these humans couldn't do?

The previews ended after a few minutes, and then *Queen Takes Pawn* began. All at once, Torval forgot he was a demon trapped on Earth. He forgot about the Roxtons, about Prelz, about Christine—about everything.

For the next two hours, he slipped into another world.

* * *

John Ramos was a genius, one of those lucky few who could play ten people at once in games of chess, all while carrying on a perfectly normal conversation with his friends or family. They all wanted him to find a decent girl and get married, but he was far too busy for that. Who had time for romance when he worked for one of the biggest security companies in the world? There was so much to do, so many secrets to hide...

His job meant everything to him, or at least he thought so. He designed and implemented new and better ways to protect corporate secrets, using all sorts of electronic encryptions and digital codes. He often worked on these while playing chess in the park, and was rather proud of his winning record, despite such distractions.

Then the dark-haired woman in the thick sunglasses came, sitting down at the board like any of dozens of other would-be opponents. She looked attractive, wearing a hip-hugging short skirt and low-cut top, perhaps thinking she might distract him with her feminine curves. Such tricks would never work on someone as intellectual as John Ramos!

They hadn't—he was sure of that. He hadn't given her décolletage a second glance as he moved the pieces. Yet she defeated him, after a long and challenging game. Then, without a word—just a coquettish smile—she sauntered off, disappearing into the early afternoon crowd.

John couldn't understand how she beat him. He replayed the game, start to finish, trying to figure out where she came up with the strategy. Was it simple luck, or could she really be that good? He had to have a rematch!

For the next several days, he simply waited, refusing all takers while the board stood open. He stayed away from the office longer than he should, letting deadlines slip, hoping she might return. Finally, a few days later, she appeared, looking as attractive as ever, her hair tossing about her lovely face in the early autumn wind. "I'll give you a rematch," she told him suggestively, in a deep and sultry voice, "but whoever loses has to take the other one to dinner."

"Deal," he agreed readily, too eager to play to consider the implications. So they began the contest, while a small crowd gathered. The game was intense, with pieces exchanged readily, sacrifices employed, probing maneuvers made, defenses tested . . . until finally only the two kings and a single pawn were left. At that, she smiled, easily countering his attempt to promote the remaining piece, trapping him in an endless series of meaningless moves that secured a well-fought draw.

"I guess this means we're going Dutch," she told him, and so they did. They had dinner, sharing the expense between themselves, talking, bantering, exchanging experiences, and he soon came to realize that this woman, Dawn Russell, might just be his equal—and more. He liked her, despite his initial reluctance. Romance blossomed.

Things went well, even as autumn changed into winter. They grew to care about each other. They were in love, as much as any two people could be. He had never felt this way before, about anyone. He couldn't remember what life was like without her.

Then, one day, he found her gone. Kidnapped! There were instructions on what to do to retrieve her. Codes that had to be revealed, codes that would compromise his company's security. If he didn't tell the kidnappers what they wanted to know, she would be killed. The woman he loved would die, if he didn't do what they asked.

John struggled with the dilemma. How could he reveal this information? Hundreds of companies would have their private data suddenly vulnerable to theft. The kidnappers would become wealthy at the expense of others, all because of John's actions. Yet if he didn't do something, Dawn would die!

He vowed not to let that happen, turning his intellect and resources to trying to find the kidnappers. Then he found something else—a coded message on his private computer. Something he read that shocked him, so much so that he exploded in fit of rage, smashing valuable equipment, screaming in pain and anguish.

After that, he became more determined. He worked throughout the night, programming, sending e-mails, processing data. Finally he was ready. He had the codes the kidnappers wanted. He met them where they told him to go—at the chess board in the park, where he and Dawn had first met.

They were there, with her. She sat down to play a game, silent, not smiling now. He, too, was pale and worried. He placed a portable disc on the table nearby as the game progressed. The leader of the kidnappers took it, put it in a computer, examined the contents. Satisfied, he left them to their chess.

Finally, John concluded the game, taking a pawn with his queen, and securing checkmate. Without a word he walked away, placing the captured piece sharply on the table before her. She called to him, but he didn't reply, getting into his car and driving away. She picked up the pawn, looking at it, rolling it between her fingers, a single tear running down her cheek.

The kidnappers used the information they'd stolen to break into company accounts, robbing them of thousands of dollars. Yet even as they congratulated themselves on their success, the police arrived to arrest them all. The disc had contained an elaborate fabrication! All the corporate accounts were fake—accessing them alerted the authorities and led them right to the perpetrators.

Dawn, it turned out, had been one of the thieves all along, but she'd fallen in love with John, even while plotting to use him for their nefarious scheme. She warned him, in her secret message, what was happening, and he used that information to thwart the robbers. But her change of heart at the end didn't alter the fact that she'd lied to him all along. She had set him up, nearly costing him his job, almost causing no end of damage through her irresponsible actions. How could he ever forgive that?

He tried to forget her, over the ensuing days, but he couldn't. She was always in his thoughts. The world seemed empty without her.

And then, finally, one late winter's day, while he waited alone in the park by the board, a gloved hand placed a familiar-looking pawn in the empty spot before its queen.

She sat down without a word, and they began to play.

* * *

The credits rolled. Torval blinked a few times, sucking in a breath. Where was he? What was going on?

The story had ended, he realized. He wasn't in that other world anymore, but back in the theater, with Christine, and all the other patrons, many of whom now filed out of the room, talking in low voices among themselves. How much time had passed? What happened to all the popcorn, and his Coke? He must've consumed them during the film, but he didn't remember doing so. He didn't remember anything after the movie started, except that incredibly captivating story.

"What did you think?" asked Christine, looking at him with curiosity.

Torval reached up and poked around his eyes. They seemed swollen and he felt wet spots there, almost painful to the touch. "It was amazing," he replied. "I was entranced. It was all so real."

"Why, you're actually crying," she remarked. "Most men wouldn't cry at something like that. A closet romantic, too, along with everything else I didn't know about you! Incredible! Here, have a tissue."

He took the piece of cloth and wiped his eyes, even as she did the same. Apparently whatever emotions overcame him weren't his alone. "I was happy they were together at the end," explained the demon, trying to make sense of it all. "They seemed to care for each other, despite her deception, and I feared they would not see each other again."

"Well," said Christine, "I thought it dragged on a lot in some places, especially when they were talking about all that encryption stuff. I never could quite understand anything that technical. It seemed like they expected us to know what it meant, you know?"

"I must admit I did not understand that either," agreed Torval, "but it did not matter. I felt I was part of their lives, for however brief a time. What will happen to them now?"

"Well, I suppose they live happily ever after."

"They do? How do you know?"

"Because that's how it ended, silly," she answered, rolling her eyes and grinning. "They got back together. I think it was sort of saying they were starting over, like from scratch. They could forget about what came before and pretend like they'd just met."

"I see," replied Torval, nodding. Yes, that made sense. Even though the movie hadn't actually explained that, he could see how Christine could draw that conclusion. "So we will not see any more of them? That is the end of their story?"

"Unless there's a sequel." Christine stood up, stretching, and sipped down the last of her drink. "I doubt that, though. It didn't do too well at the box office. I still liked it, though. It had a good message—love conquers all. Don't you think?"

"Yes," he agreed, also rising. His legs felt sore and stiff from being held in one position for so long, but a quick stretch relieved him of that pain, which was good, because it was obviously time to leave. The theater had emptied out, the credits nearly done. "That is indeed a good message," he added after a moment.

"Glad you agree," she told him. "Now, I have to tell you, all that popcorn did was whet my appetite. You promised me some Chinese food, and I've been craving it all day, so let's go!"

# Chapter 34

The China Cottage, like so many other human places and things, seemed badly misnamed. The restaurant wasn't a cottage at all, but an establishment tacked onto of one of the many massive buildings that made up the city of New York. The structure's primary purpose had something to do with insurance, whatever that meant. One of the sides, however, possessed a string of smaller businesses, including the Asian place Prelz had recommended.

Next to the arched doorway stood a human-sized green statue of an extremely overweight man wearing an ornately jeweled headdress. Upon entering the establishment, Torval immediately noted a new and enticing aroma drifting out from deeper within the building. This particular scent smelled nothing like any odor his nose had detected before. Having no idea what Chinese food should smell like, all he could do was gratefully acknowledge the odor's presence and wonder what amazing flavors its source might possess.

A short, well-dressed man of Asian ancestry greeted the two customers as soon as they entered. "Two for dinner?" he inquired graciously. His short hair was slicked back and he wore an effusive smile on his round, slightly pudgy face.

"Yes," Torval agreed immediately, with no small amount of enthusiasm.

"Excellent. Follow me, please."

Torval started after him, but recalled at once that according to the dating book, he should always defer to his date in such matters. He waited, earning an appreciative smile from Christine as she passed.

Obviously she approved of his efforts to be a "gentleman" (yet another inexplicable human term). Once again, taking the time to do some research had paid off.

The Asian man led them to a small table along a side wall, underneath a hanging lamp made up of multiple carvings of sleek, bewhiskered dragons. The light seemed unusually dim, but Christine didn't complain as she sat down in the proffered chair. Torval waited until she was seated—as a gentleman should, according to the book—before taking his own seat.

"A waiter will be here momentarily," said their host before departing. Torval watched him go, wondering if that was his entire role here at the restaurant, since he didn't seem to do anything else. Perhaps, thought Torval, the greeter-person was a low-paid trainee looking to work up the ranks, like a Fourth-Class demon before it advanced.

"I always did like this place," Christine mentioned after unfolding a large cloth napkin and sliding it discreetly on her lap. "It doesn't look like much, but they make excellent teriyaki, and the sweet and sour isn't bad either."

"I haven't tried those," responded Torval, following her lead with the napkin, "but if they taste as good as they smell, I'm sure I will not be disappointed."

"Oh, I'm sorry, I forgot, you've probably never been here before, have you?" Christine looked somewhat dismayed, putting one hand up to her mouth as if she'd said something she regretted. "I'm sorry, I didn't mean to remind you, Joe."

"It doesn't matter," he responded with a shrug, making a distinct effort to speak more naturally, like a real human would. "That part of my life is behind me. I look forward to experiencing new things. That is what you've done for me, Christine. You have helped me change the way I look at myself and at others."

"Oh, come on, I didn't really do that much," she replied, waving a hand dismissively. "You could've done any of that yourself, if you put a mind to it."

"Nonetheless, it was your aid that allowed me to successfully find a job," Torval pointed out. Another connection occurred to him then, and he decided she might like to hear about it. "Furthermore, I was not the only one you helped. Do you know my friend Hal Sommersby?"

"Yes, of course I know Hal," she answered immediately. "Why? What happened to him?"

"I told him of my success, and he decided to try to do the same," explained the demon. "He called his daughter, who agreed to help him improve himself, as I have. When last I saw Hal, he was traveling with her to her home, where he assured me he would soon seek a job of his own."

"Really?" asked Christine, blue eyes wide and shining with hope. "Do you really mean that?"

"Of course," replied Torval. "Why would I deceive you about such a thing? I spoke to him this very morning."

"Why, that's wonderful!" she gushed, almost clapping with excitement. "You're an inspiration, Joe! You're proof that anyone can improve themselves, if they only try. I should show you off some more—maybe other people will be inspired like Hal was!"

"Show me off?" He glanced about, at the half-empty restaurant. None of the other patrons, or serving staff, seemed the slightest bit interested in the two diners in their shadowed alcove along the wall. "In what way?"

"Oh, it's nothing bad," Christine insisted. "I just mean I could point you out at one of the daily meals, or something like that. Maybe you could give a little speech. Just think of what you might accomplish! None of them listen to me anymore, after so many years of hearing my nonstop nagging, but if one of their own were to talk to them—why, I bet at least some would listen. Don't you think?"

Torval nodded slowly, not sure if this was a good idea or not. Many of the bums in the shelter supposedly knew him, but he doubted he could so much as remember their names, now that Joe's memories had all but faded. Still, the idea was fundamentally sound, and besides, Christine couldn't stop gazing at him with those bright blue eyes of hers, filled with joy and enthusiasm. Furthermore, he sensed in this an opportunity to help others, with no reward for himself, save for Christine's thanks. He could repay her, in some small way, and do good besides—how could he refuse?

"Very well," he answered after a moment. "I will do as you say."

"Oh, that's wonderful, Joe!" she said as she beamed happily. "I'll see if I can get something set up for later. 'Kisha is never going to believe this!"

Torval had to agree, but before he could say anything, another restaurant employee arrived. The waitress stood even shorter than the greeter, with narrow hips, a thin frame and excessive makeup on her face. Her eyes were little more than slits, barely open underneath dark blue blotches that seemed almost painted on her eyelids. She wore a long, maroon-colored dress that hung about her in folds.

"Good evening," she said in a heavy accent, "I am Mai Ping and I am your server tonight. Here are menus." She handed over two large, brown slabs of heavy cardstock, coated in some kind of slick, clear substance. Emblazoned on the front of each was a gold image of a pagoda-like building with a sign labeled "China Cottage," along with a pair of incomprehensible symbols that vaguely resembled letters.

"Thank you," said Torval, taking the menus and handing one to Christine. "We do not yet know what we wish to order."

Mai went on as if he hadn't spoken. "We have specials tonight. Happy fam-i-we, and sweet and sour park." She seemed to be struggling with some of the words, and perhaps to remember the items in question. Plus, the more she spoke, the sloppier her English became. "They twenty percent off. Also appetizers half price until six. You order in ten minute, you get that price. You want drink?"

"I would like a Coke," Torval answered, hoping he understood her correctly, "if you have one. And she will have a Diet Coke. Is that what you want, Christine? I apologize if I'm making an incorrect assumption."

"That'll do," she agreed with a nod, continuing to survey the menu. "I was thinking maybe a margarita, but on second thought, I'd better not."

"I bring those now," replied Mai quickly. She gave a quick bow and scurried off, trailing her long dress behind her.

"What did you mean by that?" inquired Torval. "You can request a 'margarita' if you so wish. Do not concern yourself with the price."

"It's not that," answered Christine. "The last time I drank too much, I regretted it, that's all. Besides, I don't want to tempt you any more than you probably are every day."

"I see." Torval nodded, realizing now that this drink of which she spoke must be alcoholic in nature. Yes, perhaps it was best to avoid such things as much as possible. He opened the menu, surveying it briefly, and spotted the section on beverages, which listed a margarita's ingredients. The concoction did sound intriguing, he had to admit, but he forced himself to put it out of his mind.

The price of the margarita did give him a brief jolt. Almost six dollars! In fact, as he studied the menu still further, he discovered to his dismay that most of the items listed were more than ten dollars, many of them approaching twenty dollars or even higher. Depending on what Christine ordered, he might not be able to afford a meal for himself!

The lessons from *Dating in the 21st Century* were clear, though—one does not bring up the price during the meal. According to that invaluable tome, even if he wanted to, he couldn't simply suggest to her to order as cheaply as possible. All he could do was hope she remembered he was still quite poor. If the price of the meal rose too high, and he couldn't pay it…what would happen then? Would he be arrested? No, surely not—Christine would simply cover the difference, which would be embarrassing to say the least.

Torval couldn't let that happen, so he decided it might be best to simply wait to see what she ordered, before choosing his own selection. Fortunately, unlike the Italian restaurant he visited for lunch, the China Cottage included detailed descriptions of every meal. After perusing the items for several moments, he located several he at least understood. One, as Mai Ping had pointed out, was one of the specials—sweet and sour pork. The very description made his mouth water.

"See something you like?" Christine asked after a moment, interrupting the silence that had unintentionally settled over their little table.

"I believe so," he told her. "This pork item sounds most intriguing. I believe I will try that."

"Good call," she agreed. "Good value, too. I think I'll try the Happy Family tonight, since it's also on special."

Torval was about to thank her for the consideration of his finances, but before he could speak, Mai returned with their drinks. "Ready to order?" she asked in that thick, heavily enunciated accent of hers.

"Yes," replied Torval, ordering for both himself and Christine, as the book had instructed him to do. "I will have the sweet and sour pork, and she will have the Happy Family." Whatever that is, he added to himself.

"Wonton soup or egg drop?" she asked hastily, scribbling notes on a small pad she produced from one of the folds of her robe.

Torval glanced at Christine, having no idea what those items were, or that they were an option. Seeing his confusion, she came to his rescue. "Wonton for both of us," she answered with a smile.

"It not be long," Mai told them. "I take menus."

Torval handed over the two items and she hurried away, heading toward another table, where four people waited. He noted as she left that an excessively large white bow adorned her hair in back, making her look as if she wore a wide, floppy headdress. She paused, apparently taking another order, although he couldn't hear at this distance. He realized now that she wasn't serving just him, but many tables, all simultaneously. Keeping track of all those orders would definitely be a challenge, obviously why she kept a notepad handy.

"Sorry to be presumptuous there," said Christine, "but I figure you're a wonton kind of guy. You'll love it."

"I'm certain I will," he replied amiably. "Although I am not all that hungry, because of the popcorn, I am still looking forward to this meal. I have never—or, rather, it has been a long time since I have been on a date such as this."

"Well, it's already going a lot better than my last one," she said, rolling her eyes. "It's nice to be with someone who doesn't have only one thing on their mind."

"What one thing?"

She twittered at that. "Oh, Joe, I love how innocent you always sound! You know what I mean. The one thing men always think about, all the time."

Torval frowned slightly. He didn't actually know what she meant, at least not at first, but a moment's thought brought the answer to him. It's a good thing, he considered inwardly, that she doesn't know the kind of preparations I took prior to this date!

"I assure you," he replied carefully, "I do not think about that all the time."

Christine laughed again. "Just most of the time, then! Ha-ha-ha! Well, forget it, buster. I'll tell you the same thing I told Pete—I don't sleep with anyone on a first date."

Torval was chagrined. So much for his lessons! But she did say first date, suggesting if he could arrange more, he might still be able to make use of his training. However, even as his rational mind mulled that over, the emotional side of him spoke almost outside of his control.

"When you say Pete, do you mean Pete Roxton?" he asked curiously, not even realizing what he was saying. "You had this same conversation with him?"

Christine looked suddenly horrified, slapping a hand over her mouth. "Oh, no! I shouldn't have said that!" she gasped. "We met that morning, when I took you to—ah, I shouldn't have said his name! Stupid, stupid!"

"It's all right," he answered quickly, holding up his hands. "It doesn't matter, Christine. I knew you went on a date with him anyway."

"You—you did? How?" Now she looked perplexed, and then slightly angry. "Did he talk about me? What did he say?"

"He said nothing directly to me," answered the demon honestly. "I only know of your date because someone I know saw you get into his car. The next morning, I overheard him speaking highly of you to Lincoln Roxton, and how much you enjoyed Chinese food. That is why I had the idea to bring you to a similar restaurant."

"I see," she replied, mouth set in a firm line. "And what else did he say?"

"Just that he enjoyed your company," replied Torval, trying to remember exactly what he'd overheard of the conversation, "and that he hoped to get together with you again soon."

She nodded, clearly looking upset. Torval gave a slight shudder. He hadn't intended to antagonize or anger her, but he had nonetheless. Clearly he'd made a mistake by inquiring further about Pete. The book had said not to discuss other romances, but she was the one who brought it up, not him, and he just couldn't contain his curiosity.

"He would think that," growled Christine after a moment. "Why, that's just priceless! It's just what that pompous, self-absorbed peacock of a man would say! He was so sure I would just fall all over myself to sleep with him, just because he's handsome and wealthy and said all the right things! Well, that might work with the floozies he meets in bars, but not with me! When I told him as much, he made some very ungentlemanly comments under his breath, which he thought I couldn't hear. At least he had the common decency to drop me off where he picked me up, instead of just leaving me at the restaurant. That's about the only good thing I can say about him, though. And no, just in case you were wondering, I do not have any intention of going on another date with him—and you can tell him I said so yourself!"

Torval waited until she finished her rant, which seemed quite uncharacteristic of the normally cheerful Christine. What, exactly had Pete Roxton done to upset her so? Torval wanted to know, but he'd already done too much damage to the date by bringing up someone else. Perhaps it was best to change the subject.

Before he could do so, though, she put her hand on her forehead, rubbing her temple for a moment before smoothing back a lock of dark brown hair that slipped out of place. "I'm sorry, Joe," she went on, "but people like him just rub me the wrong way. I thought Pete might be different when we met that morning. He seemed so nice and pleasant, but then I found out he was just trying to get into my pants, and it really set me off. That's why I'm glad I'm here with you, Joe. I know you'd never treat me that way. I don't know how I know, but I do. I just . . . I can feel it. You're different, somehow."

Torval nodded. She had no idea how right she was! "I feel the same way about you," he responded honestly, again taking the advice the dating book offered him. "I've never met anyone as kind and generous as you, Christine. You intrigue me more than any person I have ever met. I want to know everything there is to know about you."

She smiled at his genuine compliments. "Oh, don't let me bore you with details of my life," she told him, waving a hand in his direction. "You'd be asleep in minutes!"

"I doubt that very much. I know very little about you, except that you have some sort of job, and that you volunteer at the soup kitchen. What else can you tell me about yourself?"

"That's not all you know," she pointed out. "You saw my apartment! You know where I live."

"This is true," he agreed. "You will recall, however, that I did inform you of my own profession. You can at least tell me the same about yourself."

"Oh, is that how we're going to play it, then?" She chuckled. "Okay, mister, here's the deal. I'll tell you one thing about myself, and then you have to reciprocate with something about you. Sound good?"

"Very well," he replied with a nod, eager to know more about the enigma that was Christine Anderson. "Since I already told you I was a truck driver, what is your job?"

"Fine, if you really want to know," she replied, "I'm a legal secretary."

Torval raised an eyebrow. "That sounds like a redundancy. Are there such things as illegal secretaries?"

Christine burst into laughter. "Joe, you're so funny!" she giggled. "Illegal secretaries! I can't wait to tell that one to my boss on Monday morning. No, I work for Hochman, Stein & Veehorven, precisely eighteen blocks uptown from the shelter. You know the firm?"

"No, I'm afraid not."

"Didn't think you would. They specialize in messy divorce cases—the nastier, the better."

Torval knew what a divorce was, from several of the prisoners in cells back home, and had by now determined that these people she named were lawyers of some kind—but why they would be needed in a divorce still eluded him. Something to research later, he decided. "And you help them?" he asked curiously.

"Well, I help some of the lawyers where I can, and take care of a lot of record-keeping," Christine explained. "I'm not a paralegal, but I have some legal training, and a good memory for cases. They can't just use any old secretary at a place like that, you know, which is why they keep me around." She gave a little shrug, as if that were somehow unimportant. "Anyway, it pays the bills. Plus, every so often, I get a chance to work behind the scenes a little. Maybe help patch up one of these broken relationships. It's not easy, and if they knew, I'd probably get fired, but it's worth it." She gave a sigh, gazing up at the dragon-shaped light above them, obviously thinking about some private memory.

"Okay, then," she said after a moment, "enough about me. Tell me something about yourself. It's your turn."

"Very well," agreed Torval. "What would you like to know?"

"Hmm," said Christine. "Okay, tell me about your family. Are you—or were you—married? Do you have any children?"

Torval hesitated. What could he say to that? He honestly didn't know the answer. Joe's memories were gone and he didn't remember ever thinking of kids, back when he could still access Joe's brain. He did recall images of a woman, or perhaps several women, but whether these were spouses was beyond his reach.

"It's okay," Christine interjected. "You don't have to answer, Joe. I didn't mean to try to trick you. I'm sorry."

"No, it's all right," Torval responded, deciding to focus on honest replies, at least as much as he possibly could. "I feel comfortable talking to you like this, Christine. It feels good to answer. No, I am not married, and I have no children. I never had any family or friends that I can recall. I worked in a prison and driving a truck, and I was always alone."

"You mentioned a prison before," she pressed on. "Where was it? Were the prisoners violent at all? Did you get hurt?"

"It was . . ." He paused again, trying to think of how to describe it. The memory of Gregor Pyrzeschi, the prisoner who kept trying to escape his cell despite the impossibility of such a thing, came back to him, and Torval focused on that. "It was a . . . a maximum security penitentiary," he explained after some consideration. "Each prisoner was kept in solitary confinement. I interacted with them only very infrequently, and there was never any violence. At least, not involving myself."

"That's good," said Christine. "Did it pay well?"

"Not particularly," he answered, again choosing the simple and most honest response he could think of.

"Why did you quit?"

"I did not—" Torval stopped himself just before he made a mistake. "I found another opportunity," he corrected quickly.

"Truck driving."

"Yes. Just so." He disliked lying to Christine, but had little choice now. In order to fit the facts he'd already revealed about himself, he had to tie things together. Although, in a way, he'd only bent the truth, it still bothered him, so he didn't try to continue adding more details, sensing they would only muddy the waters still further.

"Thank you, Joe, for being honest with me," said Christine after a moment, using a tone that suggested she didn't really believe he'd been entirely forthright. "I really appreciate it. Like I said, you can always talk to me about anything. I can tell you're hiding something about this prison job of yours, though. Something happened there, didn't it? Something else that made you leave."

Torval considered his response. She was right, of course, except that he didn't officially quit his job back in Hell. He went on "vacation" instead, probably because—as Prelz had suggested—he faced advancement. Would his old route still be waiting when he returned? Almost certainly not. So in a way, he had left that job, depending on how one looked at it.

He couldn't reveal any of this to Christine, though. In fact, the more she pried into this particular detail, the more he would have to lie, and that made him uncomfortable. He didn't like having to deceive Christine any more than he had to. So instead of offering any further details, he chose to avoid the question.

"I would rather not speak of it," he told her after a long pause. "It is . . . private."

"I understand," she answered with a half-smile, again employing that tone that implied she didn't really accept his answers. Still, she could tell she'd reached the limits of what she might learn at this point, so she gave up on that line of questioning. "Well, I think that's enough talk about our pasts, don't you think? Besides, it looks like our food is here."

Torval nodded, happy to get off that uncomfortable subject, and even happier at the sight and smell of a plate full of Chinese food. The silent waiter slid the oval-shaped plate off a carefully balanced tray, and swiftly followed up with Christine's food, as well as two bowls of steaming broth containing several chunks of some kind of meat. The waiter moved away, leaving only Mai standing there, looking expectantly at her two customers. "Anything else now?" she inquired energetically. "More drink?"

"Not right now," said Christine, noting that both their soft drinks were all but untouched. "We should be good."

"Okay, thank you, I come back later," she replied, buzzing away to check on another table.

Torval didn't watch her go. Instead, he focused his attentions entirely on the smoking, rumpled meat, slathered in orange sauce, half-buried in a pile of rice and vegetables that lined his plate. The food smelled wonderful. Only with the greatest of self-control could he hold off on digging in until Christine tried hers—again, following the instructions from the priceless dating book.

She nodded appreciatively as she consumed a clump of vegetables, making an "mmm" sound to indicate approval. Torval noted she held a pair of sticks instead of the usual metal implements, and in fact, he found two similar items along the edge of his plate. He picked up the chopsticks, held them as she did, and failed utterly to grasp even a tiny morsel of pork. No matter how hard he tried, the tempting food just slipped away.

Christine giggled. "Just use your fork," she told him between bites. "Don't worry, I won't tell!"

He put the chopsticks down, grateful for her permission, and picked up the more sensible piece of silverware. Why one should use those unwieldy sticks instead of a fork, he had no idea. This must be another of those strange, inexplicable human rituals that defied all comprehension.

Torval only needed one bite of the sweet and sour pork to forget all about that, though. The taste was as incredible as it was misnamed. There wasn't anything sour about it at all. Sweet, yes, and flavorful, but definitely not sour or unpleasant—not by any stretch of the imagination.

"I guess you like it, huh?" asked a smiling Christine.

"Yes, I do," Torval answered. "I have tried many foods since leaving the shelter, and this is by far my favorite."

"It does look good," she agreed. "Can I try a bite? Here, you can sample some of mine if you want."

"Certainly," Torval agreed readily.

She pulled the two plates closer together, wielding her chopsticks with surprising dexterity to spear a small chunk of pork. Meanwhile, Torval selected a couple of items from her own meal, which seemed to include a variety of different types of meat and vegetables, all covered in a thick white sauce. This, too, he enjoyed, and Torval now felt he understood why the dish was called the "Happy Family." For once, the human name for something actually made a small amount of sense!

They spent the rest of the meal consuming their own dinners and occasionally sampling each other's, which Torval appreciated. He doubted he would've tried that particular dish otherwise, and it tasted just as good as his own, if not better. So many different flavors to explore on this world, and so little time! He found himself wishing his vacation might go on a little bit longer, if only so he could sample more types of human food.

When they were finally finished, the waitress Mai brought the bill, and Torval studied the numbers carefully. She'd taken off the discount promised at the start, but once the drinks were added in, the price used up nearly all his remaining funds. He took the bills out of his wallet, counting them carefully, a crestfallen look on his face.

"Something wrong?" asked Christine worriedly. "Don't you have enough?"

"I do," he replied, "but only barely. I will only have a dollar and fifteen cents left over."

Christine nodded in understanding. "Okay, Joe, that's fine, don't worry about it. I can leave the tip."

"You should not need to," he replied disdainfully. "I did not calculate the price properly and failed to manage my funds. I have disappointed you, and I apologize."

"It's okay, Joe! You bought everything for me tonight. You spent so much on me—I'm grateful for everything. This is the least I can do." She reached into her purse and produced a five-dollar bill. "Here, give her this. That should about cover it."

"Thank you, Christine. I appreciate it."

Torval sighed again as he handed the payment to Mai, who seemed pleased as she handed each of them a small brown cracker-like object wrapped in plastic. "You gen-a-was people, you have good night," she told them with another quick bow before scurrying off deeper into the restaurant.

"What is this?" asked Torval curiously, studying the strange object that looked like a solid brown cracker somehow folded over into a dual triangle shape.

"Fortune cookie," replied Christine. "You never had one before? There's a note inside—don't eat the paper."

She removed the wrapping and cracked her cookie in half, withdrawing a small scrap from within. After munching for a moment on the hard shell, she read the printed words aloud: "You will go on a long journey with friends."

"You will?" Torval looked at her curiously. "What does that mean? Where will you be going?"

"Oh, it doesn't mean anything." She chuckled. "It's just something they put inside—random phrases that are supposed to be your fortune. They don't really happen, at least not necessarily. It's just superstition. What does yours say?"

Torval crunched down on his cookie, withdrew the scrap and studied the words printed there. The slip said something about lucky numbers, and a Chinese definition, followed by some more of those mysterious printed symbols. On the other side, he found his fortune.

"Keep your friends close," the scrap of paper warned, "and your enemies closer."

"Always good advice," agreed Christine, dismissing the words with a quick shrug as she pulled on her gloves. "Shall we go? I should get home and change, so I can get back to the shelter, and you have work tonight, don't you?"

"I do," Torval admitted with a sigh. Yet another reason nothing else would happen after the date—a detail he'd failed to consider when he planned this little adventure. Still, things were going fine, as far as he could tell, and it wasn't yet over. Anything could happen.

"Would you walk me home, Joe? It's not far, and I never got a chance to ask you about your job. The one at the Roxton place."

"Of course," he replied, standing up and pulling out her chair for her, exactly as the book suggested. She stood, collected her purse, and allowed him to lead her out of the restaurant. "What is it you wished to know?"

She wrapped an arm around his as they walked, something that made him feel quite warm inside, as if that's where she was meant to be. "I'm curious about how things are working out. I'm worried about you, you know."

"Why are you worried?" he asked, taking his time as he meandered down the chilly sidewalk, paying no attention whatsoever to the cold. The sun had set and the city lights were coming on, causing the streets and cars to glow and flicker beneath the darkening sky.

"Just a feeling," she replied with a shrug. "I don't really trust that Pete Roxton much. I'd rather not talk about him anymore, but suffice to say he's not the kind of person I like to think you're working for."

"Pete has been nothing but kind to me," explained Torval. "He and Lincoln have treated me fairly in every way. I am sorry things did not work out between you, but I have no complaints."

"That's good to hear," said Christine, "but he left a bad impression on me, so be careful. The other thing that concerns me is that they seem to have already paid you something—isn't that right? That's where you got all this money."

"Yes," he admitted. "I was given cash for accomplishing an extra task, above and beyond that which I initially agreed to do."

"I see. Well, that's rather unusual," Christine suggested, unwittingly repeating the concerns Prelz had already brought up on more than one occasion. "Normally you get a paycheck, not cash. What did you do, exactly?"

"I cannot tell you," said Torval, wishing very much that he could. "I was asked to keep that information confidential."

Christine nodded, looking a little bit perturbed that he would dodge the question. "Okay, I can appreciate your loyalty, but you can at least tell me if it was illegal, so I know whether I can stop worrying. Was it?"

Torval sighed. He wanted very much to talk openly with Christine. He didn't like hiding things from her. Besides, he'd already given this information to Prelz, and of course the police knew about it too. What harm could it do to reveal to Christine—the most honest and good-hearted person he knew—the truth of what he'd done?

"Very well," he said after a moment, "I will tell you what I did for the money, Christine, if you promise not to tell anyone else."

"Of course, I promise," she answered readily, now looking much happier that he was willing to confide in her.

So he told her all about the trip on the subway with the briefcase, and the box he took back to the warehouse—as well as the payment in cash for his services. He left out the names and the exact address, but Christine didn't press the issue, apparently not caring about such details.

"So you don't know what was in the briefcase or the box?" she asked when he was finished with his story.

"Only that the briefcase contained papers," replied Torval. "I believe the box contained some sort of car part, although I did not open it to find out. The Roxtons trusted me not to examine the contents, so I didn't."

She shook her head, obviously trying to make sense of what she'd heard. "I don't see why they needed you to do this, or why they paid you," she finally told him. "It doesn't make a lot of sense. What are they up to over there, anyway?"

Torval considered mentioning the meeting with the police, or what Prelz had suggested about the chop shop, but decided not to bring those things up. They were almost at Christine's apartment now, for he could see the staircase just ahead, underneath a faintly flickering streetlamp struggling to activate in the gathering dusk. "I don't know," he answered, "but I do not believe they are breaking any laws."

"What will you do if you find out they are?" she asked curiously.

The question seemed innocent enough, but Torval could tell she was unusually interested in hearing his response, almost leaning toward him in her eagerness. She stopped beneath that flashing streetlamp, which emitted faint buzzing sounds overhead as it tried desperately to come to life.

"I don't know," Torval finally answered. "I have wondered that myself. I suppose I would need advice, and I think I know exactly who to ask."

Christine smiled openly at that. "Oh, Joe, you say the nicest things," she told him, clutching his arm more tightly.

She looked up at him with a curiously wide-eyed expression, head tilted slightly sideways. Torval realized she probably thought he was talking about her, when in fact he intended to take that particular moral question to Father Michaels. However, thinking it over more closely, he realized Christine would be an excellent choice as well. Her moral compass was surely as straight and narrow as the priest's, and she'd be more than happy to help. After all, as she was fond of saying, he could talk to her about anything.

She continued standing there, apparently waiting for something, not making any move to climb the stairs or approach the doorway. "We are here," he told her after a moment. "This is your apartment building, is it not?"

"Yes," she answered, still looking up at him with those bright blue eyes of hers. They seemed to flicker and flash in the stuttering light. "Yes, it is."

Torval gazed deeply into those eyes, completely captivated. All at once he knew what she was waiting for, and he knew he wanted the same. He'd wanted it for a long time—since he first saw her, in fact, all those many days ago, as he coughed and thawed in the shelter on his first desperate day in the Middle World.

He had to be sure, though. He couldn't leave something like this to chance. He felt his heart beating more rapidly now as his rational mind contemplated his next move, and the emotional side of him begged him to press on.

"Christine, I—" he started nervously, realizing all at once that he was shaking like a leaf. With conscious effort he steadied himself.

"Yes, Joe?" she asked expectantly, almost eagerly. She kept right on smiling in that alluring, entrancing way of hers, and he felt his knees wobbling uncontrollably. "What is it?"

"I would—I mean, well..."

"Go ahead, Joe." She gave a little giggle at his difficulties. "Go ahead when you're ready."

Torval sighed, clenching his fists and shaking himself with frustration. With a singular force of will, he drove away all the nervousness and quivering that assailed his weak human body. "I apologize," he told her. "Let me start again."

"Of course." She was clearly enjoying this.

"Very well." Torval took a deep breath, steadied himself once more, and proceeded as boldly as he could. "Christine, I would—I mean, if you don't mind, that is—I would very much like to kiss you."

She smiled demurely and gave a little sigh. "Joe," she answered after a long, purposeful pause, "I would very much like that, too."

Above Torval, the light flickered one last time, emitting a final pop before brightening to full intensity. Eyes of purest sapphire shined brightly up at him, just as radiant as her smile.

Torval forgot all about the lessons from Shelly Mendez, or any of the practice he'd had in this particular ritual. He simply let his body take control, in the most natural and human way he could. Reaching down, he took her in his arms, and closing his eyes, he pulled her softly to him. Their lips touched, and her hands came up behind his neck, holding him close, returning the tender kiss with a kind of gentle intensity as surprising as it was comforting.

Standing there, as dusk fell on the city and another frosty gust whipped down the streets, Torval experienced sensations he'd never felt before, or even imagined could exist. His body seemed to be drifting, tingling with an inner glow that seemed likely to bear him aloft at any moment. The press of Christine against him, the feel of her face against his, was like a moment of perfect happiness, a tiny glimpse of what Heaven must truly be like.

He hovered, for that brief instant of time, locked in that amazing embrace, wondering if this feeling of contentment and belonging could ever end, and if it did, if he could ever feel this way again.

If this is what love feels like, he thought blissfully, I can understand why being human is worth all the trouble.

Then he noticed something else. Through his eyelids, which remained closed, he could sense a barely discernable glow, too bright to come from the streetlamp above. He wanted to believe that this was just an aftereffect of the deeply intense feelings brought on by their amazing kiss, but a tiny fragment of his rational mind told him that just couldn't be possible.

With the greatest reluctance, Torval ended the embrace. As she pulled away, he opened his eyes and blinked. For an instant, the briefest of moments, he saw a golden flash, like an afterimage from a bright burst of light, and then it was gone. In its place, he saw Christine's beautiful face, those wonderful lips that had just met his now twisted into an expression of shock and horror.

"Oh, my God!" she blurted out, backing slowly away from him. "Oh, dear God in Heaven, no! It can't be!"

"What?" asked a confused Torval. Everything seemed to be slipping away now. From the lofty heights of Heaven, he felt himself falling into the Deep Pits, from which there could be no escape. "Please, what is wrong? What have I done to distress you so?"

Christine all but ripped off the gloves she'd been wearing most of the night. "Joe," she gulped out in desperation, "take my hands. Please. Take them. And for the love of all that's holy, please don't be what I think you are!"

Still shaken by her completely unexpected and unwanted reaction, he reached out and took her hands in his. Her skin felt warm and soothing, as if touching each other should've been the most natural thing in the world. Yet as soon as they linked hands, it became very clear that there was nothing natural at all about it.

In that sudden, gut-wrenching moment, Christine *changed*.

That lovely face, the one that always gazed so intently at him with such kindness and understanding, simply melted away, replaced by a glowing visage of smooth, perfect beauty. The eyes were bright points of light adorning the flawless oval of her head. Golden hair shimmered, dancing on the wind, swirling about her like a shining cloak. She wore only fluttering robes of pure white, a simple, knee-length garment that nonetheless looked somehow befitting and regal. She didn't stand, but hovered in the air, bare feet floating several inches off the cracked concrete landing below.

She was beautiful—the most beautiful thing Torval had ever seen. He recognized her true shape immediately, of course, even though he'd never met one of her kind before. The sight of her both enthralled and terrified him beyond measure.

All he could do was stand there mutely, all capacity for rational thought lost as he stared in fascination at the true form of Christine Anderson.

She was an angel.

* * *

To be continued in *Demon Ascendant*, available Fall 2013 from TAANSTAFL Press!